Hi !

I hope :

MW00681401

RURAL SPRAWL
A Gloria Trevisi Mystery

by A. R. Grobbo

?? (Bonne)

A. R. Grobbo

Double Dragon Publishing

Rural Sprawl
Copyright © 2006 A.R. Grobbo

Double Dragon Press

Published by
Double Dragon Publishing, Inc.
PO Box 54016
1-5762 Highway 7 East
Markham, Ontario L3P 7Y4 Canada
http://www.double-dragon-ebooks.com
http://www.double-dragon-publishing.com

ISBN-10: 1-55404-372-7
ISBN-13: 978-1-55404-372-9

A DDP First Edition July 7th, 2006
Book Layout and
Cover Art by Deron Douglas

"The lunatic, the lover and the poet,
Are of imagination all compact."

Wm. Shakespeare: *A Midsummer Night's Dream*

Chapter 1

Normally, Constable Brian Stoker would not have been anywhere near the construction site in O'Dell Township late Thursday evening. Unpaved township roads were not part of his regular patrol route.

That night, however, he'd had to drop by a house just outside the village of East Lister to deal with a drunk husband in a touchy domestic situation.

Even so, he would not have slowed down and turned into the rough gravel drive if he had not noticed a light where it shouldn't have been. And he certainly never would have left his cruiser if he hadn't thought he heard the low rumble of a bulldozer, and wouldn't have slipped in the goop of engine oil if he had bothered to point his flashlight on the ground in front of him instead of waving it toward the collection of backhoes and other construction equipment parked near the shed.

It was not engine oil, however, he discovered as soon as he regained his balance.

On a normal day, which contained anything from checking seatbelts on motorists to cornering a runaway bull, Stoker was not an excitable man. But as he stared down at the soggy bundle at his feet, the burly six foot three police officer decided he wanted some company. Badly. In gooey boots, he hop-skipped back to the cruiser and radioed a concise message to the police dispatch thirty miles away.

Early the following morning as the young constable was filing a report at the detachment office in Plattsford, the ramifications of what he had found at 11:50 P.M. on a warm summer evening suddenly dawned on him. He glanced down at his left boot, the sole of which had been sticking softly to the floor of the staff room, and nearly lost two tuna sandwiches.

* * *

"This is the third time this has happened in seven weeks!" Gloria Trevisi wailed to the noisy little black box mounted under the dashboard of her car. "For once, I'd like something to happen *before* this newspaper's deadline, not five hours later," she moaned as she slowed to make a quick U-turn on the deserted highway.

The recently hired editor of the district's only weekly newspaper would not have known much about the incident either, if she hadn't been returning from a late-running (and deadly dull) meeting of the Plattsford Memorial Hospital Board of Governors. Tired, bored, and frustrated, she had just passed County Road One to East Lister on her route home when her police band scanner picked up the excited broadcast. Swearing at the radio, and at the fact that she was smartly dressed in skirt and good leather pumps instead of wearing something comfortable and practical, she doubled back to the county highway, floored the accelerator, and ground the gearshift of her ancient Mazda into high.

Industrial park indeed! All she had ever seen was a crudely painted sign tacked to a construction shack and a muddy hole; and tonight, traffic. An ambulance and two police cruisers were pulling into the site when she arrived five minutes later. She stepped carefully from her car onto the gravel shoulder, watching while Sergeant Dave O'Toole carefully swathed the gate with yellow tape. After eight weeks of covering local police and courts, she knew that O'Toole rarely came out from behind his desk.

"Whatever this is, it must be important, Sergeant," she called out. "What's up?"

"Can't say," replied the reticent sergeant, tying off the end of the tape and regarding her over the barrier.

"Well, what *can* you tell me?"

He paused, his hand resting on the gate post. "Not much, at this point."

Annoyed, but not surprised by his guarded response, she persisted. "May I look?"

"Look all you want," he said, blocking the view, "as long as you don't cross the line."

"For heaven's sake, I'm not a souvenir hunter." She stood uneasily beside her car, looking toward the industrial park, currently the front half of a one-hundred-acre cornfield about a mile from the village of East Lister. At the moment, the "park" looked like a muddy, stony wasteland populated with earth movers and dump trucks, and all of it barely visible in the headlights of two cruisers.

Photo prospects? Naturally, there were none. Would the readers be satisfied with a blurred, inky, seven-day-old snap of a large police officer standing beside a strip of yellow tape? Depends on what happens, or doesn't happen, between now and next Tuesday, right? Reaching into the vehicle, Gloria grabbed her camera and flash unit and walked toward the gate.

"Watch your step, Ms. Trevisi," O'Toole warned in his blandest tone. "There's a pretty steep ditch there. Wouldn't want you to take a tumble, would we?"

She quickly sidestepped back into the muddy ruts at the bottom of the driveway, ignoring the loose gravel collecting under her toes of her low-slung pumps and the splash of dirty water from a puddle that added an interesting pattern to the hem of her skirt.

"Thanks for the tip." Many, she mused, would no doubt have enjoyed watching the local newshound topple into a ditch full of sludge and muddy water left over from a recent June rain. She was, however, reasonably good-looking, and more or less single, according to local gossip, and therefore warranted a little consideration. And, of course, being a gentleman, the sergeant would have felt obliged to crawl into the muddy abyss after her. Or maybe not.

Halting beside the yellow marking tape, she peered through the darkness. The construction shack was completely in shadow, headlights of the police vehicles facing the other way. A large elm spread its umbrella branches from the ditch across both sides of the road, its summer foliage preventing the yard light at the top of the drive from illuminating the scene below. Other trees along the fence line of the property had been eliminated. Farmers, hydro workers, even developers, however, were reluctant to destroy so rare a find as a healthy elm.

She took a deep breath. The evening was warm, and the scent in the air was of damp soil and sweet grass munched by contented cattle, reminding her that she was deep in the heart of the best farmland in the province. Strangely, the air suggested life and renewal, not death by misadventure.

"Stay where you are," O'Toole cautioned. "We've called a couple of investigators to collect evidence. They won't be here for a couple of hours yet." His eyes took in her full-skirted elegance. "Got a hot date?"

Fat chance. "No, I'm working, like you. What are you doing out of the office? Had to see it for yourself?" The gray-blue beam of the solitary yard light gave the sergeant's face a grayish, pinched look; or perhaps, Gloria thought, it wasn't the light.

He shrugged. "You planning to take pictures?"

"I'm not sure." Gloria stepped back a few paces and glanced again at the murky scene behind him, where another officer was spreading a yellow plastic sheet over something pinpointed in the cruiser's headlights. She hoisted her camera and flash. "Who is it?"

"We can't say just yet."

"Can't say? Don't you know? Is he a stranger? Local? Vagrant? Employee?"

"We'll know better tomorrow when we've compiled a few more facts. Sorry." He grimaced. "Stoker should have known better than to broadcast it for you media types to pick up on your scanners. Paper's out, anyway, isn't it?" he added smugly.

"Sure. This week's issue hit the street six hours ago, but the next issue is only a week away. Look grim, Sergeant." She snapped a photo before the officer could protest, and left him muttering an impolite curse and blinking at red dots in the darkness. "Don't worry. Even if it does turn out, it'll probably do no better than the back page next week." She retreated to her car, tiptoeing through the soft ruts. "Can't say," she mused, meant "won't say" until he has been given the official nod. It was a reasonable courtesy to the victim's next-of-kin. If she were pushing a deadline, it would have been infuriating to be kept waiting. Instead, it hardly mattered.

She almost liked Dave O'Toole, in spite of his grim face and dry, humorless way of talking. He was as reticent as any cop should be, but at least respected her job well enough to answer whatever questions he could. He was also reasonably nice-looking, in his late forties, and a widower with a teenage son...not that she cared much at this point, but in a community this size, personal details were difficult to avoid.

Her predecessor on the *Plattsford Sun* would have whiled away most of the night chatting with the police officers, found out nothing in particular, then slept away half the following day. Not Gloria; as exciting as news might be, hanging around at the scene of a tragedy, or watching someone's life and dreams go up in smoke at a spectacular house fire in hopes of catching a teary-eyed survivor on film, was not her style. That was for the cutthroat competition of the city rags, and she'd already had her fill of those. Besides, the *Sun* came out only once a week, and a few days could make a world of difference in an ongoing investigation. By the time the next issue went to press, the victim, whoever he was, would be six feet down, his survivors finished all the muffins and casseroles offered by caring neighbors, and the will loudly contested. And Sergeant O'Toole would have other things not to tell her about.

She swung her feet into the car and caught sight of her shoes, once a creamy off-white, now smeared with black mud. "Probably pig dung from a manure spreader," she murmured as she pulled another U-turn and headed back toward the highway. "Serves me right for dressing up. I should know better."

Gloria did like to dress up occasionally, though most of the time decent clothes were not practical for a typical news day on the *Plattsford Sun.* One could be sitting through a town planning board meeting one minute, and climbing into the back of a pickup truck for a better photo angle of someone's prize boar the next. Back in the early days of her journalism career, the publisher of a small suburban daily had insisted that all his news staff be prepared, at all times, to meet royalty. He had stated in his pompous, chauvinistic way that every reporter, while on duty, must "wear a jacket and tie." Gloria had protested at the time that she did not own a tie. The idea of a dress code for news staff was ridiculous, she had pointed out; a news reporter had to be ready for anything. After all, the royals usually gave plenty of notice if they were coming, but riots, accidents, and fires did not. And anyway, when last had the Queen and Phil dropped into the newspaper office to check out the latest fashions?

Well, what could one expect of a newspaper that still printed a "Girl of the Week" portrait featuring photogenic, twenty-something females whose main claim to fame was an outstanding cleavage and a willingness to undress for the photographer? The photos that were too revealing for the weekly feature were plastered on the wall of the darkroom where she had been expected to process her own film.

She thought she had left it all behind, the rough beginnings on tiny newspapers that expected a writer to be on duty sixty hours a week covering every Brownie and Scout dinner. Indeed, she *had* worked her way into bigger and better things for a few years.

Two months ago, that had all suddenly, abruptly changed, and here she was, at thirty-one, the new face in the small town once again. And this community was unusually tenacious in closing ranks at the appearance of a stranger, particularly a stranger with a secret.

"The *Sun* has a very close-knit, cozy staff," explained the head-office executive who offered her the job. "They're loyal to your predecessor even though he did a poor job on the news. It isn't anything like the type of job you're used to, working in the city for a big corporation."

"My very first job was in a close-knit, small town, sir," Gloria quickly reassured him. "I've learned a few things since then." She'd accepted his offer, and his rather puny starting salary, and congratulated herself on the fact that, in this tight economy, she could still find work, and a means of supporting herself.

And once again, small town happenings were big news. Ribbon-cutting ceremonies, Chamber of Commerce luncheons, Boy Scout banquets, the rising price of pig feed, fund-raising dinners, strangely shaped potatoes resembling celebrities, and an endless round of small-town social and political goings-on were the stuff news stories were made of in Plattsford. Until tonight, that is.

Until now, she had not considered anything about the industrial park to be newsworthy, unique, or unusual. The plans for this bizarre aberration on the rural landscape of O'Dell had been set down long before her arrival, and zoning changes approved the previous autumn, among a cloud of controversy now nearly forgotten. Did the township officials even know what an industrial park should look like, let alone what services one would expect to be provided under the latest environmental protection guidelines? She doubted it. As for industry.... In O'Dell? The only industry that had shown any interest at all in this project so far was a timber-finishing plant that, due to zoning difficulties and loud protests from all the neighbors within a mile of its present location, was being forced to move. Clippings of O'Dell Township council news, sketchy though they were, had not indicated recent problems for follow-up. But an accident, especially a fatality, could turn a nondescript field of mud into a theater for drama. She would have to read up on the details of this particular piece of property as soon as she had a spare moment. And when, she wondered, would that be?

Right now, she had other worries, the biggest being her marriage of inconvenience, followed by her mildly irritating young boss, and whether the ancient farmhouse she had recently rented would stand up for the winter. And gossip.

She had never lived in a community that enjoyed gossip as much as this one did. Separating news from gossip was a minor aggravation. Protecting herself from gossip was pretty much impossible, and she was still not certain how much she wanted to tell people about her particular circumstances. They just wouldn't understand. Hell, *she* still didn't. But by not telling, she was leaving it up to conjecture, and that was even worse.

And some were, indeed, wondering. After all, a conspicuous wedding band meant nothing, if not accompanied by a conspicuous mate. Two weeks after her arrival at the *Sun*, a lady from a nearby church asked if she would like to have her name included in a weekly prayer circle for victims of spousal abuse. The offer was, at best, well meant but puzzling— what on earth had she been thinking?—and Gloria politely declined. A few days later, a middle-aged farmer with appalling teeth offered to accompany her to a meeting for widows and widowers. His eyes were not on her face, however, but a considerable distance below, giving her a good idea what *he* was thinking. The briskly refused date was soon followed by an improper pass made at a service club dinner by a local life insurance broker rumoured to be recently separated—turned down, but not so politely—then another outlandish proposition by a young man barely eighteen with pimples and a stutter. He approached her during a high school career day and asked if she was really a lesbian, as everyone was saying, and if she would give a presentation on gay lifestyles to their senior social studies class, since no one in Plattsford had ever met a dyke before.

"Who the hell put you up to this?" she bellowed. "I'll maim the son of a bitch!" Not that she had anything against people enjoying alternate lifestyles;

she was, however, tired of being an object for speculation. Nevertheless, a few additional expletives gave the local business leaders who were helping out at the career day some insight into the newspaper's newest editor: she has a temper, and when provoked could out-cuss a team of millwrights.

After that, people stopped probing, though they hadn't stopped talking. And Gloria, for her part, began to dress with more self-conscious feminine flair whenever she had the opportunity, caving in to popular stereotyping nonsense. Finally she decided to find an ally and tell all. As her confidante, she chose the *Sun's* advertising manager, Linda Grant, a cheerful, energetic, hard-working woman in her late thirties.

"Well, I was curious, and so is everyone else," Mrs. Grant admitted. "People want to know, even if they're too polite to ask you directly."

Polite? That wasn't the word Gloria had in mind. But when Linda invited her home for supper, Gloria forgave her and happily accepted. She was still nurturing a much-needed friendship with Linda, her husband Bob, two teenage sons, and favorite nephew, a well-mannered, intelligent nineteen-year-old who would not have labeled her butch for refusing to date the locals.

Headlights in a farm lane ahead caught her attention; a tractor, no doubt. She wondered about the strange hours kept by working farmers, often as erratic as her own, and was growing accustomed to keeping a sharp eye out for the little orange triangles that signified a seed wagon trundling toward the barn in the middle of the night.

But it *was* rather late, she noted, to see all the lights on in the McDaniel house, less than a mile from the industrial park. Hazel McDaniel was one of the *Sun*'s elderly, and slightly infirm, community correspondents, and she wondered idly if everything was all right in the McDaniel household. Had the noisy activity next door caught their attention? Perhaps....She snickered softly. "That does it. I'm getting to be as nosy as everyone else around here!" Instead, she drove faster up the highway toward home, ever hoping to see the side-reflectors of Tony's elegant Buick wink a greeting as she turned in the long driveway, and always just a bit disappointed when the lane was dark and empty. After all, Tony was a few thousand miles away.

***

The light was blinking on her answering machine when Gloria arrived home, having retrieved a pile of flyers and letters to "Occupant" from the new mailbox that Linda Grant's teenage nephew had installed at the end of her lane. Tired as she was, a strong wave of warmth ran through her when she heard the voice on the tape. She could picture his face, full of tender affection as he stood before her in white shirt and studs, and not much else, and later torn with regret and anxiety as he held her in a bone-crushing hug, turned and walked through a security gate in Terminal Two....

"...and the orchestra is taking a break and flying back to Toronto tomorrow morning," she heard as her mind wandered back to the present. "My car is downtown, so I'll see you sometime Friday afternoon."

Friday. Tomorrow! *Here?* "Oh, bloody hell." She experienced a momentary feeling of wavering doubt, as though after wishing fervently and passionately for something and finding out it was indeed hers, she was not so certain it was a good idea. Swallowing a feeling of rising panic, she looked around the room, mentally making a list of all the things she must do, and buy, before tomorrow afternoon. The house itself, simple white-frame with large kitchen and nicely proportioned rooms, was adequate. Her furniture, however, was still sitting where the moving truck had dumped it off, amid stacks of packing boxes, nearly two months ago. Since then she had been living out of a suitcase and soup cans, something she had never in her life done before. The windows were bare of curtains. Kitchen cupboards were nearly empty, most of them still awaiting washcloth and bleach. Her one and only rug was still rolled up and tied, wrapped in plastic, and stretched on the floor like a body bag. What was wrong with her?

Her close acquaintances, if any had bothered to venture this far from Toronto, would have come to the obvious conclusion: Gloria Trevisi, once indomitable, independent, and in control, was in shock.

***

A city-bred workaholic, Gloria had been contentedly maintaining a tiny apartment in a run-down neighbourhood in east Toronto, finishing a university degree at night, and working for a large insurance firm as a promotions writer when she first met Tony. He was a struggling concert violinist, son of one of Toronto's elite families, and probably the most unlikely mate one could have chosen for a stubbornly independent Canadian-Italian daughter of an immigrant tradesman.

Two years ago, on a dare, she had attended a dressy social event at Fort York Armoury with a brash, junior executive from her corporate headquarters. This was a formal regimental dinner pegged on the official invitation as "Ladies Dining In," and more aptly known to the regimental bar stewards as "Mixed Mess." The latter description was the more accurate, Gloria surmised as she watched the often childish and sexist behaviour of the young men in dashing red and gold-braid jackets. Officers, yes. Gentlemen? Definitely not.

She had no interest in her escort, except as one providing the opportunity for a good meal and some first class entertainment. He, in turn, had little interest in her, except as a prop on his arm that would further solidify his reputation as a ladies' man.

She had dressed elegantly, and cheaply. The floor-length black velvet skirt, a Christmas present for her eighteenth birthday, still fit her admirably, and, as her reflection proved, still showed off her five-ten height to full advantage. Even in modestly low-heeled shoes, she towered over most of the lame-mannered young officers around her. The borrowed blouse of coffee-coloured lace set off her dark gold shoulder-length hair, honey complexion, and light-brown eyes that, according to her mother, flashed golden when she was annoyed. As the latest in her date's string of female companions, she was impressive...and very annoyed. She was alone in a sea of scarlet-clad males and simpering females, her escort having disappeared for a crapshoot with two of his friends after buying her first, only, and long-gone, drink. She did not expect, or deserve, this treatment. While on the outside she remained cool and impassive, on the inside, she was *fuming*.

Her attention was caught, and held, by a quiet, dark-haired, gray-eyed young man sitting at the bar, not in flashy scarlet military mess kit but sombre black tuxedo. And evidently she had also caught his. Making his way carefully through a crowd of boisterous sub-lieutenants who were asking each other who had brought the Amazon with the great hips, he gazed down from a height of at least six-two, and said with an apologetic smile: "Do you realize, Miss, it is against the rules for a lady to be unaccompanied in the Officer's Mess?"

"In that case, *sir*," she replied with surprisingly little sarcasm, considering her mood, "if you would kindly accompany me to the bar, that pompous ass of a steward who refused to serve me might let me buy myself a glass of vermouth, and perhaps even buy one for you as well."

"Actually, it was that pompous ass of a steward who suggested I fetch you over," he pointed out, with a twitch of a dark eyebrow in the direction of the dignified, middle-aged bar steward, and immediately offered his arm. It was all the encouragement she needed to introduce herself to Tony Lambert, militia captain, whose chamber ensemble would provide the dinner music in the posh adjoining dining room. This was a bonus, Gloria noted, smiling up at the handsome violinist. She *loved* chamber music, and requested Dvoøák for dessert. Once he'd bought her a much-needed shot of sweet vermouth, she clinked her glass against his, downed the vermouth quickly, and their respective fates were sealed...

***

The ring of the telephone interrupted her frantic unpacking, and she snatched it up impatiently.

"I have to talk to you. I've missed you," Tony's voice murmured in her ear.

"Oh.... Sweetheart!" A sudden lurch in her chest robbed her of breath. "Where are you? What time is it there?"

"Very late. I wanted to be sure you got my message. It must be pretty late there too."

"I just got in a few minutes ago," she gasped, collapsing on an uncluttered chair. "When are you getting here? I haven't any food and the house is...well, still kind of disorganized." She reached into the nearest box with her free hand and began pulling out its contents: two used fuses, an oven mitt, a three-year-old calendar, and half a pound of old elastics, items from a kitchen drawer. Disorganized was not a strong enough word; disastrous, more likely. "And it's hot, and the mosquitoes are ravenous, so we can't even sit outside without being eaten alive. If only the place had a screen porch...." Her grimy shoes caught her attention, and she pulled them off, making a face as she shoved them toward the kitchen door. "You might not be very comfortable here. Maybe I should try and meet you in town, but I don't know when I can."

"Gloria, is everything all right?"

"Sorry. It's just...."

"Just what?" He sounded slightly exasperated. "When I'm not on tour, I expect to be with you, wherever it is you've chosen to live. It can't be that bad, can it?"

"I don't know." She felt almost close to tears. "I guess not. But I thought you'd be touring the Maritimes and Quebec for most of the summer."

There was a brief pause on the other end. "We're taking a break for about a week while we replace a cellist. This means I have a few days free to...well, whatever you want to do for a few days."

"I know what I *want* to do," she remarked, feeling a tiny trace of the familiar old spark, and wondering if he could feel it too. "But unfortunately, I have to work, and...." A loud meow came from the direction of the kitchen door, and Gloria was distracted as her chubby gray and white cat buried his claws in the screen. "Damn cat. It's not even my door. Tony, can you just give me a second? I need to talk to you, but Max is going to rip the screen door off its hinges if I don't let him in."

"When I get there tomorrow, we can talk as much as you want, and...look, I know you're busy, so I'll stop at the market on the way up and stock up on all your favorites. After all, I'm crashing in on you unexpectedly...."

"Idiot! You're not a guest, you know. This is your home too." Home? She glanced around the cluttered living room and bare kitchen with a sinking feeling. The sound of claws in wire became even more persistent. So did the demanding yowls.

"You haven't exactly chosen a convenient spot to live, have you? I was looking at your map, and you're not near any place I recognize."

"I didn't have much of a choice. Are you sure you can find the way?" What a ludicrous question. Of course he'd find her. Wouldn't he? They said their good-byes, and she hung up the phone and dashed to the kitchen door, wondering as she detached Max's large paws from the screen how this impractical, unpredictable mess had ever come about.

It was simple, really; Tony proposed, to her amazement. After a year of courting sporadically between her corporate commitments and night classes, and his demanding schedule of auditions, rehearsals and concerts, he suggested that marriage would be far more predictable and practical than dating. Once she recovered from the shock, she agreed—a naive and foolhardy assumption, as they soon discovered. First, a wedding: amid Gloria's Italian relatives' enthusiastic demands for a big church extravaganza, and Tony's firmly Anglican parents' loud wishes for something "tasteful," they made their plans.

The real trouble began three weeks before the appointed event when her employers handed down a state-of-the-nation decree that recommended some drastic downsizing, beginning with their creative departments. Gloria received her pink slip, and her severance, just days before her scheduled trip down the aisle. Tony's luck was running in the opposite direction. Zeroing in on a dream posting with the Upper St. Lawrence Symphony Orchestra, he was offered a contract: two years with a touring company of chamber artists, fully sponsored by the symphony. Chamber music, his life's ambition, was about to become his life.

"Damn it," Gloria muttered when she heard the news. "What do we do now?"

Tony shrugged. "I don't know about you, but I plan to get married this weekend."

They did, just two short months ago, in a mid-sized quasi-ethnic wedding in the small Roman Catholic church that she had attended nearly every Sunday since coming to Toronto. The guests, upper crust Toronto socialites and working-class Italian cousins, ate, drank, and celebrated. And the following day, after a honeymoon that lasted a matter of hours, Tony took to the road while Gloria was left to sort out her abruptly ended corporate career. Reality hit her like an express bus. Just married? Why did she feel as though she had just been dumped?

And why was it such a big deal to her, anyway? She hadn't seen her husband in two months. Truck drivers' wives put up with it all the time. But truckers' wives weren't...Gloria. And truckers weren't Tony Lambert. Apart from the obvious reasons for being crazy about him—looks, talent, and money—there was something else that compelled her to stick it out. When she had reluctantly suggested putting off their marriage to a more convenient time, his answer had been a simple, and unchallengeable "No." She hadn't pushed.

To make matters worse, the job market was not exactly brimming with opportunity. After a week of scanning want ads and contacting agencies, she threw up her hands and took the first job available to her, as the editor of a mid-western Ontario weekly newspaper. "Back where I started," she mused as she packed the belongings from her small apartment and prepared to move, not to Tony's attractive lakeside condo where her family, and his, expected her to take up residence, but into this old, rented farmhouse in the middle of a cornfield.

It was after one when she finally drifted off on the living room couch, exhausted from mentally buying groceries and physically arranging furniture. What would they need, besides a few of her favorites from the market? Coffee? Breakfast cereal? Real paper napkins? She had forgotten all about the body in the industrial park, and the mud on her shoes....

A few miles away, a murderer was still awake, anxiously pondering the day's events, and wondering what tomorrow would bring.

***

Thirty seconds at the East Lister village store the following morning told Gloria that everyone in a hundred kilometers had already heard the news via the country grapevine.

"I hear they left him lying out there in the mud for *two hours* while they waited for some bigwig police inspector to get out there in the middle of the night," an anonymous female voice hissed emphatically behind the soup cans. Gloria pricked up her ears.

"Oh, my," a second voice chimed in. "And they say he was in debt up to his ears. Maybe it was...suicide!" The voice dropped to a hushed whisper on the last word.

"You mean he was bankrupt?" A light gasp. "Well! They always went to Florida, certainly never spared the cash on cars. Oh, poor Marie, it must be *awful* for her. What will she do?" The voice was almost gleeful in its chords of woe.

"Insurance would carry them through, I suppose."

"That's if he had any. Were they really hard up for money?"

Gloria groaned as she grabbed a copy of the Toronto *Globe and Mail* from the pile near the front door and half-listened while two women dissected the personal lives of their latest victims. "And here I thought that finally, I knew something before everyone else," she muttered. She had no doubt whom they were discussing, despite the name being "withheld." It seemed that the victim's name, place of residence, and survivors were already well known...even his financial solvency or lack thereof. Even so, locals refused to believe the local newspaper had any business messing in their lives.

That attitude had its advantages, she supposed; she was spared the undignified early-morning vigil outside the home of the deceased, waiting for a family member to peep out so she could descend on him, or her, with outrageously insensitive questions. Not that rural readers were any less bloodthirsty; they could get more spectacular dirt, though less accurate, over the counter at the feed mill, or behind the cracker display at a convenience store. Were Gloria to be so impolite as to speculate on someone's financial solvency, or worse, disturb the tranquility of a mourning family by asking if the man had committed suicide—to say nothing of ask whether he had life insurance—she'd be ostracized, shunned, and blacklisted from any more potluck dinners.

The voices, echoing light "Tsk, tsks" behind the canned goods, halted as she rounded the biscuits on the corner of the aisle. Two women started in surprise. She ignored them and moved up to the counter to where a slight, elderly man with sparse white hair covered in a flat hat was unloading bags of penny candy.

"How are you today, Norman?" she asked.

"Not good," he replied, shaking his head, and spent the next four minutes describing joint aches, back aches, stomach aches, and a pounding head. "Can't eat, can't sleep. Doctors have given up. Not much point in goin' on," he concluded, chewing a toothpick.

"Tough about last night," she ventured.

Norm snorted. "Sure. Too many new people comin' to live here, bringing all their crime with them. Not like it used to be." He stared morosely from under his hat, his large flat hand slapping the counter. "Used ta know everybody that come in here."

"I see." Gloria paid for her paper, and made her exit. She climbed behind the wheel of her car, started the engine, glanced at her face in the mirror and smiled. Never mind the slight from the two women; to hell with this hypochondriac's symptoms. Her husband was coming home, and nothing would quell the singing in her head. She felt like a teenager in love, even though she'd already overslept on this warm, mid-June morning, and had to forego coffee, breakfast, and a brisk walk.

The landscape never ceased to catch her attention as she cruised through the countryside to the busy little town of Plattsford. Large expanses of soybeans, corn, and grain were turning the generally flat expanse into a checkerboard of many shades of green. Some people touted the wild growth and rock faces of Muskoka as the ideal country setting. Gloria preferred this; a yearning to work the land was firmly embedded in her not-too-distant ancestry of generations of Italian subsistence farmers and British sheepherders. Hundred-acre fields stretched to distant woodlots, home to birds of all sorts from warblers and finches to kestrels and vultures. Under warm sunshine, the grain fields were undulating slowly with the softest breeze, unable to contain the energy of growth.

The drive took her just over ten minutes, on a good day. This morning she spent that time daydreaming about every long, lazy moment of the next few days she would be spending with her husband. Parking in the large public lot behind the storefront newspaper office at barely eight thirty A.M., she headed for the rear door beside the old wooden loading dock. The *Sun's* front office opened at nine. At this hour, the front sidewalks were nearly deserted, but the lot was slowly filling up with vehicles belonging to employees and shopkeepers, florists, hairdressers, travel agents, and accountants.

Opening the door with her key, she paused to eavesdrop on more of the latest gossip from the two women who ran the *Sun*'s office, chatting over their morning coffee as they stacked newspapers and sorted bills.

"Their neighbour says that when the police came to tell Marie about her husband being killed, she wasn't even at home."

"Really? But it was after midnight when they found him, wasn't it? Doesn't *she* keep strange hours."

"Hmm, doesn't she, though? What do you suppose?"

News of the fatality had already traveled as far as Plattsford, and Theresa and Jan, the front office staff who looked after circulation, classified ads, customer billing, and hundreds of phone calls every week, already knew more than *she* did. Information from the victim's neighbours? She doubted whether even the police had progressed that far.

"Clarence and Marie never had much of a life together, did they?" Theresa was saying. "Why did they ever get married?"

"Same reason as most, I expect," Jan observed. "She had a weakness for 'tall, handsome, and dumb as a bag o' hammers.'" A flurry of giggles. "Besides, they *had* to. *You* know why," she added in an arch tone.

"True," Theresa confirmed after a pregnant pause. "And she really hasn't done too badly, since. Nicest house in the village. But he was gettin' a bit carried away, don't you think? He should've stuck with barn foundations and field drainage. McKees were a farming family. Why did Clarence try to get so fancy? Industrial park? As if the township needs one. And on his family's farm, no less."

"Yeah," Jan answered. "True, it backs onto the village, but his father and grandfather must've been heavin' up the earth, spinnin' in their old coffins." Another gurgle of laughter was quickly hushed. "Guess I shouldn't be laughing; now Clarence is dead, too."

Clarence? If Gloria's memory wasn't mistaken, Clarence McKee was owner of McKee Excavation, the local digger who had submitted an acceptable estimate to her landlord for a new septic bed for her house, since the old one backed up rather badly every time she put through a load of laundry. Nearly a month ago he had staked out the new bed with bright orange sticks and promised he'd be back within the week.

He was also the local contractor who had proposed the industrial development in O'Dell Township the previous year, rammed it through council with himself as an elected official, and moved his trucks and bulldozers onto the property in April, just after she arrived at the *Sun*. Interesting. Not only could she predict a smelly summer on the home front, but also O'Dell Township might have to wait awhile for all of that lucrative industrial assessment the council had been promised.

But most important, the victim was beginning to take the form of a person, not simply a news story to be pursued. He was a neighbour, husband, business owner, entrepreneur, and working man. Without even an official word, she could feel that his death was sending small ripples through a close-knit rural society.

The two women were silent as she clattered noisily down the long corridor and rounded the corner into the front office. She smiled a greeting, shuffled clipboard and camera into one arm and reached for her messages with the other.

Theresa moved to the front counter. "Good morning, Gloria, you're looking pretty chipper today!" Her eyes glittered as she studied Gloria's slightly flushed face.

"Thank you. It must be the weather." Better not to let them know she had eavesdropped. Friendly though they were, they weren't quite prepared yet to share their spicy stories from their local social circles like the Women's Institute, not to mention rumours about the latest tragedy, with the new editor. And she, in return, wasn't willing to give them any more material. Besides, they'd already noticed she was glowing like a thousand watts, and that was enough. She heard the rear door crash shut as she headed for the stairs, no doubt the arrival of Rick Campbell, her staff of one, with a handful of films of sports events for processing. Or.... The wattage dimmed to about five hundred.

"Just the person I wanted to talk to," Fred Russell's energetic tenor voice boomed down the corridor. The current general manager, Russell was five years her junior and always reminded her of an overexcited youngster. She heard his quick footsteps coming up behind her as she hastily swung around the corner on the landing. "Did you hear the big news? Someone was found dead—"

"Clarence McKee, I believe." She cut across his enthusiastic rhetoric. "Local contractor. I was there last night shortly after the body was found." Imparting this fact to her twenty-something boss gave her a certain satisfaction. "It's not big news, Mr. Russell. And since the paper came out yesterday evening, it will be *old* news by the time we can deal with it." She continued up the stairs. Nothing, she vowed, would spoil her good mood, not even Fred Russell.

As she headed to the desk behind the small partition in the corner designated as her office, his long stride matched hers exactly, and his pointed face was brimming with excitement. "Oh. Well, it sounds like real news. Has there ever been anything like it in this area before?"

"A workplace fatality? Probably," she answered, rounding the partition to her desk and flopping into her chair in front of the computer terminal. "Farmers, for example, have accidents all the time; it's a hazardous profession. But none have died since I've been here."

Russell, rushing behind her, stopped just short of tumbling sideways into her lap. "I already assigned Rick—"

"*You* assigned Rick?" Gloria interrupted, swiveling her chair to face him. "What have you assigned him? And did you check his schedule first?" She looked at the clipboard that contained the busy weekly assignment roster. Damn it, Rick was *her* staff, not his.

"Uh...no. I just asked him to get on top of it, pick up a police report before coming in, maybe drive past the site for a photo...Okay. You're right, we need to set up a game plan, coordinate our efforts. Coffee at ten o'clock sound right?"

"Sorry. I have a photo at ten."

"Noon, then. How about lunch?" He looked hopeful.

"It's Pizza Day at the Christian school. I need some cute pictures to round out the back pages."

"How about ten minutes from now?"

Gloria looked down at the pile of press releases and letters that needed sorting and editing, and at the Friday assignments, which listed the opening of a new hair salon in a nearby hamlet, dress rehearsal for the high school convocation, and an interview with the local Royal Canadian Legion president about the planned addition to the present hall, two photos at the truck dealership for an advertisement...all before lunch. On the other hand, he probably wouldn't let up. "How about right now?" she suggested. "I have five minutes." Her good mood would have to be put on hold, she resolved.

Fred Russell had been general manager of the *Sun* for three months, the latest in a string of junior executive up-and-comers who had cut their managerial molars on this assignment. Last summer the paper, which had been in the same family's hands for three generations, was sold to a large multi-media corporation, and became a handy place for a communications network to try out promising business school graduates who were scratching and clawing their way up from the cellars of administration. After all, what harm could they do here?

To give them credit, some probably had been reasonably adept. Then, there was Fred Russell, who couldn't quite figure out what his job was; and even *he* would be all right, she thought, if only he weren't always trying to impress her.

He wasn't a bad sort, she mused as she followed him across the large open space filled with desks, computers, file cabinets, cupboards, and tables, toward the tidy glassed-in cubicle in the corner. At first she had been patient with his assumption that since they were both newcomers to the *Sun*, and outsiders, they should be sticking together, proving that mankind was essentially a herd animal. She did not expect that attitude from the general manager of a busy little weekly.

His tactics, however, were damned annoying, sometimes dangerously close to flirting. Frankly, she would have preferred a direct approach, like: "What are you doing at midnight after you finish a sixteen-hour work day?" so she could give a direct answer: "Sleeping. Alone!"

She had made no secret of her circumstances, once she told Linda Grant. But "Married, husband absent" seemed to mean "lonely, seeking companionship" to a person like Russell. She did not want those two happy gossips downstairs to get any strange ideas. She called him "Mr. Russell," in spite of his junior years, to keep him at a distance. He called her "Gloria" to move in closer. She found it irritating. She had dealt with his type before; his type thought she enjoyed being irritated, like a high school sophomore. She didn't.

She followed him into his office and closed the door. "First," she began, preempting any attempt on his part to take control, "thank you for your interest and support. Second, keep your hands off the news and let me handle it. We need a police report—"

"Rick is getting the police report."

"Rick has other things to do. Then we will require a recent photo of the victim—that's dead-guy, to you—preferably from files, so we don't have to bother his family. Then we need someone who knows him, maybe one of our community correspondents, to gather facts for an obituary, the usual stuff: birthplace, schooling, business history, etc. That's the plan."

"But what about pictures of the scene? Rick's a crack photographer. He can take care of that, and—"

"I have a photo," Gloria asserted, "but chances are, we won't be using it." She leaned on his desk. "We're not a Sunday tabloid. We are a community newspaper. The police will have everything we need to know, and probably more than is fit to print anyway. Please, Mr. Russell, do not interfere with my work."

"But I *should* be interfering. I mean, I am the manager." His earnest gaze flickered from her face. "And I'm supposed to manage."

She swallowed an angry retort as she watched his eyes, searching for an interesting place to rest, and finding none: she dressed modestly, even in summer. "Fine. Manage. I'll keep you posted." She rose and stepped to the door, hoping for escape.

"Gloria."

She stopped, and immediately regretted it.

"I...uh...got a call yesterday from Mr. Murray at head office. He asked me how you were doing."

She turned slowly. "Really? And what did you tell him?"

"What *could* I tell him?" He smiled slightly. "That I didn't know. In fact, I didn't even know where you were."

She ground her teeth. "I was out doing my job. What do you think?"

"Well, if you *tell* me what you're doing, maybe I can let Mr. Murray know."

"Mr. Murray can read the paper." Impudent ass! His job was business; hers was the news. Wasn't it obvious? She turned on her heel and left quickly, nearly colliding with Rick Campbell as he bounded energetically up the stairs.

"Junior gymnastics starts at nine, Rick," she snapped grumpily as she recovered from full contact with the former college linebacker. "Remember?"

"Of course I remember," he replied huffily. "Fred called me just before I left home, said something happened last night, and asked me to go straight to the police station for a statement," Rick said, turning in her direction. "As your staff—"

"If I need your help, I'll tell you myself," she said, glancing into Russell's office, still stinging. She sighed noisily. "And what did the police say?"

"Nothing that you don't already know." Rick's voice held slight resentment. "Sergeant O'Toole left a message asking us—asking *you*—to call before nine. I guess you already talked to him last night. The officer on duty didn't have a report, since it's a criminal investigation. And now," he hoisted his camera to his shoulder, "if you'll excuse me, I'll go off to *junior gymnastics.*" He turned abruptly and thumped back down the stairs.

Gloria watched him descend, her good mood a distant memory. Great; not only was she getting used to a new marriage and a new job in a new community, she was lumbered with a power struggle, a manager trying to get the upper hand, and a staff reporter who resented her.

She glanced at the clock on the wall. "Oh, hell!" She dove for her desk phone and dialed the police line.

Chapter 2

"You're late, Ms. Trevisi." Sergeant O'Toole sounded grumpy when Gloria finally reached him by telephone later in the morning.

"I can't help it. You weren't available when I called, and I had other things to do. Are you certain, sir? A *homicide?* Are you telling me that this *isn't* an accident or a case of negligence?"

"*Suspicious death* is the term, though we're treating it as a homicide. Don't jump to conclusions. I am saying that we are not ruling out the *possibility* of foul play. The investigation is still being handled locally."

"Suicide?"

"If it's suicide, we wouldn't tell you anyway," the sergeant replied with a trace of impatience. "But it isn't suicide, we're sure of that."

"So you're saying it could be murder. And you're sure of *that.*" Gloria stared at the lukewarm coffee in the Styrofoam cup. This was going to be a pretty sensational headline in—what, six days? She took another gulp to ease the dryness of her throat. "Homicide." Gloria repeated the word as she jotted it down on the blank page of a large notebook. "What makes you think it's a possibility?"

"I can't tell you. It's pretty sketchy."

She drummed her fingers on her desk. If the closed-mouthed Sergeant O'Toole had said *that* much, then the sketchy part of the narrative likely consisted of suspects' faces drawn in a notebook. "Sergeant, what *can* you tell me, keeping in mind, of course, that it will be a full week before the paper comes out and likely the news will be completely different by then?"

"Well, I can tell you that the victim is Clarence McKee, aged fifty-six, resident of East Lister in O'Dell Township, owner of McKee Excavating and Tile Drainage. That won't change by next week." He paused. "Body was found at 11:50 P.M. on the premises of Lot 11, Concession 23 of O'Dell, a building site."

So far, the gossip mill is disturbingly accurate, she mused, jotting down the essentials. "And what brought the police to the scene? Were you tipped off?"

"No. Routine patrol. Cause of death is undetermined at the moment," the sergeant continued, "but between you and me, he was squashed flat by a bulldozer. Now again between you and me, Ms. Trevisi, how many people will stand still long enough for a bulldozer to run them down?"

Her coffee suddenly turned very acidy. "I see your point." After all, *someone* was driving the bulldozer, one would assume. She jotted down a quick question mark in her notebook.

"So we're looking for possible witnesses," O'Toole added, "anyone who was in the area and may have seen or heard something from five, when the crew left, until midnight when the body was discovered. And we want to know what he was doing on the building site so late at night when most men are home with their wives."

"Perhaps his wife wasn't home, either," Gloria suggested, recalling the other nugget of information she had overheard.

"Perhaps she wasn't," O'Toole replied frostily. "Until we can gather a few facts, we're only speculating, and on that topic, this is about as far as I want to go."

"All I am suggesting, sergeant, is that you were not home last night, nor was I. We were working. Mr. McKee might have been working late as well. Is his wife also employed somewhere?"

"I can't say, Ms. Trevisi."

Police were reserving their judgment, obviously. But with six days to go before the next publication, what did it matter? By then it would be old news, but with luck, good news, a case solved. She wondered if his wife drove heavy equipment.

"Squashed flat, you say?"

"Bulldozer tracks went right over him," O'Toole said in his driest tone of voice.

Gloria closed her eyes on the vision that floated through her mind. "And how was the body discovered?"

"Brian Stoker stepped in the remains while checking out something he thought he saw on the site. And that, Ms. Trevisi, is all I can say right now. Perhaps next week we'll have more."

"What do you mean, something on the site? A break-in?"

"Save your curiosity, Ms. Trevisi. It's a criminal investigation."

Jotting down his last words and underlining them three times, she thanked the sergeant, replaced the receiver, and took another swig of weak, tepid coffee.

Sergeant O'Toole had a point; why would anyone lie down in front of a bulldozer? The thing made enough racket to wake...the dead. There were other reasons, however, why a man might be lying dead in a construction site: a fall, a heart attack, or stroke. Having fallen in the wrong place, he might have been run over accidentally, though it was doubtful. Hit-and-run on a bulldozer wasn't common, not even in O'Dell Township.

Neither was murder. The police, however, seemed awfully sure of themselves. They had a reason to rule out other causes of death. Why?

And why Clarence McKee? Besides being a local building contractor, he was a member of the O'Dell township council, and one with a pretty large following, if the polling results in the last election were any indication. His overall win in the township may have been by a narrow margin, but in the small community of East Lister, he had polled ninety percent of the votes. Her predecessor, for all his failings as a news gatherer, was nevertheless well organized and had kept decent clipping files, no doubt because it made him appear busy. She had made a point of looking into the "who's who" of that particular community this morning before calling the police.

Perhaps McKee's popularity and success in local politics was rather odd as well. In rural townships, the farming community generally stuck together and kept development of any kind at bay. Even in O'Dell, people who were frankly pro-development were rarely popular. Members of council were usually local farmers, with a heavy mandate to preserve the status quo at all costs.

True, the McKees were one of those old local families who had lived here for generations, and that meant they were related to most of the people in the community, in one way or another. Plus, McKee seemed to have the magic touch when it came to mixing business with politics. Gloria had heard that certain controversial issues were pushed through council on a three-to-two vote, in spite of objections by residents, and their subsequent appeals to the Ontario Municipal Board somehow never came to anything. Clarence himself, however, was loudly touted as a model citizen. She knew how that worked; McKee attended church and was active in community affairs, and few people would dare oppose him. That wasn't all; he also ran a small, independent business that provided much-needed employment, albeit low-skilled and low-paying, for the locals. That much, if nothing else, was to his credit, even from her point of view.

She pulled out an old clipping and looked at the photo of McKee, a man well into middle age, clean-shaven, with thin, grayish hair receding from his forehead and brushed diagonally across a bald spot on the top of his head, sagging cheeks, and narrow eyes. The picture was a face shot; she couldn't see his shoulders, could not determine height or build. Only colouring, and even that was merely in black and white. She had attended one meeting of O'Dell Township Council since arriving, and had probably seen him there. She studied the photo carefully, recalling yet another piece of gossip from Jan and Theresa: tall, probably. Thick as a brick, no doubt. But handsome? To some, perhaps. A family man, likely, with grown-up children, possibly grandchildren. Did he deserve to die?

She considered her six-day-old headline. If the case were resolved before next Wednesday evening, she would have a much more immediate story. Yet, a bit of speculation never did any harm.

But not yet; Fred Russell, hovering just within earshot, stuck his face over the partition. "So, what's the news? And where were you all morning?"

"The news is not good, but it will keep. And in case Mr. Murray asks, I was interviewing a local artist for next week's crafts page and getting debriefed by a hospital board member who doesn't like the new lab forms."

"I like that last part," Russell's eyes glittered. "Next time, can I watch?"

Adolescent twit! "I'm not wasting news space on a long discussion about lab forms." *Or debriefing in front of you,* she added silently as she punched in a file number and started typing, hoping Russell would take the hint.

He didn't; instead, he walked around the end of the partition and stood behind her, watching her hands as she typed—or more to the point, staring at her wedding ring, accompanied today by a large diamond that she had slipped on just before leaving the house that morning. She could hear his breath over her shoulder, and kept her eyes on the screen in front of her. "And the police?" he asked. "Have they said anything about last night?"

"Nothing noteworthy with our deadline six days away." Gloria stopped typing and turned to face him. "They're treating the industrial park incident as a homicide. That's all." She enjoyed the comical visual response on Russell's face.

"A homicide? *Murder?*" Russell's voice rose so high it cracked. "Oh, wow."

"Yes. That means they're not talking. And I have work to do, Mr. Russell." Why was he interested? Was he considering increasing the press run for the upcoming issue to provide the people of Plattsford with more souvenir copies of a sensational story? After all, newspapers sold well during a crisis, and strong circulation figures were crucial to a newspaper's economy.

He stared curiously at the file photo on her desk. "Who's this?"

"Clarence McKee. The murder victim." She smiled, showing teeth. "Curious?"

Russell raised his eyebrows at the photo. "Huh. So that's what he looked like." He paused, still hovering. "Listen, I'm sorry about sending Rick to the police this morning. He...he should have had your job, you know."

"Should he?" Gloria asked, turning to him. She felt her breath forcing its way out of her lungs. She was beginning to get a feel for Russell: he stuttered slightly before he nipped. "Then why didn't you give it to him?"

"I would have. And I may...yet." He turned and strode back to his office.

She sat back and stared at the flickering letters on her screen. Is that why Rick seemed to resent her? She couldn't blame him, really. Her predecessor in the editor's chair had rarely lifted a finger to cover breaking news, and he must have felt a certain sense of responsibility for tasks other than sports, until Gloria took over. He was, she had discovered, a local athlete trained in journalism at University of Western Ontario, well schooled in general reporting as well as sports coverage. If Rick had wanted this job, why had the company not promoted the present staff to the editor's post and hired another junior? The answer had been carefully worded by Mr. Murray during her final interview. "We want someone in charge who has no...previous loyalties."

"In other words, someone who won't try to follow in the footsteps of his old leader?" she'd asked. "He must have been some editor."

And that was the problem, wasn't it? Ed Murray, manager of Heartland's print division, Fred Russell's boss, fired her predecessor and appointed a stranger to the post, without consulting the general manager. And not only did Russell resent the challenge to his authority as general manager, but he bore further resentment on Rick's behalf, as well.

Old loyalties aside, Rick Campbell knew his job; he was on friendly terms with all the coaches and league organizers, produced great photographs on demand, and ground out miles of copy for the front section sports pages, the pages that every household in three counties wanted to read first. In his early twenties, he was good-looking, athletic, and intelligent, and no doubt had a sweetheart somewhere. Whoever she was, Gloria hoped the young lady enjoyed sports as much as *she* enjoyed a good string quartet.

But there were other things in the world besides good music, like a good story. Even township politics held a certain intrigue.

She glanced over the notes from the previous night's hospital board meeting: a budget update, two bulletins from the province about new health care billing procedures...no, not much intrigue there. And not much in this crafts page story, either.

She returned to her keyboard, determined to have this feature finished before lunch.

***

"Lunch?" It was nearly one, and Linda Grant poked her head around the partition as Gloria was unpacking her camera and removing the Pizza Day film. She glanced at her computer, where the copy for the crafts page was waiting for a quick finale.

"Give me ten—oh, what the hell? I've said all I want to say about watercolors." Famished after watching ninety children gobble pepperoni and double-cheese for the past twenty minutes, Gloria punched a quick "30" at the end of the last paragraph, and picked up her purse. Out the back door and across the parking lot, the spicy smell of pizza was on the wind, beckoning them to Gina's Italian Food. She was sidestepping around a large blue sedan that had just pulled up near the Main Street access alley, when the passenger door opened and a large cane protruded, nearly tripping her. She caught herself from falling right into the lap of Hazel McDaniel, the East Lister community correspondent.

The woman gave her a stern stare. "Watch where you're going, young lady," she warned, waving her cane as Gloria reached out to assist her. "No need. I can get out on my own. I'm not a cripple, you know."

"Sorry, ma'am," Gloria murmured, and glanced up at the large No Parking sign above the vehicle. The two of them watched as Mrs. McDaniel swung the heavy door shut and ambled slowly toward the access, the hem of her dark, flower-print dress no doubt concealing painfully swollen knee joints. The vehicle moved away.

"She looks more tired and frail every time I see her." Linda shook her head as she watched the elderly woman making her way through the alley toward the flower shop.

"I imagine she's tired," Gloria remarked. "There were lights on in her house well past midnight, last night." Catching Linda's amused glance in her direction, she added, "I noticed as I drove past on my way back from East Lister. I thought perhaps someone was ill."

"More likely drunk. But not Hazel. She's as dry as they come. Her husband, though, is a real case." Linda watched the print dress disappear around the corner. "She's heading toward the funeral home, I expect, probably preparing to write Clarence McKee's obituary for next week's paper."

"How did you...Oh, never mind. Does she know the McKees that well?"

"Well enough, since they live in East Lister. They're related, somehow. Don't even try to straighten out family relationships in that village; in some way or another, they're all related."

"Scary thought." Gloria shook her head and turned back to the restaurant. "I'll try to watch what I say, though I can't say *they* do. You should hear what was being whispered in the store this morning."

"I can imagine. It's all right for *them* to speculate, though. They're close, caring neighbors."

"Huh!" Gloria snorted. "Did you know him? He's not a relative of yours, is he? News follows family ties. I come from a big family myself."

Linda pulled open the heavy front door of Gina's Restaurant. The air inside was warm and heavy with Italian seasonings. "Not a relative, but I feel sad for the family. Enough bad news. It has been a busy morning, and I'm hungry enough to eat the entire lunch buffet." She found a table near the window and perched delicately on one of the restaurant's light wicker chairs.

"Where would you put it?" Gloria glanced over to the tasty array of fresh pizza, six different salads, and warm garlic bread, then back at her friend's slight figure. Linda was barely five feet tall, and probably boasted size four shoes and an eighteen-inch waist.

"I eat like a bird, about the equivalent of my weight in food every day. And so do my boys." Linda had thick, bright red, curly hair and the high energy of a person well suited for sales, and probably burned off a whole wedge of cheesecake while presenting a three-issue, half-page, spot-color package to the local appliance dealer. The chief (and only) sales representative on the *Sun*, Linda was one of the locals;

she grew up on a farm, married out of high school, and brought her family into the world while she still had the youth and vigour to enjoy them. Her children were almost grown, and she was still happy to be working at something she liked. On top of that, being related to half of Plattsford made it fairly easy to sell advertising. Sometimes, Gloria envied her.

Linda glanced at the menu on the blackboard and waved to the waiter. He hurried over to their table, and blinked at Gloria's hand. "Wow. Dazzle me. Is that thing real?" He winked at Gloria and turned to Linda. "The usual, coz?"

"Yes please, Carl, and can you brew me up some fresh decaf?"

Carl looked at Gloria. "The same for me, but make it a real coffee. I need the zip."

"I've got enough, thanks," Linda said. "Caffeine makes me dizzy." She turned back to Gloria as Carl left. "And speaking of zip, you look as though you have plenty of it today."

"I feel like a married woman today." She leaned forward and smiled. "Tony's coming home, but just for a few days."

"Ha! And that's why you're glittering like a strobe light. And not just the diamond, though Theresa and Jan practically knocked foreheads every time you walked by, trying to get a better look. How come you don't wear it more often?"

"Well, it's a bit showy, don't you think?" She splayed her long, large-knuckled fingers on the tabletop.

"I think it shows that Tony has exquisite taste in jewellery. Look at the size of that sparkler!"

Gloria glanced down at the ring Tony had bought her just before their wedding, a fat gold band sporting a rock the size of Newfoundland. Even though it suited her large, sturdy fingers, she considered it a bit upscale for her lifestyle. They rose and moved toward the buffet. "By the way, I checked out the new hairdresser's in Perkins Hill today for a business story."

"Good. I'll hit her up for an ad. Maybe you should hit her up for a free trim."

"I'm afraid to get my hair cut by any of these young kids. I might just walk out of there with a fifties flip, or a biker-girl's chop and purple streaks. And the older hairdressers favour two-inch-long hair and perm rods. Anyway, I don't have time for a haircut." Gloria helped herself to a large scoop of romaine lettuce.

"Oh, I don't know. You've been at it pretty steadily for the past two months. Steve Lang, your predecessor, never covered the district as thoroughly. Is it necessary?"

"What do you think?" She shook more lettuce onto her plate and moved toward the croutons. "I found a two-inch thick consultants' report on sustainable development strategies on his desk when I first came. It was a week before I had time to go through the back issues and see what he had said about it since it was released by the county in January. And guess what? Nothing."

"Steve claimed people only care about accidents and court. And sports, but that was always Rick's territory. Once we lost our third news staffer, the one who used to attend council meetings, he never bothered, just printed highlights of the minutes. Who cares about sustainable development and land use strategies, anyway?"

"You would, if someone were building a factory beside your farm that will dump acid rain on your cash crop, or if someone wanted to put a massive pig barn right behind a village. But you're right: no one considers this important. Every township in the area simply tabled the thing, and buried it." She poured Italian dressing on her salad, smothering the croutons. "People would be wise to pay some attention, before we get more O'Dell industrial parks."

Linda waved her hand. "Lodging an objection would be impolite. You did a great job reviewing the whole report, though. Even I understood it, in the end."

"And we got two letters about it the following week."

"Which means at least two more people finally understood it. Isn't it time to let up? Go somewhere? Visit some friends? I'm certain they must be wondering what's happened to you."

I can well imagine, Gloria thought to herself. Truth was, she had few friends. Her favorite cousin and confidante, Renée, had left with her family to spend the summer in Italy shortly after serving as her maid-of-honour. Her friends in Toronto were former work colleagues, the kind with whom one did not keep up once one had left the job. As for the people she had grown up with...No, she did not even want to think about them until she had a better idea what to tell them. She took the second-to-last wedge of cheese and tomato pizza and searched for a safer topic.

"What's with Norm, the old guy in the general store at East Lister? Is he dying?"

"Since the day he was born. Or more precisely, ever since I can remember. He used to be the reeve of O'Dell, years ago. Be careful what you say about him. He has friends and relatives everywhere."

"Oh well, at least he talks to me." Gloria glanced around the restaurant. "Linda, this paper has been under the new regime for a year now. What do you think of working for a big corporation instead of a small, local dynasty?"

"Same old dung, different pile." Linda picked up a clean fork lying beside the hot peppers and waved it as though she were shoveling something heavy and sticky. "The 'family' never bothered much with the welfare of their employees. At least now we have health benefits, a dental plan, and even a retirement package, of sorts. Other than that, I don't notice much difference." Linda grappled with two big wedges of pizza and a large helping of Caesar salad. "I've never noticed a general manager taking much personal interest in the well-being of the staff, either, except Fred. He seems quite interested in you. Just this morning, he was asking me if you live with your husband."

Gloria nearly dropped her plate. "What? Why?"

"Maybe because everyone is whispering that you're really separated, or divorced, or something."

"Well, you know better, and so should he. Why this sudden nosiness about my personal life, asking about my friends, family, and...jewellery?"

"I'm just passing on what people say."

"I'm well aware of what they say."

"Glo, people are curious. And imagine how it feels to be Fred Russell, stuck in Plattsford. He's assessing his chances."

"He doesn't even like me."

"Oh yes, he does. Come on, aren't you ever curious about him?"

"No. I really don't care." Gloria teased her macaroni salad with her fork before trying some. "He's a boss, Linda, and so adolescent for his age, which incidentally is at least five years younger than I am. I know that matchmaking is a rural pastime; heaven knows, farmers arrange these things all the time with their cows, and then start on people. But believe me, if I weren't married, I'd be single." She glanced over at another table where three young men decked out in uniform of green coveralls were hunched over their coffee and sandwiches. "Really, *really* single."

"All right. I'm not really matching you up with Fred, although I do think that he's just a little bit interested...I'm kidding." The three stockyard employees were looking their way. "That's the way it is in a small town. People are interested in your private life."

Gloria leaned toward her. "I know all about small towns. My first job was in a small town, and they were interested too. Half the married men under the age of thirty-five were trying to sleep with me, and the other half were telling everyone that they already had. I was twenty, and believe it or not, I didn't know how to handle that garbage."

"No kidding?" Linda teased, dropping her voice to a whisper. "This is more like it. Tell me, if you weren't sleeping with them, who *were* you sleeping with?" She glanced at the three men, and leaned forward. "Everyone does, you know."

"Well, I don't tell," Gloria whispered back. "But I'll give you this much: not one of them was married." She relaxed, sat back, and grinned at the shocked expression on Linda's face. "I had standards. And I still do." She checked out the nearest diners, and lowered her voice. "Tell me, since everyone is curious about everyone's private lives, did you know Clarence McKee personally?"

"Sure. Everyone did. And it won't be easy finding out who murdered him."

She put down her fork. "You mean, not only did you know who had been killed before the local police had released the name, but you knew that they suspected murder? Next you'll be putting together a sponsor page and selling space around the news story to half the merchants in town."

Linda looked indignant. "I'd *never* do that. Marie McKee and I belonged to the same bowling league ten years ago. She may not be my closest and dearest friend, but she deserves my respect. Even her husband does."

"No doubt. How did you find out that police suspect homicide? I just heard this from Sergeant O'Toole a couple of hours ago."

"Would *you* lie still while someone made a parking lot pizza out of you? I suspected the worst as soon as I heard."

Gloria looked at the pizza on her plate. "*And* you know about the bulldozer. That's exactly what Sergeant O'Toole said to me today. Well, not exactly. But no one seems to think he had a stroke or a heart attack, and got run over by accident. Isn't that the most logical thing?"

Linda smirked. "You didn't say *drunk*, but that's more likely than a heart attack, knowing the McKees."

Gloria raised an eyebrow. "Right. A close, caring neighbor. I forgot."

"Well, if it had been an accident, the person driving the bulldozer would have noticed, and done something, wouldn't he? And people don't drive bulldozers around construction sites in the middle of the night, usually." Linda pressed her lips together.

"Okay, I know I shouldn't say nasty things about someone who has just died, but people have been talking about it everywhere I go. I know he was a big noise in O'Dell Township, and you'll hear everyone say he was a great guy, but plenty of them disliked him."

"Why? Was he a success? That's grounds for being disliked in some circles."

"As successful as anyone can be, who grew up, married, and did business in O'Dell Township. I say he was murdered, because that's what everyone assumes. But that's gossip, and you're looking for news."

"Sometimes, gossip's far more interesting than news," Gloria remarked. "It's not printable, of course, but it gives me a feel for the place. Tell me more. Does his wife drive a bulldozer? And why would people *assume*—"

"Not here." Linda glanced over at the farm workers who had just strolled to the salad bar. "It's too public. Gloria, you're not going to dig up dirt on the guy, or anything, are you? Because it isn't nice."

"Why? Is there dirt to dig?" She raised an eyebrow. "I know the role of a community newspaper, Linda. Murder or no murder, I'm not interested in printing dirt. I want to get a feel for the place and the people."

"That's a tall order. We're not as simpleminded as you think." Her eyes twinkled. "I promise, I'll let you know what I hear."

"Please do. Let's eat. I want to get home early this afternoon for a change."

"Obviously." Linda stuffed a forkful of salad into her mouth. "And since he's in town, you'd better bring him around so we can all get a look at him. It will stop a lot of talk."

Gloria looked at her, exasperated. "I was just thinking today that Mr. Russell is as nosy as my mother. I think you are too."

"It comes naturally. I *am* a mother. And what do you hear from your mother these days?"

"Not much. When I told her I was moving here, she was shocked, screaming 'What on earth are you doing, you should be living in Toronto with your husband,' et cetera. I tried to explain that my husband doesn't live in Toronto, or anywhere for that matter. He arranged to have his condo sublet by the symphony just before he left. I married a vagrant." She bit forcefully into the pizza. It was warm and delicious with a thin, slightly crispy crust, just the way she liked it. She began to wonder what Tony would be cooking for supper tonight.

***

There was a message waiting for her at the office, from Elisabeth, an acquaintance in Toronto. Speaking of old friends, this was a curious development, she thought. Elisabeth's forte, if one could say she had one, was trying to imagine out loud certain very personal aspects of her friends' relationships. "If trumpeters do it with brass, how do violinists...Mm?"

"Violinists do it in consort, Elisabeth," Gloria occasionally replied, and thought about those incredibly gentle fingers poised to play—well, occasionally she imagined a violin in those fingers, and not always the erogenous zones of her feet.

Still, most of the old crowd had not called her since she had married and left the city. Her old job had status; this one did not. After setting up two feature appointments for the following week, she dialled her back.

"I haven't heard from you since you married the virtuoso," Elisabeth gushed merrily when they finally connected. "Nice party. Your rich in-laws put out a great spread."

"My in-laws had nothing to do with it. How is life in Toronto?" Gloria nearly bit off the words.

"Same old stuff. What are you doing this weekend?" Elisabeth asked. "There's a Renoir film festival on at the university. I think you must be starved for some culture by now, marooned as you are in that backwater." As entertainment writer for one of Toronto's national dailies, Elisabeth was well acquainted with culture, backward, forward, and likely between the sheets as well.

"There is always something to do on the weekend when one works for a small newspaper, Elisabeth. Maybe you can't remember that far back." *Chew on that,* she thought with a wicked grin. "And this backwater is actually quite a lively little place."

"I don't know why you bother working. You married a pot of money."

"No, I married a musician." So the new job may have no status, but the new husband did. "Besides, I have all the culture I need this weekend. I have a violinist to entertain me." Was it coincidence that Elisabeth should be checking up on her this weekend after not bothering for months? Paying only slight attention to her running commentary on the social, personal, and intimately private lives of several mutual acquaintances, Gloria noted that, working in the *Toronto Star's* entertainment department, Elisabeth should know Tony's schedule better than he does. She simply wanted to know whether she and Tony were still an item. *And I worried about* rural *snoops!* she mused.

"Anyway, enough gossip," Elisabeth was saying, "I hear you have a murder investigation out there."

Gloria hesitated. "We're tracking it. Why? Don't you have your own murders to write about?" And how did this news get all the way to Toronto?

"We're interested in yours. Didn't I hear that you'd like to earn a stringer's fee?"

"No. Whatever gave you that idea?"

"Come on, Gloria. Better writers than you do it all the time. That's how they get ahead."

"Then I guess I'm not one of the great ones," she said through clenched teeth. Her father had taught her years ago to respect the people who signed her paycheque. That meant *not* feeding a daily newspaper information that they could publish before her next issue, nearly a week away.

Elisabeth sighed. "Can you at least give us a lead?"

Big-city dailies had their own resources; if they wanted this one, she resolved, they would have to work for it. She gave her Sergeant O'Toole's number, knowing he would be a lot less willing to talk with a Toronto newspaper reporter than he had been with her. They could find someone else to do their legwork; she was overworked as it was.

She mentally crossed Elisabeth off a short list of people she would be looking up, should she ever by some miracle have time to visit Toronto. The telephone rang again, this time her landlord, explaining anxiously, and in hushed tones, that the repairs to the septic bed would be delayed.

"I'm not surprised. I hear our contractor is no longer on this earth, let alone digging it." She immediately regretted her flippancy.

"That's true," he answered, with a slight hesitation that made her cringe in shame. "I'll try to make other arrangements as soon as I can."

"I realize it's awkward. Please do your best, before we have a serious heat wave." She packed up her camera and was heading off to the high school to check in on this year's grads, when Russell hailed her from his office.

"Where are you off to?" He sounded casually conversational. She told him, rather than take the chance he would tell head office that she had left early for the weekend. He looked nonplussed. "No time to fill me in? Steve Lang and I used to talk about the news, and you did say you'd keep me posted."

"My predecessor had a lot of time to sit and gossip with everyone, and very little time for actual work. That's why your company replaced him, Mr. Russell. I'll be back," she added, trying not to feel too irritated.

But she *was* irritated. The call from Elisabeth had bothered her. On her way home, after a brief detour to take a picture of Peak Township's proud roads superintendent and his new grader, she felt the stirrings of the old competition: a local weekly newspaper protecting its territory and attempting to beat a large city daily to a news story. The battle had been waged often, in the suburbs. Why would the crime beat of a paper like The *Star* or The *Toronto Sun* or even—ugh!—*The Express*, take more than a casual interest in a small-town incident? Was there no one being murdered, garroted, dismembered, and washed up on shore at the Scarborough bluffs?

She made a quick pass through East Lister and around the country block to check out the site of the previous night's homicide. Beyond the beribboned posts at the end of the drive, police activity was at its height with a trailer, a large van, three cruisers, and a swarm of officers combing every inch of ground.

Hardly a sinister place in the light of day, the site looked like a party waiting to happen.

She pulled away, glancing back only once in her rearview mirror. Well, one must admit, the bulldozer aspect of the case made the whole thing rather sticky...yuk! She geared down and swung her car onto the county road that would take her home. Her heart had already begun to beat just a bit faster in anticipation, especially when, from a distance, she caught a glint of sunlight reflecting off chrome in her driveway. But as she drew closer, the quick beat of her heart nearly turned into a major coronary. It wasn't Tony's Buick, after all. It was...a major complication.

***

"Oh, damn!" Gloria stared in utter dismay at the familiar old Chrysler parked next to the sloping side veranda of the old, white frame farmhouse. "Now what do I do?" Wine bottles clinked in their brown paper bag as she hoisted her shopping out of the back seat and dragged her feet carefully and reluctantly up the veranda steps.

Two cats stubbornly stood their ground outside the kitchen door, glaring through the screen at a sleekly dressed woman in shirt, skirt, stockings, and open-toed shoes, seated at Gloria's small kitchen table sipping espresso and looking as though she might be more at home at an outdoor café near the Hotel San Giorgio in Florence. Her abundant, light-coloured hair was pulled back in an attractive French roll to show off her emerald earrings, and her eyes were following Gloria's approach with a steely glint.

"Hello, Mother," Gloria called, her voice sounding three octaves lower than usual. She carried the bottles of wine and spirits through the door. "Not teaching this afternoon? How long have you been waiting? And what on earth are you doing here?"

"Piano teaching is finished for the year, as you well know," Carolyn Trevisi replied, rising and giving her daughter a brief embrace. "I thought it was time to find out what is going on, since you're not telling us." Her mother's diction was perfect; obviously, she had been thinking what to say. "We've heard nothing since the wedding, except that you are living here in this...uh, place, and Tony isn't. Are you married, or aren't you? Are you living together, apart, changed your minds, getting a divorce, what?" She glanced at her daughter's left hand, and her face showed relief at the sight of a wedding ring still intact, and accompanied by the big diamond that had been the talk of the old neighbourhood. "I do not wish to invade your privacy, but your father and I want to know."

"And the rest of the family knows better than to ask, I suppose," Gloria said, returning her mother's careful kiss on the cheek. "How did you get in?"

"The door was unlocked. Careless." Her mother, nearly as tall as she, represented the Canadian side of the family tree with an interesting French, Scottish, and Irish heritage, poise and manners of a duchess, and a degree in music pedagogy. She also had the large-boncd stature that Gloria had inherited along with the height to carry it off. With a deepening frown on her face she watched as Gloria carried the shopping bags to the counter and began to unload scotch, vermouth, and two large bottles of wine.

"I guess I was in a hurry to leave this morning," Gloria noted over her shoulder, crushing the paper bag. "Anyway, the landlady says no one locks doors around here. It's considered bad manners. And besides, I have nothing worth stealing."

"Certainly no food." She looked with disfavour at the paper bag crumpled on the counter. "I packed a few of your favourites, but as far as supper is concerned...." She bit her lip and rose to her feet. "My dear, I think we need to talk."

"I didn't get a chance to shop last night. And Tony's coming, with groceries. Actually, he should be here any minute now. I wanted to get home before he arrived so I could tidy up a little."

Her mother's face changed alarmingly. "He's coming *here?* Now? Good heavens, why didn't you tell me?" She gazed around at the stacks of boxes, disorganized furniture, and untidy kitchen counter. "I'll clean up the dirty dishes. You'd better wash this floor, dear. Your cats have thrown kibbles all over, and you spilled some milk under the table this..." she frowned at the old stain, "this week, sometime." Mrs. Trevisi pushed the sleeves up on her fine linen blouse and began clearing the counter.

"Let me do that, Mother." Gloria quickly grabbed a cloth from the sink and took the coffee mugs, milk glasses, and dirty cat food dishes from her hand. Filling the sink with soapy water, she began soaking dirty dishes and scrubbing off the old linoleum countertop.

Mrs. Trevisi shrugged. "Your house looks as though you moved in yesterday," she remarked. "It will take more than a few minutes to get yourself organized, but I'll help, if you want."

"I don't need...All right. I *do* need help." Why not? It was obvious her mother was determined, well entrenched and not about to be shifted out until she was certain how things stood. A stubborn woman. And caring. She wanted to hug her, but not today. Instead, she handed her a sponge from the back of the sink. "And how is Dad?" she asked as she swept up the kibble, ran water into the old porcelain laundry sink, and searched for a floor mop near the basement stairs. Her mother wiped down the small wooden table that would seat three in a pinch.

"Your father sends his love and a bottle of wine— not that you would appear to need it." She rinsed out the sponge, replaced it on the countertop, and began unpacking a carton of spices, wiping the bottles carefully and arranging them on a small built-in rack on the door of a cupboard. "The yard has a bit of a smell. Something they put on the fields today?"

"No such luck. The septic bed has problems, and the contractor who is supposed to do the work just got...got busy." To tell her he just got murdered would sound just a bit harsh. Gloria was offering up a prayer of thanks for Linda's nephew, Mike Hurtig, who had come over earlier in the week and cut the grass for her; the place did not look too wild and unkempt, at least from the outside. She rinsed the floor mop and stowed it behind the basement door, then pitched in to help her mother shift a pile of empty cartons to the basement stairs.

"There are some nice flowering shrubs in the front, but they need pruning," her mother continued. "And there is room at the back for a decent vegetable garden, a bit late for this year, of course, though perhaps some late lettuce and beans...The house could use some repair. Those porch steps are ghastly. And where is your furniture?"

"This is it, Mother." Gloria looked around the kitchen, with its tiny table and four old chairs. "The house isn't mine to repair, and I'm...*we're* not planning to stay here for long. Tony's furniture is still with his condominium, which has been sublet for a year to a musician from Europe, and I had only what was in my apartment. On top of that, I started a new job barely two months ago. I haven't really had time for any serious shopping, and this will be only the second time I've seen Tony in two months, if you count our wedding day. He doesn't get home much."

That is, if he cares to call this home, she added to herself, as she stopped for breath. Her mother's comments on the condition of her living quarters brought its inadequacies to mind. Of the three rooms upstairs, one was bare to the walls, one was full of boxes yet to be unpacked, and one contained the only good furniture she owned: a queen-sized pine rolling pin bed and matching armoire. The dining room had only a gateleg table that she had bought and refinished while she was still in college; no chairs or sideboard. In the living room were her parents' old couch and easy chair that she had rescued years ago on their way to the furniture cemetery and taken to her first tiny flat. Still rolled up was the carpet she had bought at an auction a year ago. In the midst of these odds and ends was the one luxury that Tony had insisted on bringing from his condo to her old flat on Gerrard Street before he left: a rather wonderful stereo system with a multi-disk CD player, and an enormous, eclectic collection of compact disks. The kitchen, apart from four big appliances, was large and rather sparse, with just a few dishes in the cupboards, her coffee maker, and the espresso pot that had been a wedding present from a favorite aunt.

The whole house suited her lifestyle admirably; she was used to less-than-sumptuous living quarters. But when she thought about Tony's own lakefront condo, not to mention his parents' house in an upper-crust Toronto neighbourhood, she realized it certainly was not the style to which he was accustomed.

Her mother continued giving the place a full review as she pulled open another packing box. "Your bedroom is a good size, and will be nice when you get another large dresser, and perhaps a carpet. And it could use another closet. That one's rather small, for the two of you, that is, if...." She glanced in Gloria's direction. "I'll keep my eyes open for a large wardrobe." She unpacked the rest of Gloria's old coffee mugs, lined them up beside the sink, and searched the drawers for a clean dishtowel. "You'll need decent drapes in winter; those windows look drafty. As for the other bedrooms, I don't know what you're planning to do. A den, perhaps? Or a practice studio for...."

"Mother—"

"The living room paneling is rather dismal," she continued, "but I think some pretty curtains might spruce it up. I can help you with that, but it's too late for this weekend. And I was hoping you'd replaced that old couch. Heaven knows, it was in our family room enough years to warrant a full pension." She shook her head. "Why not forget about the dining room and move the gateleg table into the kitchen where it will do some good? Where would you feed your guests, if you were to have any?"

"I don't have guests. It's just me and the cats," Gloria answered, rinsing the suds off her wrists. Dishes done, floor swept and washed, she opened a fresh can of cat food and placed some on a clean plate in the corner, then opened the screen door. Max and Buffy headed straight for the dish.

"And you haven't unpacked your wedding gifts," her mother added, hesitating over another carton of

Gloria's old apartment dishes. "It looks as though you were planning to return them." She glanced over her shoulder at Gloria, with eyebrows raised.

"Mother, this is just someplace temporary for me to stay while Tony's gone and I'm working here, which may not be for very long." She sat down at the table with a cup of espresso, and stirred in a heaping spoonful of sugar. Obviously this would be no lazy evening lying cozily in her husband's arms. She'd have to jolt herself awake and be ready for anything. "We'll find our own place as soon as things get sorted out."

"Such as?" Mrs. Trevisi was determined.

"Such as *our* things. My future...*Our* future. Tony's career. We haven't had time to talk about this between ourselves, let alone discuss it with our families." She sighed. "It has been frustrating, but I've simply had to handle things the way I always did, before...," she took a deep breath, "before I was married. It sounds lame, but the easiest way to cope, for me, is to carry on as though I'd never had a wedding."

Her mother smiled. "I brought up my daughter to look after herself. And a good thing, too."

"Exactly." Gloria laughed. "Can you imagine what I would have said if cousin Loretta's husband had left her in this fix? I would have yelled at her to smarten up, tell the jerk where to go, and get an annulment! And I am sure that is exactly what she and everyone else must be saying about me. But give him a break, Mother. He doesn't like this either." She tipped up her cup and swallowed the sweet espresso in one gulp.

"I see less of Tony now that he's my husband than I did when we were dating."

"And now he's coming home for the first time in two months, and here I am." Her mother stood up. "Gloria, I'm terribly sorry. No wonder you looked upset when you came home. Would you like to be left alone?"

"No!" Gloria almost shouted as she sprang to her feet. "Of course not. You're here, and I'm glad to see you, and he'll be happy to see you too. Please stay. You can have my...*our* room for tonight." The thought of her mother sleeping on an old mattress flung on the floor of an unfurnished spare room was, well, unthinkable. Tony would understand.

"Good." Her mother sat down again. "Frankly, I'd feel better if I were to talk to Tony myself." She shook her head. "You surprise me. During the weeks before your wedding, you two were inseparable. Now you're married, and...If you have any second thoughts...."

"Of course not. Why would I have second thoughts?" The sound of the car in the driveway coincided with the ringing of the telephone in the living room—and the sudden realization that she had just told the biggest lie of her life. "Damn," she muttered as she jumped to grab the phone.

"Gloria?" It was Linda. "Something has happened. I have to talk to you."

"Now?" Gloria heard the car door slam and watched her mother saunter out onto the veranda.

She sank into a chair. "Linda, is this important? Can it wait?"

"Yes it's important, no it can't wait. My nephew Mike is being questioned by the police."

"Questioned? About what?" Her mind had some difficulty changing gears.

"About Clarence McKee, of course!" Linda sounded panicky. "And it looks bad."

"Why? Does he know Clarence McKee?" She heard Tony's voice in the distance, and moved toward the window to see what was happening outside, stretching the telephone cord as far as it would go. *Unpack the cordless,* she reminded herself sharply.

"I didn't want to tell you in the middle of Gina's with everyone listening. He used to work for him, but not any more. They had a...Well, he has another job, but he was off with the flu all day and didn't hear the news. When his mother told him this afternoon, he went all pale, she says. He told her there was something the police should know, and called them. Next thing you know, they showed up at Mildred's door this evening and loaded him into a cruiser. She thinks...Mildred's afraid they've arrested him."

"Mildred?"

"My sister. His mother. Glo, you know the police. You've covered crime stuff before, in the city. Clarence stopped Mike from getting a job with the township a few months ago. That's why Mike quit McKee's construction company."

"There must be more to it than that, if police have taken him for questioning," Gloria pointed out, as she finally caught a glimpse of her husband's back and heard the crackle of paper bags. Groceries! Her stomach rumbled loudly. "Otherwise, they'd be questioning me, as well, since he's supposed to dig me a new septic bed. Linda, can we talk about this later?" she asked, a note of quiet desperation creeping into her voice. She didn't need this tonight, on top of everything else.

"But...Oh, I almost forgot. You and Tony probably have plans for tonight, don't you? Am I interrupting?"

That was a good one, Gloria thought, listening to the voices in the kitchen. "No, we have visitors, the family kind. How about tomorrow? I'll be there right after breakfast. No, wait. I have a fund-raising garage sale to take care of first." She made a quick estimate of the amount of time it would take to swing by the grocery store after the garage sale. "Let's make it lunch. Here." *And please don't bring your famous birdlike appetite,* she pleaded silently as she made a mental count of her cash on hand. She had already spent her mileage check on wine and liquor.

"Okay. You know Mike's a good kid. He's taking this pretty hard. He thinks the world of you. Maybe you can reassure him."

Or maybe you can simply get a lawyer, Gloria thought as she turned toward the kitchen, telephone receiver still in hand. She could hear her mother demanding to know why Tony hadn't been around at all since their marriage.

"I'm here now," he was saying as she hung up the receiver and hastened toward the kitchen to greet him under her mother's watchful eyes. So much for a few blissful days of peace and togetherness and Tony's incredible cooking. Not even a proper hello, this time, probably a shy peck on the cheek, and a wry smile, and a quiet night on the uncomfortable old couch. Were there any more surprises on the way?

***

"Surprise!" Tony whispered in her ear. They were standing in the warm moonlight in the backyard. "A housewarming gift. I had no idea what to bring, until I talked to you last night. I know it isn't personal and romantic, but I can think of a few personal uses, starting right now."

"You didn't have to bring me anything, but…" She was staring at a large screen tent, its sides waving gently in the breeze. She giggled. "It's perfect, Tony. It's absolutely marvellous. You have no idea."

"I didn't get a chance to tell you earlier, so I decided to sneak out right after supper and set it up. I've brought us the perfect escape from the mosquitoes, the heat indoors, and anything else we care to escape from." He slipped an arm around her waist.

"You mean houseguests?" She studied the shiny framework of poles and supports holding the fine mesh with the canvas roof. "So this is where you disappeared to while my mother was doing her whirlwind act, organizing the kitchen." Gloria touched the mesh gently. "You're a marvel! How did you manage to put it up in so short a time, and by yourself? I could have helped you." She stepped inside, drawing him in closely behind her.

"I was in the militia, remember?" He zipped up the door. "I remember tents, and sleeping on the ground. We talked about going camping together once, didn't we? And while you were busy changing the bed and getting your mother settled, I made up *our* bed. It isn't as comfortable, but it is private." He crouched down at the foot of a double sleeping bag spread on the fragrant fresh grass, reached up to grab her hand, and pulled her down with him. "And now, finally, I can say hello the way I had planned to." He put his arms around her, lowered his face to hers, and slid his hands inside her jersey.

She squirmed away, gripping both his hands in hers and holding them away from her. "Tony, do you realize my *mother* is asleep in the house?"

"I know she's not in here." Another prolonged embrace, and this time the jersey crawled halfway up her middle.

"But you're undressing me in the backyard!" Her clothing was becoming disorganized, and she wondered why this fact disturbed her. Suddenly she felt shy, something she hadn't felt since their third date. "Do you mean we're staying *here* tonight, you and I, and not on the couch?"

"Why not? You know how sound travels, and your mother looks like a light sleeper. And I know what you're like when we...." He stopped. "What's wrong? Would you like to say a proper hello first?" His mouth twitched at one corner.

"No, you don't need to...*Tony!*" She clutched at the hand that had just slid into her waistband.

"What?" He released her and sat up. "Gloria, we *are* alone. And we're married now, in case you've forgotten, so your mother shouldn't mind, even if she does hear us. And I've missed you like hell."

"And I've missed *you.*" She looked up and saw, for an instant, the attractive gray-eyed stranger sitting at the bar of the officer's mess. She blinked. "Tony, it has been awhile, and a lot has happened. Maybe I have to get to know you again."

He shifted, and sat cross-legged beside her on the sleeping bag, looking down at where she lay, her head propped on one elbow. "All right." He reached out and took her hand. "On my way up here today, I was thinking about the few weeks we spent together at your apartment on Gerrard Street, just before the wedding. Remember? You were working, I was auditioning and rehearsing, and in the evenings we were home, eating and talking, studying, making plans, falling asleep together and waking up together. It was heavenly. I could have gone on like that forever."

"I thought we *would*." Her eye caught the gleam of his bright, gold wedding band. His hand looked pale against her honey-gold skin. His almost black hair was perfectly trimmed. She touched his chin and cheek, only now beginning to show a trace of five-o'clock shadow, as though he had stopped on the way for a shave and a haircut and— *My God!* And she thought *she* was nervous. "Tony, this has been more difficult than we ever imagined, hasn't it?"

"It has." His mouth turned down at one corner. "And now here you are, living in a strange house. It's...I can't describe it, except that it doesn't seem real."

"I think I know," she said softly. "It's as though someone has drawn a curtain, a gauze veil, between us. It feels strange, and awkward, like a...a first date."

He stared through the screen, and Gloria followed his gaze. Twenty feet away, Max was sprawled comfortably on top of a cement slab that marked the location of a one-hundred-foot drilled well. The septic tank, fortunately, was around the other side of the house, and at the moment, the light breeze was blowing the aroma in the other direction, leaving the air only slightly tainted. A plum tree, two apple trees, and a large elm in full foliage gave the yard some shade in summer, and their leaves rustled like a petticoat. Beyond that were fields, with small sprouts of corn pushing through well-tilled soil. To her, it looked beautiful. But to him?

She sat up, taking the hand that had been resting lightly on her hip, and squeezed it. "I'm sorry. Strange as it is, sweetheart, this is the only home we have. And I guess it's time to make it our own."

"I guess you're right." He turned toward the house. "Make a list. If you're staying here, I want you to be comfortable. We need a dining room set, and—"

"That wasn't quite what I meant. And forget the dining room. I'm not planning to entertain, except my family, maybe. Certainly not yours!" The thought of his high-strung mother and formidable father standing in her cozy but disorganized kitchen gave her the shudders.

"Then maybe something for outside? Patio furniture? How about a nice Victorian garden bench for the veranda?"

"They cost a fortune," she protested. "I think this screen tent is perfect." She looked around. "But it isn't exactly private, is it? Maybe we shouldn't...." She started pulling her jersey back down.

"Gloria, who is going to see us? The squirrels?"

A soft meow was heard outside the tent. "Just Max," she sighed, relaxing on the pillow. "You're right. This is rather unique. And it's about the closest we'll ever get to a honeymoon." She looked at the sleeping bag, the best pillows—so that's where they had ended up—and underneath one, a provocatively brief nightie. Honeymoon, indeed! Pulling it out, she fingered the delicate fabric and heaved a deep sigh. "Tony, sweetheart, I *am* glad you are here."

"Are you?" He gave her a sideways glance. "May I hug you now?" He wrapped his arms tightly around her. She relaxed, feeling the welcome warmth of his slightly rough face against her cheek and his strong fingers on the back of her neck. "You have no idea how much I've missed you, wife."

"Mmmm. Show me."

***

Midnight passed, and so did a pair of raccoons, staring at the tent curiously, as yet another invasion of their territory. Mad Max wriggled under the side of the screen so he could take his usual place at Gloria's feet, admitting two or three mosquitoes in his wake. One buzzed by Gloria's ear, and she swatted it in her sleep.

A few miles away, a frantically worried mother was having a restless, wakeful night, tossing and turning. Her nineteen-year-old son, two rooms over, awoke suddenly from a bad dream.

And somewhere else, a murderer dozed off peacefully, having overcome the first hurdle.

Chapter 3

"It'll be perfect!" Gloria gazed at an old wooden railroad bench, its back painted in rainbow colours and the seat an attractive flat black with daisy and iris decals.

The garage sale fund-raiser for a local choral society was not exactly brimming with antiques and collectibles, but there were some interesting cast-offs. Two children were perched on the gaudy wooden seat, eating candy and ogling the camera. Looking at the bench from a different angle, she discovered she had found just what she needed: a cute shot for page five, and perhaps something else. She snapped the photograph, smiled at their mother, and jotted down the children's names and ages for the photo caption. As the children scampered off, she lowered herself carefully onto the seat. It seemed solid enough....

"Have you ever seen anything so ugly?" a handsome contralto voice commented behind her. "When our rehearsal pianist brought it to the garage sale I wondered who'd ever buy such a thing around here."

"You must be with the O'Dell Bells," Gloria said, standing and introducing herself.

"That explains the camera," the middle-aged woman said with a comfortable smile. "I'm Margaret Ormsford, the choir chairman...or whatever." The lady was nearly as tall as Gloria, with comfortable middle-age spread, thick, brown hair streaked with gray, and sparkling hazel eyes. "Do you like the bench? I'll check the price for you." She sent a ten-year-old in bright pink shorts to find the fund-raising chairman.

"I'd love to talk to you about the choir sometime soon." Gloria had an eye for the August doldrums when councils suspended important meetings for vacations, and news was scarce.

"We start rehearsals again in four weeks for our fall concert." Mrs. Ormsford looked at her curiously, brows raised. "You might be interested in taking part. It seems I heard somewhere that you are married to a concert musician."

Gloria smiled. "That's right. And I'm glad someone says that I'm married, and not separated, divorcing, single, gay, or living in sin!"

"Gossip!" Margaret laughed. "I'm trying to arouse some interest in the culture of the area, but gossip is all I ever get back. I've heard all those stories, by the way, but at the moment, you've been replaced as flavour of the month by what has happened at the East Lister Industrial Park, if that's the proper name for that atrocity. It's all I've heard about this morning."

Gloria sidled in closer. "What do they say?"

"People are shocked, of course." Margaret lowered her voice. "They say someone murdered the poor man.

Half the people assume he was into something illegal to prop up his failing business. The other half? Well, they'd like to think it was someone from far, far away. You know the story. Somebody came up from the city, found that godforsaken construction site in the middle of nowhere and tried to steal a bulldozer, or something ridiculous. But people in the know say that the police arrested Mildred Hurtig's son Mike last night, and folks are sure he did it. They claim Clarence and Mike had a row over money last spring when Mike worked for McKee Construction. Some even say it got down to punches." She smiled at the elderly man from the East Lister convenience store, shuffling by to examine a box of old bottles. "Frankly, I don't believe a word of it, about Mike, I mean. I know the young man. He's one of the few kids around here who finished high school as an Ontario Scholar. He's smart, works hard on the family farm, and holds down a job on top of that. But I *do* believe he had problems with Clarence. Plenty of others have. In fact," she looked about her, "I wouldn't be surprised if a few of those who are accusing Mike wish they had thought of it themselves."

"Do you think so?"

"It's not that people hated him. After all, they all voted him into office, didn't they? But they enjoy crowning their Caesars as much as they like bringing them down. The other choice villain, of course, is his wife."

"His wife?"

"Naturally." The low voice dropped to a whisper. "Clarence did a lot of bragging, and rumour has it she was pretty tired of his carryings on with certain other females."

Gloria recalled the file photo: Clarence McKee, a philandering Casanova? "What were they like, these other females?"

"One in particular, actually: a bit dotty, is my opinion. Not that a McKee would ever disgrace the family with the scandal of divorce, they say, but you likely know the kind of woman who would go for a man like our Clarence."

Gloria didn't. She dropped her head in close conspiracy. "Has no one considered the possibility that a mistress might have a motive, as well, especially if McKee was refusing to divorce his wife and...?" She stopped, suddenly shocked at her own presumptuousness.

Mrs. Ormsford didn't seem to notice the embarrassed pause. "I doubt if she could figure out how to put a bulldozer in gear," she said, "whereas his wife...." She glanced down as the young girl approached her, and straightened up.

"Mr. Jones says if we can get twenty dollars for that ugly old bench, it'll be a miracle, but he'll take fifteen."

Mrs. Ormsford turned to Gloria, her eyebrows twitching. "You heard it. Twenty dollars."

"Will you take fifteen?" Gloria asked, stifling a smile as the youngster ran to join her mother.

Mrs. Ormsford shook her head, laughing. "The child is so earnest. But watch what you say, near her. I'm sure she'll repeat everything to her mother."

"I'll remember that." The crowd was getting thicker, and only two choir members were on duty to take money and help out. Gloria was torn; she would have loved to stay and listen, but was itching to get back home and see what her mother and her husband were up to. "And I'll take the bench."

"Good. Fifteen dollars and it's yours."

Gloria handed her the bills, wondering how she would pay for the groceries for Linda's lunch. Tony had bought enough to last the two of them several days, but hadn't counted on family visits or the appetites of her neighbours. That likely would feed Linda and her nephew for one meal, or maybe not.

The two of them wrestled the heavy bench onto the roof of the old Mazda wagon and fastened it down with baler twine, and as she climbed into her car, she heard Mrs. Ormsford greeting old Norm.

"And how are you today, Mr. Weatherby?"

"Not good," the rough voice grumbled.

Gloria slammed the door and started off down the road. Perhaps the small deli counter at the general store could help fill out her food supply for now, and she could always write a check. How much money was in her account, anyway?

She drove slowly, checking the tension on the cords.

So the McKees were not so popular and well-respected, after all. And if Clarence was carrying on an illicit affair and making no secret of it, what about his wife? Didn't Theresa—or was it Jan?—mention that Mrs. McKee hadn't been home at midnight, when the police came to her door? Gloria had a lot to learn about local politics, the kind that did not appear in township council minutes, as well as the kind of family histories that weren't published by the Women's Institute.

And she had her own family politics to deal with, she recalled, before she could spend a quiet weekend with Tony. Waking up in the backyard with the sun in her eyes, wrapped in a sleeping bag and the bearlike grip of her husband's arm around her middle, all this had felt strange beyond description. Not to mention the tractor that had passed not twenty feet behind them when they were barely awake...quite barely, in fact. It was her landlord, whisking by on his way to a back field, waving nonchalantly, just as that pickup truck driver had just done. She withdrew her arm from out of the window and looked down the road ahead. And now, lunch guests. This was their first weekend together as a married couple, and considering how it was starting, she was wondering how things would proceed. "Maybe I'll be lucky," she murmured, stroking the steering wheel. "Maybe Tony has sweet-talked my mother into pleasant complacency and she is willing to pack up and go home without further interference." Not likely, even though on a good day, he could charm birds out of the trees. Carolyn Trevisi was no bird, except perhaps the kind who watched anxiously over her nestlings. And she'd been pretty cool to Tony ever since his arrival. He'd disappointed her, the look she gave him over breakfast said plainly. Gloria knew the look. As a teenager, it had had the effect of freezing her innards.

The bench seemed to be firmly in place on the roof; she picked up speed, anxious to get her shopping done and return home. For the rest of the day, at least, the news could wait.

* * *

"Bad news," Carolyn Trevisi said, stepping through the back door and onto the veranda as Gloria was undoing the ropes around the railroad bench. "You'd better sit down. There isn't much time."

"Bad news? Where's Tony?" she demanded. "Did you chase him away?" She had noted as soon as she pulled in the driveway that his car was gone, and her mother's was still there. Not what she had hoped. She grabbed the grocery bags and lugged them to the veranda steps where her mother was waiting.

"He received a phone call from a variety store in Plattsford. You have company. It's *them*!"

"Company?" Gloria would have pointed out the obvious, but poor grammar was a sure sign that her mother was upset. "Them? Who?"

"His parents, your *in-laws.* The Lamberts." Her mother curled her lip.

"Tony's parents are coming here, *now?*" She sank to the steps, grocery bags still nestled in her arms.

"They are." She lowered her voice. "I may not be pleased with Tony, but they are not happy with you. Your mother-in-law has been in touch with me already, at least a dozen times in the past three weeks. Quite excitable, isn't she?"

"An understatement."

"Well, your father-in-law is somewhat more concise in voicing his concerns—at least he doesn't rant—but they are every bit as grim, and in my opinion unjustified."

"My in-laws," Gloria groaned again. What could be worse? Setting the groceries beside her, she covered her face with her hands.

"Yes, we've heard from both of them. I'm afraid I was reluctant to give them your telephone number, under the circumstances. In fact, it's one of the reasons I decided to come out and have a talk with you, and now that I understand how things are—I think I do— *I* feel a lot better, at least. They were rather surprised when Tony answered the phone. They seem a bit meddlesome, don't they?"

Hey kettle, yelled the pot. Gloria looked up and swallowed the sarcastic retort. "Surprised?" She struggled off the step. "If they didn't know he was here, they came all this way to have a talk with me, and...Oh, bloody hell! Here they are." The sound of tires crunching on gravel caught their attention, and Gloria stood up, braced her back against the veranda post, and prepared for the worst.

Tony's mother was in the front seat of Tony's Buick, talking non-stop and pointing out the window to various scenic views. She could hear it all: her mother-in-law's opinion of the corn field, the sloped veranda, the weedy flower beds and untrimmed forsythias lining the bottom part of the driveway. She could just imagine what Barbara Lambert would say about the smell of the old septic bed. Tony's father followed behind, inching along in his sedate blue Mercedes 450 SL as if the dust from the car ahead would ruin the finish. Mrs. Lambert stopped talking as she gaped at the battered Mazda with its bizarre treasure still perched on the roof, baler twine hanging over the doors. The lacquered fingernail hovered, and pointed again. Then as Tony swung his car in beside hers, Gloria heard the tirade continue.

"Well, they are my family now, and I am certain they mean well."

"I can't say *I* am." Her mother didn't smile, but joined her, shoulder to shoulder, at the top of the veranda steps. "How did they know where to find you?"

"I imagine my father-in-law has his methods of finding people." Gloria inched backward toward the safety of her kitchen door, a hand on her mother's arm. "Mother, stay out of this, please. Tony can handle his family."

"Stay out of it? Not on your life. You're my daughter." Her mother hefted the second grocery bag and stood shoulder-to-shoulder with Gloria. "Besides, I don't like getting nasty phone calls in the middle of a busy day. The lady still thinks you stole her *baby*. Let me handle this, and you run along and fix us some lunch."

And here they were, in full voice, before Gloria could argue. Barbara Lambert was stepping cautiously out of Tony's car, and still talking. "...and for her to run out on you just days after your wedding, and now here *you* are. What are you *thinking*, Tony? And what is *she* doing? Furnishing the place from a rubbish heap, that's what it looks like. Look at this place! Maybe the Trevisi family wouldn't mind living in a dump, but surely you know better."

Tony said nothing, and Mr. Lambert hurried to her side. "Now Barbara, don't—"

"Well, isn't this cozy?" Barbara Lambert eyed Mrs. Trevisi coldly as she and her husband paused at the bottom of the steps. Mr. Lambert, his gray hair slightly ruffled and his golf shirt and slacks barely wrinkled from sitting in an air-conditioned Mercedes for two hours, looked wary. Mrs. Lambert, her short, white hair pulled back from her face, hands curled on the portion of her angular body where her hips should have been, looked ready to square off with Gloria's mother.

Think nice thoughts.... Gloria swallowed, and smiled. "Hello, Mrs. Lambert. Good morning, sir. This is a surprise."

Barbara Lambert was not put off. Swinging abruptly in her direction, she began. "Well, *you* led us on a merry chase, hiding out in the middle of *nowhere*. Gloria, I'm appalled. After all that fuss over your wedding, to suddenly walk out and go—"

"Now, wait a minute, who walked out on whom?" interrupted Carolyn Trevisi, saving Gloria from losing her temper. "Where in heaven's name has your *son* been these past two months?"

"I have *nothing* to say to you," Tony's mother hissed through her teeth. "Your daughter left town without a word—"

"My daughter *left?*" Gloria's mother bristled like a terrier. "Are you surprised? *Your* son didn't even leave her a place to live!"

"Uh oh. Excuse me." Gloria ducked quickly down the steps past them and across the driveway. Her mother, she knew, could hold her own, and plenty more besides, in a battle of words with Barbara Lambert. Her concern was for Tony, who was still standing by the Mazda and examining her latest acquisition.

"Don't yell at me. I had nothing to do with it," was his first comment as he circled to the back of her car to loosen a rope.

"Neither did I."

"I didn't think so." He turned to her with raised eyebrows. "Nice bench. Where did you find it?" He took the car keys from her hand, opened the small penknife she kept on the key ring, and cut the baler twine that fastened the bench to the car's roof rack.

"It's perfect, isn't it? It was at the choral society's garage sale. It's rock-solid, doesn't even need mending or painting, at the moment. And it was so cheap even *I* could afford it. Shall we put it on the veranda?"

He handed back the keys and glanced over his shoulder to where the others stood, arguing loudly. "Good idea." The two of them reached up and heaved it off the roof.

"How do you suppose they found out?" she grunted as she adjusted her grip.

"Don't know. I didn't tell them I was home, because I wanted some time to ourselves. I think they got a bit of a shock."

"Hmph. Do you suppose my father is going to show up as well?" Gloria asked, adjusting her grip on the armrest to keep the legs from scraping the gravel.

"I hope not." Tony glanced uneasily down the driveway. "Don't our parents understand that we're all grown up?"

"We'll never be grown up to our parents; at least, certainly not mine. In their view, they're the only responsible adults in the world. But we had better do something before a real fight breaks out." Carolyn Trevisi, she could hear, was admirably defending her daughter, her daughter's heritage, herself, her faith, and her general class of people while Ray Lambert was attempting to stick to the point, whatever that was, and her mother-in-law was hurling any abuse that came to mind. Gloria was well aware she had never been Barbara Lambert's ideal choice as wife for her oldest son.

The two of them reached the steps and elbowed their way through the howling trio, lifted the bench onto the porch, and set it down carefully against the wall.

"Why don't you sit down and make yourselves comfortable, while Tony and I start making lunch for everyone?" Gloria announced in a voice strong enough to carry all the way to Plattsford. After all, she thought, one could not effectively hurl abuse with one's mouth full. Then she spotted the pickup truck moving slowly up the drive. "Lunch! Oh, no! Here's Linda and her family."

The yelling ceased, and the five of them gazed down the lane. "Oh, dear," said Barbara Lambert. "Were you expecting someone?"

***

"More coffee, anyone?" Carolyn Trevisi was stationed by the espresso maker.

Gloria returned to the table carrying a bowl of fresh green grapes that Tony had brought, and eager hands were already reaching out. The cold cuts and buns she had bought on her way home from the garage sale had vanished, the Friulano cheese, salami, and artichokes her mother had brought with her were almost all gone, and the coffee cake that Linda had made that morning nothing but crumbs. Tony and his father had dragged in the gateleg table from the dining room and opened it up to accommodate eight people while she was hastily assembling a meal on brand new clean dishes. She, Mike, and Linda were seated on the bench, brought in to supplement the sparse supply of chairs. The Lamberts and Mildred Hurtig, Mike's mother, were occupying three of the four good chairs, the fourth just vacated by her mother. Tony was perched on the stepping stool. Only Barbara Lambert and Gloria were holding out their cups. The rest were shaking their heads and patting their stomachs as they broke off small mops of grapes and began grazing languidly in the fruit bowl.

"That settled, tell us, Mike, what the police wanted to know." Gloria turned to the tall, lean, tanned young man seated quietly on the end of the bench.

Mike winced. "Well, the police think I was the last one on the industrial park construction site before the cops found the body. I would've told the police about it sooner, but I was sick yesterday and missed the news, so I had no idea about the...about what happened to Mr. McKee, until last night."

"How did the police find out you'd been there?"

"From the other employees, I guess." He shrugged. "They all know me."

"Ah. No police sketch needed."

"What?" Mike frowned. "Anyway, as soon as I heard there had been a...an accident, or something, I called them. By then, they'd already talked to the employees, and they were planning to pay a visit. Mom was outside in the garden when they showed up. I thought they'd just take a statement at the house; instead they took me down to the station as if I was under arrest or something, and really gave me the third degree for the delay. That's when I heard Mr. McKee had been murdered."

Tony froze, Mildred Hurtig shifted uneasily in her chair, and the Lamberts looked flabbergasted. "There was a suspected homicide last week not far from here," Gloria explained, giving them the short, less grisly version.

Ray Lambert recovered first, addressing Mike in a serious, businesslike manner. "Son, are you considered a suspect?"

Mike turned to him, surprised. "Well, I don't know, sir. I suppose people are thinking—"

"Never mind people," he said crisply. "Stick with police. You were on the scene earlier, talking to the victim. Why would witnesses finger you? Did you argue?"

"No, I didn't even see him." Mike shook his head.

"But you called the police yourself as soon as you heard there had been a problem?" Lambert asked.

"He certainly did! And they have a nerve, picking him up like that," Mildred Hurtig declared. She was a big woman, quite the opposite of Linda, not tall, but broad and plump. "He had nothing to do with whatever happened there. My son wouldn't—"

"Mom, can I tell them myself?" Mike turned, exasperated, to Gloria. "It isn't that simple."

"Relax, Mike. We're listening," Gloria assured him, silently cursing meddling parents once again. The overbearing, take-charge manner of her father-in-law was annoying her. "Tell me from the beginning, why were you there in the first place?"

"Mr. McKee owed me a favour."

"What kind of favour?" She studied Mike, a forthright nineteen-year-old, tall and strong from years of farm work. His sandy brown hair and hazel eyes were much like his mother's, but his cheerful demeanour was muffled with worry and traces of anger.

"A bunch of us are helping to build a house on the old Barnes property about a mile from the site. We needed some heavy equipment to clear away an old stone fence row, and last week I asked him if we could rent one of his bulldozers for a few hours, since they're so close by. It was just too big a job for the old tractor that we had there."

"And he let you?"

"Yeah." Mike heaved a sigh. "It cost us a few hundred dollars, and we could only use it for the afternoon and evening because we all have day jobs, but he agreed to rent it to us. I went straight from work, got there just after three thirty. It took me awhile to move it, since we don't have a heavy equipment trailer...."

"And you didn't see Mr. McKee there, between three thirty and, say, four?"

"I saw his truck. He was there, all right, probably in the construction shed. But I was in a hurry. I had to drive the damn—the bulldozer all the way over to the Barnes property, around the corner, about a kilometer and a half. But it was worth it; we managed to get the fence row moved, and we did some grading for the septic system and the drainage bed while we were at it. I guess it was after eleven and pitch dark when I finally got the bulldozer back to the site, and parked it. By then I was feeling pretty rough, with this flu thing coming on, and I just wanted to go home."

"Mike, why did you say Clarence McKee owed you a favor?" Gloria asked. Her father-in-law, she noticed, was listening with interest.

Mike looked uneasy. "Last summer I worked for McKee Excavation part-time, when they were swamped with demands for foundations for new construction outside Perkins Hill. I got to know the work, and I could run all the equipment, even the high-hoe, and since I was just casual labor, I was paid in cash. When I finished OACs last Christmas I went to him for a job to tide me over until this coming fall. He said he could only hire me part-time until construction picked up in the spring, and wouldn't pay me more than minimum wage since I was just out of high school."

"And probably the only high school graduate on the site," Gloria observed. "So you were employed there all winter, and that's how all the employees knew you."

"The guys know me anyway. And Mr. McKee, he didn't actually have me listed on his payroll. Said he didn't want to pay compensation and payroll health tax, and all that, said I didn't need it anyway, since I was still living at home. I agreed to do it because I needed the job. I plan to go to university in the fall, and I have to save some money toward my first year away from home. I spent the winter working there, and what he called part-time was full-time for part-time pay. Basically, he didn't want the authorities to know I was working for him. He wanted cheap labor. Some of the others resented it, said I was taking someone else's job. Of course, they never said it to me, out loud."

"I see. Later, you found a better job, is that it? You're not working there now."

"Well, yeah, but...." Mike hesitated, and glanced at his mother, who was looking agitated. "Around March I was offered a great job working for O'Dell Township for the entire spring and summer, and mentioned Mr. McKee as a reference. I thought everything was settled, and I was going to start first of April. I don't know what happened, but Clarence either gave me a rotten reference or told someone not to hire me. One day the job was mine, next day it wasn't. I have a good job now," he added. "But no thanks to him."

"Did you quarrel about it?"

"No. Mom warned me not to mention anything, as it would cause bad blood, so we never talked about it. I was pretty mad, though, and just walked off the site six weeks ago and never went back. What the hell, anyway? He still owed me for fifteen hours, but I couldn't prove it. I couldn't even prove I'd ever worked there."

"Did you talk to the other employees about the township job falling through?"

"I didn't have to. They all knew about it, and they were pretty quick to tell *me* what they thought happened, and what I oughta say to the boss, but I didn't want to leave with a lot of bad feeling. This is a small community. People remember." He looked again at his mother. "Obviously, some people remembered, in spite of my efforts to make the best of it."

"So they did," Gloria downed the last of the sweet espresso.

"In no time, I had a decent job, without a job reference from Clarence McKee."

"You see why we're so worried," Linda said. "When word gets around that Clarence shafted Mike over the township job, people will think the worst."

"They will, won't they?" Gloria groaned. Perhaps now was not the time to mention that they already were. She pondered the rumors she had heard only a few hours ago at the garage sale. "So in spite of what people are saying, you were not arrested, and the police did not pick you up as a suspect; they just questioned you as a witness."

"Not just that." Mike heaved a deep sigh. "The bulldozer I borrowed? It's the one that ran over Mr. McKee." He stopped to clear his throat. "He must have passed out, or fallen, or something. And I think I may have killed him. At least, the police think so."

Dead silence. Even Mildred Hurtig was quiet.

"Oh, my...." Gloria stared at Mike. His face was pale under his tan, and his eyes had deep, dark circles, as though he hadn't slept. "How could you have run over him? Where and how did you park it?"

"I've been going over this." Mike took a deep breath. "I pulled into the driveway—there's a chain across two gate posts, usually, but it wasn't there so I imagine he left it open for me—and I backed it into the same spot I drove it out of, earlier. There's a bunch of heavy equipment parked near the shed, away from the gate, and it's usually lit up by a yard light. The other night there was no light there; burnt out, maybe. It was pitch dark, and I didn't have a flashlight or anything. I didn't even see anything on the ground behind me in the reverse lights. Maybe I wasn't looking very carefully. I had a hell of a headache." He looked at his hands. "Then I jumped off, left the keys under the seat, and walked straight out to the road. I must've walked right by him. One of the guys was coming to pick me up, and I started toward the village to meet him. I was almost at the corner when he finally met me in the truck, and we drove away toward East Lister."

"Was Mr. McKee's truck still there?"

"I didn't notice. Police think that's weird."

"And did you hear anything? See anything?"

"That's what the police wanted to know, but I wasn't listening too hard, to tell the truth," he said, hanging his head. "Maybe I heard a tractor, but there are always tractors running at this time of year. I didn't notice an extra vehicle on the site. Who would? There were no lights in the shed; it seemed deserted. I put the chain back up before I left, and locked it. That's all I can say for sure. The police took my boots, of course, and my fingerprints, and the clothing I was wearing."

"You just *gave* them your clothes?" Ray Lambert looked astounded.

"Even his underwear," his mother added. Mike glanced at her, slightly pink.

"What do the police think? Have they told you anything?" Gloria asked quietly. She could understand why his parents were so worried. Mike was young. The thought of having taken someone's life, even accidentally, would not result simply in a lot of unpleasant talk; it could shatter him personally.

"Well, I found out a few things. They asked me if I had been drinking that night. I didn't even have a beer with the guys; I wasn't feeling that great. Evidently they had found an empty liquor bottle in the construction shack. And they suggested that maybe I had found Mr. McKee passed out on booze, or something, and was still angry about the township thing. They seemed to know all about it, for some reason. I guess they're looking for some motive, as if *I* could deliberately run over an unconscious guy with a bulldozer. It doesn't matter how pissed off I am—

" His mother frowncd at him, and he looked away. "I couldn't possibly be *that* angry. It's only a job."

"Some people have done worse for a lot less," Ray Lambert commented dryly.

"Also, the police mentioned that it looked as though someone may have wanted to burn the shack down," Mike continued. "There were some gasoline-soaked rags in the trash can and outside the shed, but the door was locked, which was odd. That's what the investigation team is doing there now; going over everything quite thoroughly. And I hope they're finding something that will point a finger at someone else, but there's an investigator there who probably thinks the worst. It looks bad, doesn't it?" He rose to his feet, clearing his throat, walked over to the counter and picked up one of the dirty glasses.

Gloria jumped up. "I'll find you a clean glass, Mike. You mean the police officer who found the body may have interrupted the murderer in the middle of an arson attempt?"

"Either that, or I did when I came rumbling into the yard."

Gloria opened a cupboard. "But the officer who found the body was on routine patrol, according to Sergeant O'Toole; he *did* say he thought he saw a light where it shouldn't be." She searched through the sinkful of dirty dishes. "Mother, where are all my glasses?"

"If you'd unpack those wedding gifts, you'd have plenty," her mother observed. "Tony and I found at least three new sets of glasses, and two sets of dishes."

"Sorry. I haven't had time. Anyway, the constable saw a light, or a reflection of some kind, but he didn't see anything else. If someone was still on the site, he must have been pretty sure of himself to let the police officer walk back to his car and radio for backup. And he must have had an escape route. He couldn't walk past the cruiser and out the gate. What is behind the construction site?" She found a glass and washed it.

"Just an open field. McDaniel's gravel pit is over to the left, and a field of corn, then some bottomland to the right, kind of a wet woodlot near the river, and the sideroad. He could have headed toward the pit, but he'd have to know where he was going. It was pitch dark. He would've ended up in the McDaniel's back lane, but I doubt if the old folks would have noticed, and I don't think they have a dog."

They might have noticed, she thought; they were awake after midnight. "Well, what Constable Brian Stoker didn't see is possibly what kept him alive. And what he *did* see may be the only thing keeping you out of jail right now, and that's not a pleasant thought." She ran the tap, handed Mike a glass of water, and watched him while he drank. "What else is McKee Excavation working on at the moment? Could he be in trouble with some other contract? A septic system, or a foundation?"

"I could find out," Mike said, sounding hopeful.

"I'm certain the police will be looking into that, as well," she noted.

"Don't count on it," her father-in-law interjected. "Police want to build the best case they can to stand up in court. You may be their best choice."

He gulped down the glassful in two horse-sized swallows. "Well, I *am* responsible for Mr. McKee's death. That makes me the only choice."

"Nonsense. Even a man passed out from drinking ought to hear a bulldozer bearing down on him. Can your friends vouch for your whereabouts all evening?"

"Sure, until I left with the bulldozer." He slumped against the counter.

"And it probably took you the better part of an hour to get it back to the site, so all that's unaccounted for are the few minutes you spent parking the machinery and walking toward the village." Lambert sighed, and shook his head. "That might be enough to place you in the wrong place at the wrong time. Can I give you some advice before you end up in jail?" He leaned back in his chair, which creaked slightly.

"Advice?" Mike turned to him with a slight frown, and glanced at Gloria.

She smiled. "It might be the best advice you'll get. Better than mine."

"He's a lawyer," Tony said, standing up. He walked to the screen door and stepped outside.

Gloria patted Mike's arm, excused herself and followed, leaving Ray Lambert to offer what she hoped was free counsel, and Linda Grant to share her coffee cake recipe with Mrs. Trevisi. Barbara Lambert and Mildred Hurtig were no doubt bemoaning the fate of mothers with grown sons.

"I don't think Mike's family can afford your father," she noted. "Do they realize he's one of the top criminal lawyers in Toronto?"

"They'll be all right. Dad just wants to help, sometimes." He glanced back over his shoulder. "What on earth happened to our peaceful weekend?"

"Our timing was off, I think," Gloria said, slipping her arm through his. "Thank goodness for your mother's company manners. She can be very nice when she wants to be. Do you think the family crisis is over yet? Of course, there's still my dad." She sat on the topmost wobbly step and leaned back against the veranda post.

"We don't need any more visitors, at the moment." He joined her on the step. "Are we ever going to have time to ourselves?"

"Like the times we had before we were married?" She laughed softly, acutely aware of him as he sat next to her. "I'll check my schedule if you'll check yours."

He smiled. "You hardly know your schedule from one minute to the next."

"And you pay attention to yours? All you do is go where they tell you, put on your tux, and play your violin." She stretched a leg and scuffed the toe of her sandal in the gravel in front of the old steps. "What are your plans for the next week?"

"I don't know. We'll be in rehearsals again with a new cellist, and we're developing some new material for guest woodwinds. But you'll be working next week anyway. And what exactly is your involvement in this local homicide?" He glanced back toward the mob in the kitchen.

"Apart from the fact that I'm responsible for the news coverage?" Gloria told him about the police call, Sergeant O'Toole's ominous conclusions yesterday morning, and her suspicions.

"And why do you care at all, if your friends are not actually in any trouble?"

"Who says they aren't in trouble? You heard Mike. He was there in the afternoon, and again at about eleven, shortly before the body was discovered. Police think that Mike ran over the man with a bulldozer, and they may conclude it was unintentional, or they may not. Who knows? They'll be talking to his friends, confirming his whereabouts, and also trying to get an idea of his mood. Maybe the police are thinking that he had a drink or two with McKee in the afternoon to get him started."

"And you're afraid they might jump to conclusions." He hugged his knees.

"It wouldn't be the first time. They tend to go for the quickest, most obvious solution sometimes. But there's more," she said and told him about Elisabeth's call from The *Star*. "The nerve! Whatever happens, I don't want them taking this over and playing it up for the entertainment of the city intelligentsia. We're only a small weekly newspaper and we have few resources, but I can't just rely on police press reports." She looked at him carefully. His face told her he wasn't convinced. "Okay then, silly as it sounds, I won't let those people at the *Star*, or any other rag in the city, scoop my story! I've staked out my territory."

He didn't laugh. "No, it's not silly. It's serious."

"I'm not turning into Miss Marple. But I have a job."

"To hell with the job. You don't need it. Gloria, you know what I'm saying." He took her hand and squeezed it. "I am tired of traveling alone, and I want you to join me. Heaven knows, we can afford it. I should have insisted you come with me as soon as you lost your job in Toronto, but I thought you'd have another job downtown and you'd still be living in the same apartment, and it seemed reasonable then. Now, it doesn't. With what it costs to rent this place," he glanced back at the old house, "and what you're spending to keep up that old wreck, we can more than cover your travel expenses."

"Oh?" She withdrew her hand. "I'm glad you've thought about that part. But what about me? Have you thought about what I will be doing while you're performing? Sit in the back row, perhaps, and clap quietly with the rest of the chamber music aficionados? And have people who know absolutely nothing about music tell me how lucky you are to have such a gift, as if you were born with a twelve-thousand dollar violin stuck to your chin and never had fingers and wrists so sore from practicing that you couldn't even pick up a pen?" She tried to swallow her annoyance. He turned away. "As for covering expenses, what on earth do you know about that? If I leave this job, I won't have a salary. But you'll still have yours."

"This has nothing to do with money. I don't want to worry about you when I'm not here." He rose and began pacing the short walk to the cars.

"And it's important to me that I keep working. What if something should happen to...us?" She glanced behind her at the group in the kitchen, and moved off the veranda after him. "And as for worry, you never worried before we were married. Why is it any different now?"

"You have no idea, do you?" He sounded exasperated.

"No, I don't." She caught up with him as he turned back toward the house. "What is there to worry about? That I might get tired of sleeping alone? Do *you?*"

"What do you think?" His face coloured slightly. "Of course I do. I didn't get married to sleep alone. I had the idea we would be together."

"We are together, in a way. I'm here, and this is pretty much all the home we have at the moment, yours *and* mine. Why would you have felt any different if I still had been living in Toronto?" She put a hand on his arm. "Other than the location, nothing has changed. I'm working, as I always have. I'm doing all right, thank you; just lonely, sometimes, the way I was before I met you." She glanced down at her hand. "Except that now I can't go out with anyone else to pass the time. No, I don't want to, either," she added as he turned away from her and kept walking. "I want *you*. But you're a few thousand miles away, doing exactly what you've always wanted to, and I'm happy for you. Tony, this is not the best time to talk about this," she said, catching up to him again as he stopped, close to the veranda.

Silently, he stared at the screen tent in the backyard, his face set in a stubborn frown. "So this is all my fault, is it? Are you saying I shouldn't have left?"

"Of course not. There's no point spending the weekend debating about what we can't change. Besides, we're getting close to the house again and I don't want everyone to hear us arguing. That's what they came here for, after all, didn't they? We have a lot of things to discuss, when no one is here. And we have other things to worry about." She looked at the shiny Mercedes. "What are your parents' plans? Are they staying over? What if my mother stays too? And she will, if they do; count on it. Where will we put them? The only other decent place to sleep, besides my—our—bedroom is the screen tent." She raised an eyebrow as his face turned thoughtful. "Well, can you picture your parents on a mattress in the spare room? Or even on a lumpy old pull-out couch in the living room?"

"Or sleeping in a *tent?*" He pulled a face, and Gloria burst out laughing. He glanced in the kitchen door. "No, I can't picture it. But I think we'd better go back and see what's happening. I think your friends are doing the dishes, and our respective mothers are starting to search through your packing boxes for more china."

"Oh, no." Gloria groaned. "And if they all stay, what should we feed them for breakfast? We've eaten everything except the Meow Mix."

"Why not? It doesn't look as though the cats need it." Tony watched from the veranda as Buffy crossed the field carrying a rodent nearly as large as herself. "I think you'd better intercept her before she parks that carcass in the kitchen under my mother's nose."

"Oh, damn!" Gloria lunged across the driveway as cat and carcass turned toward the comfortable shade beside the screen tent.

Chapter 4

Monday was no better than Gloria expected. The rain had begun overnight, and with the extra water in the ground, the septic bed had started to smell again. "And I wonder if the landlord is even *looking* for a solution," she complained as she joined Tony at the table for an early breakfast. "And if that's not enough for me to worry about, the manager of the print division at Heartland is coming to see me sometime this week to assess my work, thanks to some cracks made by the paper's manager, I suspect."

"Good. Let's hope you stink as an editor so he'll fire you and you can join me." He smiled over his coffee mug.

"I think you're finally showing me your rotten side," she chided, rising to refill her cup.

He grabbed her around the waist as she passed by. "You never let go of work, do you? I bet you wanted to pick strawberries yesterday so you could drive by the scene of the crime once more. That officer wasn't very happy to see you." He released her and took a large bite of toast.

"Too bad," she asserted. "I merely asked him if they were investigating all possible angles before settling on one theory. I wanted to know how close they were to pinning the whole thing on Mike. He thought I was being nosy."

"You're interfering. You said you wouldn't."

"I'm *not* interfering," she insisted. "He's a nice kid. Even if they think he did it by accident, he doesn't deserve this."

"Mike likes you rather a lot, too, I notice. Maybe a bit too much."

"You're jealous!" she accused. "That's sweet of you, Tony, but you should be no more jealous of Mike than I am of your chamber ensemble."

"A lot less, I hope. What will you do with all the strawberry jam we made?"

"Eat it. It's a family tradition, not eating it, but picking strawberries and making a gallon of jam, every year."

"And smelling like strawberries, all day." He took a deep breath and his nostrils flared slightly. "It drove me nuts, you know." He glanced into the living room. "And what about that steamer trunk you bought at the garage sale yesterday? Shall I move it?"

"No, leave it right where it is, in front of the couch. I can store all the extra bedding and towels in it, and it will make a great coffee table." She stopped chewing. "Tony, are you planning to come back to see me before you head out east?"

"Of course." He hesitated, reaching for the fresh jam. "I'll call you."

There was that gauzy curtain again. She was staring across the breakfast table at a stranger.

She said good-bye to him at six thirty, standing in the rain in her nightgown. "Come home when you can," was all she could say. Her stomach turned another somersault as he kissed her once more, squeezed her hand, turned his car, and splashed through the uneven potholes down the driveway, just in time. As she stood, waving and getting soaked, she let the tears come.

***

In five minutes, it was all over. She dried her eyes, her hair, and her feet from the rain and wet grass outside, and poured herself a fresh cup of coffee. It was nearly seven A.M., and she had a week's worth of news to worry about. And what about Rick, and Mr. Russell?

By eight she was at Bud's Café, the coffee shop across from the *Sun*'s storefront on the Plattsford main street. Merchants, high school students, politicians, and police considered Bud's their exclusive meeting place, with four cozy, plush booths and several tables all served by two white-aproned young women behind a long counter. During the day, it was always busy, and always noisy. Its specialty was the freshest coffee anywhere, and homemade bagels. Linda was already at the counter, talking to a couple of merchants about an upcoming flyer.

"Gloria! You've heard me mention Doug Sullivan before. He used to be general manager of the *Sun*, and my former boss." Linda presented an interesting-looking man in his late thirties, tall, with dark hair and a full beard.

"I've seen you at merchant meetings," Gloria said, shaking hands with Sullivan. A strong, warm grip, and an attractive face, she noted. In fact, he was by far the most attractive man she'd met since her arrival in Plattsford. "What are you doing now?"

"Opening a business," he replied, smiling down at her. "I'm tired of working for other people."

She smiled back, and noticed how his warm, dark eyes met hers without wavering. "What kind of business? Not another newspaper, I hope."

"No. It took me awhile to decide what to do once I left the *Sun.* For the past year I've been working for an accounting firm in London, consulting on various businesses, particularly newspapers, and building a new house just outside of Plattsford on a country lot. Now, I'm starting my own management and accounting firm here in town. It's not as prestigious as running a newspaper, of course, but...." He shrugged, and grinned. "Let's just say it's what I do. I trained years ago as an accountant. Small businesses in small communities need help in planning financial strategies and balancing budgets as much as large corporations do."

"You're an *accountant?*" And so charming too? "I'm surprised you decided to stay here, Mr. Sullivan."

"Why not?" He lifted an eyebrow. "It's a nice town, and I came to know a lot of people during the seven years I was managing the paper. My wife has friends here, our son starts Kindergarten in the fall, and the teacher lives next door. It makes it rather homey."

Gloria hadn't so much as glanced at his left hand; naturally, a man his age, with his looks, wouldn't be caught single in a town this size. And why was she even thinking about this? Well, most of the accountants she had known on the corporate side of her career were weedy, boring, and bald, she mused as she paid for her coffee and bagel. This one was tall, had a gorgeous head of dark hair, dynamic voice, and a friendly face. His sober, dark suit didn't tone down the vitality, but enhanced it. He looked like the dashing newspaper magnate that Russell was trying to be. She imagined, for one second, Doug Sullivan in that corner office. Nice.

"Are you joining us? We're discussing Doug's advertising strategy." Linda stood by the empty booth with a grin on her face wider than the main street.

As Gloria slid into the booth next to Linda, she found herself gazing across the table at the friendly, urbane accountant and wishing her own wedding ring were not so prominent...then mentally slapped herself on the wrist. "Of course, we'll do a business introduction story for you, Mr. Sullivan, although you probably need no introduction."

"I'd say not. Doug is pretty well-known in boy scouts and service clubs," Linda piped up, giving Gloria a none-too-gentle nudge.

"I've always kept up a high profile in town," Sullivan agreed. "But a new business feature would help. The grapevine is interesting, but the newspaper is more accurate. At least, it is now. How are you enjoying the *Sun*?" he asked, stirring his coffee.

The compliment sent a slight flush to her face, and her next breath sounded more like a sigh. "I'm working my way slowly but surely into small town politics, but it has been a few years since I worked in a community like this, and I'm out of practice. The official politics are easy. The other politics, well...." She shook her head. "Tell me. You're not from Plattsford originally, I gather, yet you managed the paper quite successfully for a few years. How did you find out what was really going on?"

"The barbershop," Doug said with an easy smile. "Everyone talks to Sid."

Gloria laughed in surprise and touched the ends of her hair. "The barbershop. I never thought of that. Thanks." She favoured him with her brightest and widest smile, and ignored Linda's almost inaudible gurgle beside her.

The glow was short-lived. "Well, hello. What have we here?" a familiar voice asked. "What did you say to win a smile like that from our most glorious Gloria?" Fred Russell was approaching from the counter. "Sullivan, you must be an artist at charming women. Our editor here is not an easy one to impress." He placed a possessive hand on Gloria's shoulder.

Sullivan raised a dark eyebrow at the two of them.

"Good morning, Mr. Russell. Mr. Sullivan is giving me some research tips," Gloria said, shrugging away his hand in annoyance and getting up from the table so Russell could take her place next to Linda. "You'll excuse me if I don't stay? I have films that need developing." She nodded a quick thanks to Sullivan, gulped most of her coffee, and crammed half the bagel into her mouth so she wouldn't curse out loud. *Damn that Fred Russell!* she screamed inside her head as she pushed open the door of the coffee shop with her shoulder. It swung wide, nearly knocking over an elderly woman on the sidewalk. Gloria mumbled an apology, her mouth still jammed with warm multi-grain, and the woman stepped aside and continued toward the corner. Gloria stood in front of Bud's, feeling completely foolish.

Visibly chewing, she headed three doors down to the barbershop, pausing in front of the door as she attempted to swallow a large wad of dough without the aid of a liquid. If this works, she thought, this would be one way of gathering information that was safe and detached from an ongoing police investigation.

Sid Stanton was trimming sideburns on the face of the proprietor of the health food store and chatting about the benefits of fish oil capsules. Roy Palmer, loans manager from the local credit union, was sitting in a chair, reading *The Globe and Mail*. Gloria had talked to the barber at Merchant Association meetings, a gregarious sort, and curious, as a barber should be. She decided on a direct approach, just as soon as she was able to activate her vocal chords.

Thc trio in the shop waited expectantly while she struggled to down the last bit of breakfast.

"Mr. Stanton, when do you have a quiet minute to chat?"

"Only school kids call me mister, *Ms.* Trevisi. To everyone else, I'm just Sid. Pop in just after nine, and I'll give you a trim," Sid suggested, his clippers buzzing quietly in his hands. The store owner snickered.

She grinned. "What a good idea. Do you do bangs?"

Sid looked up, brushing the front of his clean, white shirt. He was stocky, had a marvelous head of thick gray hair, a beautiful mustache, and glasses perched on his nose. His slight middle-aged paunch didn't get in the way of his work at all as he sidestepped around the chair, clippers in hand. "Yours? Certainly."

She turned to the credit union rep. "So, Roy, I hear Doug Sullivan is starting a management and accounting business in town."

"He'll do just fine," Roy Palmer said, glancing up from his paper. "People here have a lot of respect for Doug, even though he's not from around here."

"Really? Why is that?"

"Well, when he managed the paper, he was always interested in the good of the community at large. The paper became more involved once he took over, you know, sponsoring activities and giving more free promotion to fund-raisers. He's a bit of a shy guy to talk to, but he gets involved in every worthwhile community project there is."

"Yeah," the health store manager agreed. "He's a great organizer, and he isn't afraid to tell you what's on his mind. He wrote a column, about once a month, made a few enemies, even had words with people at Rotary meetings, but he didn't compromise his own principles for anyone."

Charming, *and* a model citizen. Should she believe it? "I'll be back," Gloria said to Sid, and slipped out the door and across the road to her office.

***

"You'll be up to your neck in news today, I imagine," Sid remarked as he showed her to the large chair in front of the mirror.

Sid's barbershop was a relatively small cubbyhole, compared to the big unisex hair styling shops Gloria was used to. His combs, clippers, and dryers were lined up neatly on a counter below a mirror that stretched from one end to the other. The walls were white, countertops black, and there was a hair-washing sink at the back. The only other barber chair in the place was empty, as were the three chairs lined up along the front window with a table full of magazines, farm publications, and the *London Free Press*. It was a peaceful time of morning.

"Been up to my neck since I got here. That's why I haven't had time to get a haircut. I can see you're well set up for women as well as men," Gloria said, tilting her head as he fastened the large apron behind her neck. "I like your shop. It's not fussy."

"The customers like it that way." He narrowed his eyes as he studied her bangs. "Some are rough around the edges, but they still appreciate a good trim."

"Tell me, Sid, was Clarence McKee a customer of yours?"

"Only occasionally, but a lot of his business cronies are based in Plattsford. I see a few of them."

"Is Doug Sullivan one of them?"

"I'm not sure I should say." Sid adjusted the apron and ran a comb through her hair. "Doug would tell you himself if you asked, I imagine. Doug is the up-front type, very open. McKee never was, when it came to business, never wanted people to know exactly what he was doing. If he were alive for you to ask, he'd probably say he'd never heard of Doug Sullivan. Is that why you're here? Or do you really want a trim?" He held up his scissors.

Gloria grinned. "A trim, please. What can you tell me about Mr. McKee? His business cronies probably talk about him sometimes when they're getting their haircut, don't they? Anything interesting?"

Sid hesitated, assessing their privacy. The street outside was deserted; too early for most shoppers. "Off the record?"

"Way off. I'm trying to get a feel for the place, and the official stories barely scratch the surface. Doug

Sullivan suggested I get a haircut, and develop an ear for gossip."

"Did he?" Sid chuckled as he snipped at her bangs. "He's a good fellow." He combed her hair across the nape of her neck, and gave it a quick undercut.

"What about the people Mr. McKee did business with?" Gloria persisted. "Did they respect *him*?"

Sid hesitated again. "I wouldn't call it respect. Let's just say they were wise to him."

"Now you have my attention."

Sid checked the sides of her hair for evenness, and snipped some more. "Are you going to the funeral home this afternoon?"

"No." Gloria had decided against it. For one thing, it would mean returning home to change into something somber and uncomfortable. And unless the deceased was a personal friend, she did not think that the media reps belonged at such an occasion.

"Then meet me for coffee next door at two, when I take a break. Things should be quite peaceful. I'll have time to think about this." Sid looked at her. "I've heard a lot of things, Gloria Trevisi, and to tell you everything would take me all morning. But there are one or two little items that can sum up the whole of Clarence McKee's career in business, and politics. There." He carefully laid his scissors on the counter and handed her a small hand mirror.

"You're quick, Sid. Best trim I've had in ages."

Sid beamed. "Thanks. Actually, I've been wanting to do more women's hair, if only the local ladies could lay off the perms and curling rods." He winked. "Besides, the women have some pretty interesting things to say, if you like listening."

"As long as it's not about me, I'm happy. There are plenty of women who crave a simple haircut. I'll recommend you." Gloria paid him, and tried an experimental toss of her nearly straight, blunt cut strands in the mirror before fetching her raincoat.

He slipped the money into the till. "And if you people keep back copies of the newspaper for a few years, read up on the O'Dell community center improvement package about two years back, in March, I think. You might find it interesting."

As she walked out the door, a farmer, in clean green work wear and boots, was walking in. He tipped his ball cap with a friendly grin.

* * *

Hazel McDaniel and two other community correspondents were waiting for her, with sheets of paper and envelopes stuffed with written accounts of Institute and church club meetings, family reunions, and other activities. Six correspondents regularly contributed these odds and ends of social notes, for an embarrassingly low retainer. Gloria's only objection, of course, was that they wrote only about the meetings they wanted to, and usually mentioned only their friends and lifetime acquaintances. Perkins Hill had doubled in size since the local social news correspondent had glanced out her window.

Newcomers, however, were mentioned only rarely, probably to their relief. Would she want some nosy social columnist including a paragraph on *her* most recent weekend visitors? And surely one's houseguests were one's own business. But what could one expect from a community correspondent who was paid ten dollars per issue?

"I didn't realize you weren't into work before nine thirty," Mrs. McDaniel said with a petulant frown. The other two correspondents glanced at one another, saying nothing. Theresa and Jan, on the other side of the counter, stopped working and sat as still as watch stones. "Your predecessor certainly was always here on time."

"Steve Lang lived in the apartment above the office," Gloria noted, ignoring the rest of the insult.

"I have poor Clarence McKee's obituary written, and I'm wondering if you could print it just the way I wrote it," Hazel said. "He was a relative of ours, you know."

Gloria accepted the lengthy piece, neatly penned on foolscap. It reminded her of a university examination paper. "Thank you, Mrs. McDaniel. You've saved us a great deal of time."

"Well, sometimes we have to do your work for you so it will be right, seeing as how you're not from around here," she said loftily, glancing at the other two correspondents. "Clarence was well-respected in East Lister, you know. People will want to read about him."

"I am certain of it. And how is his family?" Gloria asked politely. She was surprised to see Hazel's ruddy, scrubbed face turn a shade redder.

"They're fine, thank you. Bearing up well, as you will see this afternoon." Mrs. McDaniel turned abruptly toward the door, adjusting her rain bonnet over her nearly white, tightly permed hair and pulling her navy blue coat more closely over her baggy print dress and white cardigan.

Now what was that about? Gloria wondered. She watched Mrs. McDaniel ease slowly and carefully across the threshold of the front door in the large, sensible shoes that were absolutely necessary for a woman of her somewhat cumbersome weight and limited physical ability.

"Mrs. McDaniel must be feeling the loss of her nephew," the second correspondent, a middle-aged matron from North Andover, said as the door closed. She handed over twenty pages of varied script. "He's been a great help to them in the past. They might've lost their farm without him, I hear. He got them a gravel pit license for the lower fifty acres so they could get extra income."

Gloria smiled back, leafed quickly through the contributions, saw the ladies to the door, checked for messages, then ran lightly up the stairs with the bundle of papers.

Linda Grant was buttoning up her raincoat by the coat rack as Gloria rounded the corner at the top of the stairs. "Do you have a minute, Linda?" she asked.

"Why? Did you want to know whether Doug Sullivan is happy with his wife? Thought no one around here was worth your notice, huh?" She glanced over her shoulder at the closed door of Russell's office. "I think we may have found a match for you, after all. Gloria, you were almost *flirting*! Fred was jealous as hell."

Gloria flushed guiltily. "Skip it. Just very quickly, tell me about Clarence McKee's family. I asked Hazel McDaniel how the family was, and got a strange reaction."

Linda chortled. "His family? Clarence's mother is still alive, but pretends not to know him. No," she added when Gloria was about to interrupt. "No dementia there. They had a falling out when she went to the old folks home for the winter, and he rented out her little house in the village."

"Ah. So she was never able to go back home?"

"You get the picture. His wife was once the belle of the county. Rumour has it she drinks heavily. People might be thinking that she's better off now. As for marriage, they've lived separately, almost, for the past couple of years. They had two daughters, no sons. And he had another woman on the side, lives in Chesterton Township, with two kids, from two different men, of course. Clarence wasn't one of them, far as I know."

"You know all that?"

"*Everyone* knows all that. They just don't talk about it to strangers."

"Like me, you mean?" Gloria grinned. "I think perhaps I *would* like to attend the funeral, after all."

"You never know, though most people around here behave themselves at funerals. And while you are touching on the subject of family fiascos, you seemed in the middle of something when we arrived Saturday. I hope it wasn't inconvenient for you that we pulled in when we did."

"Hell no! You were the rescuing cavalry. I'll fill you in when I have time, if you're interested."

"Of course I'm interested." Linda started down the stairs, and turned back to Gloria. "You never mentioned that Tony's so young. I mean, I thought violinists were all middle-aged. And so good-looking, too. But everyone knows now, because I made a point of telling Fred and Doug at the coffee shop this morning."

"You didn't. You devil!"

"Well, *someone* has to watch out for you. I also mentioned that he's charming, friendly, and very handy around a kitchen. Doug was impressed." Linda lowered her voice. "And it's just what Fred deserved, after embarrassing you and Doug. He's such a child at times. Why don't you put a photo over your desk so we can all see and admire?" She ran down the stairs with her large briefcase in hand, and left Gloria blinking after her.

Rick came around the corner with photo contact sheets. "You're here, finally. Ready to do some work?" he asked.

"I've been working since eight. Where were you first thing this morning?"

His runners squeaked on the tiled floor as he braked hard. "Sorry. I was held up by an accident on the county road."

"I hope you have a picture of it." Gloria led the way into her cubicle. "Sergeant O'Toole told me this morning that the report will be ready at noon." She wondered when she would get a chance to tell him what a great job he was doing. It seemed every time the opportunity arose, some echo of nastiness crept into their conversation. Was it Russell's doing? Did he enjoy seeing people at odds around him?

***

Photo captions written, council agenda for the evening collected, and even a story completed on a paper-recycling scheme for a neighboring township, Gloria felt she deserved an afternoon break. Lunch at her desk had been brief. A bagel and coffee, and a cozy chat with the gregarious barber, would be welcome.

As she crossed the wet street, Sid was putting a Back In Ten sign on the door of his barbershop and heading for Bud's Café.

"Well, I read up on it," Gloria said as they elbowed their way through the waiting crowd at the counter and found a booth. Sid obviously had an understanding with the woman behind the counter, a slim, young girl with long hair pulled back in a hair net. She brought two coffees and a bagel to the table. Gloria wondered whether Sid cut her hair, as well.

"You found the story about the improvements? It was two or three editors ago, but I presume it was fairly complete." Sid stirred two helpings of cream into his coffee. "What did it say?"

"It was three years back, and it mentioned that the improvements to the drainage bed at the old arena would cost nine-thousand dollars, that McKee Excavating would do the work, and the province would kick in a third. It sounded pretty mundane, until I thought to check his obit—Mrs. McDaniel wrote it, by the way. Wasn't Mr. McKee on council then? Could he serve council and work for the township too?"

"You're getting the idea." Sid smiled and nodded. "Serving on council never stopped him from picking up township contracts. He lived in East Lister all his life, and probably thinks they're his by right. And in O'Dell, anything is possible. They make their own rules. Read up on their severances some time." He took a long gulp from his coffee mug.

Gloria sipped hers while she waited.

Sid put down his cup. "First, I want to make it absolutely clear, young lady, that I do not condone murder. Occasionally, though, I can understand it, a little. Clarence McKee was a hard-working man with a family, in spite of his other sins. He was elected to council several years ago, was acclaimed only once during that time, and fought a tough election to become the deputy reeve. But we're not talking about an ordinary, run-of-the-mill, dumb rural politician here, Gloria." Sid leaned over the table and dropped his voice. "I need your solemn oath on this. If a word of what I am about to tell you ever gets in the papers, certain people will know where it came from, and I swear I'll never tell you a secret again as long as I live."

Gloria regarded him carefully. "As far as I'm concerned, you're an unquoted random source of information. After all, you're passing on gossip, aren't you?"

"Gossip?" Sid cocked an eyebrow. "Gossip claims he was cheating on his wife. This isn't gossip. This is something that everyone knows, and no one mentions."

She set down her half-empty cup. "That's exactly what I want, Mr. Stanton. I don't need what I can quote. I can get that from the meeting minutes. I need to know what actually goes on, and Doug Sullivan says you're the best source he knows."

"He's absolutely right. Does nine-grand seem like a rather expensive drainage bed?"

"Is it? Frankly, I don't know much about it, since the newspaper story didn't go into details. But if you're looking at foundation work for a city building, it's probably in the ball park."

"Well, this isn't the city. The only ball park it was anywhere near, was the park next to the community center. The price was out in left field, if you take my meaning. After council applied for the funds, they kept the whole thing quiet, didn't want anyone knowing when the work would be done, didn't want press photos, anything."

"And they likely succeeded, judging by the clippings." She lifted her mug and took another sip. "Well, no one's going to argue about the province kicking in three-thousand dollars to help cover the cost of anything, are they?"

"That's just it." Sid took a long pull on his coffee, and sat back. "It didn't cover a third. The grant covered all of it."

Gloria almost spilled her coffee as she put down her mug. "All of it? Three thousand?"

"The whole project, unofficially, of course. At least, it was supposed to. The paperwork may have made it sound like a large project, but it wasn't. Just one corner. You see..." Sid smiled and nodded to two weather-beaten farmers wearing dark suits, no doubt stopping in to Bud's after the funeral home visit. "Careful." He leaned forward again, and lowered his voice. "Clarence himself put in the estimate for the work. He was on the arena board at the time. The building inspector approved it. I think the plan was to put in a high estimate, but not too high, get a grant that would more or less cover his cost of the entire project, and then use the rest of the allocated funds for improvements to the lawn-bowling green."

"But all these province-funded projects are audited very carefully," Gloria pointed out.

"Not that carefully, but they considered that," Sid said, all wound up and using his spoon as a baton. "The books had to look good. So the O'Dell clerk issued a check for nine thousand bucks to McKee Excavating, with the handshake agreement that Clarence then would give the arena board a donation of six thousand toward its other projects."

Gloria frowned. "A bribe?"

Sid glanced over his shoulder at the two men seated close by. "Actually, it was much worse," he muttered. "It was robbery."

Gloria raised her eyebrows. "It would look bad in any light. And if the province got wind of it, the township's future grants would be jeopardized."

"Don't jump ahead too fast. The whole thing is," Sid leaned forward even further and his voice dropped to a whisper, "Clarence never gave it back." He poked a stubby finger on the wooden tabletop to emphasize his words.

Gloria sputtered as her coffee went down the wrong way. "Oh, shit!" she choked.

Sid waited until she caught her breath. "Are you all right?"

"Never mind me. He never gave it back? In a community like O'Dell? Did he think he'd get away with it?"

Sid nodded. "He did. The council had no idea how to handle it. And neither did the arena board."

"But the *minutes*! How on earth could they cover it up?"

"The minutes?" Sid waved his hand in dismissal. "You'll never read anything in the minutes. But plenty of people knew about it, and never said."

"It's peanuts, I know, but...." The entire recreation board on a list of suspects, for a lousy six thousand in public funds? Not likely. How about other contractors who might have bid on the job? "Do you think the police know about this one?"

"Maybe," Sid replied with a warning glare. "You can imagine the awkward position the council was left in, not to mention the clerk, the board. Legally, they couldn't go after him, or the province would have found out about the grant. They sent him some pretty hot memos, and some of that paperwork is no doubt still on file somewhere. But their hands were tied."

"And how do you know all this?"

"I'm a barber," Sid said with a wink. "The members of the recreation board in a township like O'Dell are just volunteers. They're not seasoned politicians; they're not even township councillors. They don't swear an oath, or even get paid for their time. The ones who were mad enough to burst, told their barber." He paused. "I don't think any of them would kill for money that wasn't even theirs. But the betrayal of trust? I don't know." He glanced at his watch. "Gotta go. My ten minutes are up. Gives you something to think about, doesn't it? After all, if he'll do it for a measly few grand, would he be dumb enough to try it with a bigger fish?" He put down his cup, still half-full, grabbed half the bagel, and slid out of the booth.

"Now please, Gloria Trevisi, swear on the best coffee in five counties that you will never tell."

"Of course, I swear," she said, smiling up at him. *I swear all the time and my mother hates it,* she added to herself as he left the restaurant without stopping at the counter. She finished the other half of the bagel, downed the coffee, walked up to the counter and asked, point-blank: "Who pays for this?"

The girl in the hairnet, jotting on a clipboard, solved that one, honestly and courteously. "Yours is a dollar and sixty cents. Sid pays at the end of the week."

***

By four thirty she was caught up on her work and ready to go home for a quick bite before Plattsford Town Council met at seven thirty. The rain had let up, and Rick was getting ready for yet another industrial league softball game—"which may, or may not, be cancelled," he muttered glumly as he stared out of the upstairs window by Gloria's desk.

Russell had held a very short meeting in which Linda had summarized the advertising prospects, and Gloria had quickly reviewed the week's news contents and assessed her space requirements. She had also handed Rick the opportunity to claim his own space for sports, and work up his own page layouts, to give him some authority along with his responsibilities. Sports coverage in a small community was vitally important, and Rick's responsibilities were not meager. She hoped this would patch up some of their past differences, and spike Russell's guns. Rick was pleased. Russell didn't seem to notice or care.

"Do you ever get tired of sports?" she asked Rick as he hovered by the window.

Rick shrugged. "I don't know. I'm used to it." He paused. "And I guess I respect it. But it's all I've been doing since you got here. With the last editor I was....well, picking up a lot of his slack, and there were no local features in the paper like there are now. I made certain we always had sports. He seemed to think that was all people would read anyway. It would be nice to cover a few other things."

"Any preferences?"

He hesitated, his hands in his pockets. "Oh, perhaps police and court coverage. That's where the action is. It would look good on my résumé."

"True. Next to sports, people like the police reports best: accidents, assaults, robbery, as long as it happens to someone else. Would you like to take care of the late-night police check for me? Call the desk at eleven to pick up on anything that evening that needs follow-up."

His face brightened. "Sure!"

"It won't take much extra work. Sometimes there's nothing going on. It's most important on Tuesday and Wednesday. By Thursday it's too late for the paper anyway, and we can pick it up Friday morning, unless it is earth-shaking news. You don't have to come to the office to do it. And it would be a help."

"I can pick it up every night, if you like." Rick grinned happily and walked quickly back to his desk, pocketed two short rolls of film, and turned back, camera in hand. "See you tomorrow, then?"

Gloria watched him head out to the park with a feeling of satisfaction. She had been too preoccupied with her own adjustments for too long; it was time to take care of business.

At home again, she found Buffy and Max staring out the window at the birds cavorting through the wet grass. She also found a message from her mother-in-law asking when Tony was expected in Toronto. No doubt she knew, by now, but she put in a call anyway, and was sorry she had.

"You must spend more time in the city, dear. It's not proper that you hide yourself in that godforsaken corner of the country. People will think there's something wrong."

Only if you tell them, she silently remarked. "I have a job here, Mrs. Lambert, and it is very demanding."

"You don't want to spend time with Tony while he's home?"

"Of course I do. But he works too, and he's not *home* at the moment." Gloria's voice betrayed her temper. "And he knows what to expect of me this week." Both rang off, bristling.

A message from Tony, on the other hand, mentioned there were two concerts later in the week and that they'd be in rehearsal for a few days, but he'd try to make it home Saturday night, before the group headed for Halifax. He sounded so aloof it brought tears to her eyes. She cursed his natural Anglo reserve, sighed, opened the fridge and pulled out some cat food. Max purred with enthusiasm as he spotted the loaded dish approaching the floor. "Sometimes, Max, I wish you were a guy. You're always glad to see me."

***

Rick was waiting at eight thirty when she arrived Tuesday. "Two accidents, and a break-in at a tractor dealership," he reported, checking his scribbled notes. "And the investigative team will hold a press conference at ten this morning, if you want me to go for you."

"No, thanks, I'll take that one," Gloria said, dumping a pile of committee reports and notes from last night's meeting on top of the growing heap of piled-up correspondence and unopened mail on her desk.

She was slitting open mail, piling most into the wastebasket by her chair and stacking some choice pieces neatly beside her keyboard, when Russell stuck his head over the partition. "Got a minute?"

"Just," she said, stabbing at the top of a large brown manila folder marked IMPORTANT.

"I'd like to come to the press conference with you."

"How did you—Oh." Gloria knew, of course, that Rick would be her pipeline should she ever want Fred

Russell to hear an interesting rumor. "I guess so. But I want to come straight back afterward. I have a council meeting to write up yet, and two more township meetings tonight to hunt down. And the county has just sent an official plan amendment that I'll have to look over."

"If we can leave in half-an-hour, I'll have you back here right after lunch."

"*Before* lunch. And we'll take my car, if you don't mind," Gloria added. "This is my job, and I'll have *you* back when I'm finished with the police."

"Your car?"

"Why not? Mileage is part of my pay package, and in case you haven't noticed the size of my weekly salary, I need the mileage checks to buy groceries." Or did Mr. Russell think that attending a press conference about a grisly murder together would make an interesting first date?

He shrugged. "Your car, then." He turned and left her to her pile of mail.

Norma Simmons peeked around the corner of Gloria's office a moment later. "Hi. Give me what you've got, and I'll get to work."

This was one interruption she welcomed. Norma was the community correspondence editor, a whiz at interpreting the scratchy and scrawling handwriting of the local news gatherers for community social bulletins, something necessary in the rural communities surrounding Plattsford. Norma also kept track of obituaries by phoning every mortuary chapel in a hundred miles at least twice a week, and was a tiger for correct name spelling.

Norma hadn't been particularly happy with her new editor, Gloria recalled. Gloria had begun her tenure with a rigorous editing job on these long, arduous accounts, eliminating descriptions of food consumed, prayers murmured, and layers of names like "Mrs. Ralph Green" that never included the woman's given name unless she was (ugh!) a spinster. Her attempts to update the church news was about as successful as Copernicus's plea to the Catholic church to accept a sun-centered universe; she and Norma had ended up in a fierce argument. She had soon given up and trusted it to Norma's judgment as to what was considered proper etiquette for community correspondence.

Gloria looked at the enormous, messy pile of written and folded sheets on the corner of her desk. She had not even had time to sort it into districts, or thumb through the entries on coming events to see if there was anything worth a photograph. She scooped up the entire pile and handed it to Norma. "You're a lifesaver. I have to be at a press conference for most of the morning. Can you also check Clarence McKee's obit for accuracy or whatever? Hazel McDaniel brought it in yesterday, and I haven't had a chance to read it over."

Norma made a face. "It will be long, flowery, and full of lies in his favor. But I'll do what I can."

Gloria watched as the woman seated herself at the wide table opposite Rick's desk to sort a large pile of pages, sometimes written, sometimes typed, always folded and crumpled and occasionally coffee-stained, and wondered what she would do if Norma took a vacation. Forty-five and self-taught, she could type like lightning.

By the time Russell was ready to leave for the police office, Gloria had compiled a list of three major and six small stories to be written up from the previous night's meeting, and was wishing she had insisted on separate cars. With the other stories needing completion and a field trip at the seniors' day care center to check on this afternoon, she'd need most of her day to catch up. By the middle of July, however, she'd be scraping the walls looking for ways to fill the news space in the paper every week, as she knew from past experience. "Enjoy it while you can," she murmured.

"Gee, I'll try." Russell, walking beside her to the parking lot, looked startled.

"I mean, a heavy news week. I don't suppose you've ever spent the summer, or even Christmas holidays, at a newspaper, when there is a shortage of newsworthy activity like council meetings. That's another challenge." She unlocked the passenger door of the Mazda and circled to the driver's side, climbed in and grabbed the end of the seat belt.

"You've been doing this sort of work for awhile, I gather."

"If you have read my résumé, Mr. Russell, you'll notice that I worked for small and suburban papers for eight years before going corporate. I opted for regular office hours so I could finish university." She started the engine.

"Actually, the personnel files are not in my department," he said, his embarrassment just barely obvious. "I have to talk to people to find out anything about them, such as why you need a mileage check to buy groceries when you're married to someone with a more-than-adequate income, as I would judge from the size of that diamond you were wearing last week."

Too late to insist on separate cars. "I live on my income, he lives on his. It's complicated, and personal. And you won't read it in my résumé, either."

"Well, it doesn't sound like any kind of marriage I've ever known," he remarked, strapping himself in. "It sounds a lot like legal separation." He paused. "Calculate the price of that rock, and I'd swear it wasn't *his* idea."

"Calculate all you want, Mr. Russell." Gloria lurched her car hard into reverse and hoped he'd bang his skinny knee on the dashboard. They had been together barely two minutes and already she was irritated. Apart from his obsession with her jewelry, however, she had found out something interesting. She hadn't been aware that her hiring was accomplished without input from the general manager; it explained a few things that she would find handy when Ed Murray, print division manager and the person who had interviewed her for this job two months ago, paid a visit later this week. They were turning onto the main street before she said anything at all. "I guess you're in the same position as I am, with regard to finding out things. Tell me about yourself, Mr. Russell. How long have you worked for Heartland Communications?"

Getting Fred Russell's life-story proved to be an easy task. It also kept him occupied at arm's length for the short drive to the police station, and could well have gone on for another hour. By the time they were inside the building, he was in an agreeable mood, and willing to remain quiet and let Gloria do any talking that was necessary.

As Gloria had feared, the *London Free Press*, K-W *Record*, and at least two television stations were on hand. Sergeant O'Toole was sitting at the front of the common room with a white-shirted supervisor of the investigation, Detective-Inspector Lawrence Gray.

The information was brief and to the point. On Thursday evening, June 15th, just before midnight, McKee's body had been discovered on the premises of what was known locally as the O'Dell Township Industrial Park, at Lot 11, Concession 23 of O'Dell Township. At first it appeared that the victim, Clarence McKee, aged fifty-six of East Lister, had died as a result of being run over by a bulldozer.

Further investigation (and autopsy, likely) had revealed that the victim had been drinking and was also heavily drugged with barbiturates, had presumably passed out, and been transported by wheelbarrow to the spot where the remains were found. Time of death estimates varied, but their best guess was prior to eleven, based on witness accounts. Forensic evidence, Gray stated, was still being analyzed at the crime lab in Toronto, and an inquest was scheduled for Tuesday, July 4th.

"What kind of barbiturates?" someone asked, a camera rolling on his shoulder.

"Enough phenobarbital to stop a team of work horses," Sergeant O'Toole replied.

"We believe the drug was mixed into the rye," Gray added, with a sidelong look at the sergeant. "The bottle we found on the premises had some foreign residue. Our forensics lab in Toronto confirmed it this morning."

"Where would such a drug originate?"

"We don't know yet."

Another reporter, tape recorder in hand, piped up. "I heard you brought someone in for questioning over the weekend. Do you have a suspect?"

"A young man came forward with information, and was questioned," Gray said. "And at the moment, there are no suspects."

Gloria heaved a deep sigh of relief. "Was Mr. McKee killed by the bulldozer, or by the drugs, Inspector?" she asked.

Gray hesitated. "To the best of our knowledge, he was killed by the drugs. Phenobarbital in this kind of dose, mixed with alcohol, will very quickly and very severely depress the central nervous system and result in coma, followed by cardiovascular failure. We believe the bulldozer mishap may have been the result of error, not of murderous intention."

"Do you mean to say that someone accidentally ran over a dead body on a construction site, and didn't know it?" A television reporter, from the back of the room, was posing the question and scribbling on her notepad.

"That's what I'm saying," Gray answered.

Other details were noted, and the question-and-answer wound up. It was the first police press conference Gloria had attended since arriving in Plattsford, and she looked around the room, interested to see who rated an invitation. Ben Cootes, reeve of O'Dell, was standing to one side of the room with George Fuller, his township clerk, and another member of council. She was surprised to see Hazel McDaniel sitting in the back row, her ruddy face slightly puffy. A few other locals were there as well. Whether they were present in any official capacity, Gloria had no idea.

While the inspector repeated his summary into their personal microphones and camera lenses, she sidled over to Ben Cootes. "What is going to happen to the industrial park now?"

"We haven't discussed it. We'll be bringing it up tonight at council."

Tonight. A meeting she couldn't miss, and another evening shot.

She was still checking local angles with Reeve Cootes when she noted Mrs. McDaniel leaving on the arm of a younger man. Her son? Her nephew? Perhaps he was another relative of the McKees. And what was Mrs. McDaniel doing attending a *press* conference? Writing it up as a social event? Gloria was curious, but didn't want to miss out on this fact-finding opportunity, either. She made a mental note to find out, and continued with her questions, asking about McKee's role on council, his political priorities for the township, and Cootes's opinion of how local politics will be affected.

McKee, she was told, had been a strong proponent of the status quo, except where his own projects were concerned. He had spoken out against the feasibility of a sewage treatment plant to serve the growing village of East Lister, campaigned vigorously against black-topping the sideroads as it would affect the business of private gravel pits, yet approved the plan to expand the limits of the village, in the direction of his property.

Still, Cootes insisted on describing his fellow politician in the most glowing terms, she noted. When she was joined by a camera and two microphones, she retreated, and looked about for Sergeant O'Toole to ask about Mike's status. O'Toole was not around, but Russell was standing to one side and chatting with a short, sweaty gentleman in a rumpled business suit that looked as though it was taken out of its wardrobe case only on special occasions. She made her way across to them and introduced herself.

"This is Joe Cameron," Russell explained. "He owns Cameron and Sons Timber-finishing, in Genoa."

"You'll be moving your whole operation to the industrial park in two months," Gloria recalled. "I suppose Mr. McKee's death has delayed your plans."

"Huh? Oh....yeah. Thought they arrested the guy on the weekend...Hurtig kid. Had a nasty fight with McKee last spring. Guess they didn't." Cameron wasn't completely following her, and it was obvious why. His eyes were bloodshot and unfocused, and he swayed alarmingly on his feet.

"Will you still move your plant to the site?" Gloria persisted.

"Uh, we still hope we can," he said, slurring his words more than slightly. "We bin gettin' pretty bad publicity where we are."

"I believe your neighbors in the village have been complaining to council about sawdust and loud machinery," she noted.

"Some people'll complain about anythin'," he replied with heartfelt belligerence. "An' the press picks it up and makes a big thing of it. We run an honest business." He blew a small tornado of Crown Royal in her direction. Gloria glanced at Russell and raised one eyebrow. If she wasn't mistaken, it was barely eleven in the morning and already this man was...well, not driving, she fervently hoped. She checked the room again for the desk sergeant. Still absent.

"I hope things go well for you. But how does this murder affect your plan to move your business, Mr. Cameron?"

"Site's been closed by police f'nearly a week now," Cameron growled. "Clarence, now, he promised me I could be in by mid-July, or August, th'latest. Don't know if we can, or whether we'll just havta find 'nuther place to go. Can't stay where we are." He drew himself up to about five-seven, but still didn't make it face-to-face with Gloria. She backed away slightly to avoid his toxic breath, and made a note to keep track of this development.

"Do you have a business card, sir?"

"Gave m'number to yer boss." He leered somewhat.

"I'll be in touch." She looked at Russell and walked toward the door. He joined her.

"Pleasant chap," he said.

"Yeah. With a twenty-six-ounce habit." And I'll bet he can operate heavy equipment too, she thought as they crossed the parking lot. "I'll need that phone number as soon as we get back to the office."

"Does this have something to do with the murder?" Russell asked as they reached her car.

"I don't know. I'm not the police. But murder or not, I'd like to check on the nature of the problem he's been having with his neighbors." She smiled. "His misfortune is our living. Remember?"

Chapter 5

It was nearly lunchtime when Gloria was finally seated at her desk. Russell knew better than to invite her out for a bite, but he did anyway, and she refused politely. The pile beside her computer was not getting much smaller. She had just pulled her notes on last night's meeting when she was interrupted by a soft voice.

"Gloria?" It was Mike Hurtig, wearing construction coveralls and boots, and an anxious expression.

"Mike!" She beamed at him. "Grab a chair and sit down. I have news. Are you on a lunch break?"

He nodded. "Did you find out anything?"

"As a matter of fact, I did. And you can breathe easy, I think. It appears that Mr. McKee's death was due to an overdose of barbiturates mixed with alcohol."

"You mean, drugs and booze killed him and not...the bulldozer?"

"That's what the police are saying. It doesn't rule out murder. They think his whisky was deliberately tampered with, and the body was moved before it was run over. But rest assured he was dead before you ever drove the bulldozer onto the site. I don't think they will consider you as a suspect much longer, unless they believe you drugged his whisky."

"Thank God!" Mike blushed with sudden embarrassment. "Does that sound selfish? I should be sorry he's dead, and I am. And I feel sorry for his family, his wife and kids, but I'm relieved it wasn't my fault."

"That isn't so selfish." She punched a few letters on her keyboard and turned to him. "We're all relieved, for your sake."

"My mother called at their place yesterday, took them a casserole. They go to the same church as we do. But Mrs. McKee didn't come to the door. Mom thinks it's because of me. Maybe they think...."

Gloria shook her head. "Don't give it another thought. Mrs. McKee might not be in any condition to face anyone just now." She thought of Linda's rundown on the McKee family.

"Yeah. Guess she'd be pretty busted up." He glanced at the mountain of papers on her desk. "I see you're busy today."

"I doubt if I'll even get a lunch break."

His face brightened. "Would you like to share my sandwiches?" He pulled his lunchbox onto his lap. "Ham and cheese? Mom makes them out of homemade bread, extra thick."

Gloria hesitated, glancing at her computer screen, the curser blinking impatiently to start. "What the hell? I could use a sandwich...or maybe half," she added as she saw the enormous chunks of whole wheat bread springing out of the lunchbox. As she accepted the sandwich, she glanced at his hands. They were as clean as hers. "Tell me, what kind of work did you do for McKee?"

"Ran a bulldozer, sometimes a backhoe. Not much going on in the winter except repairing the equipment in the yard, and occasionally digging a hole for something, and sometimes snow removal. But once April came around, we were hopping. We put in a lot of septic systems when I was there." He paused. "You asked me to find out what else he was doing. Actually, there are a few things you should know. I did a co-op term in my last year of high school with the health unit, and I used to wonder how he got away with what he did."

"Such as?" It was about all Gloria could say with her mouth full.

"Well, tile drainage in fields that ended up in roadside ditches instead of municipal drains, septic systems with inadequate tiling, lagoons for liquid manure that were too close to the river bed...Those things can affect the quality of people's well water, especially near a village. He didn't seem to care. He had no respect for townspeople, anyway, even though some were his customers. I wondered sometimes." He paused. "You wanted to know about trouble. Last year Mr. McKee gave someone a low quote on the foundation for a pig barn, because the concrete wasn't the right grade. It saved the owner a lot of money, and Clarence figured as long as it will hold up the

barn, who cares if it leaches dirty water into the creek?"
He took a large bite of sandwich.

"He didn't have much respect for farmers, either,"
Gloria noted, thinking about the proposed industrial
development and all the problems it could generate
for its immediate neighbors. "Did anyone ever check
up on these things? There are health inspectors,
conservation authority officers, people whose job it
is to make certain everything on a building site is
going according to the rules. Didn't the township
building inspector ever drop by?"

"The clerk asked Clarence for a written report,
since he was on council. And the inspector is a cousin
of his. What he didn't see couldn't fail inspection,
could it?" He swallowed another large bite of
sandwich. "But there's more. This spring, after I left,
Clarence offered a guy who was building a house the
same cut-rate deal on a septic bed that most people
go for. But when the crew rolled onto the site, they
didn't even get their equipment into the ground. The
owner said he wanted to consult the health department
with Clarence's specs, first. Well, they wound up in a
hell of an argument, and Clarence pulled his
equipment off before he even dug the foundation. I
think they wound up in court over it."

"Really? I'd have a hard time believing that. The
last thing Mr. McKee would want is a health
department assessment of his work ethics. And what
did he plan to give him as a cut-rate septic system?"

"Something that was legal about fifty years ago but is well under specifications today. It would have saved Mr. Sullivan a lot of money if he'd gone along with the plan. Instead, it might have ended up costing him big bucks in legal fees, if what Mr. McKee claims is true. Clarence swore he'd keep the guy tied up in court and he'd *never* get his house finished."

Gloria paused, sandwich halfway to her mouth. "Sullivan? Not *Doug* Sullivan?" *Ask him yourself,* Sid the barber had said. Likely, he knew all about it, she mused. And so did the choir chairman. What had Margaret Ormsford said? *Plenty of others....*

Mike nodded, his mouth full. "Not that I have anything against Mr. Sullivan. He's a good guy, helped our hockey team organize a great trip to Quebec last year, but he's not from around here. Mr. McKee didn't like him at all." He poured some milk from a carton into a plastic thermos cup and handed it to her. "If it's true, I imagine it has cost McKee more than the contract was worth." He smirked. "He must have a relative who's a lawyer, or something. Sullivan said a groundhog could do a better job on a drainage bed."

Gloria swallowed a large bite of sandwich. "Good for Doug Sullivan, I suppose. He may be a nice guy, but I'm betting he's not someone you'd want to cross." She finished the last morsel of ham and wiped her fingers on a paper towel. "There are a lot of things that bother me about Mr. McKee's death, Mike; and I hope the police aren't shy about getting to the bottom of it. Some might hesitate to tangle with good, solid citizens like Mr. Sullivan, and pick on the little guys, instead," she said, taking a gulp of the milk.

"Like me?" he asked, chewing a modest mouthful of ham and cheese.

"Like you. But there are other issues, political issues, for instance. You know, I cannot understand how someone elected to serve on a municipal council could do so much township work without ever having someone challenge him on it. I looked over the minutes, when some of those contracts were awarded. He actually voted on them, never declared a direct conflict of interest."

"He was challenged once, a few years ago. It was thrown out, or buried, or something," Mike noted. "Anyway, no one ever heard any more about it, and he's been pulling the same stuff ever since."

"Another thing I wonder about is how he gets to poll such a high percentage of votes in East Lister. Is he really that popular?"

"Hell, no. People who remember him from high school say he couldn't be trusted to carry the football from the locker room to the bench without trying to siphon off some of the air. He was always trying to get away with something."

"If he's that unpopular, how does he get elected? Who counts the ballots?"

"The clerk, I guess, makes the final tally. But I haven't had a chance to vote yet in a municipal election." He brushed some breadcrumbs from the front of his coveralls.

"East Lister seems to have an unusually high voter turnout, over ninety per cent at the three polls in the community hall, compared to sixty-five in the rest of the township. Do the people in that village really care that much about their local government?"

"Heck, I never thought so," Mike said with a shrug. "But O'Dell nearly always has some hot issue going. People can get riled up, even to the point of fighting in the schoolyard. But village kids and farm kids often fight."

"I wonder how many people cast their ballots after eight, when the polls closed?" Gloria raised her eyebrows. "Or whose names were checked off as having cast ballots when they actually never made it out that evening? No one would bother checking. You've lived here all your life. Could you imagine anyone stuffing the ballot boxes?"

"They say that in O'Dell, anything is possible."

"How about Joe Cameron? He has a timber-finishing business in Genoa, at the north end of the township. Do you know him at all?"

"Don't know him, but his kids were often in trouble at school. Their mother and father don't live together. He lives with his mother in a house across from the lumberyard. The boys lived with their mother and stepfather for awhile, out on a farm at the east end of O'Dell. They have a half brother, as well, or maybe a stepbrother. I don't hang with the same bunch of guys, but I did hear that one of the Cameron boys, the oldest, moved back to Genoa to live with his dad. Why?"

"Someone in Genoa doesn't like Joe Cameron's plant, and got a petition circulated. Mr. Cameron had a business arrangement with McKee to move the timber-finishing to the industrial development outside East Lister."

"Really? That's surprising. I've always thought they hated each other."

"Why would that be?"

"I'm not sure. You'd have to ask my mom. It's something that happened when they were in high school, I think. A lot of family feuds begin in school." He grinned. "I don't think very many people in Genoa voted for Clarence McKee."

"At least, they *said* they didn't, but I wonder," Gloria mused. "What do you plan to study in university, Mike? If I stay around here for long I may need a good lawyer."

"Not me. Besides, it sounds like you already have one in the family—your father-in-law."

She laughed. "He defends white-collar embezzlers, big-time crooks, and occasionally high-profile murderers, not lowly editors being sued for libel."

"Well, I'm not going anywhere near law, I'm afraid. General science. And then, I don't know whether to go into regular or veterinary medicine." He glanced at the clock on the wall.

"You probably have to get back to work, and so have I," Gloria said, following his gaze. "Mike, you are a jewel. Thank you for sharing this incredible sandwich, and thank your mother too. She's a nice lady, and a good neighbor." She wiped the rim of the cup before handing it back, still with some milk in the bottom. "I'm afraid all I can share are germs. You don't mind, do you?"

"That's all right." He blushed alarmingly as he finished off the milk.

He was leaving as his aunt came up the stairs. Gloria heard them exchange a few words before Linda stuck her head around the back of the partition. "He looks happy. What did you say?"

"I told him the latest in the police investigation, and he shared his lunch with me. He's a sweet kid, isn't he? Your sister brought him up well," Gloria said, glancing up from her council notes.

"He won't thank you for calling him a kid," Linda warned over her shoulder as she walked to her desk. "Believe me, he hasn't been a kid since he was twelve."

"I don't suppose so. He works hard, doesn't he? With those shoulders and arms, he could lift a tractor single-handed."

"For that, he *will* be grateful." Linda winked.

Gloria turned back to her work. Norma Simmons had put a serious dent in the backlog of community correspondence. The page make-up format was on Gloria's computer, but she still preferred a hands-on, pencil-to-paper system. Technology could only improve things so much. The second section front was the crafts page, and it was looking good. The club correspondence was coming through, and the entertainment column was finished and typeset, and floating around cyber-heaven waiting for a spot to open up on an inside page. She began rattling away at the council reports, and tried not to think about a nineteen-year-old kid who was far too honest for his own good.

**

By three o'clock Plattsford's political news had been dissected in detail, and an editorial written. Gloria was sifting through the contents of three letters to the editor when Linda came around the corner. "Break time," she said. "Come on over to Bud's and bring the blank page dummies so I can show you how the second section will look."

Settled in a booth with their coffee and half a bagel apiece, Gloria said, "It looks as though Mr. McKee died of a drug overdose. Mike's off the hook, I think. Mr. McKee was dead before the bulldozer went over him."

"That's wonderful." Linda hesitated. "I shouldn't sound so glad, should I? The man is still dead, after all, and someone...it is still considered homicide, isn't it? I'm glad Mike is out of it, that's all. I know how worried Mildred has been about him."

"Don't celebrate just yet. Police may not have any other suspects." She sipped her coffee. "You're not at all like your sister, are you?"

"Not like my brother, either. Mother said I turned out different because we changed milkmen. For the longest time I had no idea what milk had to do with it." She showed a dimple. "Now, tell me how your morning with Fred went."

"I found out everything he's ever wanted me to know about Fred Russell, MBA, top two percentile. He talked. I drove."

"You drove? I'm surprised you didn't have him do the driving just to keep his hands busy."

"His hands have never been a problem. It's his head. He thinks too much."

"Did he mention that he and his wife separated four months ago, after four years? I think it was her idea. She put him through UWO Business School."

Gloria made a face. "He did his best not to mention his wife at all. But it must have hit him hard. I guess I should try to be more patient with him." She watched Linda work quickly with pencil and ruler, checking the ad run sheet at her elbow and sketching in the major ads on the inside pages. "It's frightening. Linda, I'm barely married and I'm wondering if it was all a mistake; maybe we should have gone on dating indefinitely. But after two people have put as much time into a partnership as Fred Russell and his wife have, how can they throw it away?"

"Don't believe in divorce? You're too Catholic, Glo. I don't believe anyone should stay in a marriage they don't belong in. And believe me, there are plenty of marriages like that around here that no one talks about. Young women, still teenagers, get married because they're pregnant, or for other wrong reasons, like to get out of the house, or freak out their parents, or rebel. And they pay for it the rest of their lives. Do they do it differently in cities?"

"Some hit the streets." She sighed. "In those cases, you're right. Even to my way of thinking, that's a wasted lifetime. And speaking of Catholic: I only found out last week that the nearest Roman Catholic church to my house is about twenty kilometers away, in the next county. But there's a Loyal Orange Hall on almost every side road." She fingered the small gold crucifix on the chain around her neck. "I think I'm a fish out of water."

"You are. This area was settled by both Irish and Scottish Protestants in the mid-eighteen-hundreds," Linda explained. "A lot of families around here are still on the farms that their ancestors received as Crown Grants. There is a strong Protestant tradition in this county. That's why you'll find old Presbyterian and United or Methodist churches, and a few Anglican and Lutheran ones as well. But very few Catholic."

"Maybe it's worth a feature sometime: Religious Roots in Rural Ontario. I could dig into the religious biases that shaped rural society. I'll think about it in the middle of the summer when nothing is happening. And maybe it's the root of the problem between me and my in-laws too."

"That you're Catholic? Or that you don't believe in divorce?"

"Divorce is frowned upon in their stuffy old social circles too. No, I mean the fact that Tony and I were married in a Roman Catholic Church instead of their ritzy Anglican one. It lowered the tone of the whole thing for them." She finished her bagel and spread out the page mock-ups. "This day's not over yet. Show me what you've got in ads and let's get this section together. I have to see Doug Sullivan this afternoon about his financial management and accounting business."

Linda's eyebrows shot up. "Ah. Letting him check out your figures?"

"Strictly business, you scamp." She grinned. "Linda, I'm married. But I'm not blind, and certainly not dead."

"Neither is Doug." Linda winked. "Keep that in mind, especially if you spot a couch in his office."

***

"Nice office."

Gloria glanced at her surroundings, a comfortable, quiet two rooms above a men's clothing store on the main street, with a large, tidy desk, computer, several file cabinets, and a glassed-in bookcase of investment manuals and financial tomes. Comfortable chairs. No couch.

She had chosen one of the less plush seats, a straight-back model, lightly cushioned, with low armrests; his was a leather-upholstered swivel chair adjusted to accommodate his height. She balanced clipboard and pen; he fidgeted with a large bulldog clip, obviously not used to sitting idle.

"It will serve, at least, for now," he said, following her gaze to the bookcase. "If things go well, I'll have a larger one, street-level. Are we finished?" he asked as she closed her notebook.

"Finished. At least that part. Mr. Sullivan—"

"Call me Doug, will you?" He smiled lazily and leaned back. "Or do you prefer to be called *Ms. Trevisi* all the time?"

"I'll try. It's force of habit." She touched the ends of her hair. "Thank you for your tip about Sid Stanton. We had a great chat, and I also got a rather nice trim."

"Good." He grinned. "My wife prefers Sid to the local hairdressers. She saw you the other day at the choral society garage sale. She's vice-chairman of the O'Dell Bells. I sing in the bass section when I have time."

"I'm glad to hear it. Mrs. Ormsford invited me to join."

"You'd be in good company. It's one of O'Dell Township's more redeeming features."

"Speaking of O'Dell Township, you had some business dealings recently with one of its councillors, Clarence McKee?"

He raised an eyebrow. "Not exactly. Our building contractor suggested McKee Excavating to do the foundation and drainage, and install a septic tank, saying his prices are better than reasonable. It wasn't meant to be, however. Why do you ask?"

"Well, it seems Clarence McKee was telling everyone he was taking you to court for canceling his contract."

"And now he is dead, is that it?" His swivel chair gave a sudden lurch, and his voice dropped several degrees below warm. "Would your readers be interested in a personal vendetta?"

"Our readers are talking about it already. That's where I heard about it," she replied steadily. "Mr. Sullivan, I'm not taking notes on this. I hear gossip, and I'm curious." She smiled, slightly. "And Sid didn't have all the details."

Sullivan took a deep breath, and looked around his small office. "Well, *Ms.* Trevisi, there was no contract, and there is no court case. Is that what people are saying?"

"I'm afraid so."

He sighed and leaned back, relaxing once again. "Naturally, they wouldn't say it to me. But I'm sure they'll be whispering it over the back fences when they speculate on who killed Clarence McKee."

"I don't care what they say. The paper doesn't print rumors, so rest assured, sir, that it won't be included in this particular entry." She placed her notebook and pen on the desk in front of her and sat back. "But it might take the heat off Mike Hurtig."

"Mike's a friend of yours, is he? Nice kid. Smart." Sullivan gave her a cool, assessing look that made her cross her knees. "Normally, I'd rather not discuss it, but Clarence McKee is dead, under suspicious circumstances, and even the police will be asking me questions, no doubt. It's simple, and straightforward, and there were plenty of witnesses. He rolled up in a flatbed truck, unloaded his backhoe, and offered to put in a septic tank and circumvent the health inspection to speed up the process. He said he was on good terms with the building inspector and all the county officials. I told him I wasn't afraid of a health inspection, and suggested that if he didn't mind, I'd rather double-check the requirements with the health department before he began the digging. We had an argument, and he left, pulling his equipment off the site. Then he sent me a bill for a day's work which he didn't do."

"And you told him, more or less, to piss up a rope?"

Sullivan's eyebrow twitched again. "Something like that. Then I got a letter from his lawyer. One letter. I passed it on to my lawyer, and we came to an agreement."

"Which was—?"

"Between the two of us. End of discussion. I didn't hear from him again."

"That simple?"

"That simple. He'd like to say that it's a big thing. It isn't, in my books. But I'm not from this area originally, which makes me fair game for pushing around. And you too," he warned. "I know how they do business around here. If they can avoid building inspections, permits, environmental controls, and health regulations, they do it, and just act stupid when they're caught and hope they'll get away with it. I don't. If it costs me more to get an out-of-town contractor to do a proper job, so be it. After all, it's my house, and it will be mine for a long time yet." He rolled his chair back. "And you'll be pleased to hear, if you decide to come out to the choir, that Clarence McKee didn't sing."

"I'm glad to hear it. Between us, do you have any idea who would want to see Mr. McKee dead?"

"You sound like a police officer."

She shook her head, smiling. "Believe me, I don't carry a hidden tape recorder. Truth is, I've been concerned that the police are trying to build a case against Mike Hurtig. He's an easy solution. I've been worried about him. He cuts my grass," she added when Sullivan raised his eyebrows, and then wondered why she thought an explanation was necessary.

He read her expression. "You don't need to explain to me. But I am also curious, of course, to know why they suspect Mike."

"They have their reasons," she answered evasively.

Sullivan wasn't put off. "I know he was working for McKee Excavating over the winter, and left this spring to work for another contractor. Left under a cloud, did he?"

"Not really. But I don't like the way gossip travels around here."

"I'd be happy to help Mike if I can. I'm hoping he'll have time to referee our hockey league next year while he's in university. And speaking of gossip, and I hear plenty, Linda tells me your husband plays violin with a symphony, and is away from home quite a lot."

"Not a symphony orchestra, but small chamber ensemble that is touring, at the moment, sponsored by the symphony. And in case you've been hearing gossip, just because my husband is not here doesn't mean I'm looking for company, Mr. Sullivan," she added, standing up and picking up her notebook and camera.

"Which is what everyone thinks, I'm sure, including your friend, Fred Russell." He paused. "No, I wouldn't think that." He rose with her. "But your boss would. I can't say much for the kind of leadership the paper has had since it was sold, but perhaps things are finally looking up, at least in the editorial department."

"I think Linda does a terrific job too."

"So do I. But then, she always did. I remember hiring her when I was general manager. Well, good luck to you, and I hope you stay with the *Sun.* You're very thorough."

She smiled. "I was trained by the best. Good luck to you, too." She walked out of the small office, feeling his eyes watching her. Were they unfriendly eyes?

Suspicious, cautious? Or just speculative? She resisted the temptation to turn back.

***

O'Dell Township's cramped council chamber was not the most comfortable for extra guests. Gloria suspected it was set up that way to discourage people from attending council meetings which they had every right to attend, and like most small townships, the evening's agenda seemed set up to render any spectator unconscious in the first fifteen minutes.

Most of the topics that she wanted to hear this evening, fortunately, were not particularly controversial. Otherwise, there would have been a quick motion to have them moved to the end, forcing Gloria, and anyone else who cared to listen, to hang around until after midnight, a popular tactic practiced by councils.

One could always tell the farmers from the local businessmen, she observed soon after arriving. Even when they were in their Sunday best, the farmers, young and old, had a certain look, a sharpness of eye, a face tanned and lined from working outdoors, sinew to the hands, and a relaxed gate that could carry them across a plowed field with ease. O'Dell's council was made up of farmers. She was surprised, though, to see old Norm Weatherby from the variety store, seated at the table with the elected officials.

Gloria had not attended the three o'clock funeral service for Clarence McKee, but she assumed that all

those in the room had. She had sent Rick to the church
with strict instructions to get a picture of the coffin,
pallbearers, and chief mourners in the funeral
procession, then beat it. What was the local tradition
when someone died? A quiet, dignified gathering, or
a rousing wake?

As the group came to order, she glanced around
the room. Of the five municipal councils she routinely
covered, mostly by telephone, only two included
female members; even in this day and age, women in
positions of power in rural Ontario were few and far
between. So, it seemed, were people from the village
of Genoa. Scanning the addresses of the five
politicians present, she noted that all resided in the
southeast end of the township, and none in the
northwest. Even Clarence McKee had been from East
Lister area. Joe Cameron's political and business woes
would get no support in this room.

Reeve Ben Cootes's touching tribute to his fellow
councillor was almost as flowery as Hazel McDaniel's
obituary, and naturally called for letters of condolence
to be sent to the widow and family.

"Next on the agenda is deciding how to replace
him on council," Cootes said. "It is only five months
to another municipal election, and I would entertain
a motion that we choose an acting deputy-reeve from
among the other four councillors, and leave the space
vacant until fall."

"Isn't it traditional to appoint the first runner-up
in the last election?" asked another councillor, a short,

middle-aged man with a gravelly voice. Norm Weatherby wheezed loudly.

"It has been done that way before," Clerk-Treasurer George Fuller confirmed. "But it depends."

"On what?"

"On who it is," he answered with a stony face. Two of the councillors snickered. After all, Gloria mused, who wanted a newcomer stirring up issues so close to an election? Leave things quiet, and with any luck, these five would be acclaimed without even having to take out a campaign ad. She studied Fuller carefully, his casually well-groomed appearance, middle-brown hair, ordinary face, neat hands, possibly in his late forties. He seemed totally at ease, even slightly pleased, as the council members began bickering.

As the ponderous debate continued, Gloria began to nod off in the stuffy room. Dimly she heard Cootes suggesting old Norm Weatherby as McKee's replacement. Weatherby had retired from council before the previous election after serving several terms. It was the perfect solution; they all knew where he stood, and he wouldn't have the nerve to contradict them, thus keeping the apple cart perfectly steady for yet another few months. She tried to picture old Weatherby, wheezing and coughing as he drove a bulldozer over McKee in order to take his spot on council. The drone of the deep voices was nearly putting her to sleep....

She sat up suddenly, her chair giving a sharp creak, as another person entered the council chamber, his back to her as he stopped to have a word with the clerk-treasurer. She glanced at the agenda: there were no scheduled petitions or presentations.

As the newcomer sat next to her, she recognized the man who had escorted Hazel McDaniel out of the police press conference. He smiled, and quickly bent over to pick up a pen he had dropped, pressing his shoulder against her knee. She growled under her breath, but looked him over carefully, noting smooth hands, a well-fitted suit, a decent haircut, and potent aftershave. Not an O'Dell farmer. Businessman? Professional accountant? Lawyer? Not a lawyer, with that reek. Any right-minded judge would have held him in contempt for breaking clean air laws. The pungent scent had its uses, however; she was, at least, fully awake and not likely to drift again until long after midnight.

Reeve Cootes's gavel fell, and she cursed her inattention. Weatherby was looking pleased as Fuller handed him an agenda and a sheaf of papers. Weatherby was in.

"The future of the industrial park project?" Cootes intoned. Fuller was sorting papers again. "Councillor Owen asked that we discuss this tonight."

"Right," the middle-aged councillor with the gravelly voice spoke up. "Now that Mr. McKee is gone, I think it is in all our best interests to cancel this project."

Fuller's voice was more than a trifle patronizing. "McKee Excavating applied for the rezoning a year ago. There was only one objection at the time, from the county, actually, since it went against the current planning and zoning requirements. None from you, Garth, even though your farm is on the next concession." He checked more papers. "Clarence promised to make certain modifications to the site, and the type of industry to be brought here would be restricted to farm-friendly....for the good of the township." He gazed around the table. "There is no reason to expect the project will not continue, gentlemen. And the taxes we could gain from new businesses would be a shot in the arm to the township."

"But Clarence isn't here any more. The zoning changes don't haf'ta hold—"

"If I may speak." The man beside Gloria stood up.

The councillors swivelled their heads.

"I'm Glenn Hullett, as most of you already know." He gave Gloria an oily smile. *Hair coloring*! she realized. *That's why he appeared young at first.* Actually, his face and teeth placed him in his forties, at least. "What you may not know is that I'm Clarence's business partner in this venture." No one spoke. Everyone stared, with eyebrows raised all over the room. "McKee Construction will continue with the project under my direction. I understand the contracts are all in place. We also had partners' insurance." He paused. "Clarence is the one who insisted on it, since I am the main financial backer."

Cootes's open mouth could have caught a dozen flies. He turned to Fuller. The other councillors shifted in their chairs, while Fuller examined two pieces of paper handed to him by Hullett before passing them over to the reeve. "The terms of the zoning are guaranteed, naturally, since the property is not changing hands," Fuller said, looking up from the papers over which he and the reeve had been poring. "I think the matter is settled."

"Not so fast," the gravelly voice objected. Fuller looked at him sharply. "Where does an upstart like you...," the councillor pointed a finger, "...get the money and the brass to back a project like this?"

Hullett turned slightly red. "I...I have investors."

"Calm down, Garth. The financial arrangements are none of our concern, at the moment," Fuller said smoothly. "The project looks to be in safe hands." He nodded to Hullett.

"As for being an upstart," Cootes noted with a scowl, "the Hullett family has as long a history in this township as the McKees and the McDaniels, and longer than yours, Garth."

Gloria scribbled a note in her book: *Look up Hullett connections!* Cootes may have been surprised at Hullett's claim as the financial king-pin, she observed, but he was obviously acquainted with the man, and was now siding with him. An old, respected family connection? Was Hullett related to him? Or did he merely choose to back a winner?

Hullett sat down once again, and Gloria took advantage of a brief pause in the proceedings to get the newcomer's attention. She quietly asked him for a business card and phone number. Then she rose and whispered over Fuller's shoulder. "Can I call you tomorrow? Early?"

Fuller nodded. "Eight thirty." Gloria left.

So Clarence McKee had a business partner. And since his partner was providing the financial backing, it was possible that the other strong rumor she had heard, that McKee was in financial trouble, could have some truth. Or did his partner have enough political clout to squelch an objection to the Ontario Municipal Board about such a radical departure from the usual rural land uses? Perhaps young Hullett had a deputy minister in his back pocket; maybe Clarence McKee owed this partner for more than simply the financial backing. Had he been forced to take on a partner for other reasons? Or was he hoping to pull a fast one on this reasonably young, well-heeled businessman as he had on the arena board? Mr. Hullett did not look like the naive type. Smooth, yes; stupid? She doubted it.

It was after midnight when she finally got to bed, having written all she could and having made a list of the people she must talk to on Wednesday. During a week of council meetings, that eleven P.M. copy deadline always seemed to come too early. She hadn't had time even to think about Tony, and was thankful that there was no message to distract her for the time being. The day had begun with a cool breeze and warmed up in the afternoon, but the house was still refreshingly cool. She collapsed on her bed and immediately fell asleep.

***

She was drinking her first mug of coffee on the side veranda early next morning, relaxed on the old bench and stretching her legs in front of her, when the telephone rang. "Oh, hell!" She mopped up spilled coffee with her toes and rushed inside. It was the woman who ran the village store and postal outlet.

"The UPS courier tried to deliver a parcel there yesterday, but you weren't home. I suggested he leave it here and I've been trying to call you ever since. You're not around much, are you?"

"Afraid not. Thanks for taking care of it. I'll pick it up on my way to Plattsford." She hung up, and walked thoughtfully back out to the veranda where she had been watching a flock of cedar waxwings demolish the fruit on the cherry tree beside the house. Marge may be preferable to her father behind the counter, but she was a gossip, like everyone else, and she knew damn well where Gloria worked, what her job required, and many other details, true and false, besides. Likely, she was curious about the package.

She finished her coffee, wondering what the parcel could be. A present from Tony? More likely it contained a few of his belongings from the condo that he thought he might use. A cordless telephone, perhaps? She hadn't found hers yet. By seven she was in the car, her curiosity getting the better of her.

At the store, which opened very early in the summer months, she politely asked after Marge's father, who had been out late the night before, and got a noncommittal shrug in return. Marge handed her a large cardboard box wreathed in packing tape. It was from her mother, Gloria noted when she checked the label. Too curious to wait, and aware that Marge was also dying to know, she slit the tape with the penknife on her key ring and peered inside.

"Looks like—curtains!" she exclaimed with a chuckle. "My mother sent me a box of curtains for our windows." She signed the form, bought a *Globe and Mail,* carried the box out to the car and squeezed it through the hatch of the old Mazda. She would drop it off later, if she had time.

Fortunately, Bud's Café was also open early. At seven fifteen she was on her way in as Sid Stanton was bustling out, coffee and bagel in hand. "So Gloria, what's new?"

"Clarence had a business partner in this venture. Glenn Hullett. And he intends to go on with the industrial park project in spite of his partner's demise."

Sid raised his eyebrows. "*Glenn* Hullett! In business in O'Dell? Now there's something interesting."

"Interesting?"

"Sure. I believe he is Hazel McDaniel's nephew."

"Is there anyone in this place that she's not related to?" Gloria exclaimed. "So was McKee, wasn't he?"

"On her husband's side, yes. Hullett is Hazel's nephew of sorts, though he didn't grow up here, and he hasn't been around for several years."

"Not a born and bred O'Dellian? At least that speaks in his favor."

Sid grinned under his mustache. "Perhaps. I'm surprised he's involved in this."

"Really? Tell me more."

"No time," Sid said, looking at the town's clock tower two blocks away. "Catch me later."

"I will," she called after him as he bustled off.

Back at the office, she put in a call to Ben Cootes. Seven thirty was a good time to catch a farmer at home, she had found. The dairy farmers were finished milking and on their way in, and most hog farmers were still eating breakfast. Cootes answered the telephone himself.

"Who has been objecting to the Cameron and Sons Timber operation?" she asked, flipping open a notebook.

"Cameron put his plant on a piece of property that was fairly decently zoned for light industrial use, but timber-finishing is turning out to be a dusty business. He is on the edge of the hamlet of Genoa."

"So someone circulated a petition?"

"Right, and nearly everyone there ended up signing it. It's something we can't ignore, even if a lot of them are city transplants. We don't have much business in O'Dell, other than farming, and we were worried about losing the plant to a neighboring township."

Even if? City transplants? That explained why there was virtually no representation from Genoa on O'Dell's council. No long-time local resident approved of newcomers—especially city transplants—serving on the council of an established rural municipality, even if any of them *were* interested in running. They might bring new ideas. "When was it presented to council, and by whom?" she asked, still trying to get a name.

"It was presented to council about a year ago by one of the locals. I guess the residents thought we'd listen to one of our own people, rather than someone who doesn't come from here originally. It was Janice Poulton who spoke for the residents, and I believe she and another resident had circulated the petition."

"So she is a 'local,' not a city transplant. Who are her family connections? She's not by any chance related to the McKees, is she?"

A pause. "Actually, I believe she's a cousin. Something like that."

Bingo. "And what about her husband? What is his connection? Does he, or someone else close to her, work for McKee Construction?"

Another pause. "That I can't say, Ms. Trevisi."

I bet you can't, Gloria thought. *Ben Cootes has suddenly realized to whom he has been talking, these past few moments.*

"Mr. Cootes, did anyone from the village run for council in the last election?"

"Two people did, but they're not locals. They would've just caused no end of trouble on council anyway."

Really. She asked him a couple of innocent questions about the previous night's agenda, then rang off, and sighed. Looking at her notes, she summed up some quick discoveries. It wasn't the city transplants who had objected to Joe Cameron's noisy, dusty business. Of course not; council would have ignored them. Instead, it had been something concocted by residents with strong local connections, notably a relative of Clarence McKee. Obviously there was a political agenda at work.

She dialed George Fuller at home. His line was busy. "Wonder why?" she muttered, dropping the receiver back into its cradle. She would have to talk to him later, after he had been given a thorough report of her conversation with the reeve. In the meantime, she had other concerns. She put in a call to Sergeant O'Toole.

***

"I never thought of the McDaniel clan as movers and shakers," Gloria commented to Linda Grant over juice and cottage cheese, later in the day.

"They shake more than they move," Linda said. "Hazel is big, but Elwood McDaniel is bigger. He rarely gets out of his easy chair these days, and I doubt if his legs could hold him up."

"What's his problem? Poor health? He can't be that old."

"Booze, I think. Wrecked his heart, and probably pickled his liver too." Linda dug a plastic fork into a mound of grated carrots. "He looks healthy enough, just a bit, well, fazed, if you know what I mean. Vacant."

"And how do they feel about their relatives, the McKees, using their ancestral lands to build an ugly industrial park next door to them, in the middle of prime farmland?"

"The entire Hamilton basin was once prime farmland, and look what's there." Linda retorted. "I'm not sure how they feel. Their farm is next door, but it won't really affect them much, since their house and farm buildings are almost a mile away. The old folks, of course, are retired, and part of the land has been used as a gravel pit, right at the corner of McKee's property, so there is a bit of a buffer; but their son still has a small dairy herd there, and grows hay and grain and some cash crop as well. He lives in the village, by the way. And since they're all related anyway, they wouldn't object. Wouldn't be polite."

Gloria snickered. "So Clarence takes advantage of his family bonds, does he? And what about the Hulletts? Where do they fit in?"

"Hazel's mother's maiden name was Hullett. I'm not sure where the rest of the family is now, but they used to have a farm behind McDaniel's. And they owned half of East Lister about eighty years ago. They're probably based in London, or Kitchener."

Fred Russell interrupted their lunch, charging up the stairs two at a time. "How's the front section coming together, ladies?"

"Most of it is done." Gloria held up an almost black photo. "Behold. The scene of the crime, just after the body was discovered. Rick's good in the darkroom. I didn't think there was anything on this negative, but he actually managed to pick up an image."

Russell squinted at the photo. "Is that the sergeant I was talking to yesterday at headquarters?"

"In brilliant black and white. And looming up behind him are the construction shack and the bulldozers and heavy equipment. I guess that patch of white is the plastic sheet." Gloria took out a small magnifying glass used for examining negatives, and studied it. "My, it looks flat."

"Are we going to...to use it?" Russell's face was slightly pale.

"I doubt it. It's really not a nice thing to do in a small town." Gloria was amused at his disappointment.

"Has the guy from Toronto's *East End Express* called?" Russell asked, sitting on the side of Linda's desk beside Gloria, pressing his thigh against her arm.

"Ugh! Twice," Gloria replied, deliberately sliding her chair several inches to the left. The *Express* was a

Toronto-based tabloid that had recently started up in an attempt to pick up the less savory readership that had fallen away from the now-respectable *Toronto Sun.* It read like the tackiest police gazette or sleaziest tabloid Gloria could ever imagine, concentrating its efforts on bizarre crimes and personal tragedies. "I put him off both times. Why?"

"Oh. I...uh...told him we'd pass along what we knew," he replied with a smug smile in Gloria's direction. "Tipped off a guy I know at the *Star* too." He inched over until the toe of his neat oxford was brushing against the leg of her chair.

Gloria froze. "You didn't." Her voice was almost a whisper.

"Why not? It seems like a great idea to be on the good side of the big papers." His toe, moving toward the edge of her shoe, hesitated.

She laid down her plastic spoon and turned slowly toward him. "And have you told them anything?"

"Well, I told them about the press conference yesterday." He moved, placing one or two inches of air between them, watching her with a wary stare.

"And how much of the press conference did you pass on?" she asked quietly, rising from her chair and facing him as he slid off Linda's desk. His close proximity to her was about to become very uncomfortable.

He glanced about for an escape route, and found none. "Well, the facts, and...the question-and-answer...." Russell stood still.

"The barbiturates? The liquor? The bulldozer? Everything?" Gloria could feel her pulse thump somewhere behind her eyes. His ridiculous, startled face filled her vision. "How about McKee's biography? Did you pass that along too?"

"Well, sure," he said. "That was enough, wasn't it?"

"*Enough?*" She exploded. "Fred Russell, why the *hell* did you do that!?"

He jerked backward. "Why not make contact with the dailies? Isn't it good for your career? I overheard you talking to someone at the *Star* just the other day."

"*Overheard?* Did you overhear me telling her to take a long hike?"

"I thought I could help—"

"*Help?* Have you any idea how you have compromised our paper, our community standing, and my personal integrity by this? When Heartland hears about it, it will be *my* responsibility, and it will be *my* bloody ass hanging out a mile. Not yours."

He blinked, surprised. "Wouldn't they be happy that we are in contact with one of the big daily newspapers?"

"With a daily newspaper that will print our information Wednesday, when we can't print until Thursday? Would that make them happy?" She gasped for breath. "We come out once a week, in case you haven't noticed. Timing is everything in breaking news."

"So what?" Russell's feigned nonchalance betrayed his nervousness. "The *Free Press* has it Wednesday." To his credit, he averted his eyes from her heaving chest. One more second of staring, and she would have slapped him hard.

"The *Free Press* sent a representative to the press conference. They actually worked to get that story. All those bastards at the *Express* did was find themselves a handy stooge, Mr. Russell. You!"

"Glo, is that your telephone I hear?" Linda's voice was a distant squeak.

Gloria ignored her, as she stood nose to nose with Russell and discovered to her dismay that she had to look up to do it. "That was why you wanted to come to the press conference, wasn't it? Not out of interest in community affairs, not even morbid curiosity—I could understand *that*—but so that you could pass along information to a bunch of people who are too damned lazy to gather their own news? What kind of a bloody fool are you?" Her fingers fumbled on the desktop. If there had been an object, even a stapler, within her reach, she would have hurled it.

"What's wrong with the *East End Express?*" Russell was cornered. He backed away another step and bumped into the wall. "And what's wrong with you, anyway? You're not the only person here with an important job."

"Important?" She took a step closer. "You may think whatever you please of my job, but it is *my* bloody job, not yours. There is a line between business and news. Don't you ever, *ever* cross that line with me again." She scarcely noticed her finger, pointing like a dagger at his midriff. "Remember that your bosses hired me, not you. And they can damn well fire both of us!" She wheeled around and started walking away, teeth clenched tightly. Lunch didn't taste very good, at the moment.

"What makes you think they would fire me?" he threw after her, stepping away from the wall. He looked brave, but his voice gave a betraying squeak.

"Oh? Why *wouldn't* they fire you?" She swung around, balling her fists. "Are you the president's nephew? Untouchable by blood, is that it?"

She watched him wince, but he set his jaw and narrowed his eyes to answer. "Remember you're still on probation, and they're not all that happy about my reports," he ventured. "And they won't be happy to hear this."

"*Your* reports? Just wait until they hear *mine!*" She blew out an angry breath. "You're supposed to be managing this paper, and already they replaced the editor without your consent. It's obvious why, isn't it? You couldn't—*wouldn't*—do what had to be done to get this paper back in line. How far will you get, trying to brush the blame off onto me? I don't care if you're the *son* of the chairman of the board, Mr. Russell. You will fail. They're not stupid and blind at head office. They don't trust you with personnel, they double-check all your figures in case you screw up.

Are you on probation as well? Is that why you were sent out here?"

He drew himself to his full height. "I happen to be very good at—"

"Good? As long as you look good, that's all that matters to you." Her voice rose over a persistent jangle in her ears. "At the moment, you don't look good at all. Is this how you take care of business? Hand information to competitors?"

"I didn't mean to—"

"Would you hand all our advertising and circulation statistics to the *Kitchener Record* if they were to ask for them, just to stay on their good side too?" She was running on, she realized; his attention was straying once again to her jersey top. "I will tell head office myself. I, for one, will not stand still to have my livelihood threatened by an incompetent manager."

"Don't...." Russell looked pale. "The *Express* is going to send you a finder's fee."

"Screw them! I'll rip it up." Gloria stalked furiously back to her desk, determined to stop now before it got *really* personal, and before her language became a whole lot worse, and definitely before she felt inclined to do something physical, such as break a chair. The persistent jangle in her ears was the ringing of her desk phone. She wanted to dash it to pieces across the corner of her desk. Instead, she snatched the receiver.

"Yes?" she barked into the mouthpiece.

"Hi." It was Tony's voice. "Is something wrong?" he asked.

Gloria was still blowing like an angry bovine. "Sorry. I'm just really upset at the moment. What is it?" That sounded rather short, she noticed. "I'm glad you're on the phone just now. I need calming down." Good thing he is there, and not here, she thought, still feeling a rapid pulse beating deep in her gut; she probably would have bared her teeth, ripped his clothes off, and bit his neck.

"I have a few minutes." Tony sounded anxious. "Tell me about it."

"Never mind. I'll only get more upset." She sighed. "Why am I doing this again?"

"Something about your salary, not mine, wasn't it?" He continued before his perfectly bland observation caused her to blow a serious fuse. "I'm calling because we have two concerts at University of Waterloo later this week. It's a late booking and it's as good a time as any to try out our new cellist. Do you think you can come?"

"I'd love to." She glanced across the office. Russell had retreated into his glass cubicle. "Can I bring Linda along?"

"If she wants to come. Are you staying out of trouble?"

"I'm too busy working to get into trouble. The riskiest thing I've done all week is get a haircut from the local barber." She glanced out her window toward Sid's shop. Two people were standing outside, talking.

"You let a *barber* cut your hair?"

"The hair looks good. Really."

"If you say so. Gloria, I *am* worried. I can't stop thinking of you out there alone when people are being murdered."

"Your secret's safe with me."

"Don't be sarcastic." His voice had an edge to it. "You know I'd rather—" He broke off, listening to a voice in the background. "Don't go away," he said to Gloria just before putting the phone down.

I'm not going anywhere, Gloria thought glumly, listening to a muffled conversation as she drummed her fingers impatiently on the desk.

"I'll have to go. Someone wants to run through the Schubert again. Friday night or Saturday afternoon?"

"Let's make it Saturday. Tony, I miss you. I'm sorry everything is so messed up right now."

"I miss you too. Don't do anything...rash. Okay?"

"Don't worry." She suspected he almost said "stupid" and that only made her angry again. *Men!*

She said good-bye and rang off, looked at her chair, then at the schedule of assignments hanging behind it. It was almost time for the high school track meet, and Rick was busy printing in the dark room. She grabbed her camera, knocked on the darkroom door, and told him the track meet was covered. A muffled "Okay," could barely be heard through the closed door and black curtains. As she walked past the glass cubicle, she noticed Russell on the phone, likely calling head office, probably voicing a loud grievance against her. Did she care?

The entire office, upstairs and downstairs, was completely silent as she walked purposefully down the stairs and out the front door.

Chapter 6

By eleven that evening Gloria was home, copy written, page layouts complete, and photos printed. The extra adrenaline from her face-off with Mr. Russell had given her the momentum to finish work early. There were no new bulletins on the O'Dell murder, leaving her neck-in-neck with every newspaper and radio station in a hundred miles.

Hot and exhausted, she dumped the carton of curtains inside the back door, grabbed a glass of cold milk from the refrigerator, and searched briefly for her dressy shoes that she had thrown in a corner just a few nights before. Never again would she be shorter than Fred Russell, even if it meant wearing high heels with her shorts. That jerk!

Max and Buffy were waiting for her. "Hi, guys." She greeted her loyal roomies, filled their dishes to the brim, and watched them eat. The kitchen was hot. Upstairs, her bedroom was hotter. Changing into the very brief, sheer nightgown that Tony favored—the one that barely covered her thighs—she grabbed a pillow and a comforter and headed downstairs. What she needed was the peace of the outdoors, with the sounds of crickets and the gentle rustle of the leaves overhead, like in *A Midsummer Night's Dream*; only she wasn't a fairy queen sleeping with Bottom the Weaver, or Kevin Kline, or anyone, tonight. No chance of curling up with someone who cared. Zipping herself quietly into the screen tent, she spread a plastic ground sheet and the comforter on the cool grass, and lay down.

Max had followed her into the tent, head high, whiskers back, and tail like a banner. He settled down against her knee, purring gently. She reached down and stroked his ears. She liked cats, and Max liked her. He seemed to have a life of his own, yet found a way of adapting to hers without either of them getting in each other's way. Why couldn't a marriage fit together so easily? She wished Tony were here, purring against her knee. She was drifting, and the cat was purring, and telling her he was worried about her....

Seconds later she was awake. Max had tensed suddenly and was staring, ears and whiskers forward, at the house. She lay still, trying to sort out dreamland from reality. A soft crunch of coarse gravel; wasn't that the sound she always heard as she placed a foot on her wobbly back step? Was someone snooping on her veranda?

Had she locked her door? Of course not. She had merely dragged her bed outside and flopped into it, never thinking the house required locking as long as it was occupied.

But it wasn't occupied. She was out here, and someone was in there. She could not tell who it was.

Tony? No, she hadn't heard his car. Or had she? It purred, like the cat, didn't it? She raised her head and looked. A penlight was visible on the side veranda, barely forty feet away, bobbing and swaying like a firefly, which perhaps it was. She could not see the door from here, but she heard the familiar soft creak of its hinges, followed by a thud and a muttered curse as someone stumbled against the box of curtains she had dropped inside by the basement stairs. She froze, and prayed that Max would remain quiet. The cat, however, was creeping to the corner of the screen tent, staring. She made a grab for him, but he slithered out from under her hands.

The time. The time? She pushed the button to illuminate her watch, and quickly pushed it under the pillow. It glowed like a spotlight, and the tiny beep it made as the light switched off might as well have been an air raid siren in her ears. It was 2:26 A.M., precisely, and she had been asleep for almost three hours. If it *were* Tony, she reasoned, he would find the bed empty, the comforter gone, and know where to find her. If it weren't…. She looked for the cat, but he was gone; squeezed under the edge of the screen and loping across the lawn. *Come back!* she screamed inside her head. *Don't go in there!* But Max would creep in where angels balked. The screen door creaked again. It couldn't have been properly shut if Max had opened it so easily with a paw. *Trust a thief to let in mosquitoes*, she thought irritably.

The night was dead silent now; no crickets. No frogs. And no cat. She waited, huddled in the corner of the screen tent with her pillow and comforter, indignant over the very idea that someone thought she had something worth stealing. But she did have one thing, and it was sitting on her dresser in plain sight. And what if he—or whoever—were to come out here? Was there any place to conceal herself?

The night was dark; the gibbous moon had already set. To hell with sitting still. Perhaps she should creep closer to the house, and peep in the door or window to see what this person was doing.

In this get-up? Touching the hem of the filmy fabric, she shrugged slightly to adjust the tiny shoulder straps. Well, why not? She couldn't even see what she was wearing, in the darkness. She inched cautiously toward the front of the tent, and pulled the zipper of the door; it howled as she drew it upward, and she jumped, and tried again, hands shaking and heart hammering as she made a three-foot opening. Crouching on hands and knees, feeling the nightie bunching around her waist, she inched through the door. Once outside, she straightened up, and pulled the brief covering over her thighs, feeling foolish.

A thud. A crash, and a curse. She dropped to the grass as the screen door burst open, and the penlight waved rapidly away down the driveway, its beam diminishing with the sound of hurried, heavy footsteps and quick, labored breathing.

Gloria quickly bounded forward, heart pounding. Had the intruder left? Would he return? Running silently toward the house in her bare feet, she tried to pull her thoughts together. *First, don't touch anything!* How would she phone the police? The car phone. It was something Tony had insisted she have in case of an emergency, like this one. She sent him love and thanks, as she pulled the phone out from under the car seat, plugged it into the dashboard lighter, and dialed, her fingers automatically finding the number of the detachment office rather than punching 911.

"Where are you now?" the desk sergeant asked her.

"Outside, sitting in my car."

"Stay there, and lock the car doors. Someone may still be in your house. An officer is on his way."

She dropped the phone with a sigh. The police were coming, a whole SWAT team, maybe. The warm wave of grateful relief lasted only a second. In the light of the car's dim interior lamp, she looked down at her shell pink, barely-there nightie. "Oh, hell."

Twenty long minutes passed. The house was dark and silent. No one else had appeared on the steps. Was it safe to go inside and put on some clothes? She debated, hunched over the dashboard on the passenger side of her car.

More minutes ticked by; the police must have been at the other end of the county. She wondered if she should start the car and see if she could spot her intruder on the road. After nearly half an hour? He could be in the next township, on foot, or halfway to Waterloo, by car. Besides, the keys were in her purse and that was in the house—at least, unless the intruder had carried it away. Her spare set was still packed in a box somewhere. Perhaps she'd unearth them tomorrow. But how would she let herself into the office tomorrow morning?

She was sitting in the front seat with a small car blanket wrapped around her, feeling careless and foolish, when the cruiser pulled slowly up the driveway. She tiptoed out in her bare feet, long legs showing beneath the edge of the blanket, to meet the police car as it pulled a circle and stopped, its headlights beaming forcefully on the side door. A young constable emerged, enormous even without his jacket, flashlight in hand.

"Ms. Trevisi?"

"Um, yes." Without her own flashlight, she was at a distinct disadvantage, unable to distinguish anything except a large silhouette in an official-looking Stetson.

"I'm Brian Stoker. You called about a break-in?" He took in her strange attire with one rapid sweep of the light, as though beaming a flashlight on a barely-covered female was all in a day's—or night's—work.

Gloria wriggled inside her inadequate covering, trying to pull the short, close-fitting garment farther over her hips. It didn't work. "I'm sorry about the way I look, Constable. I woke up in the backyard and thought I saw someone on the porch, and then the cat ran off.... He was carrying a penlight, or something, and left the door ajar...." Was she making any sense? Stoker seemed to think so; he swept the flashlight beam briefly down the drive. Self-consciously she shrugged a shoulder where the tiny strap kept slipping down her arm. The bodice wasn't doing much of a job, either, and the sheer fabric across her midriff.... She pulled the meager blanket higher, baring grass-stained knees. "I didn't want to go inside until you arrived."

"That was wise," the officer answered. "Someone could still be there. Did you see how many there were?" He had pulled out a nightstick from his belt and cautiously approached the door, shining his flashlight around the jamb.

"I'm not certain, but I think it was just one person. And he's gone. At least, I think it was a he." She thought back to the sound of that low, growling mutter as the intruder tripped over the box. Clumsy. Probably a man. "The door was unlocked. I don't know what he was looking for, but if it's to rip off money and liquor, he can have it." She was surprised that she could keep her voice level.

"Nothing valuable in there? Jewelry, computers?"

"My laptop is here in the car, which was unlocked. The key is in the house with my handbag, if it's still there. No cash. It's Wednesday." *Wednesday?* She was surprised when he nodded in complete comprehension. Well, after all, police have paydays too. "My jewelry isn't worth much, except my engagement ring, and it's upstairs, and I don't know if he got that far. The noises I heard were all from the kitchen, or at least, downstairs. I haven't been in the house yet, so I don't know if anything has been taken." She was babbling, she noted. Also, she had begun to tremble.

The police officer glanced back, eyebrows raised. "You just got home?"

What on earth was he thinking? "No," she said with a smile. "I was sleeping in the screen tent because the house is too hot this evening. Something woke me up. I called police on my car phone."

"Oh. Right. Good thing your car phone works, out here." Stoker nodded, and went on checking. She edged up behind him. As he pulled the screen door open, Max hurtled past his boots and disappeared across the lawn. Gloria jumped, and the police officer shone his flashlight after him. "Yours?" he asked. She nodded. "Were both doors closed and locked when you went to the screen tent?"

"Closed. Not locked. I never expected anyone to barge in."

He nodded again, and stepped carefully through the doorway.

"The light switch is to the right as you enter the kitchen," Gloria called in after him.

The lights went on, dim compared to the cruiser's high beams. She monitored his movements as he looked quickly around the kitchen, basement stairs, living room, and empty dining room before returning outside to the cruiser. He sent a brief message through the radio, doused the headlights, then said to Gloria, "I doubt if anyone's still here, but you're safer sitting in the car. I'll look upstairs."

She glanced at the cruiser. As the constable disappeared through the living room and up the stairs, she stepped nervously onto the veranda, staying just outside the door, and peered inside. A broken saucer, one she had used for Buffy's supper, was on the floor. The table and counters were clear, almost. She moved inside toward the table, listening to Stoker's quiet footsteps on the upper floor. I shouldn't be here, she thought. If someone were to come dashing downstairs....

"Brian?"

Footsteps were heard on the stairs, and Stoker appeared, hat off, blinking in the bright kitchen light. He looked young, in his late twenties, tall and broad across the shoulders. And he didn't seem surprised that she had used his given name; *she* was. "What is this?" she asked, pointing to a small bottle with several white tablets, sitting on the counter by the sink.

He looked at it. "I noticed them as I came through the kitchen. Are they yours?"

"No. I don't have any medicine, not even Aspirin, in the house."

The small plastic medicine bottle was open, and two of the tablets were on the counter. One was partially crushed. The police officer took out a small plastic bag and carefully picked up the vial. "I'll take this. I checked the rooms, closets, bathroom. No one's upstairs. There's a handbag on the living room couch. And your diamond ring," he smiled, "is on your dresser. He probably didn't get past the kitchen. Did you scare him off?"

"Are you kidding? I was cringing in the corner of the screen tent trying to be invisible. I think I know, though." She indicated the can of cat food on the counter, and the broken dish on the floor. "My cat thought he was going to be fed and either rubbed up against his leg or jumped up on the counter. That would spook anyone in the dark. He's a big cat."

"Whoever it was could not have been an experienced burglar. Probably a lot more scared than you were." He took out his notebook and wrote a few words. "I'll be at the end of the lane looking for any sign of tire tracks. I think you can relax now. Whoever it was is definitely gone."

Gloria stared about the kitchen uneasily, fingers still clutching at the car blanket. "Can I make you coffee or something? It's all right if I use my kitchen now, isn't it?"

Stoker hesitated, looking around quickly. "Sure. If something is tampered with or out of place, don't touch it. I'll check it out when I get back."

He left on foot, sweeping the edge of the lane carefully with his flashlight as he walked.

She poured water into her coffee maker, examined the pot and basket thoroughly, set the open can of ground coffee to one side, and opened a fresh one.

Her hands started shaking again as she checked her handbag for wallet, license, credit cards, and keys. All were there. She moved around her kitchen—where barely half an hour ago a stranger had been handling her belongings—and felt as though *she* had become the stranger. What was it that she couldn't quite grasp, standing here at the counter? A smell in the air? The hint of malt liquor mixed with sweat? Thoughts of Joe Cameron lurching drunkenly into a police press conference drifted into her mind.

She emptied the cat food into the garbage and threw the unbroken dish into the sink, then wondered if she was destroying important evidence. Evidence of what? Evidence that someone was grinding up pills on her counter and putting them in...what? She stared at the open carton of milk she had just pulled from the refrigerator, set it carefully on the counter, and picked up the sugar bowl sitting beside it. She turned the sugar with a spoon, shuddered, and dumped its contents into the garbage with the cat food, then emptied the contents of the carton down the sink.

She was still puzzling about it when she heard footsteps in the drive, and raced upstairs to snatch up her bathrobe. By the time Constable Stoker walked up the veranda steps, she was back in the kitchen and decently bundled.

"It looks as though a vehicle could have parked a couple of hundred yards from the end of your lane, near that belt of trees," he said, as he stepped through the door. "Did you hear anything pull away?"

"I'm afraid I was too busy calling you," Gloria said. "You don't mind canned milk, do you? I don't trust anything that's open, not even the milk carton."

"I take it black, thanks. Relax. You're still shaking." He stepped up to the counter and gently took the rattling mugs out of her hands, poured the coffee, and handed one to her. She wanted to hug him, but that wouldn't seem right. Instead, she sat down in the chair he pulled out for her. Deftly he opened the can of evaporated milk and handed it over, and she stirred some into her coffee, and wrapped her hands tightly around the mug. It was still a warm evening, and the house was still hot, but the warm brew was a comfort. So was this police officer.

"You seem to get a lot of night duty, Constable. Did you tick someone off at headquarters?" She smiled, her lips still slightly stiff. "You don't have to tell me," she added apologetically. "I don't mean to sound nosy."

He smiled and shook his head. "Nothing like that. It's a long story," he said, sipping his coffee. "I don't really mind telling you, off the record, of course."

"Of course."

"I grew up in a town similar to Plattsford but bigger, and farther to the south. My father was, well, a drunk. A violent drunk. I used to hide in my room at night when he was drinking. In fact, my mother insisted I lock myself in. I could hear him crashing around the house breaking things, heard my mother screaming. Sometimes he'd pound on my door, and

I'd hide under the bed just in case he busted in. Then in the morning, it would all be over. The old man was passed out somewhere on the floor, and my mother was mopping up the mess, hiding her bruises, and getting us ready for school." He paused and took another long sip of his coffee.

Gloria stared at him. "It sounds awful," she whispered. "Horribly sad."

He gazed back over the rim of the mug. "Later, I escaped every night and roamed the streets, got in trouble a few times. I joined a church youth group, and got things straightened out. Then I decided to become a police officer. I think night duty suits me. For one thing, I'm home to have breakfast with my kids, and later we have dinner as a family before I go to work. At night, things happen to people. Even here, far away from the city, there's domestic violence." He glanced out the window into the darkness of farm fields and woodlots. "It looks so peaceful, but the country areas have their own brand of crime."

"Like a murder by bulldozer and...and a liquor bottle laced with barbiturates?" She took another gulp of coffee, and thought about the pills on her counter. Were they barbiturates?

"Homicide is not a big problem up here. Usually assault, burglary, kids getting into mischief." He stared into the coffee mug. "This murder was no practical joke gone wrong, though. It was the bulldozer part that got to me. When I saw what my boots looked like on Friday morning, I nearly lost my lunch." He took a long pull on his coffee.

"Your boots? Oh, I see. Sergeant O'Toole told me you had quite literally stepped in the remains."

"Slipped in them, to be more precise." He drained his mug and stood up. "Nearly fell in them. Not these boots," he added as she glanced at his feet. "Are you all right now?"

"I'm fine, but after thinking about the pills, I'm wondering just how long I'll feel fine. I'm worried about my food, my dishes, everything." She walked with him to the door.

"If I were you, I'd throw out all the food that's open," he advised. "It's a waste, but you'll feel more secure."

"I've already started." She let him out as she let Max in.

As the cruiser drove away, she looked back at her kitchen. Throw out the food...Reaching for the garbage bags stored in the alcove by the back door, she noticed her shoes, still pushed into the corner from Thursday night. She pulled one out. Its creamy leather was smeared black with muck from the sideroad. Pig manure, or some such thing, she had guessed at the time. She carried the shoes over to the sink, wet a sponge, and set to work.

The mud came off dark, rusty red.

She dropped the shoe and stared at it. What had Constable Stoker said about his boots? But he had been on the building site, and she hadn't. She had been standing on the side of the road, yards from the yellow tape, in some ruts made by a grader, or perhaps a large tractor or a bulldozer. Mike's bulldozer had approached from the other direction, she was certain. That left... She sat down at her table.

Tony had advised her, almost begged her, to stay out of it. But these shoes threw her squarely in the middle, whether she liked it or not. She sent him more love, and her apologies. Then she reached again for the phone and dialed the police, the second time in barely an hour.

***

Her second-best shoes tagged and hauled off by Constable Stoker, her night's sleep ruined, Gloria bagged her food, ate some breakfast, tidied up her bedroom and the screen tent, and as dawn was breaking, went for a long, early morning walk. She searched for tire marks on the road, footprints in the soft sand at the edge of the driveway, anything that would make this past night's experience real to her. It was slowly fading into a bad dream, and she was wondering if, in fact, it was. Like *A Midsummer Night's Dream*. This time, however, she felt more like bumbling Bottom the Weaver than the proud Titania.

When she returned, she got ready for work, making the best of a brave front with pair of black two-inch high pumps and a solid green linen dress that accented her height. In spite of all that had happened the night before, she still had not forgotten her serious grudge against her boss, and was determined not to let him get the upper hand again. And for once, Rick Campbell was solidly on her side.

"I can't believe he gave away our story," he said, shaking his head and leaning against the light table where the page flats were sitting, waiting for a final proofreading before being sent to press. "And to the *East End Express*, of all papers. What will they make of it?"

"And where did you hear that?"

"Gloria, everyone heard it. You weren't very quiet about it at the time." He grinned. "From now on, I'm staying on your good side."

First thing this morning when she arrived, after eavesdropping on Jan's gossip bulletin about people cavorting naked in their backyards, she found the photo from the murder scene pinned to her personal bulletin board with a note from Russell saying: "*I hope you'll use it. It's good.*" She was about to rip up the picture, but changed her mind and ripped up the note, instead. Russell himself was nowhere around. "Called to head office for the day," a gleeful Theresa had said. Gloria groaned. Was he making a full report on her, ending with yesterday's battle? Or had he confessed to an error in judgment? She doubted it.

As editor, Gloria considered it her duty to read every word the paper was printing before the pages were burned to offset plates and sent to press. She glanced quickly over Hazel McDaniel's obituary on Clarence McKee, suitably situated on the obit page with the births, deaths, and in-memoriams, and shook her head. If that is what Norma had left in, she could just imagine what she had been obliged to take out.

On the subject of obituaries, Norma was unmovable. "This is the last chance we will ever have to review a person's life's accomplishments. Whether he was a hard-working farmer or a prime minister, it is important to his family to give him the best send-off possible."

In this community, few people speak ill of the dead beyond whispers, she observed, but loudly exaggerate their accomplishments beyond what is real. On a hunch, she put in a call to Norma.

"I need your help identifying people in a photo," she said.

"I'll be right there," Norma said cheerfully. "Anything to get out of the kitchen for awhile. I've been canning berries since dawn."

Twenty minutes later she was poring over the photos from the funeral.

"Don't hurry. It's not for this week's paper," Gloria reassured her. "What I need are names of all these people in the photos, and their relationship to the McKees. I see a couple of council members there, but I'm not sure who they are. And you know everybody, and whom they're related to, don't you?"

"Sure do. Won't take me long. When do you need it?"

"This afternoon, if possible, or perhaps tomorrow." She left Norma to study the photographs and make notes, and went on to read through the sports.

By 11:45 A.M., it was finished. The coverage of the industrial park death was concise, and up-to-date. And all of it was fifteen minutes before deadline, she thought with satisfaction. It was nice to show head office that they don't really need a Fred Russell sticking his oar in, anyway.

"Word is out about your break-in," Linda said as the two were walking over to Gina's to pick up two large pizzas for the staff. It was a Thursday ritual that Gloria had started shortly after she arrived at the *Sun*.

"It wasn't a break-in, really," Gloria said. "The back door was open."

"And where were you?"

"In the screen tent, sleeping with the cat."

"Sleeping in the yard!" Linda hooted. "My, but aren't we getting countrified. We sleep in the tent-trailer on the really hot nights."

"Don't tell the crooks. What else did people say?"

"That it served you right. Someone was looking for your diamond ring that you've been flaunting all over town."

"You mean, they're admitting it was someone local?" Gloria held the door open.

"I'm telling you what I heard. Maybe they haven't thought about that angle."

"If it wasn't someone from out of town, then it was my fault." Gloria studied the ring, the large diamond in an intricate setting perched on a broad, gold band, adorning the finger of her large left hand.

"Whoever it was, the thief wasn't looking hard. It was sitting in plain sight. Now, I think it's safer on my hand than it is stashed in my house." She told Linda all about the intruder, the cat and the car phone, leaving out details about pill bottles and bloody shoes. Gina's restaurant, like every other place in Plattsford, was filled to the brim with big ears.

"And you were wearing *what?* Oh, my stars, girl, what would the neighbors think?" Linda gave the order to Carl and leaned up against the counter, staring at Gloria.

"Never mind the neighbors. They're too far away. What did poor Constable Stoker think?" Gloria grinned. "He was a real gentleman."

"Brian Stoker is a good man. Not from around here, though."

"And that counts against him, I suppose?"

"Actually, no. It is better to deal with police who aren't locals. The others tend to favor their friends too much."

"And they'd be only too happy to pin the whole McKee murder thing on an outsider, wouldn't they?" Yesterday, Jan's morning gossip had been about a disgruntled customer who had thrown McKee off his property. "I wonder where they'll find one? It certainly would be less messy."

"Sure would. But we're still worried that they're trying to pin it on Mike."

"The police could still make the evidence fit him if he's the only suspect they come up with," Gloria noted.

"They can make evidence fit anyone. Doug Sullivan had problems with McKee. Maybe they're working up a case against him. I saw a cruiser parked in front of his office yesterday afternoon," she added. "As for Mike, he trusts the justice system to see him through."

"Well, after last night, I have some confidence in our local police, but I agree with my father-in-law. Mike should take some legal advice."

"Oh, I don't know. Innocent people shouldn't need lawyers." Linda scooped up two large pizza boxes and Gloria paid the bill. They walked back together. "The other thing people are talking about, of course, is your run-in with Fred Russell."

"The hell! That's strictly between him and me. And the rest of the office, I assume."

"And half the town, thanks to Theresa and Jan, and Rick too, I suppose. And you can't blame me for mentioning it to Doug Sullivan when I picked up his ad last night. Wait until the next merchant meeting. Fred'll be turned inside out with mortification."

"So everyone in town knows. So now what?"

"Now every merchant on the street is wagering which one of you will be hitting the bricks."

Gloria snorted.

Linda paused, her hand on the handle of the back door. "The pool at the barbershop, by the way, is heavily in favor of your staying."

"Sid too? Well, at least he's on my side." They walked into the front office. "Lunch is served, people," she announced loudly.

Lunch was wonderful, and more relaxed than usual, partly because of Russell's absence, partly because Gloria's efforts were finally having an effect. Theresa asked Gloria about Tony's music.

"Three centuries of chamber music." She swallowed a garlic-laced mouthful of Gina's five-meat special, The Carnivore's Delight. "Chamber music is like a classical jam session, except of course that the musicians don't make it up as they go along. It's usually just four musicians playing in quartet. Like barbershop, only with instruments. Sometimes there are six or seven musicians, or occasionally only three, like in a piano trio. It's not grand, like the symphony; it's meant for easy listening in a small room with a small audience. It's nice, and very personal. And Tony loves it."

"Isn't classical music hard to listen to?"

"Not to me. I listened to classical music before I was born, my parents tell me. My father is Italian and loves Puccini. My mother is a piano teacher, and taught us all. I finished Royal Conservatory Grade Ten piano before I finished high school. We had a stereo blaring in our house as much as anyone else, but it was more likely broadcasting *Madama Butterfly* than The Beatles." She wiped her hands on a napkin. "It's no harder to listen to than country, or rap, just an acquired taste. It's his life, and when he's traveling, I miss him a lot."

"Yes, I suppose you would." Jan helped herself to another piece. "Especially if someone was sneaking around your house after dark." Her voice dropped. "You know, you should have a shotgun that you can fire out the window. Everyone else does."

"Sure," Theresa agreed. "We keep a big old Stevens twelve-gauge double-barrel behind the back door. And if Dan hears anything, like a noisy radio in some parked car, or a raccoon fight, he drops in a couple of shells and bang! He lets go."

Gloria giggled, picturing herself in her brief nightgown, waving a big old Stevens double-barrel shotgun at some poor, hapless stranded motorist looking for a telephone. "The burglar would have been closer to the shotgun than I was, since I wasn't sleeping in the house. I was in the screen tent."

"A screen tent! That's luxury." Jan laughed. "It was so hot last night that we dragged the old foam mattress off the pullout couch and threw it on the front veranda. We'd rather face the mosquitoes than bake."

"We have a couple of cots on the porch," Theresa added.

Gloria thought it was no wonder the person on the tractor Saturday morning was not surprised to see her sleeping in the backyard. Evidently around here, everyone did it.

"I'm in an upstairs flat," Rick said, morosely. "I just lie there and bake."

"So, tell us about the night prowler," Jan begged. "Did he take anything?"

"He didn't get that far. The cat scared him off."

More laughter. "At least your thief didn't get your gorgeous diamond. Gee, if I had one like that I'd wear it to bed," Theresa chimed in. She held her hand out for a closer look, and Gloria obliged. "I've never seen anything that beautiful, except on movie stars."

"I'm afraid it ripped the pillowcase once, so I had to leave it off at night. Last night I was lucky, I guess. The only thing that worried me was...well, the food. Imagine some stranger with evil intentions pawing over your bread and cereal."

"Ugh. I hope you pitched it all out."

"Bagged it up this morning, since I couldn't sleep. I'll take it to the dump on Saturday, as long as I'm not stuck working again." She took another large bite of pizza.

"So this is how you spend your work day, is it?" a voice behind them made them all jump. Ed Murray, manager of the print division for Heartland, and everyone's boss, was standing in the doorway leading from the rear entrance of the *Sun* office. Fiftyish, paunchy, and pompous in a stiff business suit, Murray looked slightly down his nose at the group gathered around the pizza boxes on the work table in the middle of the front office, all gaping, no doubt, like a herd of surprised cattle.

"Good afternoon, Mr. Murray." Gloria's words were unclear and likely accompanied by bits of parsley and flakes of pizza crust.

"Ms. Trevisl." Murray nodded, his face fixed in its usual stone mask. "When you've finished, I'll talk to you in Mr. Russell's office, if you don't mind." He twitched his dark moustache and walked carefully up the stairs.

Gloria swallowed hard, several times. "I'll be right there, sir." Shit! She probably had pepperoni between her teeth, and dabs of tomato sauce stuck to the corners of her mouth. Everyone was silent as she hastily wiped her lips, downed half a bottle of pop and gathered up the pizza leftovers for the garbage, brushing crumbs from her bodice.

Rick, finishing off the last wedge of extra-cheese with the relaxed posture of someone who had just missed a bullet, asked, "Is anything new happening in the McKee case?"

"They had quite a turnout for the funeral," Jan pointed out. "Over two hundred, I hear."

There was nothing like murder to attract a following, Gloria mused as she left the ladies gossiping, regretting that she wouldn't hear the latest theories on who might have done it. She and Rick went on up the stairs. "Any sports tonight?"

"Nothing, for a change. What are you doing?"

"Sleeping. I didn't get much last night."

"So I heard," Rick said. "Shall I call the police at eleven?"

"If you feel like it. It's not that important when the paper is out, but it's good to keep ahead of things. We never know how busy we'll be next week. There's nothing important to keep you in town, if you want to leave for the afternoon." She hesitated on the landing. "You still need a weekend off now and then. We'll work out some kind of schedule to suit both of us."

"Okay." He paused. "I've wanted to tell you that I'm glad you're here. Before you came, I thought I already knew everything there was to know about working on a newspaper. But now, I feel I'm learning something new every day."

"Glad to hear it." She reached the top of the stairs. "Wish me luck." He grinned and gave her a thumbs-up. She turned and walked to the glassed-in cubicle where Mr. Murray was seated behind Russell's desk. His back was as straight as a board as he gazed at her. What was he thinking? She couldn't tell. Had he already heard about her run-in with the general manager the day before? Quite likely. She took a deep breath and braced herself.

"The paper looks very good," he said as she sat down. "I checked the proofs this morning. The news seems well-covered, and advertising has picked up nicely in the past month, even though this is not a busy season."

"Thank you, sir." She blushed slightly. "About lunch...."

"Yes? Fred Russell tells me you treat the staff to lunch every Thursday."

"Everyone makes an effort to put out a decent issue, not just the editorial staff," Gloria explained. "They all deserve it. Even Mr. Russell."

He looked at her. "You think so? In that case, put it on your expense account from now on."

"Thanks. I will if it's necessary, but I think it means more, coming from me directly. With the number of new people coming and going these past few months, it helps boost staff morale to know that someone is on their side."

"Have you made up your mind to stay?"

"I wasn't aware that it was my decision, Mr. Murray," she said, surprised.

"More or less. You have done an excellent job, and the rest of the staff seem to accept you, even if it takes the occasional bribe of pizza." He smiled. She smiled back. "There is one other thing."

Ah, yes. Did her face reveal her apprehension? "About Mr. Russell, sir—"

"Fred Russell is young, but he is sharp, and we like to think he has a bright future in media management. But he is rather in awe of you, I think, to put it nicely. I hope you won't take advantage of that."

"I'll try not to, provided he allows me room to do my job. He tends to crowd me a little."

"So I gather. It can't be easy for staff members on a paper like this one to have a manager who is younger than they are."

"And less experienced, as well," she added. Hold on, she warned herself silently. You may actually *need* this job someday.

"I suppose that can be a problem as well." His eyes narrowed slightly. "I'm sure you can manage." Resignation. "Then yes, I will stay."

"Good. Barring your doing something foolish, such as getting sued, I think it's decided." He rose. "Thank you, Ms. Trevisi." They shook hands, and she walked out of the office, her emotions a mixed bag. Was she expected to teach Fred Russell *his* job too? Mr. Murray could not directly ask her without bumping up her salary. She drew a deep, exasperated breath. After a century of women fighting to be recognized, still this. But at least she was employed.

She grabbed her camera and notebook and headed off to the library, where a room had been devoted to a study on the North American Quilt. At least the crafts page would be filled next week. As long as she wasn't arrested or sued.

***

"The police are upstairs."

"They want to see you about last night's intruder." Jan and Theresa were a Greek chorus as Gloria came through the front door, eyes wide and curly heads nodding. "They offered to wait upstairs...at your desk."

"My desk?" Unlawful search and seizure? In Plattsford? She climbed the stairs, camera and notebook in her hands. Jan should have known better than to show just anyone to her desk in her absence, especially the police. Theresa was probably half intimidated, and Jan reluctant to leave them in the front office, cooling their heels and frightening the patrons. The editorial department, on the other hand, was deserted, Mr. Murray having left some time ago. Linda was canvassing the downtown merchants, setting up a sponsor page for the Canada Day issue. Rick was probably doing his laundry, or whatever. That was her usual chore on an afternoon off. Russell still hadn't arrived. Damn! The mileage checks would be late, and she had to replace all those groceries....

"Please excuse us, Ms. Trevisi," Inspector Gray explained, his impassive face studying her reactions carefully. "Your receptionist suggested that we wait here. I trust that isn't a problem."

Although going through her drawers would have been highly illegal, there was plenty of interesting material just sitting on her desk, or pinned to her bulletin board, to catch his eye: O'Dell's council agenda, with items circled and notes scribbled in the margin; a photo of the pallbearers lugging the casket at McKee's funeral, Glenn Hullett's phone number— no doubt police were aware of *his* connection—and most intriguing of all, the almost black photograph of the industrial park, taken at midnight, with Sergeant O'Toole in the foreground. Gray was seated at her desk, fingering the mouse from her computer and looking very comfortable. Unnervingly so. Had he been browsing through her files while O'Toole stood guard?

"No problem at all," Gloria said, shifting aside a pile of old council agendas and putting down her notebook. The inspector rose and relinquished the chair, and moved to stand beside O'Toole. Gloria glanced at the chair, and decided she would remain on her feet, as well; this way, she would be slightly taller than he was, in her heels.

"There are some aspects about the incident last night that we wish to clarify." Gray's eyes glittered. "Are you on your way home?"

"Not quite. I certainly have time to talk."

"I would like to check your house, if that's all right with you. We're interested in the bottle of pills that Constable Stoker found on your kitchen counter last night."

"Actually, *I* found the pills," she corrected, holding Gray's eyes as long as she could. "When I stepped inside the kitchen behind Constable Stoker and looked around, they were on the counter." She paused. "I am rather interested too. Did the bottle hold any fingerprints?"

"All kinds, actually. Trouble is, we haven't yet matched them to anything on record locally. Of course," Gray smiled, "we don't have yours."

Gloria held out her hands, fingers splayed. "Be my guest," she said coolly.

"We don't need to bother with that here," O'Toole said. "Since the inspector wants to see your house, why don't we meet you there in, let's say, an hour?"

Gloria's heart sank. She had wanted to get ahead on her work so she could have the weekend free for the Waterloo concert. "One hour would be fine, or I can talk to you now and save you the bother." Didn't her father-in-law say that willingness to cooperate would stand in her favor? And why shouldn't she cooperate? After all, she was the victim, not the perpetrator. Should she call him? *Innocent people shouldn't need lawyers.*

"We'll meet you in an hour," Gray was saying as he moved toward the stairs. O'Toole followed, glancing back at Gloria before following his superior.

Gloria sat down at her desk. No point in trying to work now, she thought. She unloaded her camera, set the film in the basket in front of the darkroom, and headed toward the stairs.

One thing she *could* still do in her distracted state of mind was shop for food. She checked her wallet, and was dismayed to find only a couple of two-dollar coins. And still no mileage checks had appeared. She went to the bank machine, and prayed that she was not overdrawn. It spat out thirty dollars, enough to pick up a few groceries to replace the ones she had thrown out, and a fresh bottle of scotch, a small one, in case Tony returned.

She was stepping away from the ATM when she spotted Marie McKee, drifting past her like a silent spirit as she approached the bank counter. Gloria recognized her at once from photos of the funeral, and although she received only a brief, close up look at Mrs. McKee's face, she couldn't help noticing the woman's eyes, deeply blue though red-rimmed, and her hair, obviously touched up to look less gray. Still a good-looking woman. Could *she* be the one with the lover? The face was pale, slightly puffy and dull, as if she had carefully prepared it to be completely expressionless. Her breath exuded mouthwash and mints, even at a distance of ten feet. The effort had been useless, Gloria judged; one could detect distilled spirits through the most rigorous tooth-brushing. Adjusting her handbag over her shoulder, Gloria paused long enough to hear the hushed voice of Marie talking in urgent tones to a bank attendant.

"No, I'm afraid we've had to freeze all your accounts, Mrs. McKee, until head office notifies us," the attendant was saying in a firm voice that could be heard on the street. Gloria turned away. Financial problems, she wondered, or simply the usual dilemma of a widow whose husband controlled their assets? As she slipped behind the wheel of her car and headed to the supermarket, she reminded herself to keep her bank account firmly in her maiden name.

She ran into Norma Simmons over the oranges. "I was on my way to see you," Norma said. "I have those notes from the pictures of Clarence McKee's funeral. I managed to put a name and family connection to every face on those photographs," she added with a hint of pride.

"Fantastic." Gloria bagged and paid for her groceries, packed them into her car, then waited by the entrance for Norma to emerge from the store. Hazel McDaniel appeared with a cartload of bread, cereal, and chips at about the same time as Gloria noticed Marie McKee moving toward the store, in her dark raincoat. What did it take, she wondered, to unfreeze enough money for groceries? A call to the bank manager from her lawyer? *Innocent people shouldn't need lawyers.*

Her view was obstructed as Mrs. McDaniel stopped directly in front of her. "Not working today? I see Clarence's funeral wasn't important enough for *you* to attend."

"I didn't have to, since I had both my community correspondent and my photographer there," Gloria replied, shifting slightly to spot Mrs. McKee. "The paper was well-represented." She watched as Marie paused in front of the store before dropping her handbag into Gloria's old shopping cart, and wondered if the woman cared who was there.

"Your boss came too."

"How nice." What on earth was Fred Russell doing there? Being nosy, or perhaps passing on more information to the *Express*? Her blood began to boil again at the thought as she lost sight of Marie McKee in the fruit aisle. She was glad when Hazel moved away, accompanied by a store assistant, and Norma emerged, cart overflowing with bags. Tucking the package with the photos safely in her clipboard, she headed home.

***

The police were waiting for her, in two cruisers. She was not surprised; nor would she have been surprised to see them following her through the supermarket. After all, she was not a lifelong resident of Plattsford. In their eyes, she was a transient, unpredictable and unstable, and liable to make a run for it if she had a guilty secret.

Gray followed quietly as she carried in the groceries and put them in a corner on the kitchen floor. She offered them seats on the lumpy living room couch.

"We'll stand, if it's all right with you, Ms. Trevisi," the inspector said, eyeing the nest of cat hair in the corner, Max's favorite spot. "Show us just where you were when this *alleged* intruder came."

She cursed him silently for sounding as if he did not believe her. "Or intruders. Constable Stoker hinted that there may have been more than one, sir. It was dark."

They walked out of the house, into the backyard, and she showed them where the ground sheet was neatly folded on the grass in the corner of the screen tent. Two officers scoped out angles from the tent to the lane, and the veranda steps. Returning to the house, they inspected the lock on the back door. "There seems to be no sign of forced entry," the inspector noted, glancing back in her direction.

"The door was unlocked at the time," she pointed out, again.

She took them into the kitchen, and showed them the box of curtains on the floor near the door, the clean counter, the broken cat food dish in the garbage, and the plastic bag full of perfectly good food that she had gathered up to throw out as a precaution. Gray examined the food. "Liquor bottles?"

"The open ones, certainly," Gloria said, gazing with regret at a bottle three-quarters full of Glenlivet. "I have no idea where he—or she—had been while he was in my house. I'm taking no chances."

"So I see. May we take this food and test it?" Gray asked. Gloria nodded, and an officer who was standing by picked up the bag and took it to one of the cruisers waiting outside.

"And you say nothing seemed to have been taken?" he asked. "No jewelry, no loose change, wallet, camera, computer...."

"Not that I know of," she replied. "If the intruder took anything, it was of so little consequence that I haven't noticed yet." The inspector looked skeptical. "We accounted for my valuable items that evening," she continued, impatience rising, "and I certainly was not hiding anything from Constable Stoker." She saw Sergeant O'Toole smother a smile, and wondered if Stoker had shared a joke with the detachment about how little she *was* hiding. Could they think she was kidding? Just what kind of floozy did they think she was, anyway? She was beginning to wonder just how the inspector's mind worked.

"There is one more thing." Gray's eyes were on her face. "What was your own relationship with the murdered man, Ms. Trevisi?"

"My...my *relationship* with Mr. McKee, sir?" Gloria was taken aback.

"Your association, if you prefer. Or to be more specific, why were you telephoning McKee, twice, just days before he died?"

"Days?" She thought back quickly over the previous week. "I was calling his office, a few weeks ago, to see when I could expect McKee Excavating to fix my septic bed. He has an agreement with the landlord." She hesitated.

"And why should his timing concern you?"

"Why shouldn't it? I live here." She paused. He waited. "Fine. Because I don't want my cats run over by a bulldozer or buried in a drainage pipe," she almost snapped at him, and received a raised eyebrow in return. "For a week after he staked out the ground for a new bed, I kept the cats inside during the day. He didn't show up to finish the job, so I called to find out when he would be coming. I want to protect my pets. Is that unreasonable?" She paused again, inhaling and exhaling rather noisily. He still said nothing. "What exactly are you thinking?"

Gray was studying her face carefully, his eyes half-closed. "Ms. Trevisi, this is how things stand: We are currently investigating a violent murder involving barbiturates and a bulldozer. What we have is a bottle of powdered barbiturates found in your house, on your kitchen counter, and blood on your shoes that has been analyzed to have come from the murder victim."

"Of course. I found the barbiturates," she protested. "And I *gave* you the shoes."

"We have you placed near the scene of the murder shortly after it was discovered," he continued, ignoring her remark. "And we have evidence of timely contact between you and the victim—"

"I never spoke to Mr. McKee directly. His office will confirm that," she cut in, feeling helpless.

"—who had quite a reputation as a ladies' man," Gray went on.

"A...*What?* Oh, spare me!" Gloria burst out in indignation.

"And now you are claiming to be the alleged victim of a break-in, in which there is no sign of forced entry to your home, and nothing appears to have been taken. Can you explain this situation to us? Perhaps you can start with the pills, and end with the shoes."

Gloria was very still. Surely even Inspector Gray was aware that a phone call to a business office hardly constituted a liaison. The picture of the scene flashed through her mind, where she had stood, and what she had seen. The photo on her bulletin board, if it was still there, showed that she was at least twelve feet, perhaps twenty, from the yellow tape. It showed Sergeant O'Toole's face shining forth like a startled deer. It showed a plastic sheet on the ground at least fifty feet from where she stood. And yet, she had blood on her shoes.

And what about last night? She had arrived home at eleven, fed the cats from the counter, grabbed a glass from her cupboard, filled it full of milk from her refrigerator, and later rinsed the dirty glass in the sink. She had left the counter clear. Had there been a bottle of pills on the counter then? No, she was certain. Had someone been in the house? She had seen the tiny penlight beam, heard the door slam as someone left, in a hurry. She had heard the footsteps. And Max? The cat had been in the tent with her until then. And when Constable Stoker had opened her kitchen door, the cat had run outside.

"No, sir," she answered finally. "I cannot explain it. Perhaps the answer lies in what this intruder was looking for in my house. Apart from my shoes, and that possibility is pretty remote, I have no idea. As for the barbiturates...." she paused. "Do you have any identifiable prints from the bottle?"

"Maybe," Sergeant O'Toole said.

"Then, gentlemen, as I said before, be my guest," she said quietly, holding out her fingers.

Her father-in-law would have been jumping up and down on his desk if he had heard her throw herself on the mercy of the justice system, just as Mike had done, allowing them to search her home and haul away her food without even asking for a warrant. Somehow, though, the whole thing seemed ludicrous. A farce. *Innocent people shouldn't need lawyers!* Linda's words kept rocketing through her brain.

She walked out of her house with the two senior officers, leaving her groceries on the kitchen floor, and climbed into the back of the cruiser. O'Toole and Gray climbed in the front, O'Toole murmuring "...nothing to hide, for Chrissakes" and the cool inspector answering, "....checking every angle, a thorough investigation to eliminate suspects." Gloria groaned.

"I guess I'm the outsider, am I?" she asked. The two officers said nothing. She sighed, rested her head back against the hot vinyl of the back seat, and closed her eyes. The cruiser rolled out of her lane.

Chapter 7

"Coffee?"

The OPP office outside Plattsford was small, and there was no official interrogation room. Seated in Inspector Gray's office, Gloria looked up at the sound of a friendly voice. Constable Brian Stoker was filling up most of the doorway and holding a large Tim Horton's coffee cup and a small paper bag. "The desk sergeant told me you were here. You take cream, right?"

She smiled at him. "Thank you. It's the second time you've served me coffee in the last twenty-four hours." She accepted the cup from his steady hands, and put it down on the table in front of her. "How long does this usually go on, anyway?"

It was after midnight. She had twice reviewed the intruder incident with Inspector Gray, Sergeant O'Toole, and a tape recorder, and explained, once again, her two casual telephone calls to McKee Excavating more than two weeks before. The inspector had appeared not to believe that an attractive, articulate young woman with a fascinating husband would not have jumped at the chance of a liaison with a bleary-eyed, pot-bellied, middle-aged contractor who was rumored, no doubt by himself, to be quite a masher. Well, she lived alone, didn't she?

Then she had explained how she had come to be near the scene of Clarence McKee's murder, taking photographs at midnight. And then she had been driven out to the industrial park, and had shown them approximately where she had been standing when she'd snapped the picture. The recent rain had washed away the footprints, but two police officers were diligently taking samples from the sides of the road. Twice she had slipped in the soft, rain-soaked gravel at the edge of the ditch, her arm and elbow saving her from a serious tumble into the mud. She was frustrated, scraped, and dirty. She had even told them about the trouble that Joe Cameron had been having with one of McKee's relatives over the finishing plant in Genoa. They had listened, taken notes, recorded, and asked questions. Her fingertips were black with ink. She was tired and hungry. No one was telling her whether she was considered a valuable witness or a prime suspect, and it was too late to clam up and ask for a lawyer; she had spilled everything she knew, and was regretting her innocent willingness to cooperate with the authorities. Fortunately, McKee's office had corroborated her concern for her pets; so had John deVos, her landlord. To the police, it meant nothing. She was considering asking permission to telephone her father-in-law when Stoker appeared with coffee.

Was this a well-orchestrated intrusion by an officer who had befriended her? She looked around the room: just a desk piled with paperwork and looking a lot like her own desk at the *Sun*, a couple of chairs that creaked, and two filing cabinets. No two-way mirror, probably no hidden microphones. The white walls and overhead fluorescent lights turned her skin tone a sickly gray as she looked at her fingers.

Stoker's sympathetic gaze took in her dirty hands and mud-streaked dress, and her shoes, scratched by gravel and streaked with dirt. "Looks like *your* shoes managed to get you into hot water too," he said, sitting on the edge of Gray's desk while she ate and drank.

She crammed a full third of the doughnut into her mouth, swallowed hard and slurped the coffee. "I cannot believe this is happening," she declared between large bites. "Does Inspector Gray think I was so desperate for company that I'd throw myself into a...a bloody filthy septic bed with, of all people, *Clarence McKee?* Does he think I bumped off a nickel-and-dime contractor that I've never even met or talked to? Or is he just in a bad mood?" She swallowed another large mouthful, and took a large gulp of liquid to wash it down. "He even asked me how many O'Dell council meetings I had attended since I started working here, and what I knew about heavy equipment. I told him that going to council meetings, even the dull ones, is part of my job, and the heaviest equipment I know how to operate is a church organ, and that's about the limit."

"You sure?"

"Of course! I wish I had never come out here and taken this job. I wish," she downed more coffee and heaved a deep, shaky sigh, "I wish that I had simply packed up and gone off with my husband on a musical tour of the east coast." She finished the doughnut, wiped her dirty hands on a napkin, and looked at Stoker. "Thanks. You're a rock." She sipped more of her coffee, and closed her eyes.

"If it's any consolation, the inspector was grilling Joe Cameron this morning. You know, the guy with the timber-finishing business in Genoa. Same routine. Picked him up and brought him here. Mr. Cameron was mad as hell; kept him away from his lumberyard for half the day."

"I can well imagine. Why the interest in Mr. Cameron?"

"According to what I hear, he had been on the building site earlier that day."

"Well, he had a perfectly legitimate reason to be meeting with Mr. McKee, since his plant is supposed to be moving there before the end of the summer. Who else was at the building site?"

"McKee's business partner, also questioned today, I gather. The inspector is checking him out too."

"Has anyone questioned Doug Sullivan? I'd bet no one has the nerve."

"You'll have to ask the inspector, or Sergeant O'Toole."

"Sure. As if they'd tell me anything. And what about last night, when my house was—"

Inspector Gray came into the room, and Stoker slipped off the desk and stood at attention. Gray looked at him with raised eyebrows, then said to Gloria, "We reached the chairman of Plattsford Hospital Board. He can vouch for your whereabouts last Thursday from eight to about midnight," he said. "The partial fingerprints that we can make out, Ms. Trevisi, are definitely not yours. The dirt on the side of the road shows traces of Type A blood, same as that of the victim. That means you may leave when you're ready. And, by the way: your food, what we checked, was fine. Thanks for stopping by," he added, and walked out.

"Huh. Just because it isn't drugged doesn't mean someone didn't spit in the milk," Gloria muttered at his back as she rose from her chair and turned to Stoker. "May I speak with Sergeant O'Toole for a minute?"

"I'll see if he's still here."

He returned with O'Toole a moment later. The sergeant had his jacket on, ready to leave. "Sergeant, you know I am willing to help out an investigation in any way I possibly can. But this?" She drew a deep, shaky breath. "This was a bit over the top."

"I'm sorry. But this is a murder investigation, and the inspector is pretty mad that the investigators missed the blood on the side of the road."

"Really?" She sniffed. "Nice to know this isn't my fault." She walked slowly toward the door. "By the way, what does the blood on the side of the road tell you? Does it mean that Mike Hurtig may have arrived on the scene before the body was dumped outside, and that his bulldozer was moved after he parked it, or could it mean that it wasn't the only vehicle that ran over McKee's body?"

O'Toole's bland expression didn't change. "It means that whoever ran over him left the scene along the side of the road. Possibly someone was there *before* Hurtig returned the borrowed bulldozer. The body may have been run over already. Or it may have happened afterward." He paused. "Either way, whoever killed McKee felt strongly enough to want him crushed into the ground before he—or she—left the scene."

"Bloody hell."

"Well, you were there at about five minutes past midnight," O'Toole recalled. "Did you pass anyone? Did you see anything? A bulldozer, or a tractor?"

She thought back to that night, a week ago. "The highway was deserted, as far as I recall.... No, wait. There was a tractor heading up McDaniel's driveway, but that was when I was on my way home, about ten minutes later. And it had to be almost two hours after Mr. McKee died, don't you think? Maybe someone at McDaniel's saw someone."

O'Toole looked at Stoker; the young officer took out his notebook and jotted it down. "Thank you,

Ms. Trevisi," the sergeant said. "We appreciate your help."

"Do you appreciate it enough to give me some information?"

"Such as...?" The sergeant looked wary.

"Well, Inspector Gray seems to be satisfied with my own alibi, for the time being. Is he satisfied with Mr. Hullett's alibi? And what about Mr. Cameron?"

"Not that it's any business of yours, but Mr. Hullett was having dinner with business associates. Mr. Cameron has no supportable alibi."

"And who might Mr. Hullett's friends be, Sergeant?"

"One was a citizen whose word we don't doubt."

Whose word, she wondered, wouldn't they doubt? Doug Sullivan's, perhaps? "Who is driving me home, Sergeant? As you may recall, I arrived here without my car."

"No need. You *have* a ride."

Gloria emerged into the main office, and stopped dead in her tracks. "Oh, no," she groaned.

Standing at the counter, his thin face serious and pale, was Fred Russell. If Sergeant O'Toole knew what everyone in Plattsford knew, the look he cast over his shoulder could have said, "Enjoy."

Russell was bubbling over. "My gosh, Gloria! Are you all right? I tried to call the company lawyer, but I couldn't get hold of him." Eyeing her bare arms, he swept off his suit jacket and threw it over her shoulders. "Geez, you look awful."

Awful? How gallant. She angrily tried to wriggle out of it. "Spare the effects, will you, Mr. Russell? I am not cold, and we're not in the movies."

"Sorry. You do look tired."

"I've hardly had any sleep since Tuesday. How do you expect me to look?" She stalked out ahead of him, listening to his footsteps as he quick-marched behind, reaching out every now and then to touch her elbow and steer her to his car. Halfway across the parking lot she halted and wheeled to face him, nearly knocking him off his feet. "You called someone in head office? Not Mr. Murray, by any chance?"

"Well...Yes."

"Damn it! You couldn't have shut up, for once, or at least kept it between us?"

"Sorry. I didn't know what to do. He told me to find out what charges are being laid before contacting the lawyer."

"In other words, before deciding whether I'm worth the bother." She wondered if this constituted doing something "foolish" in Mr. Murray's view. She turned and continued walking. She had no idea what he cruised around in, and wasn't surprised when she saw it. "An Audi. Nice. I guess your paycheck is a lot bigger than mine," she snipped as he rushed to open the passenger door for her. She folded herself carefully into the passenger side and stretched her legs; and in spite of herself, she relaxed into the seat with a deep sigh and pulled his jacket around her. "I'd been looking forward to having an evening to myself.

Instead, this turned out to be one hell of a day. How did you find out I was here, Mr. Russell?"

He switched on the ignition and backed out of the parking space. "Rick called the police station at eleven o'clock, and the desk sergeant told him you were being questioned, so he called me. And I wish you'd call me Fred."

Rick had called at eleven, she mused, just as he said he would. Good God, what time is it? She looked at her watch. Nearly one.

"It wasn't a great day for me, either, I'm afraid," Russell continued. "I'm sorry about the *Express*, Gloria. I feel like a fool. I wanted to help, but it seems I don't know about these things." He steered the car down the highway.

"Never mind, Mr. Russell. I doubt if anyone at Heartland gives a damn."

"I don't know. While I was at head office today I...I asked to see your file in personnel." He smiled. "It took some coaxing. I guess you know what you're doing."

"Does this mean you're going to stop hinting to head office that I'm incompetent and lazy?"

"Incompetent...Oh." He took a deep breath. "I didn't really. I just needed to...I don't know, feel like I was in control of things."

"And I'm not good at stroking the male ego, it seems. Sorry." There was that stutter again. Gloria didn't want to seem ungrateful, as she wrapped his jacket more closely around her and slid farther down in the seat. He was, after all, driving her home in this quiet, luxurious, smoothly running automobile which seemed to be moving rather slowly. She tried to keep her eyes open.

"Anyway, Rick told me about the break-in last night at your house. Look, I know you're living alone at the moment," a thin, reedy voice from far away was murmuring. "You're pretty isolated out here. Do you think this is a safe place for you to stay? Is there anything at all that I can do to make it...more secure?" The car seemed almost stopped. An arm crept across the back of the seat behind her head, and a hand touched her right shoulder. "I'll stay with you for a while if you need me."

"Mr. Russell, I don't need anyone to stay with me." *Am I dreaming this?* She tried to pinch her arm.

"Or we can go to my place, so you can..."

Gloria was awake with a snap. "So I can wear this dirty, muddy dress to work tomorrow, and hear Theresa and Jan speculating on where I spent the night? Are you flaming nuts?"

"You've had a tough night. You don't need to go to work tomorrow if you don't—"

"The hell I don't!" She half turned to him in the seat and noticed his arm was still stretched across the back of it. No, she hadn't been dreaming. She glared at him, and he moved his arm, slightly, in the right direction. "If I don't get the pictures of the sod-turning at the Legion, write up the quilting exhibition, and organize a duty schedule for the weekend—

because if you haven't noticed, the news keeps on happening even on Saturdays when you're out playing golf—then the paper will be one big advertising flyer with no news and no pictures. That's exactly what it looked like before I got here, if you can remember that far back! Mr. Russell, are you giving me a ride home or aren't you?" The effort cost her some energy. As the car jerked ahead, she sank back into the soft leather seat. "Turn at the next concession road. The house is half a block up this line. And step on it, will you please? I'm very tired."

"Okay, I guess you're right, but, hell, Gloria, right now you have no one else. I know."

"I'm married, Mr. Russell. That means I have a husband. And I don't like this conversation at all."

"You're married to someone who doesn't live with you and doesn't support you, and you're the only one I know who thinks that's all right."

"That's none of your business, or anyone else's. Turn in the next driveway."

"But I want to make it my business. I talked to the police about what happened last night. You shouldn't be alone in this deserted old farmhouse with people being murdered a few miles down the road, and some maniac harassing you. It isn't safe. If the guy you're married to had any brass at all, he would be here. But he isn't. I am, and I...I'd like to look after you." His arm was slowly edging back behind her shoulders.

This was too much. Turning to face him, she said with careful deliberation, "Excuse me, Mr. Russell, but there is only one maniac harassing me at the moment, and it is time to end this. I don't wish to sound ungrateful for the ride, but what on God's great, green earth makes you think I want to go home with *you?* Or have you stay here with me when—oh, damn!"

They were halfway up her lane. Tony's Buick was parked beside her car, and Tony, she could see, was parked on the veranda bench, waiting for her. Naturally. Because where would she be, without her car, except in someone else's?

As they pulled up to the house, he rose and walked out into the driveway, passing through the vehicle's headlights. Gloria struggled with the strange seatbelt, while Russell leapt out and scurried around to the passenger side. Tony, however, beat him to it, swung open the passenger door of the Audi and stood, waiting. Gloria stepped out, stumbled, and would have fallen, whether from fury or fatigue. He reached out to catch her. "Are you all right?" he asked. His face, in the beam of the car's interior light, showed no expression at all, which exasperated her even more.

"No," was all she said, and walked carefully up the wobbly porch steps, and into the house. She was strongly tempted to lock the door and leave the two men outside to howl at one another like tomcats. She was reaching for the refrigerator door when she remembered she hadn't put away the groceries. The bags were no longer where she had left them. She was rummaging for fresh milk when they came through the door.

"....Tony Lambert, Gloria's husband." Tony was, as usual, very properly introducing himself to a stranger and offering a hand to shake. "You picked her up *where?*" No howling; both were too civilized. She detested them.

"The police station. I'm Fred Russell, her...I work with her, manage the paper. I'm afraid Gloria has had a rather bad time this evening and needs to—"

"I've been 'helping the police with their inquiries,' for the past seven hours," she said, turning to Tony. "I wasn't out having a *good* time, never fear."

"I didn't think you were—" Tony began.

"I don't care what you thought. Someone broke into the house last night and left a bottle of barbiturates on the counter, which happen to be the means of choice around here for putting a victim into a coma before driving a bulldozer over him." Tired as she was, she struggled to keep a grip on her temper. "Whether the idea was to poison my food, or simply to implicate me as a possible suspect to take the heat off someone else, I don't know. But I've just wrecked a second pair of good shoes," she indicated her wrecked black pumps, "and spent seven hours as a guest of Plattsford OPP convincing them that I am not a murderer."

"Surely they don't—" Russell began.

"And all because *someone*," Gloria continued, ignoring him, "might have entertained a notion that I could hold incriminating evidence against him. Now whatever gave anyone that idea?"

Tony silently walked to the other side of the table and leaned back against the counter, arms folded. Gloria zeroed in on Russell, standing alone by the door, and was grimly pleased that she was looking him straight in the eye. As she took a step toward him, he backed up, looking startled. "Fred Russell, you've been showing up in the strangest places and blabbing your idiotic head off to everyone all week. The paper only hit the streets a few hours ago, and the picture of the scene was never used. But someone knew, Wednesday night, that I had been there, someone who might have been worried enough to come out here last night and search the house. How many people did you talk to?"

"Do you really think it was someone I talked to?" His voice cracked slightly on the question, and he averted his gaze from her eighteen-karat temper. "I'm not certain; Joe Cameron, at the press conference. And the township reeve at the funeral. I guess the clerk-treasurer was there too. I'm not sure who else."

Gloria moved in closer, and Russell cowered slightly by the coat rack. "In other words, everyone that was within earshot in both those places." She folded her arms and tapped the toe of her ruined shoe on the floor. His eyes had wandered to a streak of mud on the green linen dress that appeared like a dark bruise on her left thigh. "So besides giving my best work to a daily news rag who will never, never credit me for it, your indiscretion also compromised my safety, perhaps even put my life in danger. I've had an intruder in my home, pawing through *my* belongings, possibly trying to poison *my* food, because you can't keep your mouth shut." Her voice was low. "And now, thanks to you, I've just spent half the night talking to police because I was suspected of killing someone I didn't even know. And it isn't over. Tomorrow I have to explain to head office why you thought I needed a lawyer to bail me out of jail and why I still deserve to have a job. And you think that I would actually trust you to look after *me*?"

"I thought they should know before it got reported on the evening news, that's all," Russell protested.

"Oh? Why? Did you call the radio station too?"

"Of course not. As for looking after you," he drew himself up to appear at least a half-inch taller, "you should thank me."

"Thank you for what? Making a perfectly ludicrous pass? You've been hitting on me ever since I arrived. That kind of harassment, Mr. Russell, is grounds for litigation, not to mention immediate dismissal. Have I ever once encouraged you? How can you think for a second that I would fall swooning into your arms and go home with you tonight, or perhaps, as you also suggested, let you stay here? Has it worked for you before? Is that why your wife kicked you out?" It was cruel, but she was too angry and tired to care.

"Gloria, please." He glanced quickly at Tony, who had stepped away from the counter. "I didn't mean it that way."

"Oh? How *did* you mean it? I did not ask anyone to call you to the police station. I did not ask you for a lift home. You showed up, acting as if I were your personal property. And all that stuff in the car? Just how dumb do you think I am?"

"I am truly s—"

"I've heard it. Thanks for the lift, Mr. Russell. Now get out."

Russell backed toward the kitchen door. "I'll see you in the—"

"*Good night.*" Gloria stepped toward the door. He quickly backed through it, and strode off the porch. She banged the screen door shut, slipped the hook on it, and spun around to face Tony, seated in one of the kitchen chairs, his jaw clenched tightly and his eyes brimming. "That *wasn't* for your benefit." She looked at him more closely. "You cad, you're laughing. This isn't funny." The Audi had already turned at the foot of the driveway, and she listened to the whine of the motor with a slight pang of guilt as she kicked off her shoes and headed toward the staircase.

Tony reached out from his chair and caught her as she tried to slip past him, pulled her in and buried his face in the front of her dress while he shook with helpless laughter. She grabbed his shoulders, ready to push him away, but his breath against her body brought a reluctant surge of warm feeling. Soon she, too, was laughing.

"Ah, Gloria, how I adore you," he mumbled against the fabric. "But you're a terror, you know? Remember those officers at that lovely banquet where we met? Terrified as mice!" Finally, he looked up. "And so is Fred Russell."

She stroked his hair gently. "You think so? I think he was more scared of *you*, especially after what he was suggesting in the car about your shortcomings." She paused, a hand on his collar, and gazed at the huge bouquet of roses sitting in a crystal vase on the counter. "The flowers are beautiful."

"I wanted to surprise you. I stopped at your office, but you'd already left. I came to the house and found the door unlocked and groceries rolling all over the floor. So I waited, and waited, and got kind of frustrated. I'm not even going to mention what I thought when the two of you drove in."

"It was pretty obvious what you thought. I don't know why I'm being so nice about it." She gave him a soft cuff on the side of the head. "You should know better."

"Well, you do look as though someone rolled you over in a ploughed field." He brushed some of the mud from her dress. "You never told me you were having a problem with a...a coworker. I was surprised."

"Surprised? That someone might be attracted to me?" She shook his collar in mock anger. "How dare you."

"Spare me the temper, please. You're kind of hard on people, sometimes."

"I simply look after myself. Isn't that what you want?" She kneaded his shoulders with her fingers.

"And now that you know what's been happening, I don't need to stay up any longer, do I? I am really, really tired."

Tony rose, his arms still about her, and kissed her lightly on the temple. "In that case, I am taking you upstairs to bed right now."

"It's hot upstairs," she whined, leaning against him. "But I really do need some sleep."

"And you'll get some. I promise." He let her lead the way up the stairs. The last thing she remembered, after Tony gently helped her shed the muddy linen dress, was asking if he had put the groceries away.

***

Joe Cameron looked at the empty whisky bottle in front of him, the third or fourth he had downed since Monday. It was no use. Sleep wouldn't come, drunk or sober.

Today had been pretty lousy, even without the police. His largest crane had broken down. His lead hand, a wizard at keeping old machinery running, had called in sick for the second day in a row. A flatbed truck had been sitting in the yard since Tuesday, waiting to be loaded with a large order from a pre-fabricated home builder east of Toronto, and if he didn't have it on the road by tomorrow, he would risk losing a valuable, bread-and-butter customer. He stood unsteadily, leaned heavily on the table and accidentally knocked over the bottle. It bounced off the chair and hit the linoleum. Fortunately it didn't break, but rolled under the table. He shrugged, reached down and picked it up. It would take a harder knock than that, obviously, to smash a whisky bottle. Well, he too could take some hard knocks.

Upstairs, his mother was sound asleep, hearing nothing. She had slept heavily for years, since her epileptic condition forced her to take strong tranquillizers. Luckily, he hadn't inherited her particular illness. Police had wanted to know all about that condition of hers, what she was taking for it, where her pills were kept, when last she had renewed a prescription, and where. And they had returned to the house with him later to account for all her medications.

What did they think? That he had stolen his mother's medicine, drugged a bottle of liquor, and given it to Clarence McKee? He told them he wouldn't have wasted good booze, or valuable medicine, on that smug asshole. After all, it was no news to the police that he and McKee did not like each other, even if they *did* have a business arrangement.

He stumbled into the front room that had been his bedroom since his marriage, twenty-odd years ago. His wife and two boys had moved out; she preferred someone who didn't have a mother leaning on him. What could he do? Send the old woman to an old folks' home? As if he could afford *that!* The oldest boy, a welding apprentice in Plattsford, had moved back with him last winter. The younger, finishing high school this year, still lived with his mother and had just started working at the lumberyard this summer, and had a lot to learn. It would be nice to have a son permanently in the business. That is, if he still had a business at the end of the week.

That was the problem. He needed new equipment and a new location, and had already exhausted all avenues of finance available to him. Clarence McKee, it was rumored, had milked his in-laws every time he came up against a setback. Like, they owed him a favor. Lucky. Joe's in-laws, however, weren't interested in his problems. Perhaps some other family connections might help. Perhaps Marie, now that she was a widow....

The thought of Marie in younger days, cool and lovely, still affected him like a knife twisting in his gut. She'd been unreachable until that night by the river. They'd both been pretty drunk. She'd made him swear never to tell. But now she was free, and it was time. Hell, people must've known all along, anyway.

His hand shook slightly as he reached for the telephone beside his bed. It was late, but the drink was making him foolishly brave, tonight. After all, she was vulnerable when she was lonely. That's how he'd reached her once before. Perhaps he'd find a way again....

***

"So now you've heard the short and the long version." Gloria was sitting in bed, comfortably propped up on pillows and sipping espresso next morning at half-past seven. "And now I've slept in, and I'm going to be late. Sweetheart, it seems we never have time for anything but a brief cuddle and a few words before we jump up and go our separate ways. I need more."

"That's because you're a passionate Italian." Tony took the cup from her hand and leaned toward her. "What do you want me to say? I want to have you with me, but," he smiled and shrugged, "I know. You have a life of your own."

She sighed. "And so have you, don't forget, and that's what started this whole mess in the first place: your job, not mine. If I were to ask you to give it all up and stay here, would you?" She watched his face as he looked at her, blinked and looked away. "I wouldn't expect it. What you do has beauty and meaning, and I know you love it. But I want to live with you too. Isn't that what we had in mind before all this happened?"

"That was the idea."

"Well, what are we going to do? I don't want you to give up anything for me, and I can't abandon my own life and start living yours. I wouldn't be the same person."

"In other words, you're torn. And so am I." He shut his eyes and inhaled deeply.

"Exactly." She rubbed her hand gently over the stubble on his cheek. "I know you're having trouble concentrating on the tour. Are you sorry that we went ahead with the wedding, instead of waiting until things had simmered down a bit?"

"No. Are you? Gloria, I couldn't bear the thought that you might lose interest, while I was gone."

"Or develop *another* interest? And what about you, thousands of miles away?"

"You know better. But I thought it might be easier to get through the next two years if we made that commitment now, so we had something to hold on to. It isn't. Nothing makes it easy, does it?"

"I don't know. Perhaps if we were still single I wouldn't feel nearly as deserted as I do at times. But I wouldn't be changing my mind, and dating Fred Russell, or anyone else. I love you, and I know where I want to be in two years' time. I want to be with you."

"And I want to be with you." He took a deep breath. "Who would have thought it could be so difficult?"

"So we do have a lifetime ahead of us, don't we? We work well apart, but we're great together."

He smiled. "I am counting on it."

She reached out and pulled him down beside her. He felt solid, and warm, and familiar. "What time do you have to be in Waterloo?"

"Early this afternoon." He propped himself on one elbow, his hand in her hair.

"I hope you play some Dvoøák tomorrow. And some Walton."

"I've rehearsed a piece just for you, and it's neither, so don't be disappointed."

"Your music never disappoints. And neither do you." She moved slightly under his hands. "Did you feed the cats?"

"Of course. Relax." He leaned toward her and pressed his lips softly against her collarbone. She squirmed, and her pulse quickened.

"Tony, why did you come home last night?"

"I was worried about you."

"Damn you." She sighed, lay back, and let him kiss her again.

***

At nine thirty she was breezing through the back door of the *Sun*. Theresa and Jan, heads together and whispering, were only slightly goggle-eyed as she waved a greeting and ran lightly up the stairs, Fred Russell's jacket over her arm.

Linda met her at the top. "Have you been to the café yet?"

"No." She glanced into Russell's office. He was on the phone, his back turned.

"Goodie!" She rubbed her hands in glee. "Let me get my purse." She disappeared behind her partition and Gloria went to her office to check the schedule. She had time.

Rick was typing up a soccer report. He looked up. "Hey, glad to see the cops let you go. Mr. Murray has been calling every fifteen minutes." He frowned at the jacket. "Fred wouldn't tell me anything."

"*Now* he keeps secrets," groaned Gloria, hanging the jacket on the nearby coat stand. "I was *not* in jail, and I'll be happy to tell you all about it. We're going to Bud's. Can I get you anything?"

"Yeah!" said Rick with a big grin. "You can bring me one of their new bagels."

When they arrived in Bud's she understood. On the counter was a box of extra-large bagels. Over it was a sign: BOSS BAGELS: Eat your Boss for Breakfast, and Have a Great Day.

Gloria exhaled sharply and turned to Linda. "Whose idea was this?"

"Come on, Glo, it's a great promotion. And it has nothing to do with you, honest. Okay. Maybe a bit." Linda giggled.

"I am trying hard not to be amused, but I must know. Are they whole wheat, extra chewy, or heavy on the bran?"

She leaned over the table. "So you're out of jail. What happened? Did you refuse to divulge a source?"

"I was *not* in jail." Gloria quickly summarized the previous evening.

"That creepy inspector actually thought you'd do such a thing?"

"No. I think, actually, it was a warning. He wanted to let me know where things stand with this investigation, and that's the way he chose to do it, just in case I thought I knew more than he did."

"He oughta be shot with his own gun."

"Shhhh! Speaking of guns, here's one now." She nodded toward Sergeant O'Toole, who had just walked into the crowded coffee shop. "Good morning, Sergeant. Would you like to join us?" she invited.

He sat down, coffee in one hand and bagel in the other, his face as deadpan as ever.

"We won't tell, sir," Gloria promised. "To me, it's just a bagel. But tell me, who is Inspector Gray? Where did he come from, and has he been here long?"

"Just transferred to this region from Toronto, possibly looking for a nice retirement spot," O'Toole answered after swallowing a mouthful of bagel. "Why?"

"Perhaps I should interview him for a human interest story. You know, a personal profile. Especially if he's fairly new to the area."

O'Toole made a derogatory noise. "Not a good idea."

"No?" Gloria took a sip of coffee. "I simply want to get to know him a little better."

He grinned slightly. "Ms. Trevisi, I don't think he wants to know *you* any better."

She took a deep breath. "Fine. I won't try. How is the investigation going, keeping in mind that today is Friday and the paper won't be out for seven days?"

"We've widened our field of suspects," he said, and sipped his coffee.

"Since last night? Who are you harassing this time?"

"Can't say." He bit his bagel and chewed slowly.

"What are you doing in town?"

"Talking to the pharmacist. We've been tracking the barbiturates from your house, if you want to know, since we've figured out that they're not yours."

"No luck with fingerprints?" She saw him hesitate. "Sergeant O'Toole, I would like to understand why I was...well, fingered yesterday. I have a right to know."

He took a long pull on his coffee. "Most were old, and too badly smeared. No doubt the person who left them on your counter was wearing gloves."

"Was he trying to plant evidence, or did he simply get interrupted while he was trying to drug my food?"

"Take your pick," the sergeant answered with a shrug. "Though I think if he had been trying to frame you for murder, he would've wiped the old prints off the bottle."

"If he'd been planning to take it with him, he wouldn't have been worrying about fingerprints at all."

"Or he wasn't too smart. Some criminals aren't."

"This one hasn't been caught yet. He's not too stupid. But why me?"

"Well," the sergeant stood up, "because likely he thought that you know something that could incriminate him. Inspector Gray did his best, for your sake, to find out what it is. Personally, I think the shoes are a long shot. Maybe he thinks you saw something, since you were there shortly after midnight. It could be the place, or the time that is significant. But we'll find it." As he clumped toward the door, Gloria studied his back, thoughtfully. The boots, tough and thick, certainly added an inch or two to his height. Not that he needed it; he was tall, and large, like Stoker.

"Are you certain you're safe at home alone?" Linda asked as Gloria drained her cup and stood up. "Maybe you should come and stay with us."

"I certainly will if I have to. I'm not a hero, and I don't feel particularly safe just now." Gloria paid for her coffee and returned to the office with Rick's bagel.

First, she had to search for Glenn Hullett's phone number. It took her awhile to find it, since it had fallen off her bulletin board and had somehow become shuffled into the disorganized pile of notes on her desk.

Then she drove out to take a photo of a ribbon-cutting over the home plate of O'Dell's newest baseball diamond. She and Reeve Cootes exchanged looks, and she sized him up. Could he have been in her house Wednesday night? Did he know who was? Possibly. And in the background, serving coffee to the softball aficionados, were the two women from the general store, their heads together behind the table: "...and her daughter says he's been callin' every night since her husband died. Isn't that somethin'?"

"Heh!" the other big woman chortled. "Doesn't surprise me. The lout's always held a torch for Marie."

More gossip. And country coupling. Couldn't a widow of barely a week find any peace? Gloria shook her head.

She was back at the office less than an hour later. After three or four busy signals, a tape recorder informed her that Hullett Enterprises was closed Friday at noon, and would reopen Monday morning at eight thirty. She looked at her watch: quarter past eleven. Nice. Mr. Hullett's office liked to start the weekend early.

Mr. Murray's call came through while she was sifting through the accumulation of mail in the basket on the corner of her desk, and she briefly explained that the police merely needed her statement, and, unfortunately, several hours of her time. He seemed satisfied, and she breathed a deep sigh of relief.

By four, things were looking good. The crafts page was completed, and the day care picnic covered. A heady cry for funds for a children's playground downtown was launched, twenty government press releases sorted, and the weekend's work had been divided. Fred Russell, however, troubled her conscience. If he had noticed that she was there, he had not made any move to acknowledge her but remained closed off in his little glass cage. They had not talked, and she feared, from past experience, that he was up to something. Had he taken her threat of litigation seriously? She hoped not, but she had no great desire, at the moment, to offer any reassurance; he might take it as encouragement. Let him stew for awhile, she thought. His performance the previous night had been inexcusable, and his skills wooing women on a par with a high school senior.

She was walking through the back door from the Legion's groundbreaking ceremony, when Jan hurried to intercept her. "There's a strange man waiting to see you," she announced bluntly.

"How strange?" she asked, wondering if Jan ever bothered to ask for a name. Likely, she'd never had to.

"Well, he's not from around here. I don't know who he is. He's foreign, speaks with an accent, but a real gentleman."

Gloria felt her heart pitch into her sandals. "By 'gentleman,' you mean, not the police?"

"I mean, nicely dressed. But he's polite, if that's any help. He's upstairs."

"Upstairs? Oh, shit!" Gloria pushed her aside and hurtled toward the staircase. Polite? If not the police, who? The *Express*? No, they wouldn't be polite. Fred Russell's attorney? The axe-man from Heartland? She reached the top of the stairs and peeked around the corner. Standing beside her desk was a middle-aged, heavy-set man with thinning gray hair and an almost white mustache. He wore immaculately pressed baggy white pants held up by suspenders, beige jacket thrown casually over his shoulders, crisp white shirt with cuffs rolled backward exposing strong wrists and work-worn hands that held a wide-brimmed, panama hat. Well-dressed? Gentleman? Gloria laughed out loud. "Dad?"

Joe Trevisi's pie-round face softened into an affectionate grin. "Hi, pumpkin! How've you been?"

She bounded up the last two stairs and into his arms, squealing like a four-year-old.

***

To most people, Joe Trevisi did not look or sound particularly Italian. He spoke English in a soft, matter-of-fact voice with very little trace of old-country accents. He did not shout "Mama Mia!" or wave his hands about. His manners were not as smooth as Marlon Brando's, and he made no offers that one couldn't refuse.

He was a hard-working tradesman, short, barrel-shaped, with a rough face and bright, intelligent eyes. And like many Italian men, he had a flair for the dramatic, a fondness for good wine, and strong feelings for the women in his life, particularly his stubborn, thirty-something daughter who had taken so long to settle down and marry. As Gloria finished summing up the past week and watched him mop up the last of the salad dressing with a chunk of pizza crust, her heart nearly burst with gratitude that such a man was her true, rock-steady guiding light.

"And so," she said, folding the cardboard pizza container into a compact bundle and stuffing it into a garbage bag, "that's where the whole mess stands, right now. Whoever killed Clarence McKee is angry with me, and was even in my house. I want to know who it is."

Her father heaved a deep sigh and perched on the edge of the kitchen chair, a juice glass full of red wine in his hand. "I don't like it, *Tesoro*. I know it's pointless to suggest you come home," he frowned.

"And it's no use telling you to be careful." He rose, and walked to the side door, gazing out across the cornfield in the early evening. Max and Buffy, awake and well-fed, were sprawled on the porch steps. "This is beautiful, but it is very secluded. No one can hear you, no one can even see you."

"I know. Sometimes I feel quite alone here." She stood beside him. "Are you staying tonight? We haven't talked in ages, and I have a lot on my mind."

"That was my plan, but I didn't want to insist." He tilted his head toward the old Chrysler. "Your mother gave me a project." He stepped carefully over the cats and out to the car, sprang open the trunk and hauled out a paper bag full of curtain rods.

"Mother is relentless, isn't she? I'll find you a hammer and a screwdriver, and then I'll throw sheets on my lumpy old couch."

"You know me. I can sleep anywhere."

By nine thirty that evening, they had living room and bedroom windows decently, even attractively covered, and her father was ready to rest.

"Let's have some more wine, not that imported stuff you've been drinking. Here's some of your uncle Nino's from last year." He unearthed three bottles from an overnight bag that had appeared out of nowhere. "I came prepared. Good, homemade variety from hundred-percent fresh Niagara grapes." He filled the glasses she set out on the kitchen table, and clinked hers. He downed half of his in two gulps.

She sipped carefully. Years ago she used to try and match him, belt-for-belt; she learned her lesson. The clean, fruity flavor brought back a flood of good memories; foremost was the sharp reminder, as she swallowed the liquid and felt it slide smoothly and delicately down her throat, just how potent her uncle's wine could be.

Her father glanced at the envelope that had been sitting by the door ever since he had arrived. "Do you have work to do?"

"Not really. That's a photograph of the funeral of Clarence McKee, the man who was murdered. I wanted to get a closer look at the people. The relationships are very complicated around here," she began to explain.

"You don't need to tell me about complicated relationships. I'm from a tiny village, remember, and a lot of the people whose families had lived there for hundreds of years emigrated all over the world." He made a wide sweeping gesture with his arm. "But if all those people who have left it were to return, that little village would be the size of Rome. And everyone would be related. Let's see." He held out his hand. She hesitated only a second, then took the photograph from the envelope, with Norma Simmons's notes, and passed it over to him. He put it on the table and studied it. "Yes, as I thought," he said. "Look at the family resemblance here. This man," he pointed to Glenn Hullett, "and this woman here." He indicated a middle-aged woman in black, standing beside the coffin.

Gloria glanced at the notes. "Dad, that's the widow, Marie McKee. Glenn Hullett is actually related to Hazel McDaniel."

"Yes, and a few more people besides, isn't he? A small village, indeed. How about this one?" He indicated a homely girl in a subdued flowered print dress, standing at the top of the steps.

"According to Norma, that's...Gladys McKee, the daughter. Christ almighty, I think I would have hated a father who gave me a name like that!" She caught her father's frown, and had a sudden recollection of her older brother reeling from a smart slap to the side of the head for taking the Lord's name in vain.

"Perhaps she did," he replied quietly, then looked back at the picture. "A frightful name, but perhaps a family name from the other side of the family. And a face too, no doubt. She doesn't look at all like her mother. I'd say she looks a bit like...." He pointed to a dark-suited gentleman standing to one side, talking with the funeral director. "Is he an uncle, or someone?"

"No, that's Joe Cameron. Of course, he's old enough to be her uncle, or her father, even, I suppose."

Joe Trevisi raised his eyebrows and glanced at Gloria. "And this one standing here?"

"I know him. George Fuller, the township clerk. Not a nice guy."

"And next to him, that looks like his son."

Gloria looked again at the notes. The name registered. "Interesting. His wife presented a petition against Joe Cameron's timber-finishing business. Dad, this is amazing. Ben Cootes hinted a relationship between the Poultons and Clarence McKee through their wives, but not a relationship to George Fuller. What an incestuous little gang that council is! I wonder..."

"Nothing amazing about it. Keep a bunch of families in one area long enough, and they'll all be related. And blood will always be thicker than water." Joe Trevisi sat back, and placed the photograph carefully on the table where Gloria could view it.

She sat still, silently fingering her empty wine glass and looking at the photograph, the casket in the center, the people gathered around it as though posed for a portrait. Hazel McDaniel was there, with a very puffy-faced, obese man who was probably her husband. Even in shirt, tie, and trousers, he was obviously very fat, and likely unsteady on his legs. Mrs. McDaniel, beside him, was hunched over and propped on her cane, her face set in a disapproving frown as she stared across the casket at Joe Cameron. A few other familiar people were milling about, including Plattsford's newest business accountant. What was his connection, Gloria wondered, besides unsatisfied customer? Or did he happen to be walking by?

Her father looked up from the photograph. "In our village, Gloria, people fought with their neighbors, families feuded with other families, and when they had no grievances with others, they fought among themselves." He drained his glass, and gazed at the bottom. "They fight over property, business, someone's wife or daughter. Love and money. Always the same thing." His eyes were serious and sad. "The way I see it, this isn't a crime of convenience, to get rid of a business partner who is a liability to everyone. This is a crime of passion."

"How do you see that?" Gloria was curious. She watched as her father slowly shifted toward the bottle and poured them each more wine. She didn't refuse, even though she was already feeling its effects.

Once he was settled, glass in hand, he looked up. "Well, to kill someone with barbiturates, that's a crime of convenience. Get someone to drink a bottle full of laced liquor, then quietly slip out of the way and let the poison do its work. Poison is supposed to be a woman's weapon. I don't know about that." He looked at the picture. "But a person who would return later, carry the body to a place where it can be demolished by a bulldozer, and then perhaps even run over it himself, is a person who is very, very angry, don't you think?"

"Yes, I see your point." She studied the face of Marie McKee in the photograph, and recalled the pale, baggy-eyed countenance she had viewed yesterday at the bank. Angry?

"So love, or sex, and money are the two most volatile subjects in any partnership, whether you're in a business or a marriage—how is your marriage, by the way?"

"The money is manageable and the sex is great, when he's home." Gloria swallowed more of the potent wine. *My God,* she thought, suppressing an urge to giggle. *Did I just tell my father that I'm having sex?*

"Glad to hear it. I promised your mother I would touch on the subject, so consider it touched. Where was I?"

"Sex, money, marriage, and business."

"So who has the most to risk? Not the business partner, although he has a lot of money tied up in this. Or certainly that's not his motive. And he wouldn't destroy someone so completely. That is a hot, emotional response, not a cool, businesslike one. Check out the relatives. There are plenty of them, and they're hiding something."

Gloria drained her glass and picked up the picture. Her father refilled the two wineglasses while she studied the people in the photograph as closely as her father had. "Now that you point it out, it looks to me as though they're all related. Makes for a lot of confusion, doesn't it? What if someone were to wind up marrying one's cousin?" She snickered. "That's one problem I don't have."

Her father growled. "*Tesoro,* if you had married your own kind, you may have been faced with a distant cousin, but you at least wouldn't have been deserted at the altar by a husband who loves his job more than he loves his wife." Trevisi heaved a deep sigh. "But there is no reasoning with you, is there?"

"All the nice Italian boys over twenty are already married, with children," Gloria reasoned, sipping the fresh glass of wine. "Don't worry, Dad, I'll catch up to all my school friends in no time. Tony might not be around much, but when he is...." She giggled. "Sorry. It's the wine talking. I haven't had much lately. Wine, I mean. Or...."

"Enough said." Trevisi took a large swallow from his glass.

She followed suit, taking another strong gulp. "Dad, were you ever in the Mafia?"

He smiled. "Where we come from, there's no such thing. The people from our village who came to Canada earned their money the hard way, working for minimum wage in ditches, foundries, and restaurant kitchens, sending money back to help their families who were still in Italy. They saved until they could afford what they needed, then later, what they wanted. There was no short cut. They were well off when they died, but they didn't enjoy it much. Those people did it all for their children." He took another long gulp of wine. "Your great uncle, *Zio Pietro,* sponsored me to come here when I was barely nineteen. I had a trade, but I didn't know English. He got me my first job in the foundry so I could learn. And when I could afford it, I brought your grandmother to stay for awhile."

"I remember Nonna Trevisi," she recalled, the hazy face of her grandmother coming to mind. Her father's face was slightly out of focus, as well. "You told me once that she made some tremendous sacrifices for her family."

"Even in a small village like ours, life was a dog-eat-dog existence." His eyes were slightly misty. "And people who had the upper hand never let you forget it, from one generation to the next. Your grandmother had an iron will and great courage, and an enormous heart. And a temper. You remind me a lot of her, you know." He drank more wine.

She watched him for a moment, then quickly finished her glass, and set it on the table with a thump. "Sex and money is possible. But what about family honor?"

"What about it? A poor marriage, an illegitimate child, or the loss of an inheritance, these things involve honor. They also involve—"

"Okay, I see your point. And I agree: this is not a cold-blooded murder; it's a hot-blooded one. But family honor isn't just an Italian thing. A crime of passion, you suggest?" she mused. "A wife or a mistress? Evidently, he had both."

"Too obvious, don't you think? And always the first suspect." Joe sipped more wine. "Or a hidden hate, one that no one shows to the neighbors."

"It would have to be well hidden. People who have lived here for generations probably know a lot more than the police, or anyone. They're probably adding up the circumstances, considering family histories, and coming up with some very accurate guesses. I've been dismissing gossip, but I should pay more attention to it." Gloria blinked. Her head was fuzzy. "Dad, I haven't had a lot of sleep lately. Maybe some fresh air will help clear my head a bit. Let's go for a walk."

"As you wish." He finished off his glass, rose, and offered his arm to Gloria, who took it gratefully as the porch steps wobbled beneath her unsteady tread. They were partway down the lane, arm-in-arm and picking their way carefully on such a dark night, when they saw a vehicle approaching slowly up the road. Trevisi watched with interest. "Is this trouble?"

"God I hope not. I'm in no shape to meet it," Gloria said, standing a trifle off-balance in the middle of the lane. A light-colored pickup truck drifted lazily along the sideroad, slowed near the top of the drive, and continued slowly by. A few yards from the bottom of the lane, the engine roared and the truck sped up quickly, a cloud of road dust forming haloes around its dim taillights.

Another car was coming from the opposite direction. After the truck passed it and disappeared, it too slowed; and as it passed the end of the lane, Gloria could just make out the dark, horizontal stripe and the crest on the door. She sent a silent message of gratitude to Constable Brian Stoker, champion of the innocent, though not usually the inebriated. Leaning heavily against her father, she murmured, "I think we'd better go in now. Not only am I sleep-deprived, but I'm quite sloshed."

Indeed, she felt quite a comfortable buzz in her head, she noted as they turned back toward the well-lighted veranda. But not so comfortable that she failed to notice the look on her father's face as he glanced back over his shoulder at the dark, deserted road.

***

Gloria opened her eyes, and closed them again quickly. A shaft of light from the early sun was shining with blinding brightness through a crack in the newly hung bedroom curtains. She was sprawled in a nightgown that she didn't remember putting on, across a tangled heap of sheets and pillows. Her bedside clock read six.

Rolling slowly out of bed to find her slippers, she stared with dismay at an untidy array of clothing scattered on the floor. Her entire bedroom was, at the moment, a disaster. Had her house been ransacked once again? Or was that where she had dropped her clothes the previous night, and the night before that? With a deep sigh, she gathered up the well-worn array of loose socks, last weekend's shorts, jerseys, blouses, and underwear, carried it across the hall and stuffed it into a brimming bathroom hamper. Tomorrow, she decided, had better be a laundry day.

She doused her face several times to wake up, drank three glasses of water straight from the bathroom tap, then decided a shower and a shampoo might be wise. Twenty minutes later she slouched downstairs in Tony's RCM sweatshirt and her old track pants. Her father was lying on the couch, wearing undershirt and boxers, comforter untidily thrown partway over, snoring gently with Max at his feet. How intoxicated had she been, not to pull out the couch and make up a proper bed for him? Washed in guilt, and cursing her upset stomach, she edged closer. Her quick inspection of his overnight bag revealed change of underwear, razor, and pajamas seldom worn but nevertheless packed by her mother for decency's sake. She replaced the comforter that was half on the floor, blew him an affectionate kiss, and tiptoed into the kitchen to make coffee. God, she needed it.

She was halfway through her first mug when her father stirred from the couch. Pulling on his pants, he ambled lazily into the kitchen where Buffy and Max were munching down their breakfast. Gazing down at the two cats in mock disgruntlement, he grumbled hoarsely, "These two got me up at four in the morning, scratching to come in."

"I'm amazed you heard them," she noted. "I think a pride of lions could have ripped the door off, and I'd never have noticed." She glanced at the clock. "I remember talking your ear off until after midnight, but I don't recall what I said."

"Well, you told me what I wanted to hear. Didn't you want to sleep in?" He squinted at the clock on the kitchen wall. "It's only seven."

"I haven't slept in since I was sixteen."

Growling softly, he thumped heavily toward the stairs. Ten minutes later he was more presentable, his wet hair brushed back from his round face, and a mug of coffee in his hands. He looked about. "This isn't a bad place, you know."

"Dad, it's just a rented farmhouse. I don't even know if it has decent insulation, and every now and then a bat falls down the chimney and has to be rescued from the furnace."

"Don't apologize for a rented house. You should have seen some of the places we lived in before we bought our first house. In fact," he sipped his coffee, "you should have seen that place. This one's a palace in comparison."

"You mean Nonna Trevisi didn't set you up?" She remembered her grandmother's formidable personality. Few had the nerve to cross her.

"She wanted to, but your mother wouldn't hear of it. She preferred to sit on her pumpkin and have it all to herself, if you know what I mean."

"...'Than be crowded on a velvet cushion.' I remember my Thoreau. Yes, I imagine she wanted to make her own way, and owe no one, even if it meant having less for awhile." She gazed, smiling, at the placemat in front of her. "It doesn't seem right to start with everything, does it? Do you think I'm *too* independent?"

"Probably. But it's not such a bad thing." He gave her arm a squeeze. "I handed all the money matters over to her so I'd never have to worry, because I knew she would see us through anything. She did too. Don't be afraid to take the reins when you have to, sweetheart. I think you have your mother's good sense, and even a man who has plenty of cash needs a wife with good sense to manage it." He leaned toward her, elbows on the table. "*Tesoro*, your trouble isn't independence, or stubbornness; it is loneliness. You do not see enough of your husband to be happy."

She shook her head, and slowly sipped her coffee. "When we are together, Dad, we're very happy! You'll see. Tony is playing a short concert in Waterloo this afternoon, and I hope you'll come with me. It's on your way home, after all."

"Certainly I can. I would like to have a talk with him."

"First, I have a lawn-bowling tournament to photograph. It shouldn't take me long, though. Then we can dress and head to the city for lunch, if I can find something to wear that isn't mud or blood-spattered."

"I can set those front flower beds to rights while you're gone."

"You can relax. Don't get yourself all grubby. You don't have a change of clothes. I do." She poured them more coffee. "I'm glad you came, Dad. But why? Cambridge isn't exactly around the corner."

"I was worried about you. There's only one way to find out what's going on in my daughter's life: pay her a visit. And, of course, bring wine." He smiled.

"*In vino veritas?*" She grinned. "And just what did you find out?"

"That you seem all right. Otherwise you wouldn't be interested in someone else's problems, would you? Don't meddle, pumpkin. This place is like a little village. You could be in more danger than you know."

Chapter 8

"I think you've inspired me," Gloria remarked, sipping juice with a plump, dark-haired pianist swathed in light gray satin. "When I was younger, I could not really appreciate a Nocturne or Polonaise by Chopin until I had learned to play it myself. But I've never played a Schubert piano quintet with strings. This would be a real challenge."

The pianist smiled warmly. "No doubt you'd enjoy it immensely, but I would suggest you just accompany a single violin first." The woman's eyes traveled around the room to where Tony stood, deep in conversation with Gloria's father. "I think you two would play a beautiful duet."

Gloria shook her head. "I haven't practised or played in years, and Tony is so good, it would be hell for him." She glanced at Tony with a touch of pride. "I love to listen to him. Sometimes I imagine he plays just for me, and I wonder if everyone in the audience feels that way."

"Tony has become an intuitive performer in the last few years. It could be why the audiences on the east coast are so enthralled with chamber music."

"Perhaps. Chamber music is special, isn't it? Whether it's Mozart or Walton, there is something beautiful about the interweave of the voices of four instruments; the harmony and the counterpoint are all there in structure, yet it seems to be so...instinctive."

"There is a very cozy and personal feeling communicated through chamber music that one does not feel with a full orchestra. When you are one of sixteen first violins, your individuality is drowned out. In a string quartet, there is only one first violin, and one second. Each musician represents a distinct voice." She caught the eye of the second violin. "Through the music you exchange your ideas and feelings with your fellow musicians and with the audience. It's like having a very intimate, personal conversation."

Gloria beamed. "Intimate. That's what makes it so appealing. And speaking of appealing, your new cellist seems to be fitting in well."

"Yes, and she fits into that gown a little too well," the pianist observed with a twitch of her eyebrow. The cellist was dressed in fetching black with a plunging neckline that left little to the imagination, certainly when she was sawing her way diligently and enthusiastically through Schubert. "Our viola player gets distracted at times. It's a shame *he's* not playing cello. At least if he were, he could hide behind something. You, however, have nothing to worry about, I assure you," she said with a mischievous wink. "Tony is not interested in playing that kind of duet with a cellist, not that she hasn't given it her best effort."

Gloria snorted. She liked this woman. "And I thought small towns were bad for gossip and intrigue. Small orchestras are worse."

"Try the symphony. It's *big* trouble," the pianist said, laughing. "My husband played in one for ten years while our children were young. But enough of the bad news. Your wedding, incidentally, was the nicest I have attended in awhile: the best music, best food, certainly best party. Your family knows how to have a good time."

"I'm glad you enjoyed it. I'm afraid it was a bit of a blur to me. We'll talk again, I'm sure," she said, excusing herself and making her way toward Tony. "Your pianist—I forgot to ask her name, but evidently she was at our wedding—tells me the new cello player is doing just fine."

"Yeah. What we need now is a viola player who can keep his mind off the new cellist." Tony grimaced. "And you thought you were the only one with problems at work." A bell sounded, and the audience began drifting back to the small auditorium. "You look tired. Is everything all right up there?"

"What do you expect?" Gloria whispered, leaning against him briefly and sniffing the musky aroma of his tux. "Dad brought some wine with him, and you know how alcohol affects my sleep."

"I know how your father affects your consumption of alcohol. I'll bet you and your dad stayed up half the night and tied one on, didn't you?" He grinned, placing his finger on her lips. She bit it, winked, turned, and walked back to her father.

The rest of the concert went without a hitch, so to speak. When Tony had changed and joined them, Joe Trevisi made his departure.

"Do you realize that my parents adore you?" Gloria remarked as she watched him pull out of the parking lot. "And your parents can't stand me? It means if anything goes wrong between us, it certainly won't ever be viewed as *your* fault." She climbed into Tony's Buick and settled into the comfortable seat.

"I don't know about that. I'm never completely sure of your father," he said. "But my parents like you. At least, I know my father does."

"When I was stuck at that police station for seven hours, I thought of your dad, and wondered whether he would help me out of a mess like that."

"He'd be there in the blink of an eye. I'm only sorry that *I* didn't know where you were."

"*You* thought I was partying with my impossible boss."

"Don't remind me."

"Remind you? I should knock your block off." She leaned her head back and closed her eyes, drifting.

"You're quiet." His voice interrupted a reverie. "And you're smiling. What were you thinking?"

She had been thinking about how well Tony filled out a tux. "I was thinking that when we settle down,

I'd like a piano. Does that terrific pianist tour with you?"

"Charlotte Gatsby? Yes, and so does her husband. He's our second violin, substituting occasionally for first. I've known them for years. Nice couple, with two teenagers in private school."

"She thinks that with a bit of practice on my part, you and I could play well together."

"We *do* play well together, but if you feel you need more practice....." His hand groped for her thigh. She slapped it. "Okay, later."

"Later." She touched his knee gently. "And I need some quiet time with you before you go away...you know. Sit on the porch and watch the sun set, hold hands, take a bubble bath, whatever...oh, damn!"

"What now?"

"The landlord was going to rent a backhoe today to try and repair the septic bed himself. I hope we can still use the bathroom."

A half hour later they were staring at a massive, smelly hole outside the dining room window, and an ugly, yellow contraption squatting beside it.

"Ugh! I think I liked it better when the sink backed up." Gloria's eyes watered. She groped in her handbag for a Kleenex while Tony covered his nose with a handkerchief. "Here's another dress I won't be wearing until it's been dry cleaned."

Later in the evening, lured by a spectacular sunset, they sat on the porch sipping homemade wine and stubbornly ignoring the lingering odor that drifted from the other side of the house. She noted his silence. "I know I mentioned quiet time, but this is a bit quieter than I meant."

"The day after tomorrow, we fly to the east coast for the summer. If you were living in the city, I would be able to fly back and see you more often. Out here, well, you're two hours and some out of Toronto. How long is this job going to last?" Tony watched Buffy stalk a hapless grasshopper.

"Indefinitely. Mr. Murray asked me if I could stay." She stood up and stretched, and walked to the veranda steps.

"Do you really want to stay here? It's just...I don't like the idea of your being alone. Neither does your father. It's isolated."

She leaned back against the post, facing him. "Fred Russell offered to keep me company, you know."

"I'll punch his lights out. He already gets to spend every day with you, and I don't."

"Don't blame him for that. I wonder if Ed Murray knows about this latest conflict." She grinned at the thought of Theresa and Jan spreading the news faster than mayonnaise on buttered bread. "I'll have to deal with that on Monday, among other things, such as updating this whole fiasco at the industrial park. And judging by all that has happened since, I wonder if the approach we've taken is all wrong."

"Why? The police tell you something that's printable, you print it. Isn't that your job?"

"You make it sound like taking dictation." She squirmed to her feet. "And that's the way I've approached it, so far, and look where it's left me: almost in jail. There's more to it than that. It's follow-up, fresh angles—"

"Why make the effort? It's only a weekly newspaper."

"Exactly. And we want to cover more ground than a radio station can give you in a thirty-second news spot; it's the only advantage we have. Last week's paper nearly sold out of copies because everyone wanted to read about this, even though they had been hearing about it and gossiping about it among themselves for a week. So we have to come up with something more in-depth to add perspective to the whole thing." She joined him again on the bench where she could lean cozily against him, and sipped her wine. The evening was warm.

"What other angles are there to cover?"

"All the little waves in the pond, people who are affected in some way by the absence of Mr. McKee. Dad thinks there is a strong emotional aspect to this murder," she continued. "Maybe that's just the hot Italian in his nature, but I know that murder is often a crime of passion, committed by a person close to the victim. A close, personal killer means someone local, someone everyone knows. And I know that this community would rather go into complete denial and blame it on a random act of violence by some outsider than pinpoint one of its own. After all, it's not polite to accuse one's neighbor of murder."

"It's not manners, Gloria. It's fear."

"Okay. You're right, so now I wonder. He wasn't a particularly nice guy on any level, neither personally, politically, nor in his business dealings. He could have scads of enemies, even in his own family. It's amazing what kind of personal resentments can be harbored for years, especially in a tight little place such as this, where people don't forget. You can't leave your troubles behind; someone is always ready to remind you of past mistakes and failures."

"Are you thinking someone doped him up and ran him over for a personal slight?"

"It sounds more likely than having someone run a bulldozer over him for money. According to gossip, he had a mistress, and his wife barely spoke to him. People have hinted he wasn't nice to her. I've seen Mrs. McKee up close, and she looks...bruised, not physically, but emotionally."

"All that really interests me is, why does it involve you? And last week, it certainly involved you."

"I'm damned if I can figure that one out. I don't think that having blood on my shoes has a thing to do with it, other than giving Inspector Gray a reason to hector me. It has to be something else, something I would have seen from the place I was standing, or passed while I was driving over there. Whatever it is, I can't put my finger on it."

"Don't try. It's dangerous."

She laughed, and squeezed his knee. "I'm speculating, not snooping. I'm not an investigative reporter. But when someone leaves a murder weapon on my counter, I get a mite curious. Wouldn't you?"

"I'm very curious. But my motives have more to do with your safety than anything else."

She turned to him. "I won't do anything stupid, since that is really what you want to say, isn't it?" *Don't be afraid to take the reins,* her father had said. She took a deep breath, and stretched her toes out in front of her. "Tony, can we go to mass tomorrow?"

"Mass? You mean, church?" He looked at her, puzzled.

The good Catholic girl regarded him with a touch of exasperation. "If you prefer, I'll go alone, the way I always did before we were married."

The lapsed Anglican squirmed uncomfortably. "The hell you will."

"It's not that bad, you know." She tugged on his arm, and the two rose and as evening deepened, stepped inside.

A few miles away, O'Dell Township's most recent and best-known widow was contemplating *her* dresses, particularly one of bright cornflower blue, wondering if it was too bright to wear to a Sunday service, her first public appearance since her murdered husband had been buried less than a week before. Would people talk? Did she care?

***

Monday morning just after dawn they were saying good-bye, Gloria trying to be brave and cheerful, Tony looking apprehensive.

"Don't worry," she assured him. "Things will be fine and I'll be very careful. And wasn't it nice to meet Brian Stoker and his family yesterday at church? I think his boys are beautiful."

"If he's the local night constable, I just hope he lives closer to us than that church is," Tony remarked, putting his suitcase in the trunk of the car and setting his violin carefully on the floor of the back seat. "It's certainly a long way to drive for a Sunday service."

"It was worth it. Seeing Constable Stoker there makes me feel a bit less, well, foreign. He knows I'm worried about being alone, and he says he'll look out for me." She was suddenly silent.

"I'll call every night," Tony promised, putting his arms around her. "If I don't get an answer by midnight," he warned, "I'll call the police."

"What if I decide to stay with Linda?" She raised one eyebrow. "Or maybe Fred Russell?"

"Don't be funny. If you go somewhere else, and I hope you do, leave a message with the symphony office. They'll relay it to me, wherever I am."

She hated long good-byes. She hugged him fiercely. "Take care of yourself. Maybe I'll be able to take a holiday later in the summer and visit you."

"Try. Mmmm. Don't hug me like that or I'll have to stay at least another ten minutes."

"Only ten? It's hardly worth it." She smiled. One last kiss, after that he was in the car, driving away and she was waving him off, and wondering what their future would bring. She was becoming defensive about her choice of job, her preference for this old, worn-out house. Tony was used to more comfortable surroundings. He didn't belong here; she did. Were they facing some major adjustments ahead? It would be so much easier if he were to stay around for awhile, so they could get used to each other again. Next time he returned after a few months of touring and performing, he would be changed even more. She retreated to the house for her five-minute cry.

* * *

It was a few minutes before Fred Russell looked up from the letter that seemed to consume all his attention. Gloria sat by the desk, waiting patiently, even politely, as reluctant to begin this conversation as he was.

"We have to discuss this sooner or later, Fred Russell. The Conservation Authority meets at ten. If I can get out by noon, and pick up the library board minutes on my way back, we could get away for a one-o'clock lunch. Would you prefer Gina's or can we just get something across the street?"

He slouched in his chair, looking just a little sulky. "Do you think it's wise? My lawyer would advise me to avoid you."

"No kidding? My husband advises me to talk to you. But if you care to bring your lawyer to lunch, I'll bring mine." She leaned forward, placing her elbows on his desk. "I like my job, and I'm certain you like yours too. So let's hash this one out between us." She stood up. "One o'clock? You've been angling to have lunch with me for ages, but don't think for a moment that this is a date."

He looked resentful, and wary. "I'll think about it."

"Please, Mr. Russell, do more than that. My future here depends on us getting along, and as far as I'm concerned, so does yours. If it comes down to fighting, I'm more than ready."

"I'm not." He stared at the letter in his hand. "In the past few months I've had enough fighting to last me forever."

"Then let's talk about it instead. Lunch?"

He heaved a deep sigh and looked up, a bit less sulkily. "Okay. And I'm sorry."

"So am I." She walked out.

Hazel McDaniel was waiting for Gloria downstairs, with her East Lister notes in hand. "You're in early," she remarked, looking over Gloria's casual walking shorts and sandals. Her gaze came to rest on her engagement ring.

"So are you, Mrs. McDaniel. What can I do for you?" She held her hand up to take the pages, and to give the woman a better view of the beautiful diamond.

"I have a write-up of poor Clarence's funeral here," she said crossly. "I hope, this time, it will be printed just like I wrote it."

Last week's news. "Thank you. Norma Simmons handles these things very carefully, Mrs. McDaniel," Gloria assured her. "She knows as well as I do that death is a sensitive issue in a small community like East Lister."

"That's right. Families have been here for four, five generations, some of them. They don't take kindly to strangers minding their business and telling them how to live."

"How long has your family been on your farm, or your husband's family?" Gloria inquired casually.

"The property came down from my side of the family," she said. "My mother was an only child, and she inherited it from my grandparents, then my brother died when he was very young and when the folks were gone, I inherited it." She stood as tall as she could and looked pleased. "We had one of the best dairy farms in the area, sixty head and two hundred acres under plough. Then my first husband died. For a few years, I ran most of the equipment myself," she added. "The children helped, of course, as did the hired hand in summer. But it was a great deal of heavy work. I finally got married again, to Elwood, when the children were still teenagers. But he wasn't handy with the animals, so I did most of the milking. Elwood worked in the fields, some, till his legs gave out. I was usually driving tractors during haying and driving the combine at harvest time."

And I'll bet you can run a backhoe and fix your own septic bed, Gloria thought. Jan was beckoning her to the telephone, and she had to cut their conversation short. Promising she would do her best with the funeral write-up, she watched the elderly correspondent hobble through the door, and returned upstairs to her desk. The woman must have worked like a Trojan to keep a farm like that going. It's no wonder she was in such bad shape now, walking stiffly with a cane. And if her mother had inherited the farm from her family, the farm was originally part of the Hullett landholding. Interesting. So if she was an only child, and her mother an only child, where did Glenn Hullett fit in? Gloria pondered the question while she collected the weekend fire reports.

***

With no "boss bagels" in sight, Gloria figured it would be safe to meet Russell at Bud's. At ten minutes past one, they were eating ham sandwiches and drinking iced coffee. "I wanted to speak to you, Mr. Russell, because I know we haven't had a good start to a working relationship," she said. "I also wanted to tell you that I'm aware of your personal problems, as you are no doubt aware of mine. I'm sorry."

Russell was eating silently. He sipped some coffee, and swallowed carefully. "I am too. I was only trying to help. So we can wipe the slate clean?"

"Promise me first that you will never, never hit on me again. I don't like it, and it makes it very difficult to work together under these circumstances."

"I promise. Your husband seems like a pretty decent sort." He grinned nervously.

"For someone with no brass?" Gloria's eyebrow twitched, and his face fell, slightly. "Very decent, apart from the fact he's never around. A hell of a boxer too. And promise that you will not interfere with *my* running of the news unless for some obscure reason your job dictates that you must, which is probably never?"

He smiled, brushing crumbs off his chin. "In other words, you want me off your turf."

"Exactly."

"Can you call me Fred, please? We must be friends now, or we wouldn't be talking at all. In fact, if you had complained about me—"

"I'm not that vindictive. And I think it's better if I stick to calling you mister, for the time being."

"Agreed. And what about the rest of this mess?"

"Shall we just forget it? There was no real harm done, you meant well, even with the *Express*, and—" Her eyes widened as she stared past him. "Keep your head down!"

"Keep my— Ow!" Russell's puzzled look dissolved in a painful gasp as Gloria's sandal dug into his shin.

"Sorry. George Fuller just walked in with Glenn Hullett, and they're looking pretty cozy." What had her father noticed in the funeral photo about Fuller?

"Interesting, for two people who were acting like strangers last week. They gave me the impression they didn't know each other, or at least, that they weren't buddies, but I'm sure other people around here know better. Did I kick you too hard? I didn't want them to notice us."

"Just call it assault, and now we're even," Russell replied, talking into his plate. "Why are you interested?"

"Well, call it research, but Joe Cameron's business has to move to what is now Glenn Hullett's industrial park because Clarence McKee's wife's niece or cousin circulated a petition among her neighbors, if you can follow that at all," Gloria said. "And I have a sneaking suspicion that there is also some family connection with George Fuller, the township clerk-treasurer. Possibly a nephew. It's complicated. I thought Clarence McKee was behind it, and that's what angered Mr. Cameron. But now I'm beginning to wonder." She watched them for a few seconds.

"What?"

"What came first? The industrial proposal, or the protest against Cameron Timber?"

"You're asking whether the industrial park was proposed to accommodate Cameron's business, or the protest engineered to benefit the industrial development? Hmmm." Russell squinted at the two men.

"Well, how would withdrawing that protest benefit the industrial development? Not much, so that can't be it." She saw Russell trying to hide a smile behind a large bite of his sandwich. "Well, surely if Hullett has all the money tied up in it, he wants to see the project through."

"He may, yet, unless his whole scheme was to keep it from happening," Russell said, sneaking a look over Gloria's shoulder to where the two men had taken a booth. "Maybe he simply wanted control of that particular land parcel for his own reasons. Eat, Gloria. Don't stare."

"I'm not the one who keeps ducking behind a bagel," she intoned. "Well, it does back on to property that once belonged to his family, and still might. Who knows? Perhaps his intention all along, in becoming a partner and investing the money, was to stop it from happening. Does that make sense? Of course, in O'Dell, anything is possible. Mr. Russell, you're still ducking your head. For heaven's sake, try to look natural. People are going to wonder." She bit off a large mouthful of sandwich.

"Don't worry. They'll just think I'm embarrassed to be seen in here," he replied, glancing at a couple of merchants in the next booth. They looked up, saw him looking, and ducked their heads together. "See? No one even notices we're watching Fuller."

Gloria snickered. "Sure. They're too busy talking about us! Let's just finish our lunch, shall we? I already tipped off the police to the petition last Thursday, not that they ever thanked me. Inspector Gray acted as though I was trying to divert their suspicion elsewhere. I have to wonder if he grew up around here."

"Why is that?"

"Because local police never want to hassle their old school buddies. That's what Linda says. It makes sense." She paused. "Mr. Russell, now that I've asked you to keep your mitts off my territory, I have a favor to ask."

"Anything."

"Could you check with Heartland's print division and see if they can loosen up my budget enough to hire a summer student? It would give both Rick and me just a bit of free time this summer," she said. "I would like to get away to join Tony on the east coast for a few days. With a summer student to pick up the slack, we could manage."

"I'll see what I can do. It's about time they let me make some of my own decisions, anyway." Russell smiled.

"Thanks. Lunch is on me. Come on. I have a lot of writing to do before the Moms and Tots picnic in the Rotary Park."

She couldn't help but wonder about the meeting between the clerk and McKee's partner, as she and Russell returned across the street to the *Sun* office. She thought about what Sid had told her. Could McKee and Clerk George Fuller have been cooking up another underhanded deal when McKee was murdered?

Fuller knew all the township business and its needs, whether land expropriation, maintenance or construction, before the council did. He and McKee could have had a great thing going for years. After all, the entire rezoning of that land was suspect. What was in it for the township clerk? And could Fuller now be covering his bases by setting up the same agreement with the new industrial park owner? She would probably never know, and speculation, interesting as it was, would not fill this week's issue.

***

This was an off-week for most councils, so Gloria had to find more photos, news, and material for an editorial, from other sources. She pumped Sergeant O'Toole on the status of the investigation, to no avail. Unwilling to push him too far, she backed off.

"Any leads on the whereabouts of the second bulldozer?"

"Not really," he answered.

"Did you ever find out about the drugs?" she asked as a parting shot.

"No, but we're working on it. Good-bye, Ms. Trevisi."

Glenn Hullett's office still appeared to be closed, according to the answering tape. She tried Ben Cootes, to see if any news was pending on the status of the industrial park. "Has construction been resumed?"

"Not that I am aware," he said cautiously.

"Mr. Cootes, why was construction started only this summer? The place was rezoned and waiting more than a year ago."

"Guess Clarence was in no hurry."

"Did he have other prospects for industry that would be willing to move to the township?"

"I never spoke to him about it."

"When was Joe Cameron scheduled to move his plant? Had he made any moves to close his timber-finishing operation at Genoa?"

"You'd have to ask him."

"Doesn't the council know these things?"

"No."

"Thanks, Reeve Cootes. You've been a big help." Gloria waited until he had hung up before she slammed the phone down and cursed.

She wasn't looking forward to another interview with Joe Cameron, but obviously she couldn't avoid it. Grabbing her camera in hopes of a late news shot, she headed out the back door to the parking lot.

***

Joe Cameron ran his business out of two buildings that looked as though they had been there for at least a century. The front of the nearer building was whitewashed barnboard. An old feed sign swung and creaked from the peak of the roof, indicating it had once been the location of a farm supply store. The roof itself was new steel, and the new steel-reinforced doors on both buildings were the type with security windows. Two rottweilers were chained to the front of a nearby shack, regarding Gloria with certain hostility as she pulled up in front of the nearer shop.

Dust and noise aside, Cameron's neighbors had several good reasons to sign a petition protesting this operation, Gloria noted. "Just imagine having your six-year-old walk past this every morning to catch a school bus," she murmured as she gazed up the shady street. Most of the homes were old, with large trees overhanging the roofs. It would have been a peaceful place but for the noise of heavy machinery that could be heard in the rear of the timber-finishing plant. What had Ben Cootes told her? That the hamlet was populated largely by people who were city transplants, or at least, not locals? She could imagine the reaction of people from Kitchener, having moved to a quiet little backwater and finding a sawmill next door. It would not be difficult to stir up animosity against a business such as this one, even if the mill had been there first.

She tried the door of the shed marked "Office". It opened, and in its dark interior was a small room with two desks, one occupied by a tired-looking older woman in a cotton dress and rolled-down knee-highs. The other was vacant. The office had been well soundproofed; the scream of the equipment in the back shop was reduced to a persistent hum that reminded Gloria of the vibration of a dentist's drill.

"Excuse me. Is Mr. Cameron about?" She introduced herself.

The woman turned to her, looked her over, then pushed a button on an intercom. The noise feeding back was deafening. "Joe, there's a lady to see you."

"What?"

"I said, there's a *lady* from the paper in here!" the woman almost bellowed into the mouthpiece.

"What the...I'll be there in a few minutes." The blurry, raucous voice of Joe Cameron was recognizable. At least she had found the right place, Gloria thought. She was surprised when the woman rose and shambled over to the door. "Tell him I'll be back when you're done talkin'," she said over her shoulder as she departed. His mother? Gloria assumed she was. Her eyes had looked glazed over and trancelike. Perhaps a fifth of rye for breakfast?

The office smelled of garbage and stale cigarettes. The desks were littered with papers and coffee rings. Cardboard cups were evident in the waste baskets. Three clipboards hung on the wall over the vacant desk, with torn, stained pages of inventory, shipping notes, and production estimates, with hand-scribbled notes in the margins. Comparing it with her own cramped, cluttered, untidy workspace at the *Sun* office, Gloria found it dismal. Hers, at least, had a window, and a view.

She waited at least five minutes, and was about to give up when Cameron came in, his overalls dusty, his face covered with grease and sweat. "Sorry I took so long," he mumbled, and sat down heavily in the chair at the vacant desk. He didn't invite Gloria to sit, but merely peered up at her, looking tired. "We have a machine broke down in the back. Trying to fix it since yesterday so we can get a load out by tonight."

"I'll try not to keep you," Gloria said. "How long have you been running your shop here?"

"Three years, if it's any business of yours," he answered.

Hung over, or just grouchy, she wondered? "I'm sorry I didn't call ahead, but I was in the area and thought I'd save myself another trip out. Is there any word yet on when the new site will be ready for you?"

"Signed contracts with McKee last week. Haven't talked with this Hullett yet. Don't know if they've even started on the building I need."

"What will you do if the project is canceled?"

"Really don't know. Mebbe I won't hav'ta move at all. But let me tell you," he leaned forward, and his breath was even more repulsive without the malt, "there's somethin' pretty strange about the whole thing."

"Strange?" Gloria swallowed and raised her eyebrows.

"At one time I employed twenty people in this shop, twelve from the village here. Then they started quittin' on me. Then when I finally managed to find more staff that would work for me, and not just stand around, puttin' in their twenty weeks till they could collect pogey, I got more trouble. Someone broke my fence down, let my dogs out, and then my windows got busted as well. Next thing I know, the people got this petition saying that the saws and sanders are creating too much dust and noise for them." He wiped his mouth with his sleeve, licked his lips, and continued. "Someone had it in for me. And I know who it is."

"Do you? Who?" Gloria asked.

"It was Clarence McKee, the all-mighty township politician who had the clerk in his back pocket. Clarence, he could do whatever he wanted. And you people blew this whole thing outa proportion." He poked his finger toward Gloria's chest but stopped before he made contact. She stood her ground with an effort. "He prob'ly had *you* on his payroll too."

"This is the first I have heard of it, Mr. Cameron," she said quietly. *Move that finger one more inch, pal, and—*

"Listen. I'm tired of people trying to cause me trouble, with police crawlin' all over here accusin' me, just because I happened to be there Thursday at his shack to sign contracts. Maybe I got tired of him puttin' the screws to me too. God knows, his own wife couldn't stand him much."

"Mr. Cameron—"

His voice rose. "You have any idea what I was gonna hafta pay to lease that new building? About three times what I pay for this place. Oh, sure, it would've been a much bigger and better shop, as long as that snake wasn't paying the building inspectors to approve a shoddy job. I wouldn't put it past him."

He fumbled over the desk until he found a half-crushed pack of cigarettes, then patted his dirty pockets to locate a lighter. The dust flew everywhere, and Gloria had to hold her breath to keep from sneezing.

"He was tryin' to ruin me, y' know," he continued. "But look where he is now. I got the better of him in the end." He rose from his chair, and stepped around the desk toward her, unlit cigarette stuck between his fingers. No matter how hard he tried, he still had to look up to meet her gaze. "Now I think you'd better go, miss. Go back to that boss of yours that you're prob'ly screwin' around with, and tell him I ain't playin' along."

Gloria said nothing. She turned and left, closing the steel door behind her. *What an unpleasant customer!* What had he thought? She climbed into her car and pulled out of the yard, the dogs watching her silently. Was he threatening her? Did he think she was threatening him? Or was he a man who had watched his business suffer from one calamity after another for the past year, and was finally sick and tired of it? Was this his way of fighting back? She tried to make some sense of this brief interview, but she had taken no notes whatsoever.

Could he have poisoned McKee? Visited the construction site that evening with a bottle, and come back later with some heavy equipment? He was angry enough, certainly, to do something rash, and he had suspected that McKee was behind his problems. Was he certain, or had he simply guessed? And was Joe Cameron in her kitchen early last Thursday morning, crushing phenobarbital tablets to lace her orange juice? He certainly sounded as though he held a personal grudge against the newspaper. And he had said something about Clarence's wife. How well had he known Marie McKee? They likely had gone to school together, she reasoned. What had her father said while he was looking at that picture? He'd noted that Gladys, the oldest of the two McKee girls, looked more like Joe Cameron than she did her mother. Was Joe related to Marie? She needed to talk to someone knowledgeable to sort this out.

But first, there was a paper that needed filling. And here, on the side of the road, was a park full of children on swings and slides, another photo opportunity.

***

"Sure, I knew Marie in high school," Norma Simmons recalled. "She was a beautiful, intelligent girl from a good farming family. We all thought she was destined for college, or nursing school, or something. She even won a scholarship to the college of her choice in the county fair when she won the corn princess competition. And then it all ended."

Gloria sipped tea at Norma's big harvest table. It was after six, the end of a long day. She hadn't had a bite to eat since her lunch with Russell, but Norma's family had finished supper and were doing evening chores when she stopped in, carrying some pictures from Saturday's strawberry social, to which she had sent Rick for photos. She needed names, she told Norma, praying she wouldn't repeat it to Rick, who had diligently filed all the photo captions complete with names that morning.

"What happened to Marie?" she asked, trying to keep her mind off the lingering meat-and-potatoes aroma of the cozy farm kitchen.

"What usually happens? She got pregnant, and had to get married, as they say. They left the wedding rather late, had the baby only three months later. Some people said Clarence was reluctant to do the right thing by her. Perhaps he wasn't all that fond of her, after all."

"Had they dated in high school?"

"Yes, they were pretty thick right up through to their senior year. Then they broke it off for a bit, gave each other some space, I suppose, and she kept to herself for awhile, didn't hang around with the old crowd. That was after she won at the fair, and some said she was getting a bit big for her boots. But she and Clarence still saw each other occasionally. It was what her parents wanted," Norma explained.

"Her parents?"

"They farmed near Genoa. Eakins. Marie Eakins. Her mother was a Connor. They went to the same church as the McKees," Norma recalled. "I believe Marie stays on the family farm quite often now."

"What about her oldest daughter, Gladys?"

"Gladys never married. She was always a frail girl, never did well in school either. She had poor health, missed a lot. She still lives with her parents, or at least her mother. Has a part-time job bookkeeping for a feed mill."

"So Marie McKee certainly has a lot on her shoulders. Does she come from a big family? Does she have siblings in the area who can help her out?"

"A brother, running the family farm, I know. As a matter of fact," Norma scratched her head, "I think her sister, or a close relative of some sort, married one of the Fuller boys."

"So Marie is related to the Fullers by marriage, plus Janice, her niece, is also married to a Fuller relative."

Norma looked at her in surprise. "Yes, the clerk's nephew. George Fuller's sister's son. The sister lives in the city, but they live in Genoa. How did you know?"

Gloria smiled. "My dad. Never mind." With all the intermarriage going on among five leading O'Dell families, the gene pool must be the size of a shot glass, she surmised as she finished her tea. "I guess one can't say anything bad about anyone in this whole county without a relative hearing it and relaying it back," she said, standing up.

"It keeps us polite."

And all the rattling skeletons firmly in the family closets, Gloria added to herself as the thanked Norma and left. She hadn't been home yet, and the cats needed tending to. Besides, she thought, Tony might phone and wonder where she was. What time was it in Halifax, anyway? she wondered as she drove toward home.

She had told no one of her meeting with Cameron. It was just too bizarre, and somewhat frightening. She felt sorry for him, but perhaps he was getting his just desserts, according to...whom? Glenn Hullett? George Fuller? Someone was pulling the strings now. Was Cameron a murderer, or a victim?

As she pulled into her driveway, she tried to recall anything she could about her intruder of last Thursday morning. Could there have been more than one person? No, she was quite certain it was just one. Was it a large shadow? A thick, stocky one? A heavy footfall? There was the hint of an odor of liquor, she recalled, an impression rather than a direct gust of malt-breath. And that could have been anyone, even Marie McKee, if gossip were accurate. Max was seated patiently by the side door as she pulled up. "You saw him," she said to the cat as she unlocked her door. "Who was it?"

Max marched silently to his dish.

The phone rang as she was spooning out cat food. "You're home, finally," Tony said as she picked it up. "Is everything all right?"

Should she tell him? "Everything is not all right. It's damn boring. No news fit to print."

"That's the way I like it."

"Only when you're not here," she said, holding the cordless phone to her ear as she searched her refrigerator for a snack. Having spent the last half-hour smelling Norma's supper, she was famished. Either she would bite into some bread and cheese quickly, or eat the telephone with Tony on the other end. They talked for a few minutes, and hung up.

She found some soft Friulano cheese and cut off a thick wedge. Then she spotted her uncle's wine sitting, chilled and ready, on the top shelf. She poured herself half a glass, and held it up to the setting sunlight streaming through the west window. It was nearly opaque. "Why not?" she said and took a long swallow. It tasted comforting, like home. She picked up the phone and dialed her parents, assured her mother that the curtains fit perfectly, had a cozy conversation, did a spot of vacuuming and cobweb-dusting, and went to bed, wrapping herself around Tony's pillow.

She slept soundly; so soundly that she didn't hear someone knock her mailbox off its new post and flatten it by hitting it repeatedly with a heavy tire iron.

In fact, she wouldn't have heard them if they had used a road grader.

Her mailbox wasn't the only victim of the night. At five the next morning, Joe Cameron's body was found in a pile of sawdust behind his factory. By eight, Marie McKee, Clarence McKee's widow, had been arrested.

Chapter 9

"I knew there would be a story in there somewhere, but this was definitely *not* the one I expected," Gloria said to Sergeant O'Toole on the telephone.

"Believe it. This one was obvious, the evidence conclusive. The man was struck a blow to the head by someone wielding a heavy tool. Victim's blood was later found on one of Mrs. McKee's shoes."

That was what they called conclusive? No doubt Inspector Gray considered it so, she thought. "How was this body discovered?"

"Anonymous tip."

"And how did you end up checking on Mrs. McKee?"

"Anonymous tip." Again.

"What kind of anonymous tip, Sergeant? An employee? A neighbor? A family member?"

"A-nonymous," O'Toole repeated. Gloria sighed.

"Did Constable Stoker have the honors again?"

"No, it was his night off. Sheila Miller got this detail."

Gloria hoped that Constable Miller's stomach was stronger than hers. The mental image of Joe Cameron, lying in the sawdust with his skull bashed in, was not a happy one, nasty though he had been when he was alive. "Are you investigating the possibility that Mrs. McKee committed both murders?"

"We're looking into the possibility, yes," O'Toole answered.

Gloria couldn't help but hope Marie McKee had a damn good lawyer. Perhaps she could suggest one. O'Toole was about to sign off, and she had one more matter to discuss with him.

"Sergeant, what do you do about vandalism? Someone destroyed my new mailbox last night."

The sergeant grunted. "It's a rural pastime. Maybe you pissed someone off with an editorial."

"In other words, you don't care."

"In other words, Ms. Trevisi, it isn't a priority at the moment. Sometimes we get reports of twenty mailboxes downed in one night. We do what we can, but unless some kid squeals on his pals for a cash reward, we usually come up empty-handed."

As she hung up the phone, Russell came around the corner. "Is it true? Was it the wife?"

"The police might think so. Certainly everyone else does. It's not for me to say," Gloria added. "But at least we have news." She punched up her computer screen and started typing.

"I guess you don't have to worry about being alone at night any more." He sounded almost disappointed.

"I guess no one *else* has to worry about me, anyway," Gloria noted, not taking her eyes off the computer screen. He tiptoed away. She tried to pull the threads together in her mind: George Fuller, his nephew, his nephew's wife, Marie McKee, Joe Cameron, Clarence, and Glenn Hullett. And who else? All in one neat little bundle? No, not quite. She kept writing, and tried not to think about it.

Not thinking, however, was difficult to achieve. What about Joe Cameron himself? What had he been doing in his lumberyard, late at night? From what she had seen on that brief visit to his timber-finishing yard, she could guess: he was probably repairing a crane. Or he could have been meeting someone, Mrs. McKee, perhaps. Had he been drinking? Had he been too drunk to fight off his attacker?

And Marie McKee? Was she truly guilty of a bloody, violent, cold-blooded killing, or had she been framed? Once again, she thought about the pouchy, glistening deep blue eyes and the too, too minty breath; had she killed him in a drunken rage?

And why kill Joe Cameron? Did she suspect, as Gloria had, that Cameron may have been responsible for her husband's death? If the gossip was accurate, Marie would not have cared that deeply.

There had to be some link between the two deaths. There was the industrial development, of course. And that development was now controlled by Glenn Hullett, not Marie McKee, widow of the deceased.

Jan came up the stairs with a message from Hazel McDaniel about a special presentation to be made Wednesday night at nine to a church group member, at a meeting at her house. Gloria groaned. The presentation had better be quick, she thought. She didn't intend to stay around for the entire meeting when there were no doubt other things to be done, and a late night copy deadline to meet.

The conservation authority meeting had yielded two stories, one important enough to rate page one on a slow news week. The library board had finally agreed to purchase a series of mysteries for the entertainment of Plattsford area readers, and had released the schedule for the summer children's reading program. Registration would begin the following Monday. Gloria marked the date and time on the schedule for a photo. Norma was cutting through community notes like a hurricane, and the second section was coming together like clockwork. By two o'clock she was ready for a break. As she walked through the front door of the *Sun* and onto the sunny sidewalk, she spotted Sid hanging the inevitable sign on his shop door, and quickly crossed the street to intercept him.

"Well, Gloria, you have some interesting news this week," Sid said as they swung through the door of Bud's Café.

"It's my treat today, Sid. I owe you. And yes, it's interesting, but not as conclusive as the police are implying. What do you think?"

"I don't have to think, this time," he noted as she picked up her coffee at the counter. "I believe Marie McKee has confessed."

Gloria turned to him, her coffee almost spilling onto the flowered print skirt that she had fetched home from the dry cleaner's the day before. "Confessed?"

"One of the night officers came in this morning after his shift. He said it was all down on paper." They eased their way into a back booth.

"How neat and tidy for them. Did she admit to killing her husband too?" She examined her skirt carefully, searching through the splashy print for splashes that shouldn't be there. "Or do they think Cameron killed McKee because he was robbing him, and Marie killed Cameron, and so on?"

"Police are definitely looking into both those angles, and Marie is at the moment the favored one. After all, domestic violence is a common motive for murder. Their troubles were no secret. Marie had motive, and also knew where to find her husband, had access to the construction shack, the equipment, everything. Joe was in touch with Marie shortly after her husband's death. Perhaps he knew something and was blackmailing her. Of course," he regarded her with an impish smile, "police assumptions aren't always accurate, are they?"

"Not even when they can make the evidence fit," Gloria agreed. "But this doesn't fit the rest of the facts at all. Where does the break-in, for want of a better term, at my place fit into this? Even if I were betting on Joe Cameron instead of Marie as the killer of Clarence McKee, and I definitely am, it still doesn't fit."

"They can deal with that as a separate incident altogether. Perhaps it doesn't mean anything at all."

"But that isn't the only thing. They've already ascertained through statements and other evidence who was on the building site when Clarence McKee met his end. Do they have anything to show that his wife was there?"

"Maybe she went over to clean up the shack, gather up old, moldy coffee cups and the like. Sounds reasonable."

"C'mon, how many wives clean their husbands' offices, especially wives who aren't on great terms with their husbands?" Gloria grimaced. "Okay. Maybe she had another reason for checking up on him. But she doesn't admit to drugging her husband with phenobarbital, does she?" She watched as Sid slowly sipped his coffee. "Damn it, how do you know so much when I get sweet fluff-all from the police?" she exploded, threatening to spill her coffee once more. "It's ridiculous! And if everyone in town knows all of this—and I assume they do—why do I bother putting out a paper? I have so little to go on with their *official* statements that even the neighbor's dog knows more than I do."

"Because deep in their souls, people know that gossip is not necessarily fact. And in the end, they want the truth. So they rely on you to get it." Sid smiled at a banker who had just walked in to pick up an order of bagels for a business meeting. "And you're not letting them down, so far, so don't give up, like your predecessor did." He winked. "In fact, *rumor* has it you'll go pretty far to get your story."

"Oh, really? And which constable was in here for a haircut recently, and spilled the beans?" Gloria demanded. "Oh, never mind. What puzzles me is, why did Marie McKee confess to killing Joe?"

"Why did she confess? She couldn't have hidden that one if she'd wanted to, and obviously she didn't. There was plenty of evidence. As to why she killed him, well, that takes me back a few years. They kind of had unfinished business."

"As in Marie's daughter Gladys?" She smiled at Sid's surprise. "My father made an observation. He's usually right."

Sid nodded to two merchants who had just entered the coffee shop. "You father, eh? I'll have to meet him some day." He returned his gaze to her. "Do you really want to hear this? It isn't a pretty tale, and certainly not for publication."

Gloria nodded.

"Marie was a real beauty back then," Sid recalled. "And smart too. She had been dating the football hero, Clarence McKee, for a couple of years. He was a good-looking guy, believe it or not, but not that smart. Even so, he managed to slide through most of high school. Some people said he let one of the other kids take an exam for him, and the football coach of the day simply looked the other way."

"I don't remember high school ever being that easy to fake," Gloria recalled.

"People see only what they want to," Sid remarked. "Anyway, Joe Cameron was always on the outside of the circle. His father died in one of those rural accidents you hear about. Tractor rolled, I think. Joe was still in high school at the time, left school to run the family farm. His mother and his younger sister and brother did their best to help Joe keep the place going, but eventually they were in debt up to their ears and lost everything. It was sad, but it happens more than you might think."

"So they moved into town?"

"Joe's mother got a job in the general store in Genoa, and the store owner let them take the apartment above it. Joe and the other kids dressed in whatever the store owner couldn't sell, usually work khakis and flannel shirts. Joe picked up high school again, for about a year, then eventually dropped out and got a job."

Gloria's heart went out to the man who struggled to keep his own business afloat against a barrage of abuse from his neighbors. "So how did he and the sweet Marie ever get together?"

"Something happened between the corn queen and her prince, and they broke up for a while, and Marie stayed with a cousin of hers in Genoa for a summer, to cool things off. It was kind of a crummy little village back then. Marie started hanging out with Joe and a few of the locals that she knew from high school. They were a crude bunch, not at all what she was used to. I guess things got a bit out of control, what with drinking and wild parties by the river, and all that. Those parties were rough. I heard stories."

"I can well imagine. And next thing you know, she was pregnant, likely with Joe's child," Gloria suggested.

Sid sat back and took a deep breath. "It wasn't widely known, and her parents tried to keep it that way, but we assume it was so."

"How did you know, Sid? Lucky guess? Deduction, or did you perhaps hang out with the same crowd, you dog?"

He grinned. "I didn't exactly flunk mathematics, or biology. I could count. Plus, after all, look at Gladys." Sid took another bite of bagel. "Give Clarence his due, he married his high school sweetheart in spite of it, probably after the Eakins family made a tempting offer to set him up in business, thus buying respectability for their beloved daughter. It was Marie's family who bankrolled McKee Excavating, digging septic tanks, liquid manure tanks for pig barns, foundations, field drainage ditches, you name it. And in the fullness of time, people set aside their suspicions and assumed the child was his, after all. They had been pretty thick for a long time, and the break-up had been barely a month or two. But he knew the truth, and so did Marie. There was always an edge, a mood, about them. He was always a bit of a bully. They had a miserable marriage."

"He was abusive? Was there ever a sign of physical violence?"

"He didn't have to knock her around to intimidate her." He leaned forward. "My wife belonged to the same institute for awhile. One evening she dropped in to ask Marie a question about the previous month's minutes, and found Marie in her kitchen, crying, surrounded by broken, dirty dishes. Every dish in the place, Gloria, every plate, cup, and glass, was smashed on the floor. And Marie herself was, shall we say, not herself? No telling what shape Clarence was in. He'd driven off somewhere." He shook his head. "Not a happy couple."

Gloria shook her head and thought about her own marriage, a problem to her, but a fairy tale in comparison. Then there was her parents' marriage, the rock in mid-stream to which she had so often clung, in her volatile teenage years, her troubled twenties, and even now. How did the McKees' children fare? "A sad tale, Sid. What about Gladys? Does she know she's the result of, at best, date rape?"

"Date rape?" Sid looked nonplussed. "I never thought about it in those terms. There was no such thing in those days, at least not in the legal sense. But it's possible, when you consider Joe and Marie. As for Gladys, who knows what she knows, poor girl? That's possibly the reason she's so shy."

"And what about Joe?"

"Joe eventually married, had two boys. But he carried a torch for Marie. At some point, I heard, he even wanted to acknowledge Gladys as his own. I got that tidbit from a cousin."

"Why?"

"Why not? If you were a man like Joe, wouldn't you want everyone to know you'd had it off with the belle of the county?" He winked.

"Did he threaten to do that? It sounds like a great motive for Marie to want to club Joe, but no reason yet to kill her husband too."

"Marie had left the door open by naming the girl after Joe's mother. She refused to have anything more to do with Joe, but someday she might need his support financially, so she had to be prepared. Yes, it could have been date rape, and perhaps that's why Clarence agreed to marry her after all, and why Marie put up with him. People around here never completely forget a scandal like that, even if they pretend to."

"So Norma says. It keeps everyone polite, she claims." She shook her head. "I think this 'politeness' must keep them all suppressed and frigid. Imagine how Joe Cameron and Clarence McKee must have hated each other. Joe had plenty of reasons to want to see Clarence dead. And vice versa. I still think it's possible that he killed him."

"If it had been the other way around, everyone would have thought Clarence had killed Cameron. As it was...." He shrugged. "Marie may have been fond of Clarence in their early years, but the pressures of their life together killed whatever affection they had for one another. Even if she was under the impression that Joe Cameron killed her husband— and I doubt it—she didn't kill Joe for Clarence's sake. She killed him for her own reasons."

"Why didn't Marie and Clarence simply move away and start a new life where no one knew their past troubles?"

"Because Clarence had great expectations. He had property coming to him through his family, plus whatever he was milking out of hers. He had plans that didn't involve the hard work of farming. And, frankly," Sid leaned forward confidentially, "the guy wasn't smart enough to hold his own anywhere but here. And now, I must get back to the shop before I miss more gossip."

"Wait. I haven't asked you about Glenn Hullett."

"What about him? He is a nephew of sorts to Hazel McDaniel. Hazel had a brother who died of pneumonia as a child, but years before, her mother had another child under not ideal circumstances, if you get my drift. The birth was hushed up, and the baby sent to relatives near Woodstock. Glenn is the result of that particular offshoot. The Hullett family owned a lot of property in East Lister at one time. Glenn has been speculating in land for years, operating on both sides of the law, so I've heard. I was surprised to hear he was in partnership with Clarence McKee. He's a shifty one."

"I'll say. And now he controls the industrial park project."

"Well, I've heard of him pulling fast deals, but I don't think he's up to killing someone for a hundred acres of undeveloped property. Still...." He raised an eyebrow.

"Sid, you're full of stories."

"Full of something." Sid got up. "Chew on that one for awhile, and this whole mess starts to make a bit of sense." He smiled, saluted, and left. Gloria finished her coffee, picked up two take-out orders at the counter for her cohorts still glued to their keyboards in the office, and left, mulling over Joe Cameron's powerful motive for killing Clarence McKee as gruesomely as anyone could.

Sex *and* money! Why not? She smiled. Perhaps police would have this one sewn up before this week's deadline. It would be a neat solution, neater than pinning the blame on Mike Hurtig. Plus, they'd save the taxpayers the cost of at least one trial. How much time did they need?

***

"I hope there isn't much more of this tragedy left to play out," Linda said, in a subdued voice. "It is sad, isn't it? All those lives gone to waste."

"Oh, knock it off! I think it's about time this whole fossilized community opened the doors of its stuffy little minds and let in some fresh air and sunshine," Gloria replied in disgust. They were drinking herbal tea on her side veranda, sitting comfortably on the railroad bench. Mike Hurtig was cutting her grass, using the lawn tractor that he had brought over in the back of the family pick-up truck, having replaced the post, knocked out the dents in her mailbox, and re-attached it. "The police will have a bit more news for me in the morning, I hope. But I don't think this is over. I think it's just warming up. What can you tell me about Marie's oldest daughter?"

"She's fairly close to my age, but I don't think she finished high school," Linda admitted. "Marie and Clarence were barely married when she was born, which means...well, you can guess. She got quite sick when she was a teenager, I remember that. Seizures, I think. Epilepsy, probably. She never married, works with a couple of church groups, has a part-time job at a feed mill, and lives with her mother. I imagine that she'll stay on at her parents' home, and she and her sister will inherit the estate."

"Why? Do you really think Marie killed her husband?"

"Who knows? She already confessed to one murder. What gets me is the violence. Gloria, how could someone like Marie beat a man over the head with a baseball bat?"

"You'd be surprised. When I was a teenager, I got into a lot of fights. Once you've been hit a few times, and someone has caused you deliberate pain, you desensitize yourself. I became so violent that my father had to put a stop to it before I maimed someone. What if Joe Cameron had forced himself on Marie, all those years ago, and she had never forgotten it? What if her husband had been miserable enough to hurt her a few times? Slapped her around when he was drunk? Mentally and emotionally abused her? I can imagine that it would come out in violence."

"Did you grow up in a rough neighborhood?"

"No, I grew up with an older brother and a gang of male cousins who teased me a lot. I'd rather not be reminded about it, or talk about it. Suffice it to say, the rage that can lead to physical violence scares me, but it doesn't surprise me."

"Did you ever tell Tony about it?"

"Some." Gloria was silent. "I know it's still difficult for you to fathom marrying someone you haven't known since birth, like you and Bob, and like most of your school friends. But I think if Marie and Clarence had been able to keep some secrets from each other and from the rest of their social circle, perhaps life would have been easier for them."

"And what will Tony say when he hears? About this latest murder, I mean."

"If my luck holds, he won't." She put her cup carefully on the planks of the veranda. "I want him to concentrate on his music. We probably won't see each other until the end of the summer, barring some act of God, or Heartland. I've been hoping that they'll send us a summer student for about a month. Otherwise, it'll be fall, or maybe later, before Tony and I can get together."

"That's a long time, and you're barely married. How do you stand it?"

She shrugged. "I always did before we were married, though his trips were more like days and maybe weeks, not months. We were close in many ways." She smiled at the memory. "But we never lived inside one-another's pockets. And now, I have his parents inviting me to dinner next Sunday, if I can get away, and my mother planning to spend a weekend putting up wallpaper in our bedroom. The clan rallies around. Believe me, I'll have all the family I need this summer." She sipped her tea.

"If you get lonely in between, you can always join *our* family. My boys like you a lot, and so does Mike."

"Thanks. I've been on my own for awhile, but I'm glad of the company, now and then." The evening was dry, with a brisk breeze. The mugginess of the previous week was gone. "I appreciate your nephew doing the grass for me, Linda. How much should I pay him?"

"I don't think he expects a thing, Glo."

"He's a good kid. Margaret Ormsford said so even when he was under suspicion, when everyone else in the neighborhood had him arrested, tried, convicted, and hanged, behind their hands, of course."

"Some still do. But not all the people up here have nasty, dirty minds," Linda said with a laugh. "We just hear more from the ones that do. Speaking of nasty minds...." She hesitated. "It's about Mike. You know he likes you a lot. And his mom frets. Perhaps I shouldn't say—"

"Then don't," Gloria said tersely, watching the young man on the mower. "And with luck, no one else will, either."

Max shook the screen door behind them. Linda reached over and opened it. The two cats marched out, sniffed the gasoline fumes from the lawnmower, and sat on the steps to watch the progress, ears and whiskers waving back and forth. Gloria watched them for a moment. "I don't know whether they like short grass, because they can find the grasshoppers and mice more easily, or hate it because they can't hide as well from the birds."

"Nice cats," Linda noted.

"I'll accept the compliment on their behalf," Gloria said. "Max came with me from the city. Buffy followed me home the first week I was here, and a good thing, too. An old house needs a vigorous mouser, and she is relentless."

"Females usually are more efficient hunters. They have babies to feed."

"Not that female. Sherry at the vet clinic checked Buffy thoroughly, gave her shots, and spayed her. There will be no little Buffies running around here this fall. I almost regret it. I love babies, puppies, kittens, humans. But I couldn't bear to part with them, I'd be overrun." She giggled at the thought. "I'd be the crazy woman who lives alone with forty cats. Every community has one."

The lawnmower had stopped, and Mike had climbed off and was bending to study something in the grass. He reached down and picked it up. "Did you lose a pocket knife, Gloria?" he called.

"Not that I know of. Let's have a look."

He walked back to the veranda and held up a small penknife with a slim blade, extended and partially smeared with mud. "I wonder if your burglar dropped it when he was leaving? It would be pretty easy to miss, lying here in the grass."

The knife blade, thin and almost flexible, was unfolded, and Gloria wondered if it had been intended to slide the lock from her back door. Or had this been used to crush the phenobarbital tablets? She looked carefully for traces of powder. "Maybe I'd better drop this off at the police station tomorrow morning," she suggested. "I'll get a plastic bag."

"Do you think it's important?" Mike asked, frowning.

"Well, maybe it has been there for six months, or maybe just six days. I don't know. But they might be able to tell." She laid the knife carefully on the veranda step and turned toward the door.

"Gloria, about that hole in the backyard—"

"I know. It smells awful. You don't have to cut the grass on that side if you don't want to."

"The smell? That doesn't worry me. But if your landlord doesn't mind, I could take care of it this weekend, grade the weeping bed, lay in new tile."

"You could? Oh, Mike, you're a prince! I'll tell Mr. deVos. He'll be pleased to *hire* you and pay the going rate, never fear. He's pretty handy with a lot of things, but a septic bed is beyond him."

"And I can do it according to the health regulations too," he added, forcefully. "I've worked for excavators for a couple of years now, and I know the difference.

The health inspector won't find a thing wrong with it."

"What would I do without you? I'd live in a field of weeds and smell like a sewer." She patted his arm. Mike stared at his feet for a second, grinned, and returned to the lawnmower.

She made a quick call to the deVos house, and the landlord gratefully accepted Mike's proposal, offering to deliver the equipment and supplies on Saturday morning. Gloria returned to the veranda, where Linda was watching Mike load the lawnmower on to the back of his pickup. "Soon when I flush the toilet I won't hear its gurgling progress all the way to the bottom and splashing under the window. It is pretty disconcerting."

"Not always," Linda pointed out. "Come winter you'll look forward to that sound. It means the pipes aren't frozen."

Tony's call, just after ten that night, was brief and reassuring, but it was an uneasy night. The knife reminded her of things that had conveniently slipped to the back of her mind. The open blade.... A weapon? Would the intruder have used it on her, small as it was, if she had reached the door as he was leaving? Did he think about violence? Was he a murderer?

What was it about the barbiturates that bothered her? In grade school, a young classmate had experienced an epileptic seizure and had been heavily dosed with something like phenobarbital. The girl had never been the same after that. Who, in this area, suffered from epilepsy? Gladys McKee? Her mother? Her father? It could be anyone, and if it actually ran in families, well, it could be virtually everyone. She was still awake three hours later, and every peep, squeak, and creak set her on edge.

She climbed out of bed, descended to the unfurnished dining room, and stared out of the window. Her view was partially obscured by a load of gravel, dumped on the side yard last week, ready for spreading in the new septic bed. She opened the window to catch a breeze, then quickly closed it. Saturday, after Mike's work was finished, that smell would be gone. Back in her bedroom moments later she pushed back the heavy curtains to let fresh air from the opposite side of the house into the warm bedroom. Outside, everything was still, and quiet. No vehicles passed on the road. No tractor could be heard. Peace at last? Or just a moment of calm before a violent storm?

A few miles away, for the first time in over a week, a murderer drank a brief toast to success and fell into a deep, calm sleep.

***

"I want to talk to you." Inspector Gray beckoned to her from his office behind the front counter of the police station Wednesday morning.

Gloria did not move from her position in front of the counter. "May we talk out here, Inspector Gray? I am in a hurry." If she were Buffy, she would have laid back her ears, arched her back, and hissed.

He narrowed his eyes, then stepped out to the counter. The officer at the desk was inspecting the penknife that Gloria had wrapped carefully in a plastic bag the night before. The inspector took it from him and she watched him turn it over in the bag and examine the marks on the side.

"I have no idea whether you want to test it for prints or not, but it has been handled by Mike Hurtig, who was cutting my lawn, and by me," Gloria explained. "The blade was open when we found it, and I left it that way. Could it have been used to crush the tablets that we found on my counter?"

"We'll check it more thoroughly. Did you mark the spot where it was found?"

"More or less. What else would you like to know?"

"You were at Cameron's factory Monday night."

"Actually, sir, I was there Monday afternoon sometime after three." Why did he interpret her simplest, most routine actions as some sort of underhanded, criminal activity?

"May I ask what you were doing, unofficially?"

She raised her eyebrows at the word. "You may ask officially if you like. I was following up on last week's coverage of the industrial park murder, asking Mr. Cameron whether he had any idea if and when he was moving his business to the new site. I imagine you know, Inspector, that Cameron Timber was supposed to relocate there."

"What was his answer?"

"He had no answer," Gloria replied in all honesty. "He was upset about some machinery that had broken down, and I did not stay long. He wasn't having a good day." Why bore the inspector with Cameron's ramblings? If the police weren't interested last week, they weren't interested now. In the long run, Cameron's suspicions of McKee's motives meant nothing at all.

"Did you see or hear anything unusual?"

Unusual? The dogs, and the elderly woman? The dirty coffee cups, the sour smell.... "I have never been there before, but nothing struck me as unusual," she answered truthfully.

"Thank you, Ms. Trevisi." He turned on his heel and marched smartly back into his office.

She glanced at her watch as she was leaving the station: quarter-past eight. And she had not yet buttonholed Glenn Hullett. *Let's hope he's an early riser,* she thought as she arrived at her office twenty minutes later. She had plenty of questions for him.

Theresa and Jan were already installed behind the counter, talking about a friend of Jan's whose husband hadn't received a paycheck in two weeks. "If they don't get back to work soon they could lose their house," Jan was saying over her shoulder to Theresa, as she handed Gloria her messages. "I *told* her not to go hog-wild and buy one of those big fancy subdivision homes in Perkins Hill. But she had to be the first in her family to have a brand new house. Now, who knows?"

"I wonder how many people at McKee's are in the same boat?" Theresa mused, picking up a ringing telephone.

Gloria thought about this as she walked up the stairs to her desk. As usual, the terrible two were one jump ahead of her, but she was catching up fast.

The industrial park had been deserted when she passed by earlier this morning, and although it may have been too early to see any construction happening, the site looked about the same as it had last week, when the yellow police tape had been pulled off to allow access once again. Was Hullett planning to continue? Or did he have some problems with his "investors" now that Clarence McKee, the experienced contractor and builder, was out of the picture? She found his phone number under her council notes, and tried it. No, a female voice said, Mr. Hullett was away at a meeting with officials and wouldn't be back until tomorrow. Gloria hung up. "Hullett Enterprises" had an office, and a secretary, of sorts, unless that was how his wife or daughter answered the phone. A meeting with officials? On an outside chance, she tried the O'Dell Township office.

"Mr. Fuller is in a meeting at the moment," his deputy said.

"When they're through, would you ask Mr. Hullett to call me?" Gloria asked.

"Sure. I'll give him the message as soon as they've finished," he assured her.

Good guess.

She was buried in government press releases when the phone on her desk rang again.

"Ms. Trevisi, what can I do for you?" Glenn Hullett's smooth delivery automatically got her back up.

"Mr. Hullett, you assured O'Dell Council last week that the industrial park is going ahead without your partner, Clarence McKee. Even without him, is McKee Excavating still involved?"

"Of course. McKee Excavating is a partner in this development."

"This development has just lost its one and only tenant. What are your plans now? Are you continuing with the project?"

"There will be other businesses who need a decent location," Hullett replied.

"Are you saying there are other prospective tenants who want to put their businesses in such a remote location? What types of industry are interested?"

"Nothing specific right now, but I have every confidence we'll find plenty of people interested in the site once it is completed. The industrial park is a long-term project that will benefit the township greatly in future years."

"And when will it be completed, Mr. Hullett?"

"I can't say offhand. We haven't started back yet. But when we do, things will come together."

Dodgy customer. "Such as?"

Hullett hesitated. "Maybe someone will take over the timber-finishing business. Cameron's widow and sons could still run it."

"It sounds as if Cameron was your only prospect."

"Better than a prospect," Hullett asserted. "The contracts are signed. Whether they are in force now that Joe is gone, I can't say. As far as I'm concerned—"

"Can the project continue without a firm commitment from its only prospective tenant?"

"There will be others come forward, I'm sure."

"'There will be', you said. So no one has come forward yet?"

"Not yet, but...." He faded off, sounding vague, Gloria thought.

"But you are continuing to build? Have you considered abandoning the project until you have a few more firm commitments?"

"The project will not...." Hullett paused. "The police investigation has held us up."

"The police investigation was finished last week. Your one and only expected tenant died yesterday morning, and your partner died nearly two weeks ago. Are you seeking another business partner before you continue? A sub-contractor? What is the hold up? When are you planning to get back to work?"

"Well, we've had some problems, which you have already mentioned, that need ironing out first."

"Mr. Hullett, all I am asking, to round out this particular news story, is this: When are you planning to call back your employees to the site?"

Hullett hesitated again. "We're not sure. Soon, I imagine. Quite soon."

"Do you know what you're doing, Mr. Hullett?" she asked, exasperated.

He paused. "Of course. We will be starting back to it soon."

In other cases, Gloria recalled, delays like this one cost money, and contractors and investors were tearing their hair out to get started back to work. This one couldn't care. Not wishing to push him further, she thanked him and hung up. And cursed.

Had Clarence McKee actually embarked on an industrial development without prospective tenants? She had heard from many people that he wasn't the brightest bulb in the marquee, but she refused to believe he was that dull. Give the man his due: at least McKee knew how to organize a work force and get a job done. Now that he was gone, Hullett may not know where to start. If that last conversation was any indication, he had no idea what he was doing. Talk about dull bulbs! Could Hullett be that thick, or was it just an act? Maybe Russell was right, and Hullett was planning to stop the project. Perhaps he had something else in mind for a hundred acres that backed onto East Lister. Gloria knew one thing, however: Glenn Hullett was as slippery as they come. A speculator, on both sides of the law, Sid had said, cozy with the clerk of the township in which he had a controlling interest in a land development. Which side of the law was he on this time?

She was beginning to suspect that Hullett, not Cameron, held the key to this strange case, the partner who had been kept secret until last week.

It stank.

***

Provincial Court was in session most of the morning, and Gloria, with two interesting cases to write up, was arriving back in time for a quick lunch when Rick met her on the stairs. "George Fuller is waiting for you."

"Mr....he's *upstairs?* Did Jan send him up to my desk?" She glared back down the stairs toward the front counter.

"He asked to see Fred. Then he waited for you. Don't worry. He's not alone." Rick hesitated as Gloria pushed past him, then followed her back upstairs at a distance.

The O'Dell Township clerk was pacing back and forth through the editorial department, under the watchful gaze of Linda, sitting at her desk, and Fred Russell, who looked as though he would like to crawl under his. No doubt, Fuller had already taken a piece out of him. Gloria mounted the last step. "Mr. Fuller? Is there something on your mind?"

"What do you think you're trying to do?" Fuller exploded, confronting her at the top of the stairs.

Gloria was surprised. "I'm simply following an ongoing story, Mr. Fuller. If you have anything you would like to add—?"

"I have nothing to add, and I want you to keep your nose out of township business from now on." He followed her to her desk by the far window. "This has nothing to do with you and your damned newspaper—"

"With me, Mr. Fuller? With the newspaper? How about what it has to do with public concern and public funds?" She stood beside her desk, facing him. They were just about the same height, the slight advantage to Gloria.

"What public funds? This is a private venture that could have netted the township some nice industrial taxes. The public does not need to be concerned. Everything is under control."

"The only tax you were going to get is what you're already getting from Cameron and Sons Timber. As for public responsibility, are you saying that the rezoning of farmland against recommendations of the county's planning department is not of concern to the public? Or that the establishment of an industrial complex in the middle of nowhere is not of public concern when it would have required the township to pledge funds for additional drainage, upkeep, and the improvement and construction of roads?" She dropped her notebook onto her desk, and held her camera in her hand.

"The developer takes responsibility for that," Fuller pointed out.

"And no doubt would do it himself, and a shoddy job, at that," Gloria countered. "And in a few years, environmental protection regulations will tighten up, won't they? And when environmental hazards generated by these industrial operations become an issue, what about the public then? Is that not anyone's business either?"

"It's in the contracts. Only light industry would be allowed. McKee Excavating knows all about environmental and health regulations. They dig foundations, drainage, and septic tanks all over the county."

"McKee Excavating is known for flouting those regulations all over the county, Mr. Fuller. Didn't you know? What is going to happen when the township needs major sewer and drainage work around the site, possibly even sewage treatment? Did you already have an agreement with McKee Excavating to determine just how much of that township work would be coming his way over the next few years? And who is pushing for those plum township contracts now?"

"We're a long way from needing sewers out here. We're talking farmhouses and villages, and maybe a couple of businesses, not a chemical valley."

"Maybe you can tell your councillors that kind of garbage. I don't agree. What runs into the aquifer comes back in people's wells. Perhaps the people of East Lister would like to know what to expect."

"Fine. Disagree if you like. As long as you stop making dangerous insinuations about the township's involvement in Clarence McKee's death. You're treading on thin ice."

"The township's involvement? What about the township's future? This whole industrial development is an ill-conceived disaster that goes against every planning strategy the county has introduced in the past decade, from the time the rezoning was forced through until now. Do you think the public shouldn't know that, as well?"

"The future well-being of our township depends on a sound financial base—"

"Well-being? And what about the harassment that Joe Cameron had to put up with from *your own nephew*, Mr. Fuller, and his neighbors? What about the rights of someone who is forced to move his business, a business established on a properly zoned site, at his own expense to a location not of his choosing, or lose his livelihood?"

"Cameron's business wouldn't have survived anyway without more cash coming his way."

"He didn't survive, cash or no cash, and certainly no thanks to you. Anyone in the township might be facing that kind of treatment some day, if people in the right places decide to push. Don't you think the public should be warned about that as well? I do." She stepped closer, and Fuller sidled backward.

"The township had nothing to do with Cameron's death either. What are you implying?" Fuller's face had paled considerably since Gloria had first encountered him at the top of the stairs.

"Who's accusing anyone of Joe Cameron's death?" Gloria asked. "I didn't. All I want to know is what kind of games you people are playing in O'Dell. And which side are you betting on these days, Mr. Fuller?"

"Ah. You don't know anything about our township business, do you?" He breathed heavily. "You don't know what really happens."

"No, but I'm dying to find out. Why don't you tell me?"

"I'm not telling you anything. You're barred from attending our meetings from now on."

"Will you refuse public access to council business?" Gloria caught a glimpse of Russell as he edged out from behind his desk.

"I will tell your employers that you are not welcome in O'Dell Township." Fuller turned toward the stairs. "And I will tell them that you've been stirring up trouble by printing lies."

"I imagine you have already told Mr. Russell, our general manager. I won't be made welcome, but I'll be there anyway," she said, biting off her words. "Mr. Fuller," she added. He stopped, and turned. She continued, deliberately. "I am not snooping, and personally I wouldn't care if your whole township dropped into a crater tomorrow, except that it would miss our press deadline. I am paid to cover the news in this region. You may tell my employers anything you want." She turned and looked at Russell, who was standing behind her, his eyebrows bouncing off the ceiling. Fuller continued to thump heavily down the stairs as she returned to her desk.

"He doesn't like you much, does he?" This comment came from Russell, still behind her.

"No, he doesn't." She glanced out of her window at the street below.

"Do you have to get people angry with the paper? Handling angry customers, or employees, isn't exactly my forte, as you've probably noticed."

"Get used to it; it's one of the hazards. As careful as I am in covering the news, I still can't make everyone happy." She sat down with a deep sigh. "I was hoping to ask him about Glen Hullett's ties to O'Dell Township. But I'll get no cooperation from him ever again, of that I'm certain. Frankly, I don't care. Do you still prefer my job to yours?"

"You can keep it." He pulled a newspaper out from under his arm. "The *Star*, by the way, has a two-inch story on Monday's murder. The *Express* hasn't picked it up yet." Russell returned to his office and settled back behind his desk.

Gloria turned back to her computer and opened a file for her court story. Her employers didn't care one way or another, so what did it matter? Traveling with Tony looked a whole lot better to her than handling petty squabbles with these people. Why should she care if O'Dell Township went bankrupt through graft, corruption, and murder?

It was the murder part that was disturbing her most, the fact that two people had lost their lives, and at least one life, Marie McKee's, not to mention the lives of her children and Joe Cameron's family, had been completely ruined—all because of a ridiculous building project that never should have been started in the first place. Besides, her employers didn't give a whit what she covered as long as their circulation could justify their advertising rates. And the worse the news was, she reasoned as she typed up a drunk-driving conviction, the better the circulation figures.

What was scaring George Fuller, anyway? His job was perfectly secure, no matter what happened to the industrial development. Clerks were rarely blamed for the bumbling decisions of their inept councillors, and whether the property was developed or left to become a tract of weeds, the land was still there to be taxed, more or less; a bit less if it reverted to farmland. And now that McKee was dead, and Cameron was dead, what did it matter? Had the entire industrial complex been started as another way for McKee to sting his archenemy? Not likely. Surely there was a great deal more to it that perhaps involved the township more thoroughly than she was aware. Fuller had mentioned cash for Cameron's business. Had Cameron been in the market for an investor? Maybe he had found one. A widow? A township official? Or a speculator who worked both sides of the law?

Gloria was reaching for the telephone to call the county land registrar when it rang.

Ed Murray's voice crackled through the receiver. "Ms. Trevisi? I'm getting some disturbing reports about what is happening up there."

"Disturbing?" She glanced at Mr. Russell's office. He hadn't moved.

"Your trouble with the police, for a start. Then some mumblings from Fred Russell about a pending lawsuit last week. Now I just received a call from a county official—"

"You mean a township official, a rather unimportant one," Gloria clarified, "and someone who is trying to throw weight around." Fuller had wasted no time, she mused.

"I mean someone who thinks your idea of news coverage is irresponsible, to say the least, dangerous to the public good, and possibly even libelous," Murray continued.

Gloria glanced at the clock on the wall. Did no one else in this company, or in this district, have to put in a workday? She had a pile of unfinished business to cover, and not much time to do it. Why couldn't Fuller simply have written a letter to the editor? "Mr. Murray, if you have been reading the *Sun* lately, you will know some rather sensitive issues have come to light, and some of the politicians and officials here are scared that I might blacken their reputations by printing something unsavory. Once the newspaper comes out, they will be reassured, believe me."

"We have worked hard to bring back the circulation and advertising in that area," Murray noted. Gloria wondered exactly whom he meant. "I wouldn't want to hear that local businesses are pulling ads because of the way you are handling news."

Ah. The bottom line. "Mr. Murray, you told me last week that I am doing an excellent job. One of our local businessmen praised me for being thorough, although I don't suppose he telephoned and told you. Are you saying that you do not want me to do *too* good a job covering news?"

"I am warning you not to ruin the credibility that we have managed to build during the past few months."

"That *I* have managed to build in the past two months? I know what I am supposed to accomplish here, and believe me, it is a fine line between producing a credible newspaper, and scraping up issues that people do not wish to know, especially when dealing with local small-town politicians and public figures. I am being as careful as I can."

"As long as I don't get any more complaints. And about Mr. Russell—"

"We have worked out our differences, as you instructed last week, and we understand each other now, sir. You needn't worry." At least, she thought so. She looked again toward his office. Was he up to his old tricks?

"Perhaps I should be extending your probation."

Aha! *Finally,* she thought with a surge of annoyance, *he is being honest.* "Mr. Murray, do whatever you think is best, and let me know what you decide. My deadline is in a few hours, and I assume you want your paper on the streets tomorrow night. Shall we discuss this later in the week? By then, the situation may be clearer."

Murray hesitated. "As long as it isn't worse. Make certain that the general manager knows what is happening. Carry on, Ms. Trevisi."

She took a deep breath after she hung up, and looked around the partition at Fred Russell's glass cubicle. Well, she thought, he's the manager; Mr. Murray is right. Better give him something to manage, and see whether he is for me, or against me. She walked over to his office and tapped on the glass door.

***

By six most of her work was done, including the editorial for Page Four, and a full schedule of upcoming Canada Day events to fill up Linda's sponsor page.

"Canada Day is a handy excuse for everything under the sun, it seems," she noted, reviewing the list at Linda's desk. "There's a pub night, at least two local parades, three fireworks displays, two special church services, a red-and-white fashion show, and a bicycle rally for the kids."

"Not to mention free family swimming at the pool all day Saturday, a Monte Carlo night, and a poster competition by the legion," Linda added, looking over the page mock-up. "That flag will look great with spot color. And isn't it nice to have something cheerful in the paper? It beats those black-bordered tales of death and horror that we had on our front page last week."

Gloria agreed. After her earlier conversations with Hullett, Fuller, and Murray, and hashing out her strategy with Mr. Russell, she definitely needed cheering up. When she had driven to O'Dell to pick up the minutes of a roads committee meeting, Fuller had demanded two dollars for a copy. "Handling fee," he had grumbled.

She had slapped her money on the counter and asked for a receipt, since it was an allowable business expense and one that she was certain the company auditors would be pleased to point out to Revenue Canada in a pinch. He had looked angry, but complied. It would be interesting to know whether the toonie ended up in the township coffers, or his own pocket. And she was wondering just which one of the many people she had ticked off this week would show up at midnight to bust up her mailbox again. Cringing cowards!

Rick was developing some track and field photos, and there was still a women's softball game to cover. But it could hold until next week, if it ran late.

"I really do not need any more news to fill us up, so unless a tanker truck spills ignited gasoline over the county highway, or—"

"Or someone else gets murdered?" Linda added, helpfully.

"Let's hope not," Gloria groaned. "I have a presentation photo to take around nine tonight, by the way. It'll hold until next week as well. Tell Rick I'll be back by ten to drop off the film, do a last-minute police check, and write up tonight's dinner speaker. And I'll finish off the McKee story then, as well, and write up the last few headlines. Our front page isn't short of news."

The Women's Business Network for Plattsford and Area was holding its monthly dinner meeting around the corner from the newspaper office. Gloria was glad to get a bit of a walk, notebook and camera in hand. The late afternoon was warm and still dry. Merchants were locking up their stores for the night, and the town was looking deserted. Would she care to trade the nightlife of Toronto for this sleepy routine on a permanent basis? She did not know. How much of that city nightlife had she actually enjoyed? The city was becoming a dangerous place, different from the way it had been when she had first moved there a decade ago. This community had peace and quiet when she required it, and as much excitement as she cared to handle at the moment. She took a deep breath. Even the air at the main corners of Plattsford smelled cleaner than city air. As she was taking another lungful of fresh air a large, tandem gravel truck roared by on a yellow light, belching exhaust and trailing dust, and spoiled the illusion.

The banquet room was air-conditioned and the cold buffet was a nice, light summer treat. The travel agent from the shop next door to the *Sun* was pumping Gloria for information on the McKee and Cameron murders. She, in her turn, was asking how long a flight it was from Toronto to Halifax, just in case she could arrange a short-term getaway this summer.

Most of the women, however, were hungry for news. "I heard from a friend in Genoa that Joe Cameron's timber-finishing business was going to go bust whether he moved or not," Allison Templeton, a real estate agent, said. "At least his family still has their property, though unless he had good insurance, they may lose it to pay his bills."

"Did you hear anything about Mr. Cameron taking on a partner, or borrowing money, to keep his business going?" Gloria asked.

"The Camerons kept pretty close. I know he hadn't listed his house for sale, or any family property. That's usually a sure sign that someone is in trouble."

"Did Marie McKee kill both of them?" Joan King, the travel agent, asked. "What would drive a woman to commit those horrible murders?"

"I really can't say," Gloria replied. "One murder, she may well have committed, but two? I'm not convinced she did." She hesitated to elaborate. After all, what if Joe Cameron's aunt were seated next to her?

"But they found blood all over her shoes, I heard. That's a sure thing, don't you think?"

"No, not really." Curious, with the grapevine so heavy with news, no one had heard of her experience with the police the week before, besides her barber. Or perhaps they had, and wouldn't say, at least not to her face. After all, she noted, isn't that how people in this area remained "polite"? Again she wondered, listening to the rate at which news traveled at these gatherings, why this community even bothered with a newspaper. By the time the *Sun* was printed and on the streets Thursday evening, all the news had been known, talked about, speculated on, and completely hashed over. Never mind; it paid her salary. She settled down to enjoy her dinner and take notes.

This networking group had originally begun with local merchants, and expanded. The bookseller, the gift shop owner, and other women whose expertise covered everything from accounting to window-dressing met once a month to compare business strategies, and encourage newcomers, among which were two farm-women starting a catering business, another who put together gift baskets of uniquely labeled home preserves, and yet another representing her family's gardening center. Gloria regarded this dinner as a convenient way to dig up some summer features. She had three lined up before the speaker hit the floor, including a small family-owned seed business on the verge of a major expansion.

"We had considered the industrial site in O'Dell, but Clarence McKee told us he was already filled," Billie Sanders explained. "It's just as well. We'd need practically the whole site for our new plant, the elevators and storage bins, and I don't think seed cleaning and lumber-finishing would go well together."

Interesting, Gloria noted. Had the industrial park been filled? Not to her knowledge, after her conversation with Hullett this morning. It sounded as if the park was virtually without a tenant. Yet, McKee had turned away a large, farm-related industry that would have suited the area perfectly. Why? Was it that important to him to have Joe Cameron's timber business under his indirect control? Perhaps McKee wasn't about to stop until he owned Cameron's business outright. And how did Joe Cameron feel about it? Angry enough to—

Billie was asking her a question. Gloria blinked. "Where do you go after this dinner? I suppose you're finished for the evening?"

"Still working. Tonight is our news deadline. And I have a presentation photo to take at Hazel McDaniel's. Some church women's group is gathering there to make a special presentation."

"Really? That's strange. The women haven't met at Hazel's for five years." Billie laughed. "They threatened revolt. They're used to a good feed at these meetings—sandwiches, cake, cookies. I hear she could barely produce a pot of weak coffee."

"Damn it. And I just skipped dessert."

Seven prize draws were made, the guest speaker provided everyone with some interesting statistics and predictions about the phenomenal growth of opportunities in local agri-business, and Gloria filled three pages of her notebook and took two photos.

At eight thirty the meeting broke up, and the thirty-odd women went home to their families, children, and probably, housework. Living alone might have its advantages after all, Gloria mused as she walked back to the public lot in the warm evening.

The car was stifling. Sliding behind the wheel, and rolling down both front windows, she headed out of town on County Road One and turned down the sideroad to the McDaniel farm, and the ill-fated industrial park. She hesitated at the entrance to the farm lane, and continued past to check out the scene of the first murder, a mile beyond. The site was deserted, as though everyone had completely lost interest in this unsolved crime in favor of the one that had just dropped into their laps. McKee's murder, only two weeks ago, was now old news. And yet....

She stepped out of the car and walked to the gate. A sturdy chain was strung between two posts, with a new sign hanging from it that read: No Entry. Was that an indication that this project truly had no future? She returned to her car, turned it around, and headed back down the sideroad.

***

"Am I early, or did I misread Jan's message?" Gloria pulled into the McDaniel's lane, expecting to find it full of cars. Besides the inevitable pick-up truck, only one other vehicle was parked in the drive, a dark blue Cadillac the size of an ocean liner. She stared at the big dark sedan; something about it tugged at her memory. She pulled up beside the truck, shut off her engine, and glanced down at the pink message slip attached to her clipboard. The date and time were perfectly clear. Sighing, she grabbed camera and clipboard, and stepped out of the car.

It was the first time she had ever been close to the house, a rambling red brick two-storey affair with a square roof. The window frames were a creamy white, recently painted, with small window boxes of red and white impatiens sitting on the sills. The steps wobbled briefly. "Just like home." She smiled. Perhaps if no one else was here, it would be a good opportunity to ask Mrs. McDaniel a few questions about her nephew Glenn, her husband's nephew Clarence, and their reasons for going into business together. Surely with close family connections, and the McDaniel farm's close proximity to the industrial park, she would have some knowledge.

The side veranda had a slight slope and bounce to the floor that made her feel a bit tipsy, but the gray porch paint looked fresh. Waiting for her at the door was Mrs. McDaniel, draped in the usual flower print dress and cardigan.

"You're early," was her flat greeting.

"I'm afraid I am. I hope it's not inconvenient for you, Mrs. McDaniel." Gloria stepped inside the door to a neat kitchen. No meeting here; just one car in the drive, and a familiar one at that. Hadn't Mrs. McDaniel been climbing out of that car in the town parking lot just a couple of weeks ago?

Through the far door she could hear a television blaring at considerable volume. Draped in a large easy chair like a shapeless beanbag, a tray table in front of him, Elwood McDaniel was snoring loudly, his head fallen over to one side, the slight glisten of drool on the right side of his chin.

"At least you remembered to come," she said crisply. "Would you like some tea?"

"Certainly, if you are making some," she said, looking about the kitchen. The usual preparations for the meetings, such as coffee pots, plates of cookies or other treats, were absent. Either Billie Sanders was not indulging in catty gossip, after all, or she had come on the wrong night. No, Hazel was expecting her. Gloria sat on the carefully-preserved vinyl and chrome chair pulled up to the table. Genuine fifties' furniture, she observed, and in mint condition; she knew a couple in Toronto who would give a right foot for this set.

"Can you tell me what the presentation is about?" Her back was, mercifully, to the sitting room; she didn't have to watch that corpulent carcass in its noisy slumber.

"We'll talk about it later," Hazel said, tending to the kettle. She was stubbornly reticent, for someone about to entertain a gaggle of her friends. Gloria wondered where she would entertain them; would she awaken her husband and nudge him out of the sitting room? Would she set up more chairs in her spacious, precise kitchen?

"You have a well-preserved house." Gloria tried another tack. "How old is it?"

"Quite old." Mrs. McDaniel cast a gaze around the large room with its linoleum floor. "This house replaced the original log homestead near the turn of the century. It has been expanded over the years, of course. Most old houses have. This part," she indicated the kitchen, "used to be the woodshed. In my mother's time, it was made into a summer kitchen." She smiled. "The outhouse used to be in that corner, where the refrigerator is now. Milk? Sugar?"

"No, thanks." Gloria wondered where the outhouse had been in her own house, and almost wished it were still there. "You told me once that this farm has been in your family for generations. What about the farm next door, the one with the construction site? Is it an old family farm as well?"

"An old farm. House an' barn been gone awhile though." The kettle on the stove began to sing, and Mrs. McDaniel busied herself with the teapot. A bag of store-bought chocolate chip cookies appeared out of a cupboard. At least the ladies would not starve,

Gloria noted, wondering what had happened to the old tradition of home-baked goods.

"It must be comforting, having lived in the same house since you were born. It would be a heartbreak to leave it."

Mrs. McDaniel almost dropped the cup she was setting on a saucer in front of Gloria. "And why should I leave it? Just because someone thought he could build a factory next door doesn't mean we would give up our family farm, does it?"

Gloria was surprised at her strong reaction. "I wasn't thinking that. I suppose one of your children might want to move his family in here someday...."

Her pale eyes glazed over. "Yes. This farm'll never leave my family. I won't let that happen," she vowed, fumbling with the teapot on the countertop. She carried it back to the table and set it in front of Gloria with a thump. "We have kept this farm intact since the land grant in 1860," she said as she eased herself into one of the vinyl-cushioned chairs.

"Very commendable." The cookies, Gloria noted, were still on the counter. *I guess they're not for me,* she thought. And immediately, her stomach began to ache for food. That was all she needed: a tummy rumbling like a bulldozer in front of a dozen proper, elderly ladies. Hadn't she eaten only two hours ago? Maybe three? That kettle of Mrs. McDaniel's had been a long time coming to the boil, and the woman moved about the kitchen slowly. She glanced at her watch: nearly nine thirty. She peered through the door to the driveway. The sun had set, and the gloom that was gathering had been enhanced by dark clouds on the western horizon. She was growing impatient. "Glenn Hullett is one of your family too, isn't he? A nephew, like Clarence McKee? It must be reassuring to have these people nearby."

"I don't know what you're talking about," Mrs. McDaniel replied shortly. "Help yourself to the pot when you're ready," she urged, rising heavily from her chair and crossing the kitchen.

"I noticed that Mr. Hullett escorted you to the police station last week." Gloria reached over, poured the brew into her cup, and gave a gasp of surprise. It appeared Hazel had forgotten the tea bag. Her cup was filled with clear, steaming hot water. No, Mrs. Sanders had been speaking the truth. She looked up at her hostess, and met a cool gaze.

"No point in wasting the tea, now, is there? Go ahead. Drink it down," Mrs. McDaniel said from beside the counter. "It's not drugged."

Chapter 10

Gloria stared at the teacup, then at her hostess. "Not—*drugged?*"

"Of course not." Mrs. McDaniel placed a hand on her hip and looked over at her husband, still sprawled in the chair, noisily comatose. "I have none left. That fool lost the bottle of pills, as no doubt you know."

"What pills?" Gloria wondered if the man in the chair would ever rise again. Was he the fool in question?

"That's a man for you, isn't it?" Mrs. McDaniel ignored her query. "He's good for some things, like getting Clarence drunk so he'll sign away a partnership in his business, and taking him a laced bottle of Crown Royal so he'll drink himself to death. But don't trust him with a real job."

Drunk? Gloria stared at the snoring, untidy heap on the living room chair. Not Elwood, surely.

The woman faced Gloria. "I wasn't about to let that lout of a nephew of Elwood's get his hands on my farm after he'd wrecked his own, no matter what Elwood said. They'd made a deal, he said. Support the rezoning, and he'd take the farm off our hands and see that we had a comfortable retirement. Keep it in the family, he said. 'Cause he was Elwood's nephew, he considered himself *family!* He wasn't no family. My kids, they're family. Glenn, he's my *kin.* Clarence just thought he could get this farm. He had plans for it."

Gloria eyed Elwood, still asleep in his chair. He hadn't moved since she arrived. "You mean, Mr. McKee was—"

"He would've turned our farm into a parking lot, that's what he planned. He wanted to develop the whole block, join it to the village and become the king of East Lister." Her face twisted. "Comfortable retirement? Not with ancestors spinning in the cemetery, strangers crawling all over our land with bulldozers and trucks, turning it into a desert. I made sure he went into the ground and stayed there."

"*You* made sure?"

"Sure I did. But you saw me, didn't you? You went by just as I was pulling off the road." Hazel's watery eyes had a hint of the accuser in them, and her sagging cheeks twitched.

Gloria shook her head. "I didn't...." She slid her chair back. "Mrs. McDaniel, you're not well. If the other women are not coming, may I just...."

As she stood up a noise behind her caught her attention. She spun around in time to glimpse Glenn Hullett wielding a baseball bat. And that was all.

***

Noise. Low-pitched, rumbling noise filled her head. And lights. Glaring lights. That was strange, because her eyes weren't open. And voices, shouting above the din.

"...hit her pretty hard." A woman's voice. "You didn't need the rope."

"If I hadn't socked her good, she'd of fought us, and we don't want the house showing signs of a fight." A man's voice. Were they talking about her? She listened harder, but it wasn't easy. A brisk, cool breeze had come up.

"...don't want blood an' brains, neither." Woman's voice, again. Complaining. "If you hadn't lost those pills, she would'a drunk tea and conked out."

"Wouldn't of had to at all, if you'd done what I said. I told you to find out what she knew, not tell her a story. I wanted to get her out of the house nice and quiet, take her out of the way."

"But why here? Isn't it too close?"

"It's perfect. We don't have to go far, police will find the body in a day or so, and think she was snooping around the industrial park looking for clues, or some damn thing, and slipped. Write it off as an accident. We got time. She's got no one to miss her for awhile."

Gloria was coming to, slowly. She was in the front loader of a bulldozer or farm tractor, bumping roughly down a road. Or maybe a lane. She didn't dare open her eyes until she knew where the voices originated.

She tried to move her left hand, and couldn't. Her right? She was tied up, trussed from chest to feet, her skirt wrapped around her thighs and held in a wrinkled, bunched disarray by several bungie cords and a strong, scratchy hunk of twine that one might find on an old tent. She couldn't move; her captor had done an excellent job. She took a deep, slow breath. Her head hurt savagely. She took another breath, and the pain lessened, a little.

"Why not dump her somewhere else, like the other side of the township?" It was the woman's voice again. Hazel? She wasn't certain; the engine made a lot of noise, and the voice, shouting above the din, was distorted. "....too close, police will be askin' me questions." They were still arguing. "....a bad idea," the woman declared. Yes, it was Hazel McDaniel.

"So? All you gotta say is you didn't see a thing. They know she was coming here, and they know how nosy she is about the industrial project. So she got the wrong night, went snooping, had an accident. Take her far away, it looks like she was killed deliberately, or something. We'll take her car over to the industrial site, later."

Or *something?* Gloria clenched her teeth. Where am I going? Are they dumping me? Disposing of my body? But I'm not dead! She stopped herself just before screaming it out loud, and tried to make sense of it.

Hazel was in danger of losing her farm to Clarence McKee. Is that why she took part in his murder? "That lazy nephew of Elwood's," she had called him. No relative of *hers*, at any rate; she wouldn't acknowledge him. And she said that her husband and McKee had made a deal. But fat Elwood hadn't left the drugs on her kitchen counter; Glenn Hullett had done that. So what was Hullett's interest in all of this? McKee's business? Cameron's business? She could see it all now. His father, or more likely the grandfather, sent off in disgrace, an unwanted child. Glenn, the grandson, returned to claim what should be his.

Was he helping his aunt, or helping himself? He was now owner of an excavation business, and a muddy field that could someday house some nice farm-related industry, like the seed plant. Or it could be subdivided and sold off, if he played his cards right. It was right next to the village. But perhaps he didn't want to stop there; was Joe Cameron's business to be his next acquisition? Maybe he had his eye on his aunt's land, as well. Sex or money, her father had said. And here was another minor scandal that no one talked about.

Scandal, just like Marie McKee and Joe Cameron. Marie obviously had good reason for killing Joe: rape, a ruined marriage, and his threat to go public, either with Gladys's heritage, or something else. Marie would hardly care about her husband's part in the scheme to force Cameron out of Genoa and into the industrial park, under Clarence's nose. But she would care about her family's honor, and Clarence McKee was, if nothing else, her husband.

Hazel McDaniel also had a good reason to kill Clarence: her farm, *her* family honor. Her husband had his nephew to look out for his interests; she thought she had a nephew looking after hers, as well. But what was her reason for harming Gloria? "Why me? Why lure me to the farm, and kill *me*?" Sex or money? Certainly not sex; Hullett hardly knew her, was not the least bit interested. But obviously, he was interested in—how did Hazel put it when she described McKee?—becoming the king of East Lister, or with more businesses under his belt, king of O'Dell. Hullett was no longer a small-time speculator; with McKee's business behind him, he had security, and his aunt solidly on his side. And judging by what she had seen a few days ago, he also had O'Dell's clerk-treasurer, George Fuller.

The noise dropped in pitch, and the motion slowed. Good thing. All the lurching and bouncing, not to mention the bump on the head, had made her stomach queasy. The motion stopped. They expected her to remain unconscious; best to make them believe it, she decided, and play dead until she could determine what they were about to do. She closed her eyes and swallowed hard as she felt herself half-tipped, half-dragged out of the tractor bucket. Yes, she decided, it sounded more like a tractor.

The man grunted. "Christ, she's heavier than she looks. Solid sucker."

Jerk! Maybe you're not as strong as you think, she thought. She fell limp onto hard gravel, and lay as still as she could, sharp rocks pressing into her face and bare arms. Clumsy oaf! Playing dead was not going to be easy.

Play dead. Someone, she had read years ago, escaped a murderer by pretending she was already dead, then dug her way out from under a pile of rocks, a shallow grave. A grave; is that where she was heading? Had they dug a grave for her? They said they wanted her body found quickly. By a work crew? But there *was* no work crew on the industrial site, unless Hullett called them back to work. And he wouldn't want her found like this, all trussed up like.... She felt a hand on her breast, a rough squeeze. *If I get through this,* she resolved, *I'll kick this bastard so hard, he'll be the last of his line!*

"Gotta leave the bloody rope on 'er. Might be easier to haul," a male voice gasped from somewhere above her, out of breath with the bending and pushing. Definitely Hullett, now that she could hear him more distinctly. She resisted the temptation to squirm as she was half-dragged, half-rolled along the ground: three feet, four feet, over and over. Where was she? Would she fall into a hole? Were they digging one now? Or would they back a bulldozer over her too? She heard the tractor revving up, and felt a sudden fright.

The ropes came loose, and she tensed herself to spring up.... But where was *up*, anyway? She had rolled so many times that she wasn't certain anymore. He had given up rolling her and was tugging her arm, wrenching it hard and dragging her across impossibly rough ground that certainly wasn't a well-cultivated farm field.

"You couldn't 've pulled up closer, could you?" The man's voice again, directly above her, she surmised. Definitely Hullett. "She's a dead weight."

"Closer? You already lost the pills, Glenn, and your penknife," Hazel McDaniel's strong voice grated close above her. "Do you want to lose the tractor in the gravel pit too? Don't want to explain it to the kids...."

The gravel pit? *Oh, shit!* Gloria reached up suddenly toward the source of the deep, gasping breath and grabbed a fistful of clothing. Too late.

"Bitch!" he grunted, and gave her one hard shove. The clothing ripped off in her hand, and then suddenly she was falling, bouncing through the air, and rolling. Her shoulder struck a rock, and she screamed in pain. Then she bounced off something soft, and felt her head hit the ground. The ground gave way. She tried to break her fall, but she was spinning, and it was a long way to the bottom. She kept tumbling, tucking her head under her arm to protect her face, trying to wrap her other arm around her body, although it was not willing to move without more pain. She dropped the piece of fabric to which she had been clinging. Her hair, caked with gravel, lashed across her eyes and she tasted blood in her mouth, probably from biting down on her tongue after one of those jolting knocks on the ground.

It seemed like hours before her body came to a jarring halt. She gasped, and caught a mouthful of cool, damp gravel. She tried to spit it out, but the gravel kept rolling over top of her, threatening to bury her. Had her fall started a miniature landslide?

The bottom of the pit was dry, thanks to a lack of rain for the past ten days. Too bad, she thought as she struggled through the coarse sand. She preferred taking her chances in a pool of water. She recalled a time when, as a four-year-old, she had nearly drowned at her grandparents' cottage. After that, her grandfather had taught her to swim. As she fought hard to keep her head free of the spongy gravel that threatened to envelop her, she wondered if, by chance, this was her life passing before her eyes. And she wondered if anyone would find out what had happened to her. Would they bother? Would they want to bring her killers to justice, or would they simply want to cover it up and go on with their pitiful lives, convinced they lived in a peaceful, law-abiding community?

She thought of Tony, much as she didn't want to, and a strange feeling of guilt swept over her. She could see him in front of her, telling her in a cold, expressionless voice that she shouldn't have become involved. She stretched her left arm forward as far as it would go, and screamed: *But I didn't mean to!*

The image faded. There were lights at the top of the pit, yellow flashing lights, white lights, red lights. Did bulldozers have red lights too? She wasn't certain. The pain in her right shoulder was paralyzing, but she kept clawing her way through the gravel, ripping her blouse and snagging her hair on sharp, jagged rocks. She had lost one sandal somewhere, and the bare foot was bruised. Several minutes went by as she fought to remain conscious, and went on crawling, sprawling, and sliding to the cool, damp bottom of the pit, following the slippery tumble of falling sand and rock, until her arms were raw.

A light suddenly blazed just in front of her, at the bottom of the slide of gravel. Was this Hullett, making sure she was buried? Before she could yank back her outstretched hand, someone grabbed onto it, steadying and guiding her, pulling her free.

"Easy. I've got you," a familiar, masculine voice said. Definitely masculine.

Who? She felt her body go limp again. Someone tugged on her good arm. She slid heavily through the gravel and finally rolled onto solid ground. Someone was gripping her under the shoulders, dragging her into a pool of light so bright it seared through her eyelids like a cutting torch. *Don't move a muscle,* she kept thinking. *Play dead.* And at this point, it wasn't difficult. Every movement brought more pain.

No good. "She's alive," the voice shouted.

Hands were carefully sweeping the grit and mud from her bruised face and cradling her head. She opened her eyes into the glare of a flashlight. When the spots cleared, she saw Constable Brian Stoker looking down at her. She was lying on her side at the bottom of the pit, illuminated by the headlights of the cruiser.

"Constable...." the words stuck in her throat as she coughed up sand.

"Easy. Lie still. Someone is coming with water."

More footsteps. Another face. "Is she all right?" A woman's voice.

"She's conscious, Sheila." Stoker said over his shoulder as he tilted a bottle to her lips. "Take a sip," he told Gloria. "Try and rinse out the dirt."

Stoker. Giving her something to drink. She nodded and tried to smile at him, wondering if he'd get the joke. Then she took two sips, turned her head, and retched gravel over his boots.

***

"I'm all right, really, just shaky. Sorry about your boots." Gloria was strapped to a backboard on a gurney, staring at the ceiling of an ambulance, still hanging onto Constable Stoker's hand. She wanted to cough up the rest of the coarse grit she could feel in her throat, but she couldn't move her head sideways.

He smiled. "They'll wash."

"They were going to bury me in the gravel pit. I heard them talking, Glenn Hullett and Mrs.....Mrs. McDaniel." She started to cry. The tears stung; her eyes were still full of sand.

He squeezed her hand lightly. "I know. They threw you in from the top, and shoved some gravel down to cover you up. They didn't think you could fight your way out after the fall, but they didn't count on your being so tough."

"It was a long way down. I hurt all over."

Stoker glanced at the attendant on the other side. "Good sign. Your clothing is in shreds, and you have more scratches than a winning lottery ticket."

"Oh sh...shit!" She stifled a laugh as a sharp pain stung through her side, winced, and swore more forcefully.

Stoker grinned at her. "You'll be fine."

"Hazel asked me to come over to take a photo. Then she served me hot water. She said her husband....no, not her husband, someone else poisoned Clarence and lost the bottle of pills. And then Mr. Hullett knocked me on the head with a...with something. Like he was whacking a mailbox. Did he do that too?" Did this make sense? Gloria's teeth chattered. The attendant spread another blanket over her. "And later they were arguing, Mr. Hullett and Mrs. McDaniel...." She paused. Her mouth hurt.

"Good. You're remembering." The police officer glanced out the window. "I think we're here."

"How did you know?" She felt so helpless, strapped to the stretcher and feeling pain in every tiny movement.

"I saw the lights at the gravel pit. No one works one of these pits at night in this neighborhood; it's unsafe." He gently eased his hand out of her grasp as the ambulance pulled up to the door. "Can we call someone for you? Your family? Where's your husband?"

She shook her head, and it hurt like the devil. "Call the office. Tell Rick. He's expecting me back. I need to see him."

"I will. Right away."

"Th...thanks." Gloria shivered. The back doors of the ambulance opened, and she saw the lights of the emergency entrance at Plattsford Memorial Hospital. But there was no need for Stoker to call; Rick Campbell and Fred Russell were standing just inside the door.

***

"Picked it up on the police scanner," Rick explained. "We wondered why you hadn't come back by ten, figured you were held up by a bunch of church ladies sipping tea and chowing down cupcakes. Then it came over the radio."

Gloria was lying in a hospital bed in a small curtained area not far from the emergency nursing station, with the head of the bed rolled halfway and two pillows helping her to sit up. She had been examined, treated for a dislocated right shoulder, bruised ribs, and head-to-toe lacerations. Her arm was immobilized in a sling, leaving her left hand free. The concussion was not serious, but she was being kept in overnight, regardless. Her head hurt, and her scratches stung with disinfectant. "Where's Mr.

Russell?" she asked Rick. "Didn't I see him when I was brought in?" Her lips hurt when they moved.

"He took one look at you and left. I hope you don't mind if I go too? I want to make sure the production people know they'll be waiting at least another two hours for the rest of the front page news. I think you have a story to tell."

"Good boy." She watched him leave, and closed her eyes. *Poor Fred. I hope he's not about to lose his dinner,* she thought. *Do I look that rough?*

When she opened them, Russell was standing beside her, looking pale. "I'll try to get hold of your husband as soon as—"

"Don't. I don't want him to worry." Gloria tried to smile, but her face felt as though it were packed in dry ice. "Just get me a pad of paper and a pen, will you please? Has anyone found my handbag? It was probably in my car." She started to tremble again. "They said they were moving my car to the industrial site, to make it look as though I was snooping, and...Someone would have found my body, in a couple of days. And Tony would have...he would have had to come home again."

"Take it easy, will you? You're lucky to survive." He sat down on the bed. "He's not the only one who would have missed you."

"But I don't snoop," she protested. "You know that."

A nurse poked her head through the curtain. "Are you ready to talk to the police?"

"The police? Depends who it is," Gloria said, trying to see past the gray curtain. Sergeant O'Toole walked in, wearing civvies, accompanied by a female officer in uniform. Russell began to move out, but Gloria held onto his sleeve, pulling him back. "Stay, please? Unless you have somewhere else to go?"

He shrugged, and seated himself at the head of the bed.

The questioning took the better part of an hour. Gloria hashed over as much as she could remember, and the police constable dutifully copied it all down. When O'Toole was finished, he stood up and glanced over the uniformed officer's shoulder at her notes. "I think that's as much as I need right now."

"Oh, no you don't. Sit down, Sergeant." Gloria picked up the notepad and pen Russell had found for her and propped it against her well-bandaged, blanketed knee. "My turn. We're holding our front page for this, and we haven't much time. I have a few questions to ask you."

"The inspector is waiting for your statement."

"The inspector has wasted enough of my time this past week. I think I've earned the right to waste ten minutes of his."

O'Toole hesitated, then sent the officer and notebook away. "Five minutes."

With Russell looking on, Sergeant O'Toole filled her in: The knife she had found in the grass outside her house belonged to Glenn Hullett. "You identified the fingerprints?"

"His name was etched into the side of one of the blades."

"You mean you *knew* this morning that Glenn Hullett was the intruder in my house, and yet you didn't arrest him earlier? And if you had, would I be lying here now?" Gloria felt her temper rising and struggled to sit up. No use. "I should have taken a better look at it myself, rather than trusting the police. No wonder Gray isn't here." Her pounding headache prevented her from yelling.

"The inspector is busy interrogating suspects," O'Toole answered in a flat voice. "He left the less important part to his sergeant."

"Did you find the source of the barbiturates?"

The sergeant grimaced. "We were tracing prescriptions all over the county. Phenobarbital is not widely used anymore, because of its side effects. But when we checked with a couple of pharmacies we found several prescriptions to veterinarians. Once we had the knife, we found the link."

"The link?"

"Well, Glenn Hullett, McKee's business partner, was also a relative of the McDaniels, had even escorted Hazel McDaniel to the police press conference. It seems Mrs. McDaniel had a small dog that had epileptic seizures, and was treated with phenobarbital. We figured Hullett may have got the drugs from his aunt's house without her knowing."

"Partly right. It's more likely that she knew all about it, probably planned it herself. But I know she doesn't have the dog now," Gloria said. "I guess the seizures finally got him."

"Or the drugs," the sergeant added. "That, Ms. Trevisi, was for your benefit. *This* is for your newspaper. And you're damned lucky to get it this early, since it won't be released until Thursday afternoon." He rattled off the official statement: Glenn Hullett, of London, had been arrested, along with Hazel McDaniel of O'Dell Township, following an incident at the gravel pit that linked them with the ongoing murder investigation of Clarence McKee. At the moment, he added, the two were being held on a charge of assault; other charges were pending.

"Attempted murder would be more suitable. If you have any doubt that he threw me off that precipice, look for a piece of his shirt near the bottom. I held onto it as long as I could."

"It was right beside you," O'Toole said. "Seems the loose threads caught on your diamond ring. Don't worry. Constable Miller stayed behind to check the scene, and she's very thorough."

"Thank God for women," Gloria mumbled as she wrote it all down. She was deftly left-handed, but still had trouble steadying the notepad. Impatiently she tore off the sling, then swore when her subluxed shoulder gave her grief as she handed the notes over to Russell. "Would you please put that over on the table, run to the office for me, and bring me my laptop?"

"You're kidding, right?" Russell was staring at her.

"No, I'm not kidding. It's late, we're pushing a deadline, and I still have my encounter with a murderer to write up."

Russell sighed. "And here I thought you needed my strong, masculine support."

"Get a life, Mr. Russell." She turned back to the sergeant. "Has Mrs. McDaniel confessed to anything else since I've been incapacitated?"

"She has been talking our ears off, not that much of it makes sense," O'Toole said. "First she said they drove the tractor over to the gravel pit, and surprised you snooping, and you slipped. So we pointed out that your car was in her driveway, your handbag and camera in her kitchen, and you evidently had an appointment. She said you got the wrong night, or the wrong place. She's changed her story at least three times. It won't wash." He shook his head. "Hullett is a different matter. He was the only person, besides McKee himself, who had a key to both the padlock on the chain that went across the driveway, and to the construction shed. Mike Hurtig claims he locked the gate when he returned the bulldozer. Yet it was open when Stoker pulled in, after Mike had gone. We can only conclude that Hullett was on the scene, searching for his whisky bottle, when Stoker arrived, and that he escaped on foot through the fields. His vehicle must have been somewhere nearby, at McDaniel's gravel pit, for instance."

"Or at the farm. Maybe he and Mrs. McDaniel returned by tractor. I saw one in the lane as I was leaving. After all, a tractor leaving the gravel pit and heading up a farm lane wouldn't be as noticeable as Hullett's Cadillac. Or the township bulldozer."

"Well, it will take some sorting out, but we know where to look now. As for tonight, Constable Miller has confiscated the shirt Hullett was wearing, and she also found the ropes that were used to tie you up, and the weapon he hit you with. They'll tell a tale. And the mud on your clothing matches the stuff in the bucket of the tractor, at least by smell. But Hullett himself has clammed up tight."

"He broke into my house with phenobarbital and then he threw me into a gravel pit. But I never heard him mention McKee. Only Mrs. McDaniel talked about it." She looked down at the notepad propped against her knee. "And what about Marie McKee now? I guess you won't be considering her as a suspect in her husband's murder. Are you certain that she killed Joe Cameron? I hear you have a signed confession."

"More than that," he intoned. "It was Mrs. McKee's daughter Gladys who called police when Marie arrived home, covered in blood. But that's not for publication."

"Uh huh. And why did she kill him?"

"That's not for publication either. I gather Mr. Cameron put certain pressure on her that, under the circumstances, caused her to snap."

"Not responsible for her actions? And it sounds as though Mrs. McDaniel will be excused for the same reason." She sighed. "Sergeant, when can I have my camera back? It's probably still in Mrs. McDaniel's kitchen."

"Inspector Gray says nothing will be moved from the crime scene until it has been thoroughly inspected."

"The hell he does." Her teeth snapped shut, on more gravel. "Fine, Sergeant. The camera is not evidence of anything in particular, just a guest speaker at a business dinner, and I'll need it for next week's paper. If he exposes my film, I'll sue him."

It was well past two a.m. before all her copy was typed, one-handed, and the laptop sent to the production plant with instructions for downloading her story for the front page. Then she reached up, touched her chin where a painful abrasion stung under her fingers, and lay back with a groan. "I wonder what I'll look like in the morning?"

***

"You look terrible." Linda was standing in the doorway of the small washroom watching Gloria while she examined her face in the mirror above the sink. Her headache had subsided a little, but there was a large lump on the back of her head that was sore to the touch. The scratches and bruises weren't improving her appearance, and the gash above her right eyebrow looked downright ugly.

"I *feel* terrible. Someone woke me up every hour all night to take my pulse and blood pressure. It was torture." She blinked at her reflection. "And look at my hair! There's something smelly and gooey caked in the side. I've been trying to rinse it out. I'm going to have such a case of split ends." She picked up a small, inadequate plastic comb the nurse had found for her. Several chunks of gravel fell out as the comb became snarled in a mat. She shook her head, and turned to Linda. "Never mind me. How does the paper look?"

"I haven't been over to see it yet. It's only seven thirty. Is there anything you need?"

"Can you get me a cappuccino from Gina's? I have to wake up somehow, and the coffee here is downright awful." She limped painfully back to the bed, and allowed Linda to tuck her in.

"Will you accept coffee and a bagel from Bud's? It's on the house this morning. I told them I was bringing it over to you." She reached into her enormous handbag, pulled out a paper bag, and produced a Styrofoam cup. "Everyone's talking about it at the coffee shop. I guess the night cops were in earlier."

"Linda, why do we even bother with a paper? People get all the news faster than we can print it! What are they saying?"

"That the new newspaper editor accused poor, crippled Hazel McDaniel of breaking into her house, and Mrs. McDaniel's nephew came to her rescue." Linda grinned. "At least, some are. After all, if they're not related, they're her church buddies."

"Great." The coffee, in spite of the Styrofoam, was terrific. "What would I do without you, and Fred, and Brian Stoker, and everyone?" She bit into the bagel, and apart from the soreness of her face when she chewed, enjoyed it immensely.

"The news on the radio, by the way, is about as up-to-date as our paper will be," Linda pointed out. "No one is saying much more than the police told you last night, and you have that great inside scoop, fresh from the bottom of the gravel pit."

"Yeah. I was wearing only one sandal when they brought me in. I'd better get an award for this story, because it has cost me two dresses and three pairs of shoes." She groaned as she turned her head on the pillow. "Will you please see to the pizza today? I'll make it up to you as soon as I'm better."

"Gladly. Get some rest." Linda patted the bedclothes and left.

Gloria sipped her hot coffee and began brooding. "I don't want to rest. I want to get out of here."

At eight thirty sharp, Rick was at her bedside. "Instructions?" he asked, raising his eyebrows at her glum expression.

"Could you sneak away the front-page proof for me to look over? I want to see what the paper is going to look like."

He grinned. "Sure, if it will cheer you up. You look awful, by the way."

"Thanks. There's a press conference at the parks department this morning at eleven to introduce their summer staff. I'm not sure how we're going to cover it."

"Norma is pitching in today with the proofreading, says she knows how fussy you are. I think I can get away." Rick hoisted the ever-present camera onto his shoulder, and left. Two minutes later, Sid Stanton poked his head through the door. "Well, how's the hero of the day?"

"Not feeling too heroic."

"Well, everyone's talking about you," he chortled gleefully as he pulled up a chair. "I thought you'd like to know. Sergeant O'Toole told me this morning that the killer bulldozer was found in the McDaniels' gravel pit, and the keys in Hazel's kitchen," Sid said.

"So all the evidence points to Hazel McDaniel. I'd say Mr. Hullett wasn't careless at all," she remarked. "But the bulldozer? From the gravel pit? It wasn't the one Mike drove?"

"The bulldozer that ran over Clarence McKee's body was not Mike's. That one belonged to the township, and was kept at the McDaniel's pit. But McKee borrowed it for the afternoon while he rented his own equipment to Mike and his friends. He pocketed a few hundred bucks and didn't lose a moment's work."

"Bastard!"

"You're excused. Hazel, as you may know, can drive almost anything, and decided to drive it back, so no one would notice anything strange that would link McKee Excavating to McDaniels' pit. She moved it directly over top of Clarence, out the gate, and down the road. But, she had just pulled out and put a hundred yards or so between herself and the gate, when Mike Hurtig chugged up the road and pulled in, masking the sound of *her* bulldozer with his. But as soon as he shut off, she had to shut down as well, and wait on the side of the road with the lights off for him to be picked up so he wouldn't hear her."

"But bulldozers sound like tractors to me. Who would know the difference?"

"Mike would. She couldn't take a chance. She had barely got moving again when the cruiser came, then more cruisers and an ambulance, all from the village road. She was a half a kilometer from the industrial park, and had just pulled into the lane leading up to the gravel pit, when you came by."

"O'Toole told you all that?"

"I was cutting his hair at seven this morning, and he was talkative."

"You pumped him." She grinned. "Good work. Well, since *you're* so talkative, maybe you can tell me more about Glenn Hullett's connection. Did he simply appear out of the blue?"

"He has been keeping in close touch with his Aunt Hazel for years. Police found a stack of letters in her desk, the latest ones explaining his plans for partnership with Clarence McKee. He was planning something, all right." Sid chuckled. "I think Hullett was planning to bilk his aunt out of her property, one way or another."

"Nice nephew. How is Mrs. McDaniel doing? Did O'Toole spill that, as well?"

"Her lawyer is trying to get her declared nuttier than a fruitcake, and may succeed. Don't worry," he reached out and patted her hand. "There's enough evidence to point a finger, but police are relying on you." He stood up and looked at his watch. "Must go to work. A customer of mine is up in the cardiac ward. I promised to give him a decent haircut this morning." He was gone, and Gloria sank down under the cover.

She was dozing and dreaming of tumbling off a cliff, and someone high above was shouting her name—in a hoarse whisper. "Gloria?"

Don't hospitals have visiting hours? She opened her eyes. Mike Hurtig's scared face was looking down at her. He was dressed in coveralls and carrying a perfect pink rose bud. She smiled, conscious of her black-and-blue face. "Hi, pal. What are you doing here?"

"I heard about it in the coffee shop. Did someone really try to kill you?"

"Afraid so. I'm sorry I look so dreadful." She looked at the rosebud. "This is sweet of you. Thanks." She filled the glass by her bed with the water pitcher, and watched as he placed the bud in the glass. "Well, I guess you are well and truly cleared of suspicion." She frowned at the pale face; it reminded her of Fred Russell's face the night before. "Are you okay?"

"Just kind of shocked. Not that you look that bad, but...." he took a deep breath. "You actually do look pretty bad. I didn't expect you to do what you did. I thought the police would get to the bottom of it. Not you. I'm sorry."

"Yes, I believe I got all the way to the bottom." She reached a hand out and patted his arm. "Not your fault."

He got up. "I have to get back to work. I'll come and see you when you're feeling better." He left quickly.

She fell asleep again, probably the result of the painkillers that were doled out just before Mike's visit. When she opened her eyes, a beloved voice on the other side of the bed growled: "I thought you told me you could look after yourself."

"Oh, shit!" Gloria struggled again to sit up, and immediately regretted it. She lay back and groaned. "I thought I told Mr. Russell not to call you."

"That coward? He didn't call. I did. I told you I'd call the police if you weren't home by midnight. Your friend Stoker told me, and his sergeant helped me bump a very irate businessman off an early flight to Toronto."

"And here you are." She looked at Tony, sitting by her bed in his once immaculate white shirt, black studs, and black tuxedo trousers, the wrinkled jacket of his tux thrown over the back of the chair along with an attractive maroon cummerbund. His face was rough and unshaven, his eyes red-rimmed and bloodshot from rubbing. She smiled, and her face cracked painfully. "You look like a runaway bridegroom. No wonder the guy was mad. I hope you didn't leave in the middle of a performance."

"No, not in the middle. But I'll miss one tonight at Dalhousie, not that it matters." He glanced at the rose, ran his free hand, the one that wasn't holding hers, through his hair and shook his head. "Why did you do this?"

"Do what? Jump into a gravel pit from the front of a moving tractor?" She turned her face away so he wouldn't see her eyes fill up.

"I mean nearly get yourself killed when I'm a few thousand miles away. I thought you were staying clear of this business. Now look at you. My God, will you ever...." He drew a deep, shaky breath. "Gloria, I'm not sure I can handle this."

She sighed, and tried pulling her hand away from his, but his grip tightened. "I hope you can," she replied. "Because I need you, Tony." She swallowed. "My hair is still full of gravel."

"I can help you with that when we get home."

She felt her sore face twitch as she turned to meet his eyes. "Darling, this might not be a good time for us to take a shower together. I have an awful headache." She took a deep breath, and glanced at the wall clock. "A doctor is coming in any minute now to check my vitals, and then, probably, discharge me, and I'll need something to wear. My clothes are ruined."

He smiled, finally, and stood up. "All right, if it will make you feel better, I'll leave. I'll run to the house and get you some clothes."

"Just come right back. Please." She let go of his hand. He picked up his jacket, blew her a kiss and left.

The doctor came in a few minutes later, declared her fit to return home, and departed on his rounds. When Tony returned, his clothes changed and looking less dilapidated, she was propped up on pillows, and scribbling notes on a proof copy of the *Sun*'s front page. Rick, sitting beside her, jumped out of the chair, his eyes popping.

"For once, Rick, I'm not blaming Mr. Russell for this. My husband has his own sources of information." She handed him back the page. "It's fine. Really, you've done a magnificent job without me. Now, off you go to that press conference so Tony can help me out of bed and I can get dressed and out of this place."

***

"You should be in bed," Tony said, looking down at her from the kitchen doorway.

Gloria, hair damp, was bundled cozily in a bathrobe on the living room couch, studying the slowly spreading petals of the rosebud sitting in its vase on the small table beside her, and sipping soup out of a mug. Buffy and Max were both curled up beside her. She reached down with her bad arm, now temporarily free of its sling, and stroked Buffy's ears.

"And you should be in Halifax." She couldn't believe she had actually said it, but there it was. Apart from helping her wash gravel out of her hair, he had barely spoken to her since picking her up in Plattsford. The awkwardness she was feeling finally found words.

"Of course I should be!" he roared suddenly, and her head began pounding all over again with the sudden rise in volume. "You scared the hell out of me! When I saw you lying there in the hospital and you looked so terrible, I thought...." He took a deep breath. "How do you think it feels? I don't want to have to come home someday to your funeral because you didn't have the courtesy to tell me you had died. You have no right to do this to me." He flopped into the ancient easy chair and glared across at her.

"I'm sorry." Gloria stared into her soup mug. "You're angry, and I deserve this." She looked across at him, with tears in her eyes. "I should have known better than to try to keep this from you, but...I felt I had worried you enough lately. And I could handle it. God knows, I've handled my own life up to now."

"And you suppose I can't?" He took several deep breaths. "You're right. And I never will, if you won't let me. It isn't just *your* life you're handling. It's *our* life! We are married, in case you're forgetting, and that gives me a license to worry, whether you like it or not. I love you, Gloria." He sank down on the couch beside her and reached an arm out to gather her to him, then stopped. "But is there any way I can show you right now without touching a bruise and hurting you?"

"I'm afraid not," she said, and put her head back against the couch cushion. "I think I'm going to hurt, whatever you do." She closed her eyes. "If it makes you feel better, I was scared too. At some point, I actually thought I was going to die, and the worst part of that was...well, I felt I had let you down, somehow. Your parents have the right idea. You deserve a good, devoted partner who will follow you around and not keep thinking about herself. I'm not very good, but...." She looked up at him. "I am devoted." She reached out and took his hand, and held it against her heart.

He sighed deeply. "And I suppose I'm stuck with you, now." They would have stayed that way indefinitely, if the telephone hadn't started ringing. Tony reached over and picked it up.

"Tony, thank God! Is Gloria all right?" It was his mother, and Gloria could hear her voice clear across the couch.

"How does she know?" Gloria hissed, struggling to her feet against his grip on the cord of her bathrobe. "Not the *Star*! The *Express*? Did that rag scoop my story?"

"She's just fine, Mother. A bit stiff, but dying to get back to work." He adjusted the telephone more closely over his ear so he could hear over Gloria's angry muttering.

"Damn that Fred Russell!" Gloria whispered. "If he talked to the *Express*, so help me I'll—"

"She found out," Tony said, hand over the mouthpiece, "because I left my wallet in the dressing room and had to wake them up at some gawdawful hour of the morning so I could charge my ticket home to my father's firm's account—What was that, Mother? Just a minute. I'll ask." He covered the mouthpiece again. "My mother wants to know if you are still coming to dinner Sunday."

Gloria shrugged, winced, and nodded. "I'll look like hell, but I'll be there."

"She says she's looking forward to it....Yes, I'll be able to bring her down when I return Dad's car....No, it's a long weekend, and I don't have to be in St. John's until Tuesday night, but she has to work so she'll have to come home....No, she might as well drive *my* car back. Hers seems to be misplaced at the moment, anyway....I'll tell her. Bye." He hung up and looked at her. "Mother—the one who hates you—says you can bring the Seville back with you for the week, if you need it."

"Her *car*?"

"In case you didn't notice, I brought you home in the Mercedes. Dad met me at the airport and loaned me *his* car, and a hundred bucks, to get me home fast, since I couldn't rent one without a driver's license, and that was in Halifax with my wallet." He shook his head. "If I'd known you would be this much trouble, perhaps I would have remained a bachelor for life."

He walked into the kitchen, filled a pot with water to set on the stove, and began chopping vegetables. When the telephone rang again, Gloria picked it up. It was Fred Russell.

"Mr. Murray wants to see you as soon as you're fit. He's flipping mad. He says he doesn't pay you to go snooping around and getting involved in police investigations."

"And where did he hear that, Mr. Russell?" she asked coldly.

"Don't blame me. I told him it was all in the line of duty. He won't take my word for it, though, keeps rambling on about lost advertising. You'll probably have to tell him yourself."

"Great," Gloria mumbled to herself as she hung up the phone. "Tomorrow I have to fight for my job, once again." She sank back in the cushions, eyes closed.

"You don't need the job. How could you possibly think of staying here after this?"

"Not everyone here is a murderer. I like this community, this house, such as it is, and I'm making some good friends here, friends that I'll probably have for awhile. It's as good a place as any to stay, while you're traveling and making a name for yourself."

He shrugged.

"You know, you surprised me today." She rose carefully from the couch, limped into the kitchen in bare feet, and stood beside him. He slipped an arm cautiously around her waist. "Once," she recalled, "I broke my arm during a school ski trip, and my father drove eighty miles and showed up in the hospital's emergency department still wearing his tool belt from work. It's so typical of Dad. You are usually so...I don't know, controlled and reserved. Coming home to me today, the way you did, without even stopping to pick up your wallet or change your clothes, is the sort of thing my Dad would do."

"And I suppose you assumed I didn't care enough. Do you really think so little of me after all this time?" He frowned at the steam rising from the water on the stove.

"No," she replied. "I think I'm a major pain to you—ouch! Don't squeeze. I am trying not to distract you from what you love to do. How are you ever going to get through this concert thing for the next two years if you are worrying about me all the time? I'm trying to keep a low profile in your life."

"But I *do* think of you all the time." The water began to bubble, and he threw in a handful of vermicelli. "How do you think I finally got this opportunity after all these years? I am a better musician now than I ever was, because you are a part of what I do. Sorry, but it's too late to back out now." He leaned over and kissed her forehead, very lightly.

She rubbed the back of his neck, and winced as her shoulder hurt her again. "In that case, what do I have to do to make you stink as a violinist so you'll stay home with me?" He was silent. She laid her head against his shoulder, and felt his breath disturb her damp hair. The gauze veil had disappeared; she could see him, and feel him, clearly. "Tony, you are a wonderful musician. I'd rather take no credit at all for it."

He just smiled, and returned his attention to the pot.

The End

Now Available
8.5x11 Paperback
Special Edition Hard Back

A Celebration of Cover Art
2001 to 2006
Five Years of Cover Art
[Companion calendars also available]
www.double-dragon-ebooks.com
www.derondouglas.com